In this dazzling new trilogy from the incomparable Jane Feather, a trio of spirited sisters harbor a secret that could scandalize all of London...

English society knows them as the Honorable Misses Duncan. But what society doesn't know is that these elegant—fiercely independent—young beauties make it their business to ignite romance as the clandestine founders of a discreet matchmaking service. And a rewarding business it is, as one by one, they meet their own matches...

Constance

The eldest and most like their suffragette mother, sophisticated Con would rather be a spinster than marry Mr. Wrong—although she's somewhat vague about what constitutes Mr. Right...

Chastity

Wickedly funny and naturally flirtatious, young Chas attracts suitors as honey draws bees. But, like her sisters, she's in no hurry for marriage...

Prudence

Bookish middle sister Prue has a head for business—and a heart for mischief—wherever and whenever it's least expected...

This is her story...

A Main Selection of Rhapsody Book Club
A Featured Alternate Selection of Doubleday Book Club

Also by Jane Feather

VICE

VANITY

VIOLET

VALENTINE

VELVET

VENUS

VIXEN

VIRTUE

THE DIAMOND SLIPPER

THE SILVER ROSE

THE EMERALD SWAN

THE HOSTAGE BRIDE

A VALENTINE WEDDING

THE ACCIDENTAL BRIDE

THE LEAST LIKELY BRIDE

THE WIDOW'S KISS

ALMOST INNOCENT

TO KISS A SPY

KISSED BY SHADOWS

THE BACHELOR LIST

The Bride Hunt

Jane Feather

BANTAM BOOKS

THE BRIDE HUNT
A Bantam Book / March 2004

Published by Bantam Dell
A Division of Random House, Inc.
New York, New York

ISBN 0-553-58619-X

Manufactured in the United States of America
Published simultaneously in Canada

OPM 10 9 8 7

The Bride Hunt

Chapter 1

"Here you are, Miss Prue." Mrs. Beedle took a pile of envelopes from a top shelf in her kitchen. "Quite a few of them today. This one looks very serious." She selected a long thick vellum envelope from the sheaf and peered quite unselfconsciously at the printed heading.

Prudence sipped her tea and made no attempt to hurry her hostess. Mrs. Beedle moved at her own pace and had her own way of doing things . . . very much like her brother, Jenkins—a man who combined his duties as butler with those of friend, assistant, and sometimes partner in crime to the three Duncan sisters in the house on Manchester Square.

"Any news of Miss Con?" Mrs. Beedle inquired, finally setting the envelopes on the well-scrubbed pine table and reaching for the teapot.

"Oh, we had a wire yesterday. They're in Egypt at the moment." Prudence pushed her cup across to be refilled. "But they've visited Rome and Paris on the way. It seems like a wonderful trip."

She sounded slightly wistful, and, indeed, the six

weeks of her elder sister's honeymoon had passed very slowly for Prudence and her younger sister, Chastity, left behind in London. The sheer effort of keeping their household running smoothly, eking out their meager finances, all the while ensuring that their father's willful ignorance of the family's financial situation remained undisturbed, took a much greater toll when there were only two of them to manage it. On occasion in the last weeks, Prudence and Chastity had both had to fight the temptation to force their father to acknowledge reality, a reality that he had caused by a more than foolish investment just after their mother's death. But the memory of their mother had kept them silent. Lady Duncan would have protected her husband's peace of mind at all costs, so her daughters must do the same.

When they added to that struggle the burden of putting out the broadsheet, *The Mayfair Lady,* every two weeks, without Constance's editorial expertise, and trying to stay on top of the Go-Between, their matchmaking agency, it was no wonder she and Chastity fell exhausted into a dreamless sleep every night, Prudence reflected.

The doorbell from the shop at the front of the house chimed as a customer entered and Mrs. Beedle hurried away to attend to the counter, smoothing her pristine apron as she did so. Prudence drank deeply from her refilled cup and helped herself to a second piece of gingerbread. It was warm and tranquil in the kitchen behind the shop. She could hear Mrs. Beedle's chattily cheerful voice interspersed with that of another woman, rather shrill and high-pitched, complaining about the poor quality of the butcher's lamb chops.

Prudence stretched her legs towards the range and sighed, grateful for the brief respite from the workaday concerns, and idly riffled through the envelopes addressed to *The Mayfair Lady* that were sent poste restante to Mrs. Beedle's corner shop in Kensington. The editors of *The Mayfair Lady* had to preserve their anonymity at all costs.

The thick vellum envelope had a distinctly official feel to it. The printed address in the top left-hand corner read *Falstaff, Harley & Greenwold*. Prudence felt a chill of apprehension. It sounded like a firm of lawyers. She reached for the butter knife, intending to slit the envelope, and then put it down again with a quick, unconscious shake of her head. The sisters had an unspoken convention that they opened correspondence relating to their shared endeavors together. And if this one brought bad news, and Prudence found herself fancying a miasmic vapor oozing from the vellum, it was most definitely not to be opened alone.

She thrust all the letters into her capacious handbag and drained her teacup. Mrs. Beedle was still engaged with her customer when Prudence went out through the shop, drawing on her gloves.

"Thank you for the tea, Mrs. Beedle."

"Oh, it's always nice to see you, Miss Prue." The shopkeeper beamed at her. "And Miss Chas, of course. Bring her with you next week. I'll make some of my lardy cake, I know how she likes that."

"She'll be sorry she missed the gingerbread, but she had to visit an old friend this afternoon," Prudence said with a smile, nodding politely to the customer, who was regarding her curiously. A lady with a Mayfair accent wearing a rather elegant afternoon gown was something of a novelty in a corner shop in Kensington, particularly when she appeared from the owner's quarters in the back.

Prudence picked up a copy of *The Mayfair Lady* in the magazine rack at the back of the shop. "If you're looking for something to read, ma'am, you might enjoy this publication." She held it out to the woman, who was so surprised, she took it.

"Well, I don't know," she said. "Mayfair Lady... sounds a bit hoity-toity for the likes of me."

"Oh, it's not at all," Prudence reassured warmly. "Mrs. Beedle reads it, I know."

"Aye, that I do, once in a while," the shopkeeper said. "You try it, Mrs. Warner. Just the ticket on a cold afternoon when you're knitting by the fire."

"I don't have much call for reading," the customer said doubtfully. "How much is it?" She turned the broadsheet around in her hands, as if unsure what to do with it.

"Just twopence," Prudence said. "You'd be surprised how much of interest there is inside."

"Well, I don't know, but I suppose..." The customer's voice trailed off as she opened her purse for two pennies that she laid on the counter. "I'll try it."

"You do that," Mrs. Beedle said. "And I tell you what, if you don't like it, you just bring it back and I'll refund the twopence."

Mrs. Warner brightened visibly. "Well, you can't say fairer than that, Mrs. Beedle."

Prudence raised a mental eyebrow. How were they supposed to make money out of the broadsheet when people read it "on approval"? But she couldn't say that to Mrs. Beedle, who only meant well, so with a cheerful farewell she left the shop, going out into a chilly afternoon that was already drawing in even though it was barely four-thirty. Autumn seemed to have come earlier than usual this year, she thought, but perhaps it was only in contrast to the long and unusually hot summer that had preceded it.

She hurried towards an omnibus stop, thinking again of Constance in the desert heat of Egypt. It was all right for some, she concluded as the motorized omnibus belching steam came to a halt at the stop. She climbed on, paid her penny fare, and took a seat by the window, watching the streets of London crawl by as the bus stopped and started at the behest of passengers.

She wondered how Chastity's afternoon had progressed. Despite what Prudence had told Mrs. Beedle, her sister hadn't been visiting an old friend. Chastity, in her role as Aunt Mabel, was in fact writing her responses to a trio of problem letters from beleaguered readers, for publication in the next edition of the broadsheet. Prudence had left her chewing the top of her pen, bewailing crossed nibs that splattered ink all over everywhere, and trying to think of a diplomatic way to shoot down *Desperate in Chelsea,* who seemed to think that her elderly parents had no right to spend any of their capital on frivolous pursuits while their daughter was waiting for her inheritance.

She hopped off the bus at Oxford Street and walked up Baker Street towards Portman Square. She turned onto Manchester Square, her cheeks pinkened by the freshening breeze, and ran up the steps to No. 10. Jenkins opened the door for her just as she put her key in the lock.

"Thought that was you, Miss Prue, when I heard the key."

"I was visiting your sister," she said, stepping into the hall. "She sent her greetings."

"Hope she's in good health."

"She certainly seemed to be. Is Chas upstairs?"

"She hasn't put her head out of the parlor all afternoon."

"Oh, poor love," Prudence said. "Did she have tea?"

At that Jenkins smiled. Chastity's sweet tooth was a family joke. "Mrs. Hudson made a chocolate sponge this afternoon. Miss Chas had three slices. It bucked her up a little, if I might say so. She was looking a little peaky before."

"Inky probably," Prudence said with a laugh as she hurried to the staircase. She paused halfway and asked over her shoulder, "Is Lord Duncan dining in tonight, do you know, Jenkins?"

"I don't believe so, Miss Prue. Mrs. Hudson's made a nice shepherd's pie for you and Miss Chas with the cold lamb from Sunday's roast."

If one had to eat leftovers, mutton was infinitely more palatable than fish, Prudence reflected. She opened the door to the parlor that she and her sisters had shared since their mother's death just four years previously. It was a pleasant, lived-in room, somewhat shabby and faded, and rather cluttered. Even more so this afternoon. Chastity sat at the secretaire, knee deep in scrunched-up balls of paper, evidence of frustrating literary effort. She turned as her sister came in.

"Oh, I'm glad you're back, now I can stop this." She ran her hands through her curly red hair that had escaped its ribbons during the throes of composition and now fell loose to her shoulders. She stretched and rolled her shoulders. "I never thought I'd lose sympathy for these tormented souls but some of them are so childish and spoiled . . . Oh, wait. I have something to show you. Jenkins brought it up half an hour ago."

Her tone had completely changed and she jumped up, walking energetically to the sideboard. "See here." She flourished a newspaper. "The *Pall Mall Gazette*. Con said it would happen!"

"What would happen?" Prudence ran her eye over the paper and saw the answer. She whistled soundlessly at the headline. PEER OF THE REALM IN VICE SCANDAL. She began to read the text. *"'The earl of Barclay has been accused in the pages of the anonymous broadsheet* The Mayfair Lady *of violating his youthful maidservants and abandoning them pregnant and poverty-stricken on the streets.'"*

Her voice faded as she continued reading under her breath, aware that Chastity probably knew the article by heart by now. When she reached the end she looked up at her sister, who was regarding her expectantly. Chastity said, "They actually interviewed the women Con used in the article."

"And they offer their own condemnation of the *licentious peer,* in their own inimitable style," Prudence observed. "Full of almost religious fervor, trumpeting condemnation for such lewd behavior while titillating their readers with scandalous details."

"It's exactly what we all hoped would happen," Chastity said. "Just four weeks after the original *Mayfair Lady* article. That only produced a few behind-the-hand whispers and the occasional glare for Barclay from strait-laced Society matrons. His own cronies didn't turn a hair and he seemed to ignore it totally. I thought it had all blown over now. But when this hits the streets and the clubs and the drawing rooms, he'll be pilloried."

"Yes," Prudence agreed, but she sounded uneasy. She opened her handbag and took out the official-looking envelope. "This was in the mail."

"What is it?"

"It looks like it's from a firm of solicitors."

"Oh," Chastity took the envelope and turned it over as if she could intuit its contents. "I suppose we'd better open it." Prudence handed her a paper knife and she slit the envelope, withdrawing a densely covered sheet of vellum. She began to read, Prudence at her shoulder.

"Oh, hell!" Prudence said when she'd reached the end. Even through the dreadful, obfuscating legalese the message was clear as a bell.

"Why's Barclay suing us for libel—or rather, *The Mayfair Lady*—and not the *Pall Mall Gazette*?" wondered Chastity. "It has much more clout than we do."

"The *Gazette* only came out today," Prudence said glumly. "We came out guns blazing a whole month ago. He's had four weeks to put this together. And if he wins this case he can go after the *Gazette*."

"So, what do we do?" Chastity nibbled her bottom lip as she reread the letter. "It says they will be seeking punitive damages of the highest degree possible on behalf of their client. What does that *mean*?"

"I have no idea... nothing good, you can be sure of that." Prudence flung herself into the depths of the chesterfield, kicking off her shoes. "We need advice."

"We need Con." Her sister perched on the arm of a chair and crossed her legs, swinging one ankle restlessly against the corner of the sofa table.

"What in God's name is Max going to think of this?"

"It won't do his career much good if it comes out that his wife wrote the original," Chastity said gloomily.

"We're going to have to make sure it doesn't come out, for the sake of all our enterprises, but I don't see how we can keep it from Max." Prudence picked up the letter from the table where Chastity had let it fall. "Oh, I didn't see this, right at the bottom here . . . 'In addition to damages for the libel concerning our client's relationships with his employees we will be seeking substantial damages for innuendo and inference regarding our client's financial practices.' "

"Did the *Pall Mall Gazette* pick up those hints we dropped?" Chastity reached over for the discarded paper. "I didn't see anything."

"No, they probably had the sense to leave it alone. There's no evidence for it, or at least none that we offered. I'm sure there's some somewhere, but we were all so fired up about nailing Barclay, we just threw everything in." Prudence sighed. "What naive idiots we are."

"No," Chastity said. "Were. We were, but I don't think we are anymore."

"A case of shutting the stable door after the horse has bolted," Prudence pointed out with a dour smile. She turned towards the door at a discreet knock.

"Would you like the sherry decanter in here, Miss Prue? Or will you be using the drawing room this evening?" Jenkins inquired.

"No, I don't think we're in the mood for the drawing room tonight," Prudence said. "We'll take sherry in here, and we'll eat shepherd's pie in the little dining parlor."

"Yes, I rather thought that would be your decision." Jenkins entered the room and set down the tray he was carrying. "What time shall I tell Mrs. Hudson you'd like dinner?" He poured two glasses and carried them over on a silver salver.

"Eight, I should think?" Prudence looked a question at her sister, who nodded her agreement. "And I don't think we shall dress, Jenkins. We'll serve ourselves, if you like. I'm sure you've got things you'd rather do this evening."

"When I've served you, Miss Prue, I shall go off duty," Jenkins stated with a note of reproach. He bowed and left them.

"He's only going to the pub for his pint of mild-and-bitter," Chastity said, taking a sip of sherry. "It doesn't warm up there until around nine o'clock."

"All the same, elaborate service for shepherd's pie seems a little unnecessary," Prudence observed. "Why don't we eat up here on trays beside the fire?"

"Because Jenkins and Mrs. Hudson would be horrified," Chastity said, laughing slightly. She set down her glass and went to throw another shovel of coal on the fire. *"There's no call for a lowering of standards, Miss Prue, just because times is hard."* It was a perfect imitation of the housekeeper, Mrs. Hudson, and Prudence laughed and applauded.

The moment of levity, however, died a swift death. "How do we find a barrister?" Chastity asked.

"I think we're supposed to find a solicitor who will then instruct a barrister on our behalf. I'm sure that's the way it works," Prudence replied.

"You know more than I do." Chastity took up her glass. "Father would know someone, of course. Could we sound him out, d'you think?"

"You mean ask a couple of casual questions?" Prudence leaned forward, her light green eyes sharp.

"He's not going to put two and two together," Chastity pointed out.

"No." Prudence pursed her lips. "I just wonder if he'll know the kind of lawyer we're looking for."

"Someone inexpensive," Chastity stated the obvious.

Prudence shook her head. "This kind of barrister comes expensive. However we can but try. There might be some way around it."

The sound of impatient footsteps in the corridor outside reached them just before the door was flung open after the most perfunctory knock. Lord Arthur Duncan stood on the threshold, his whiskers awry, his cheeks rather redder than usual, his bowler hat clutched to his striped waistcoat. "I have never heard the like," he declared. "Bounders, absolute bounders. Should be hanged from the nearest lamppost. Oh, I see you've seen it." He gestured to the *Pall Mall Gazette*. "Disgraceful, disgusting calumny. It was one thing for that effeminate gossip rag to point the finger... no self-respecting red-blooded man gives a tinker's damn what a group of airheaded cowards have to say... but when that sanctimonious, tub-thumping twit in the *Gazette* starts pointing the finger, there's no knowing where it will lead."

He sat down heavily in a wing chair beside the fire. "If that's sherry, I'll have a glass, Prudence."

"It is, and certainly, Father." She poured and brought him the glass. "Is Lord Barclay very upset?"

"Upset?" his lordship boomed. "He's beside himself." He drained his small glass in one sip, and glared at it. "Not enough to slake the thirst of a butterfly."

"Would you like Jenkins to bring you whisky?" Chastity asked with customary solicitude.

"No... no need to bother him." He wiped his moustache with his handkerchief. "Just fill it again for me." He gave her the glass.

"What is Lord Barclay going to do about it?" inquired Prudence, leaning over to stir the coals with the poker. "He must have some redress, surely."

"Well, he's suing that *Mayfair Lady* disgrace, for a start. That'll fold once Barclay and his lawyers have finished with it. Won't have a penny to its name and its editors will be lucky to escape gaol."

"I imagine he must be using the best lawyers in the business," Chastity said, bringing a recharged glass over to the earl.

"Oh, yes, you mark my words... best money can buy."

"Are there many good libel lawyers in London?" Prudence asked. "We never meet any."

"Hardly surprising, m'dear." He regarded his middle daughter with a benign smile. "Not saying that you and your sisters couldn't compete with the brightest brain, but these men don't frequent the kind of circles you girls like. You'll find 'em in clubs, not drawing rooms."

Prudence looked askance. "I wonder if that's true. Give us some names of the really good barristers and Chas and I will see if they ring any kind of a bell."

"Party games," he scoffed, but he seemed to have calmed down somewhat in the soothing companionship of his daughters and under the equally soothing influence of the sherry. His cheeks had taken on a less rubicund hue.

"Well, now, let me see. Barclay's solicitors, Falstaff, Harley, and Greenwold, have briefed Samuel Richardson, KC. Any name there ring a bell?" He gave his daughters a smug smile. "I'll wager not."

"We don't expect to know the solicitors," Prudence told him. "But Samuel Richardson . . ." She shook her head. "No, you win that one. Give us another."

Lord Duncan frowned, thinking. "Malvern," he said finally. "Sir Gideon Malvern, KC. Youngest KC in a decade, knighted for his services to the bar." He chuckled suddenly. "I believe it was for services to the king . . . one of His Majesty's friends found himself in a spot of bother, you know the kind." He tapped the side of his nose significantly.

"Malvern defended him . . . man came out smelling like a rose garden. But I'll wager you haven't heard of him either, for all the royal connections. They say he's the brightest candle in the Inns of Court sconce these days. Man's far too busy to mingle."

He set down his glass and rose rather heavily to his feet. "Well, I have to dress, I'm dining with Barclay in Rules. Must show solidarity, you know. Can't let this kind of . . ." He waved a disdainful hand at the *Gazette*. "Spiteful rubbish . . . that's all it is. Can't let that rubbish win the day over honest men." He dropped a paternal kiss on each forehead and left them.

"Honest men," Prudence said with heavy scorn, taking her glass to the decanter for a refill. "It's not as if Father's either blind or stupid. What is it about Barclay that so captivates him?"

"Oh, I think it has something to do with the fact that the earl was there when Mother died," Chastity said quietly, gazing into the fire. "Father was distraught, and so were we. Distraught and exhausted after nursing her those last few months."

Prudence nodded, crossing her arms over her chest in an involuntary hug. Their mother's final days had been excruciatingly painful, and all the laudanum available to them hadn't been sufficient to ease her suffering. Lord Duncan hadn't been able to bear his wife's pain and had retreated to his library, where Lord Barclay had kept him company while Lord Duncan's daughters had shared vigils at their mother's bedside. They had had no energy to spare for their father's grief—not until many months later, by which time Lord Barclay had become Lord Duncan's most intimate confidant.

Prudence let her arms drop and raised her head. "Well, there's nothing we can do to change that now. Let's see what we can discover about this Sir Gideon Malvern."

"If he's made King's Council, he has to be at the top of the tree," Chastity said. "I wonder what it means to be the youngest KC in a decade."

"We need a recent copy of *Who's Who,*" Prudence said. "At least that'll tell us which of the Inns of Court he's affiliated with. The volume in our library is decades old; it probably predates his law degree. We'll go to Hatchards in the morning and take a quick look under the M's."

"*Who's Who* won't give us an address, though."

"No, but once we know which of the Inns he belongs to, we can go there and find his chambers. I'm sure if he's that important and well-known he'll have chambers somewhere around the Temple."

"But we can't just beard him in his chambers," Chastity pointed out. "I thought we had to go through the proper channels, get solicitors to brief him."

Prudence shook her head. "I think if we have any chance at all of getting his help we're going to have to jump him . . . surprise him. If we give him time to think for one instant, he'll laugh us into the street."

" 'Be bloody, bold, and resolute,' " Chastity quoted with an upraised fist.

" 'Laugh to scorn the power of man,' " her sister continued.

"If only," Chastity said, getting to her feet. "We'll go to Hatchards first thing in the morning." She stretched tiredly. "I'm hungry and it's nearly eight. Shall we go and eat shepherd's pie?"

"I wonder what Con's eating for dinner," Prudence mused as she accompanied her sister downstairs.

"Goats' eyeballs," Chastity said promptly. "I read that's what the Bedouin nomads eat in the Sahara."

"Oh, I can imagine Max's reaction faced with a goat's eyeball. Can't you, Jenkins?" Prudence took her seat in the small dining parlor they used when they were alone.

"As I understand it, Miss Prue, the eyeballs of sheep are a delicacy. I believe that the goats are roasted whole and the meat is considered most succulent." Jenkins held the steaming dish of shepherd's pie at her elbow.

"I'm not sure goat or sheep make much difference to the concept," Prudence said, helping herself. "This smells delicious . . . thank you, Jenkins."

He moved around the table to Chastity. "Mrs. Hudson used grated cheese on the potato. I think you'll find it nice and crispy."

Chastity cut through the crisp crust, and the butler presented a dish of buttered cabbage before filling their wineglasses and quietly removing himself.

"It is actually very good," Prudence said after a forkful.

"Mrs. Hudson does remarkably well with what little she has to work with much of the time," Chastity said. "Did we manage to pay her this month?"

"Oh, yes. I had to pawn those little pearl earrings of Mother's, but we'll redeem them as soon as we get the *charitable donations* from Lady Lucan and Lady Winthrop."

"That's such an outrageous idea of Con's," Chastity said. "To ask them to donate to a charity for indigent spinsters as a means of collecting our Go-Between fee."

"Well, they have no idea that they—or rather, their progeny—received the services of the Go-Between," Prudence reminded her, helping herself to more cabbage. "It's going to be a most useful way of collecting payment... should we find ourselves setting up other couples for their own good."

Chastity couldn't help a grin. "For their own good. How altruistic that sounds, when all we want is their money." She took a sip of wine and pulled a face. "This is a thin and ungrateful beverage."

"I know," Prudence agreed with a rueful headshake. "Jenkins found some bottles of a burgundy at the back of the cellar that are clearly over the hill. We thought we ought to drink them up, those that Mrs. Hudson isn't using for cooking."

"Don't let Father get a sniff of them."

Prudence shook her head again and took a sip from

her own glass. "It's not too bad with food, but you couldn't possibly drink it alone."

"So, when are we going to receive these charitable donations from *La Lucan* and *La Winthrop*?"

"They promised to bring checks to the next At Home. I suggested around fifty guineas apiece would be suitable," Prudence told her blithely.

Chastity choked on a forkful of potato. "Fifty guineas apiece! That's outrageous, Prue."

"Con thought it was a little much too, but I thought it was worth a try. It isn't as if they can't afford it," her sister declared. "The wedding is to take place in December, and it'll be the biggest, most lavish Society affair of the year. Hester and David are so absorbed in each other it's nauseating. And their mothers are pleased as punch. We did them all a great service. Not to mention you," she added with a grin. "Anything to give David an alternative love interest."

"The adoration *was* getting a little tedious," Chastity admitted. "By the way, were there any other letters for *The Mayfair Lady*? Besides the legal one."

"Several. They're still in my bag. We'll look at them after dinner."

"I wonder what's for pudding?" Chastity mused.

"Apple crumble and custard, Miss Chas." Jenkins answered the question as he reentered the parlor on cue. "Mrs. Hudson was wondering if you'd like her to make some scones for the At Home?" He gathered up their plates.

"Oh, yes, please," Prudence said. "We're collecting money at the next one, so the sweeter the tea, the better."

"Yes, Miss Prue. I'll explain to Mrs. Hudson. I imagine she'll make another chocolate sponge." Jenkins was quite matter-of-fact as he bore away their discarded plates. The dubious moneymaking activities of Lord Duncan's daughters met only with his approval.

Chapter 2

The sisters entered the bow-windowed bookshop on Piccadilly within minutes of its opening. They headed straight for the reference section at the rear of the shop and found what they were looking for. "We probably ought to use the lending library for research," Chastity said in an undertone. "It seems like cheating to use a bookstore. I'm sure they'd rather we bought the up-to-date *Who's Who*."

"I'm sure they would," Prudence agreed. "But it's five guineas that we don't have, and we only need one entry." She leafed carefully through the pages. "Ah, here we are, the M's." Her finger ran down the entries. "Maburn... Maddingly... *Malvern*. This is it. 'Sir Gideon Malvern, KC; Member of the Inns of Court, Middle Temple; Appointed to the bar, 1894; Appointed King's Council, 1902; Education: Winchester, New College, Oxford...' Predictable enough." She raised her head. "Well, that gives us what we need."

"Isn't there anything else, anything personal?" Chastity inquired, peering over her sister's shoulder.

"Oh, look at this. It says he's divorced. 'Married Harriet Greenwood, daughter of Lord Charles and Lady Greenwood, 1896; Divorced, 1900. One daughter, Sarah, born 1897.' "

She looked up with a frown. "Divorced . . . that's unusual."

"Very," Prudence agreed. "But it's not going to affect us. We know where to find him, or at least his chambers. Let's go to Middle Temple Lane and look at some nameplates." She closed the tome gently and replaced it on the shelf. Outside, they jostled with the shoppers crowding Piccadilly until they found an empty hackney cab.

"Victoria Embankment, please," Prudence called as she climbed in, Chastity on her heels. "The issue now," Prudence said, her brow furrowed, "is how to approach this famous man. D'you have any ideas, Chas?"

"Nothing specific," her sister said, adjusting the brim of her straw hat. "We need to make an appointment first. Isn't he likely to be in court . . . the Old Bailey or somewhere? The Bailey is open for business now, isn't it?"

"Early this year, I believe," Prudence said vaguely. "Even if he's not practicing there, he's most likely to be in some criminal court this morning. We probably won't get further than his law clerk today, always assuming, of course, that we don't get thrown out onto the street before we can open our mouths."

"Well, we look respectable enough," Chastity said.

That was certainly true, Prudence reflected. Her own neutral tweed jacket and skirt with a plain black straw hat was understated, unfrivolous, respectable, and unremarkable. Chastity's day dress of dark brown silk was a little more adorned, but still could not be called frivolous. She had debated their both dressing to the nines in an attempt to overwhelm the barrister with their elegance and femininity but had decided in favor of a more moderate approach. Once she had some idea of the kind of man they were dealing with, they could adapt accordingly.

Divorced was interesting, though. It was very unusual in their circles, and carried considerable stigma. But, of course, more for the woman than the man, she thought acidly, hearing in her head Constance, the suffragist, railing against the injustice of society's laws when it came to women, both openly in the courts and in covert daily convention. Who had been the guilty party in this case? Sir Gideon, or his wife? If they could discover that, it might give them some clues as to how to deal with the barrister.

The hackney stopped on Victoria Embankment and they got out, pausing for a moment to look across the gray sweep of the Thames to the South Bank. The sun was struggling to emerge through an overcast sky and a few faint rays lit the dull, rolling surface of the water. A brisk gust of wind sent colored leaves tumbling from the oak trees in the Temple Gardens behind them.

"It's too cold to stand around," Prudence said. "Let's walk up Middle Temple Lane. You take one side and I'll take the other."

Every door on either side of the lane bore copper nameplates listing the occupants of each tall, narrow building. Each name was followed by the insignia *Barrister At Law*. Sir Gideon Malvern's name was found midway up the lane.

Prudence waved at Chastity, who crossed over towards her. "This one." Prudence indicated the nameplate.

Chastity tried the shiny brass doorknob and the door swung open into a gloomy interior that could barely qualify as a foyer. A set of wooden stairs rose directly in front of them. The sun had gone in again and there was little enough natural light at the best of times from the narrow window at the corner of the stairs, but someone had thoughtfully lit the gas lamp at the top, so a little illumination showed the way up the ancient, rickety staircase.

The sisters exchanged a glance. The shiny nameplate and doorknob facing the street belied the shabby interior, but Prudence knew enough about the practice of law to realize that she should not judge the barrister by the air of dilapidation in his chambers. Rooms in the ancient Inns of Court were highly prized and available only to the select few. It was a matter of pride and tradition that no modern conveniences should invade the hallowed chambers.

"I'm surprised there's a gas lamp," she murmured. "I thought they hadn't progressed beyond oil lanterns and candles."

"Shall we go up?" Chastity asked in a similar undertone.

"That's what we came for." Prudence sounded more confident than she felt. She set foot on the stair, Chastity behind her. It was too narrow for two to climb abreast.

The door at the head of the stairs stood slightly ajar. Prudence knocked, thought it had been too timid a knock, and rapped rather more smartly. A creaky voice bade her enter. Presumably it did not belong to Sir Gideon Malvern, KC, she reflected. Her father had described him as the youngest barrister to achieve that accolade in a decade and she remembered from the entry in

Who's Who that he'd been appointed to the bar twelve years ago. He couldn't be more than forty, she calculated. She went in, leaving the door ajar, and failed to notice that Chastity didn't follow her.

"Madam?" An elderly man in a threadbare frock coat and frayed collar looked at her in surprise from behind an overloaded desk. He glanced up at the clock, which chimed eleven o'clock as he did so. "Can I help you, madam?" He rose from a tall stool and peered at her in the gaslight.

"I would like to see Sir Gideon Malvern," Prudence stated, glancing around her with interest. The walls were invisible behind bookshelves groaning beneath the weight of thick leather-bound volumes. A telephone hung on the wall behind the clerk's desk, an expensive piece of modernity that surprised her even more than the gaslight. It stood out like a sore thumb. On a coat rack beside the door hung the barrister's working garb, a black gown and an elaborate white curled wig.

The clerk opened a ledger on his desk, slowly turned the pages, and then peered through pince-nez at the entries. He looked up after what seemed an interminable length of time. "Sir Gideon has no appointment for this time, madam."

"That's because I haven't made one," Prudence said, an impatient edge to her voice now. She took off her gloves, aware that the gesture felt almost symbolic. The man was playing games with her. "As I'm sure you are well aware. I would, however, like to make one."

"You are a solicitor, madam?" He stared at her, and she saw that his eyes were a great deal sharper than his rather bumbling manner might indicate.

"Hardly," she said. "But, nevertheless, I wish to brief

Sir Gideon on a libel case. One I think he will find both interesting and profitable." The last lie slid off her tongue as smoothly as water off oiled leather.

The clerk pinched his chin, regarding her in silence for again an unnerving length of time. "This is most unorthodox, but if you have the documents pertaining to the case, I will look them over and consider whether Sir Gideon might be interested," he said finally, holding out his hand.

"Do you make up Sir Gideon's mind for him?" Prudence inquired, the same acerbic edge to her voice. "I would have thought such a distinguished barrister would be capable of making up his own mind."

"All briefs to be considered by Sir Gideon are presented through me," the clerk stated.

They seemed to have reached an impasse. Prudence knew that if she turned and left she would never be able to return, but if she meekly handed over the papers she had in her handbag she had no guarantee that they wouldn't go straight into the already overflowing wastepaper basket beside the clerk's desk. So she simply stood her ground.

Sir Gideon's clerk continued to regard her with that same shrewdness from behind his pince-nez. He was thinking that his principal had a rather eccentric attitude to some of the cases he took. Sir Gideon frequently took on a brief that Thadeus considered a complete waste of time, quite unworthy of his principal's attention. When he expressed his reservations they were always met with a careless shrug and the comment that a man's brain needed something out of the ordinary now and again to keep it alive and well.

Thadeus was wondering what Sir Gideon would

think of his present visitor. A lady of undeniable quality, and some considerable strength of will, he decided. She wouldn't stand out in a crowd—but then, Sir Gideon didn't care for the flamboyant, except when it came to the exotic dancers he seemed to prefer as mistresses.

Prudence glanced at the closed inner door, and then at the barrister's court dress on the coat rack. If it was there, then the barrister was presumably not in court. "Is Sir Gideon in chambers?" she asked.

"No, madam, not as yet."

"When do you expect him?"

"Sir Gideon's personal arrangements are no concern of mine, madam."

"Ah." So, whatever had taken him from his office this morning was not related to the law, she inferred.

"Leave me the brief, madam, and I assure you that Sir Gideon will see it," the clerk stated. "Otherwise, I must ask you to excuse me. I have work to do."

There seemed nothing for it. Prudence opened her bag and took out the copy of *The Mayfair Lady,* with the article marked, and the solicitor's letter. "The suit concerns this broadsheet," she said. "You will see that I have marked the relevant piece."

The clerk took the thin sheaf of papers. "This is the brief?" he asked, raising incredulous eyebrows.

"No, I wouldn't call it that," Prudence said. "I'm not a solicitor, as we've just established. But everything Sir Gideon will need to understand the situation is there."

"With the exception of your name, madam."

"This libel suit is filed against *The Mayfair Lady,* that's all the name Sir Gideon needs."

Thadeus looked at her and the semblance of a smile touched his thin mouth. "You do not know my principal, madam. I do assure you he will need a great deal more than that."

"Well, if he decides to take the case, he shall have more than that," Prudence declared brusquely. "In the meantime, a message sent to this address will reach me." She handed him a folded paper.

Thadeus unfolded the sheet. "Mrs. Henry Franklin, Flat A, Palace Court, Bayswater," he read aloud. He looked again at her, his gaze drifting to her ringless fingers. This was not a lady with a Bayswater aura. She exuded Mayfair, for all the simplicity of her dress.

"A message to this address will reach you?"

"That is what I said, I believe." Prudence put on her gloves, her movements crisp. "I will expect to hear from Sir Gideon by the end of the week. It shouldn't take him very long to make up his mind. The issue is very straightforward."

"Libel is rarely straightforward, madam," the clerk responded. He offered her a small bow. "I bid you good morning."

"Good morning." Prudence turned back to the door, only then realizing that Chastity was not immediately behind her. She went out onto the landing, pulling the door closed behind her, revealing her sister, who had been standing in the shadows behind the door. "Chas, why didn't you come in?" she whispered.

"It was so cramped in there," Chastity explained. "It seemed better to stay outside. Did you mind?"

"No. To tell you the truth, I didn't realize you weren't in the room," Prudence said, still keeping her voice low as she descended the stairs. "Didn't you think he was an obstreperous man?"

"Yes, but you stood up to him beautifully. He obviously sees himself as Cerberus, guarding the gates to *his principal*."

Prudence chuckled, then shook her head. "I only hope he shows the papers to that *principal*." She laid a hand on the handle of the street door, talking over her shoulder as she did so. The door opened abruptly, nearly knocking her sideways, and she reeled back, still clutching the knob.

"Oh, I beg your pardon, I didn't realize anyone was on the other side." A male voice that was both well modulated and unusually quiet spoke above her.

She looked up at the owner of the voice, too startled for a minute to respond. It was hard to get much of an impression in the dim light of the narrow hallway, but she thought his eyes were gray. "Sir Gideon Malvern?" she asked directly.

"At your service, madam." There was a questioning note to the courteous response. The gray eyes moved beyond her to Chastity, who still stood on the bottom step.

"The Mayfair Lady," Prudence said, holding out her hand. "Your clerk will explain the situation."

"Indeed." He took her hand, his clasp firm enough to be called a grip. "How intriguing." He dropped her hand and consulted the fob watch that hung from his waistcoat pocket. "I would ask you to explain it yourself, but unfortunately I have to be in court in half an hour."

"Your clerk knows how to reach us," Prudence said, smiling faintly. "Good morning, Sir Gideon."

"Good morning, madam." He bowed and stepped aside so that she could pass into the street. He smiled at Chastity with the same inquiring air as she stepped down from the stair. "Two Mayfair ladies?"

Chastity merely inclined her head, murmured, "Good

morning," and followed her sister into the street. The door closed behind them.

"At least that will ensure that the obstreperous clerk won't withhold the papers," Prudence said, looking at the closed door, tapping her lips with a gloved forefinger. "Sir Gideon said he was intrigued, so he's bound to ask what we were doing. His clerk can't deny we were here."

"No," agreed Chastity. "That was a good morning's work. I don't see what else we can do until we hear from him."

"I think we've earned coffee at Fortnum's," her sister declared.

"It was an inspiration to use Amelia and Henry's address," Chastity said as they walked towards Chancery Lane. "No one will connect the Franklins with the Duncans of Manchester Square."

"Unless the barrister hires a private detective. He could discover the connection between Henry and Max in the blink of an eye. Politicians' secretaries are not hard to trace." Amelia Westcott and Henry Franklin had been the Go-Between's first official clients. Now happily married and expecting their first child, they had kept close connections with the Duncan sisters, and Henry worked as secretary for Constance's husband in the House of Commons.

"He's hardly going to go to those lengths," Chastity protested. "If he wants to take the case, he'll get everything he needs from us. If he doesn't, why would he go to the trouble and expense of investigating us?"

"There's truth in that," Prudence agreed. But she felt vaguely uneasy. Although it had only been a momentary encounter, and a perfectly pleasant one, something about those gray eyes had disturbed her; but she couldn't put her finger on it.

Sir Gideon Malvern entered his chambers and greeted his clerk in his usual fashion. "Coffee, Thadeus, as strong as you can make it."

"The water's already heating, Sir Gideon. I trust your meeting at Miss Sarah's school was satisfactory." The clerk had risen from behind his desk to attend to the water on the spirit stove.

"Yes, Sarah's headmistress had only good things to say," Gideon said.

"Not surprising, sir. Miss Sarah is as bright as a button."

"And as sharp as a needle." Gideon's laugh was both proud and affectionate as he capped the cliché. He took off his gloves and bowler hat, laying them on the bench by the door. "So, tell me about our visitors."

Thadeus poured boiling water onto the coffee in a copper jug before he spoke, then he straightened slowly, the jug in his hand. "Visitors, sir? I only saw one."

"Oh, there were two, all right." Gideon went into the inner office. "Mayfair ladies, they called themselves. In other circumstances with such a name I would have thought they were a pair of madams seeking business." He went behind the massive oak table that served as his desk but didn't take a seat.

Thadeus permitted himself a frown of disapproval as he set the coffee and a cup on the table. "The only one I met, sir, was very respectable."

"How dull." Gideon poured coffee, inhaling the aroma with a sigh of pleasure. "I couldn't see them clearly in the gloom downstairs. I wonder if we should install another gas lamp in the hall."

"We have sufficient gas lamps, sir," the other announced repressively. "But I would consider an additional oil lantern on the hook beside the door."

"No . . . no, leave it as it is." The barrister waved a dismissive hand. "So, enlighten me."

Thadeus went into the outer office and returned with the papers Prudence had left him. "A libel case, sir. But the lady wishes to act as her own solicitor. She wishes to brief you herself."

"Oh, now, that's novel. Not in the least dull; just goes to show how appearances can be deceiving." Gideon drank his coffee and glanced at the copy of *The Mayfair Lady*. He nodded his comprehension. "We have an explanation for our Mayfair ladies, it seems."

"I have not, as yet, had the opportunity to read the details of the suit," Thadeus said, as if conscious of some dereliction of duty.

"How could you have done? They've only just left you." Gideon set down his drained coffee cup in the saucer and gathered up the papers. "I'll read these while the jury's out at the Old Bailey. It's an open-and-shut case. I'm hoping they won't be out more than an hour, so it won't be worth going back to chambers while they're discussing a verdict. I may as well use my time profitably." He strode energetically into the outer office, swinging his black gown off the coat rack.

"There's an address in Bayswater, Sir Gideon. The lady said we should contact her there."

"Bayswater?" Gideon turned in surprise, his wig in his hands. "Neither of those ladies carried the mark of Bayswater."

"No, I didn't think so either. I'm assuming the address is purely in the nature of a poste restante, to preserve anonymity."

"Now, why do they want to preserve their anonymity?" Gideon crammed the wig on his head and took a cursory glance in the mirror to check its position. "Every brief I've had in the last six months has been utterly tedious. I'm in need of a change and a challenge, Thadeus. Maybe this will furnish both."

He turned the wig a fraction so it no longer sat askew over his left ear, and mused, "Of course, what I'd really like is a nice juicy murder, but our two ladies didn't look like murderers. However, as I just said, appearances can be deceiving. We must live in hope." He raised a hand in farewell, and left in a whirlwind of energy that Thadeus regarded with approval and a faint sigh of vicarious exhaustion.

"I could wish we didn't have to deal with an At Home this afternoon," Chastity said as the sisters returned home. "It's so much more tedious without Constance."

"Don't forget, this is a fee-collecting occasion," Prudence reminded her. "We're working." She put her key in the door. "Just imagine a hundred guineas in the bank account."

"Oh, that'll keep me at the grindstone," Chastity said. "Hello, Jenkins," she greeted the butler cheerfully as he came into the hall from the library.

"Miss Chas, Miss Prue." The butler had a smile on his face.

"What is it, Jenkins?" Chastity demanded. "You have a secret. Don't deny it."

His smile broadened. "A telegram, Miss Chas."

"From Con?" the sisters asked in unison.

"So I believe." He walked with stately tread to the table that held the mail. "Postmarked Calais, unless I'm mistaken."

"*Calais?* They must be on their way home." Prudence took the wire. "When did it arrive?"

"About an hour ago. I've laid a cold luncheon in the small dining parlor for you. Lord Duncan is lunching at his club."

"Thank you." Prudence tore open the wire.

"So, when are they arriving?" Chastity tried not to hop with impatience.

"She doesn't say exactly . . . the boat is . . . was . . . supposed to leave yesterday morning, but the sea was rough, so they decided to wait . . . except she can't wait. Oh, here, you read it." Prudence thrust the wire at her sister, her eyes dancing with delight. "Any day now, I think."

"The sooner the better," Chastity said jubilantly as they went into the dining parlor for luncheon.

"We have to give them a day to get settled in," Prudence said, surveying the table's offering. Cold ham, a beetroot salad, bread, and cheese.

"You know Con won't wait a moment before she comes over," Chastity said, slicing bread thickly and passing a hunk to her sister on the tip of the knife.

"She might regret being in a hurry when she hears what we have to tell her," Prudence observed, buttering her bread and taking several slices of ham from the platter. "I wonder how soon we shall hear from Sir Gideon. It can't take him too long to read the article and get the picture."

"It might take him longer to make up his mind." Chastity speared beetroot. "Shall I pour coffee?"

Prudence nodded her thanks through a mouthful of bread and ham. Her mind turned now to the afternoon ahead. There was nothing that could be done to hurry the barrister's decision, but the two hours a week when the Honorable Misses Duncan were At Home had proved fruitful ground for acquiring clients for the Go-Between. They were gathering quite a register now of eligible men and women, who were, of course, sublimely unaware that they had been chosen as possible partners for some future unknowns should the opportunity present itself.

"I wonder if Susanna Deerfold will come this afternoon," Chastity said, tuning in to her sister's thoughts. "I thought she was getting along rather well with William Sharpe last week."

"We sowed a few seeds," Prudence agreed. "If they do come, I thought I'd suggest they visit the Elgin Marbles together. Susanna was extolling the virtues of Greek sculpture the other night, and I'm sure I heard William lecturing someone on the glories of the Parthenon."

"And once we've set them on the merry course to matrimony, do we demand a charitable donation?" Chastity inquired with a grin.

"Oh, definitely, but maybe not for indigent spinsters, maybe some fund to help preserve the treasures of Greece," Prudence said airily.

"Isn't this illegal . . . something akin to fraud? Raising money under false pretenses?" Chastity asked.

"I'm sure it is. But what's a working woman to do?" Prudence tossed her napkin on the table and pushed back her chair. "I'll go and change, then check the flowers in the drawing room."

"I'll join you."

By half past three the sisters surveyed a pleasantly humming drawing room. "No sign of Lady Lucan or Lady Winthrop," Chastity murmured as she passed her sister carrying a platter of scones.

Prudence offered a minute shrug in response and turned as Jenkins announced Lady Letitia Graham and Miss Pamela Graham. "Letitia, how lovely to see you." She went forward to greet Constance's sister-in-law with a brushing kiss, then bent to the small girl who stood beside her mother. "Good afternoon, Pamela." She shook the girl's hand and refrained from commenting that children of Pamela's age were better employed, not to mention more amused, in the schoolroom on an autumn afternoon. A drawing room full of adult gossip was a tedious place for a six-year-old.

"Oh, the governess left," Letitia said with a sigh and an outflung hand. "No notice, would you believe? She just packed and left straight after breakfast. And this is Nanny's afternoon out and the nursemaid has the toothache . . . so inconsiderate. So, here we are, aren't we, Pammy?" She gave the child a brittle smile that the child received in stolid silence.

"Oh, how tiresome for you, my dear." Lady Bainbridge beckoned imperiously from her armchair. "You seem to have so much trouble with governesses, dear. Perhaps you need to try another agency. Do come and sit by me . . . I'm sure I can remember the agency who sent me the treasure who took care of Martha and Mary . . . what was her name?" She swung her rather large head towards her daughters, who sat primly side by side on the sofa opposite.

"Miss Grayson, Mama," supplied Martha.

"She was with us for more than ten years, Mama," reminded Mary.

Chastity noted the faintest hint of sarcasm in the daughters' responses, not enough for their mother to notice. Lady Bainbridge was deaf to all such nuances, but it was quite heartening to hear from a pair of downtrodden sisters who hadn't managed to look their mother in the eye from the moment of their births.

"Lady Lucan and Lady Winthrop," Jenkins announced as the two dowagers sailed into the drawing room.

Chastity set down her plate of scones and went over to where Pamela, now abandoned by her mother, stood beside Prudence. "Would you like to help me pass around the cream for the scones, Pamela?" She took the child's hand and led her off to the sideboard, freeing her sister to greet the donators to the charity for indigent spinsters.

"Lady Lucan . . . Lady Winthrop . . ." Prudence smiled her best smile. "How delightful to see you. How are the wedding plans progressing?"

"Oh, very well," said the Dowager Lady Lucan.

"Quite splendidly," said the Dowager Lady Winthrop. "Hester is an angel in her wedding gown. The train is nearly ten feet long." She took a tiny scrap of lace from her sleeve and dabbed her eyes. "Winthrop would have been so proud . . . to have walked her down the aisle. Such a loss for a poor girl on her wedding day."

"But her brother, Lord Winthrop, will support her admirably, I'm sure," Prudence said. "And of course she will have David waiting for her at the altar." She smiled at Lady Lucan. "It must gladden your heart, Lady Lucan, to see your only son so happy."

"I won't say that it doesn't," the dowager countess allowed herself to say. "And Hester's a good girl."

How to prod these two dowagers for the promised fifty guineas apiece?

"Let me get you some tea," Prudence said with a nod at Jenkins, who was circulating with the silver teapot. She steered the dowagers to an empty sofa beside the French windows opening onto the terrace and sat down on a lower chair beside them. When they had teacups and cucumber sandwiches, she said, "I had a wire from my sister Mrs. Ensor. She's having her honeymoon in Egypt—"

"Egypt!" Lady Bainbridge exclaimed. "What a strange place for a honeymoon . . . all that sand and dust."

"Yes, quite ruinous for the complexion," put in Letitia. "And dear Constance has always had such a lovely skin."

"I doubt it's suffered, Letitia," Chastity said, guiding Pamela's rather wavering hand wielding clotted cream. "But we shall discover soon enough. They're on their way home."

"Oh, how delightful it will be to see dear Constance again, and Pammy misses her uncle most dreadfully, don't you, Pammy dear?" The mother smiled fondly at the child, who rather firmly shook her head and licked the remnants of clotted cream from the serving spoon.

"Constance has always been so devoted to the charity she supports." Prudence doggedly turned the conversation in a more useful direction. "She said in her wire that she has been gathering support from diplomatic circles in Paris and Rome, and, of course, in Cairo."

"Oh, yes . . . yes . . . of course. The charity." The

Dowager Lady Winthrop opened her tiny silk reticule. "I was forgetting, dear. I had promised a donation . . . such a worthy cause. Fifty guineas, wasn't it?"

"Thank you," Prudence said in an undertone, taking the bank draft. "I cannot tell you what a difference this will make to the lives of these poor gentlewomen. They are destitute through no fault of their own. Without what little we can give them they would be obliged to sell themselves on the street."

Lady Lucan put up her not inconsiderable chins and opened her own reticule. "Well, I had thought fifty guineas at first, but in the circumstances, I decided seventy would be more appropriate."

Lady Winthrop stared into space as her neighbor with an air of quiet triumph handed a bank draft to Prudence.

"You are both so kind and generous," Prudence said, rising gracefully, both drafts tucked into her palm. "I can't thank you enough . . . and these poor women will be eternally grateful." Smiling, she moved away to the sideboard, where surreptitiously she opened the linen drawer and dropped the two drafts softly among the tea napkins.

"Outrageous," whispered Chastity at her ear.

"The devil drives, sister dear."

Chapter 3

Gideon laid aside the copy of *The Mayfair Lady* with a frown. He reread the solicitor's letter and glanced again at the broadsheet before reaching for a silver cigarette box. He took a cigarette, lit it, and pushed back his chair, going over to the narrow window that looked on the street. He smoked thoughtfully, gazing down at the few pedestrians still about at this hour of early evening. Law clerks for the most part, hurrying home to lonely garrets or wives and children in humble terraced houses on the outskirts of London. It was not a profession that paid well.

As if prodded by the reflection, he left the window and went into the outer office, where Thadeus was sifting through a pile of paper on a small table. "Do I have an opening for an appointment with this Mayfair Lady?"

Thadeus abandoned one pile of paper in favor of another and unearthed the appointment book. "The case interests you, Sir Gideon?"

"Not so much interests as irritates me," the barrister said, throwing his cigarette into the fire. He tossed the broadsheet on the table. "I've seen this publication lying around, of course, but never bothered to look at it. I assumed it was full of female gossip and clothes talk."

"And is it, Sir Gideon?"

"It has its share of that," Gideon said. "But it also seems to be some suffragist tract as well."

The clerk's upper lip curled in an involuntary gesture of disdain. "What would women do with the vote, Sir Gideon?"

The barrister shrugged slightly. "As far as I'm concerned, Thadeus, the jury's still out on that question. But this article . . ." He tapped the paper with a forefinger. "It seems to me Barclay's well within his rights to sue. This is a piece of unadulterated malice."

"But what if it's true, Sir Gideon?" The clerk tilted his head to one side like an inquiring hedge sparrow.

The barrister waved a dismissive hand. "Maybe there's no smoke without fire, but this kind of sensationalist trash is worse than the sins it's intending to expose. I am going to tell whoever wrote this piece of scandal-mongering libel exactly what I think of this *Mayfair Lady*. The very idea that they would approach *me* to defend such a disgraceful malignant torrent of slanderous rubbish is insulting. Who the hell do they think I am? Some half-trained lawyer grubbing for clients in the gutter?"

Sir Gideon had quite a head of steam up, Thadeus reflected as he consulted the ledger. He was beginning to feel sorry for the woman who was going to walk unknowingly into that wall of fire. "Next Thursday afternoon, Sir Gideon. You have an opening at four o'clock."

"Then send a message to that Bayswater address requesting the presence of the Mayfair Lady in my chambers at that time."

"As you say, Sir Gideon. I'll send it by messenger right away."

Gideon reached for his greatcoat and muffler on the coat rack. "Oh, and make sure they're aware that my fee for an initial consultation with no guarantees is fifty guineas."

"I would have done so anyway, Sir Gideon." Thadeus sounded faintly reproving.

"Yes, of course you would," his employer said, heading for the door. "I'm on my way home now, Thadeus. Sarah invited some school friends for supper and I have strict instructions to be home in time to be introduced. I gather their parents need to know that even though Sarah has no mother, her father is perfectly respectable. Don't stay overlong yourself." He raised a hand in farewell and hurried out into the dusk.

The shiny green motor drove around Manchester Square and drew to a halt outside No. 10. Max Ensor turned to his wife with a slightly quizzical smile.

"Don't forget you don't live here anymore, Constance."

She laughed and shook her head. "As if I would."

"Oh, I wouldn't be so sure," he said, still smiling. "You haven't seen your sisters for six weeks. I'll lay odds that the minute you're in their midst you'll forget everything that's happened since you saw them last."

Constance shook her head again and laid a gloved hand on his as it rested on the steering wheel. "That I could never do, Max." Her dark green eyes were serious now, although they held a sparkle in their depths. "Every moment of the last six weeks is indelibly printed on my memory . . . and not just my memory," she added with a quick and slightly mischievous grin. "My body bears its fair share of imprints."

Max laughed and got out of the motor to come around and open the passenger door for her. "You're not alone in that, my love. There's something of the female leopard about you on occasion."

"The female leopard?" she inquired with raised eyebrows. "Now, why would that be?"

"I read once a very vivid description of the mating habits of the leopard," her husband informed her solemnly as she stepped to the pavement. "It seems to be a very violent coition, in which the female spends most of her time growling and scratching her mate, finally flinging him off her back with an open-clawed wallop."

"Did I do that?" Constance said in mock awe. "I have no recollection. It doesn't sound at all like me. I have such a mild temperament."

"Now, that, my dear wife, reveals a staggering level of self-deception," he scoffed. He lifted her chin with his forefinger and looked down at her, not so very far since she was almost as tall as he. "I'll come back for you in two hours."

"Don't be ridiculous, Max. I'll take a hackney home."

"No, I'll come and fetch you. I don't trust you in your sisters' company. Besides," he added, silencing her incipient protest with a finger on her lips, "I've missed them too, and I should certainly pay my respects to your father."

Constance considered this, then shook her head in

resignation. "Very well, but there's no need to hurry your business at Downing Street."

"I won't. I merely intend to bring myself back into the Prime Minister's sights, just in case I slipped his mind during the summer recess."

"I doubt you did that," Constance declared. "Once met, Max, you could never slip anyone's mind."

"You flatter me," he returned with a dry smile. He kissed her mouth, his lips lingering for a moment despite the fact that they were standing on the open street. Then reluctantly he raised his head. "I'll be back in two hours."

Constance turned to the steps leading up to the house. "Don't hurry," she said, blowing him a kiss over her shoulder as she walked quickly to the door.

He watched as she used her own key to let herself in, and when the door had closed on her he returned to the motor and drove off towards Westminster and the Prime Minister's residence at 10 Downing Street.

Constance had barely closed the door before Jenkins appeared from the shadows of the staircase. "Why, Miss Con . . ." He coughed. "Mrs. Ensor, I should say."

"No, no, Jenkins, I couldn't get used to anything but Con," she said, coming towards him with swift step and kissing his cheek. "How have you been? It seems I've been away an eternity. Is Mrs. Hudson well?"

"Everyone is well, Miss Con," the butler stated, his delighted smile belying the formal tone. "Miss Chas and Miss Prue are in the parlor upstairs."

"No, we're here," Chastity's light and cheerful tones chimed. "Con, we didn't dare to expect you so soon." She came flying down the stairs, followed with as much haste by Prudence.

Constance disappeared into their embrace and Jenkins nodded his satisfaction as he watched the three heads of various shades of red bob and blend in the way he knew so well. "I'll bring coffee to the parlor," he announced.

"Oh, and some of those almond slices that Mrs. Hudson made yesterday," Chastity emerged from the tight circle to call after him as he walked back to the kitchen.

Constance hugged her. "I didn't expect you to have lost your sweet tooth in six weeks, Chas."

Her youngest sister gave an exaggerated sigh. "No, I'm a lost cause. And I seem to be getting rounder." She pulled a comical face as she traced the swell of her breasts beneath her muslin blouse and plucked at her hips that curved voluptuously beneath the wide belt of her striped grosgrain skirt.

"Sometimes, sister dear, I think you suffer from the besetting sin of vanity," Prudence stated, even though she was laughing. "You know perfectly well it suits you."

"For the moment," sighed Chastity. "But soon it will turn to fat, and then, alas, what shall I do?"

"Give up cakes," Constance said, linking arms with her sisters. She looked closely at Prudence and saw that she had a drawn look about her eyes. She looked again at Chastity, and realized that the light banter had merely masked a similar unquiet air.

"Let's go upstairs," she said. "I want to hear everything that's happened since I left."

"First we want to hear everything about your honeymoon," Prudence said as they went upstairs. "Your telegrams were so brief. Did Max really take you to the pyramids?"

"Yes, but we visited them on horseback, not by camel. Could you imagine Max on a camel? And we went down the Nile on the most luxurious riverboat all the way to Alexandria." Constance opened the door to the parlor and gave an involuntary smile at the welcome familiarity of the room. "Oh, I've missed home," she said.

"We've missed you," Prudence said, hugging her. "But I have to say, Con, that there is nothing Egyptian about that dress." She regarded her sister's outfit with a knowing eye.

"Well, we did go to Cairo via Paris and Rome," Constance reminded her.

"That would explain the unmistakable mark of a Parisian modiste." Prudence closed the door behind them. "I saw in one of the fashion magazines that those straight skirts are becoming all the rage on the Continent. Do you have trunksful?"

"Not quite." Constance drew off her gloves and tossed them onto a console table. "But I do have several for you both. The trunk's following me here in a hackney. There wasn't room in the motor." She examined her sisters. "I don't think they'll need altering, although Chas might have grown a little rounder since I last saw her."

"Calumny!" Chastity exclaimed, laughing. "But I can't wait to see them. And that hat, Con! Is it a hat?"

Constance unpinned the small pillow of mink that sat atop her head. "They call it a hat on the Rue de Rivoli, but I think it looks more like a rabbit's scut. Max liked it, though."

"How *is* Max?" Prudence asked, trying not to put too much emphasis on the question as she geared herself for the revelations to come.

Constance smiled and tossed the fur pillow to join her

gloves on the table. She perched on the wide arm of the chesterfield, smoothing out the creases in the tawny silk skirt that stretched tight across her thighs, and unbuttoned her wasp-waisted black jacket to reveal a lace-trimmed blouse of ivory silk. "I believe him to be in fine health."

Chastity threw a cushion at her. She ducked, caught it, and threw it back. "We had a wonderful time."

"So, we can assume he's in a relaxed frame of mind," Prudence said.

Constance swung her gaze sharply towards her sister. "What is it? I knew something was wrong the minute I walked in."

She paused as a knock at the door heralded Jenkins's entrance with a tray of coffee. "How's Mrs. Beedle, Jenkins?" she asked as she rose to clear space for the tray on the paper-littered table.

"Very well, I thank you, Miss Con." Jenkins poured coffee into three cups and judiciously added sugar to the one that he handed to Chastity.

"I hope she's received lots of letters for *The Mayfair Lady.*"

"Prue collected the last delivery a couple of days ago." Chastity selected an almond slice from the plate as the door closed behind the butler. They couldn't wait forever before putting Constance in the picture.

"Yes," Prudence said. "Some quite interesting correspondence."

Constance's expression was serious. "What is it?" she asked again.

Prudence went to the secretaire, where a mountain of paper threatened to tumble to the carpet. "You remember the piece you wrote about the earl of Barclay?" She removed a sheet from the pile.

Constance rose to her feet too. "Yes. How could I forget?" Her tone was hesitant. "I knew it would cause a stir . . . we all knew that it would."

"He's suing us—or rather, *The Mayfair Lady*—for libel," Chastity told her, getting to her own feet.

"But he can't. It was all true and well documented," Constance said.

"Here's a copy of the solicitor's letter." Prudence handed her the document that she had painstakingly copied before leaving the original with Sir Gideon's clerk.

"He doesn't have a leg to stand on," Constance said. "I had the names of three women whom he'd seduced and abandoned."

"And the *Pall Mall Gazette* picked up on it as we'd hoped," Prudence said. "But their article has only just come out. It's going to put Barclay in the pillory." She leaned over her sister's shoulder and jabbed with a forefinger at the paragraph at the bottom of the letter. "I think that's where the real trouble lies."

Constance read it. "Oh, God," she murmured. "The financial stuff. I should have left that out. I didn't have any hard evidence, and yet I know it's true." She steepled her fingers at her mouth as she looked at her sisters. "I'm so sorry."

"It's not your fault," Prudence said, removing her glasses and wiping at a smudge with her handkerchief. "Chas and I stand behind what you wrote. We know he reneged on gambling debts and we know some of his financial dealings have been suspect." She replaced her glasses.

"But we had no evidence," Constance said. "I got carried away by the excitement of exposing his philandering and I thought I could throw in the dishonesty and no one would question it because the rest was incontrovertible."

"Well, he questioned it," Prudence said flatly. She pushed her glasses up the bridge of her nose with a jab of her forefinger. "Obviously he thinks that if he can sue us successfully for libel on this, then he'll be vindicated on the other accusations as well. And then he can go after the *Pall Mall Gazette*. After a court triumph, no one will dare to whisper about his sexual peccadilloes."

Constance tossed the document back onto the secretaire with an air of disgust. "Any ideas?"

"Well, we've got the ball rolling," Prudence said, and explained about Sir Gideon Malvern. "Amelia Franklin came around this morning with a message that he'll see us next Thursday at four o'clock," she finished. "Obviously, I didn't want to give him this address, at least not at this stage, so I gave him Amelia and Henry's as a contact."

Constance nodded. "I'm sure they didn't mind."

"No, quite the opposite. Amelia's always offering to help with *The Mayfair Lady*."

Constance nodded again. "Then there's not much we can do until we see him. I wonder if Max knows him. He's bound to be expensive if he's a KC."

"We'd come to that conclusion ourselves," Prudence said gloomily. "He's already said that his initial fee will be fifty guineas. But apart from that, how do we keep our own names out of this? Barclay can sue *The Mayfair Lady*, but someone's going to want to know whose hand actually penned the so-called libel."

Her sisters made no immediate response to that truth.

The heavy slam of the front door downstairs broke their silence. "Father," said Chastity. "He'll be so pleased to see you, Con." Her tone was a trifle lackluster.

"I imagine he's totally taken Barclay's part in this," Constance stated without question or surprise. She walked to the door. "I'll run down and see him." She reached the top of the stairs just as Lord Duncan began to ascend them.

"Constance, my dear," he said, hurrying up towards her, a smile splitting his face. "Your sisters weren't sure when you'd be here. Your wire said something about the boat being delayed by the weather."

"Oh, it cleared up and we sailed on yesterday morning's tide. We got back to London late last night, but I couldn't wait another minute to see you all," she said, opening her arms to him. She hugged him as he kissed her soundly. "Are you well?"

"Oh, yes . . . yes, indeed." He stood back, holding her shoulders as he examined her. "Marriage suits you, my dear. You have quite a glow about you."

She laughed. "I believe it does. Max will be coming round in an hour or so to pay his respects."

"I look forward to seeing him. I'd welcome his opinion on a bad business." He shook his head. "A very bad business."

"Prue and Chas were saying something about—" Constance began, but Lord Duncan swept on.

"That disgraceful rag . . . *Mayfair Lady* . . . libeled Barclay, would you believe? The brass nerve of it." Lord Duncan's already ruddy complexion took on a deeper hue. "Absolutely outrageous. And now this wretched *Pall Mall Gazette* has taken it up."

"Yes, we told Con all about it, Father," Chastity said in soothing tones from behind her sister.

"It's a disgrace. That an honest man can be pilloried by some scandalmongering underground broadsheet... Anonymous writers, don't even have the courage to declare themselves honestly to stand by their lies. I don't know what the civilized world is coming to."

He shook his head again and made a visible effort to compose himself. "But we don't need to spoil your homecoming, my dear. I'm sure you have much to tell your sisters, but when you're ready to come down to the drawing room, we'll open a bottle of the vintage Veuve Clicquot in celebration. There are a few bottles left, I believe. I shall tell Jenkins to put one on ice." He patted his eldest daughter's cheek, nodded benignly at her sisters, and returned to the hall.

"*Do* we have any of the vintage 'widow' left?" Constance inquired.

"No, but there are a couple of bottles of Taittinger that Jenkins put away. He'll produce those instead," Prudence said. She found their father's refusal to believe, let alone accept, the general depletion of his wine cellars a particular source of anxiety among her many financial worries. She danced a constant ballet of the bottles with the able assistance of Jenkins, who knew the contents of the cellar down to the last label and exactly what substitutes Lord Duncan would accept.

Constance picked up her coffee cup again. "Let's talk about something more cheerful. Give me an update on the magazine. Have we any more paying clients for the Go-Between?"

"Speaking of paying," Chastity said, "you should have seen the way Prue squeezed fifty guineas out of *La*

Winthrop, and then, would you believe, not to be outdone, *La Lucan* chipped in seventy. Prue was masterly."

Constance laughed. "I wouldn't have expected anything less. Have Hester and Lucan set a date yet?"

"Christmas Eve," Prudence told her. "Have you decided on an afternoon for your At Homes?"

Constance shook her head with a grimace. "There's no need just yet. Everyone's going to be making bride visits. As soon as it's known that I'm back in town, Society will be beating its curious and gossipy path to my door. You know what it's like, they'll be scrutinizing the furniture and the general decor of the house and asking me pointed little questions while they try to decide whether I'm content with my lot." Her tone dripped sarcasm.

"Or in the process of giving your husband an heir," added Prudence, regarding her sister with a lifted eyebrow.

"The only babies I'm going to be producing are in print," Constance declared. "At least until *The Mayfair Lady* and the Go-Between are truly solvent."

"Which won't happen at all if we can't beat this libel suit," Prudence said, her expression once more grave. "I'm just praying that this Malvern isn't going to be prejudiced against three women operating a *scandalmongering, underground rag.*" Her tone was a fair imitation of her father's.

They were silent for a minute, then Constance said, "We'll ask Max if he knows him. Maybe he could put in a good word for us. You look doubtful. Why?"

"Oh, I'm just wondering whether you want Max to read the piece in question," Prudence said, with a hesitant little shrug. "You know him best, of course, but . . ."

Constance grimaced. "You have a point. But I can't see any way of keeping it from him."

"His wife as defendant in a libel suit isn't going to advance his career any," Prudence commented.

"Which is one of the major reasons why it *can't* come out."

Another silence fell, then Constance said with effort, "Let's not think about it anymore, just for the moment. You still haven't told me if we have any new Go-Between clients."

"Two possibles." Chastity followed her sister's cue and went to the secretaire. She came back with two letters. "This one from a girl, at least she sounds more like a girl than a woman, who says she's desperate for a husband as a means of escaping a tyrannical stepmother who's determined to marry her off to someone old enough to be her grandfather. She wants to elope. I suspect she's been reading too many romances."

Constance took the letter and read the somewhat passionately incoherent screed, the writing liberally splattered with stains that one had to assume were tears.

"The poor child does seem to fancy herself between the pages of some melodramatic romance, doesn't she?" Prudence remarked, watching her sister's slightly derisive expression. "I doubt she's even of age. In my opinion we should just write her a sensible response saying we only accept clients who are over twenty-one."

"Except that's not strictly true. We found Hester Winthrop a husband," Constance pointed out.

"Yes, but that was to give Lucan a love interest other than Chas, and we knew it was a perfect match for both of them. We wouldn't have promoted it if we'd had any doubts. I don't want to meddle in the affairs of someone this young, about whom we know nothing. This so-called stepmother could be the most devoted and considerate woman, whose motives have been totally misunderstood by a spoilt gaby."

"Yes, you have a point." Constance folded the sheet and tapped it thoughtfully into the palm of her hand.

"Apart from anything else," Prudence continued resolutely, "we don't have the resources to offer a youth-counseling service. We'll be wasting an entire afternoon, not to mention the train fares to Wimbledon, if we agree to see her." The glance she shot at Chastity told Constance that her sisters had been around this maypole several times already. It was hardly surprising. Chastity's soft heart and truly empathetic nature frequently clashed with her sister's pragmatic nature and unsentimental opinions. Constance, as the eldest, was often required to cast the deciding vote.

"I'm with Prue," she said. "Sorry, Chas, but we have to be practical."

Chastity merely nodded. Despite her gentle inclinations, she knew when to fight a battle and when to yield. In this instance, the damsel from Wimbledon would have to find her own salvation.

"So, that's settled." Constance set the letter on the table. Prudence looked relieved—she hated being at odds with either of her sisters. She offered Chastity a rueful smile that her youngest sister returned with a tiny shrug of resignation.

"What about the second letter?" asked Constance.

"Rather more promising, I think." Chastity handed her the second letter. "Prue and I think we know who it's from, although she's using a pseudonym." She pointed to the signature at the bottom of the neatly penned letter. "She can't really be called Iphigenia."

"Unlikely," Constance agreed. "Wasn't Iphigenia sacrificed by Agamemnon to get a fair wind to sail to Troy?" She read the letter. "Oh, I see. You think it's written by Lady Northrop," she said when she'd finished. "She's always peppering her conversations with totally inapposite classical allusions."

"Doesn't it sound like her? Widowed, if not sacrificed, four years ago, in her prime . . . not yet ready to settle for a loveless future—"

"By which, of course, she means sexless," Prudence interrupted Chastity. "And look how she describes herself. Wealthy, brunette, brown eyes, well-endowed figure, impeccable dress sense, attractive to men. Isn't that Dottie Northrop to a tee? Apart from the dress sense," she added with the authority of one who knew her own was beyond reproach. "That I'd quibble with."

"She's certainly not one to hide her charms," Constance agreed. "And she's certainly well endowed."

"She's also the most notorious flirt," Chastity added.

"So, why does she think she needs help finding a suitable husband? She's a veritable mantrap already." Constance rose to refill her coffee cup from the tray on the sideboard.

"The men she attracts are not of the marrying kind," Prudence pointed out.

"But whom do *we* know that she doesn't that we could put in her way?"

"We'll have to think about it. If we can come up with a few possibilities, we can get them together at an At Home, as we did with Millicent and Anonymous."

"We could always suggest she moderate her necklines

and be a little less flamboyant with the perfume and the diamonds," Chastity suggested. "We could make it sound as if it were the sort of general advice we give all our clients."

"We'll leave that to you, Chas. Tactful advice is right up your street. One thing we do know: Dotty can afford the finder's fee." Prudence turned at a knock on the door. "Come in."

Jenkins opened the door. "Mr. Ensor is with Lord Duncan, ladies. They would like you to join them in the drawing room for champagne."

"Thank you. We'll be down straightaway." Constance examined her reflection in the mirror above the mantelpiece, tucking a loose strand into her elaborately piled mass of rich russet hair.

"It's not like you to check your appearance, Con," Prudence said with a mischievous grin. "Marriage has certainly worked some changes."

"There's quite a wind blowing," Constance declared with an air of mock dignity. "It was gusting as I left the motor."

Laughing, they went downstairs. Lord Duncan's raised voice reached them as they crossed the hall to the drawing room. They exchanged comprehending glances. His lordship was expounding with great fervor his indignation at the libel of his friend. Judging by the speed of the monologue, his son-in-law was making no attempt to respond.

"Oh, hell," muttered Constance. "He's bound to have shown Max the article and I haven't even had a chance to prepare him." She swallowed slightly, stiffened her shoulders, and opened the drawing room door. "You're early, Max. You said two hours. Did you see the Prime

Minister?" Her eyes darted to the table that stood between the two men. Both the *Pall Mall Gazette* and *The Mayfair Lady* lay there, their pages turned to the incriminating articles.

Max followed her gaze, then regarded her with a less than loverlike air. "I saw him," he said shortly. He greeted his sisters-in-law with rather more warmth, although there was a certain hint of reserve that was not normally present in his dealings with them.

"I've just been telling Ensor about this disgrace," Lord Duncan thundered, gesturing to the papers on the table. "If I ever discover who wrote that first piece of trash, I'll take a horsewhip to him. Thrash him to within an inch of his life."

"I can't say I'd blame you, sir," Max said aridly, casting another glance at his wife. Constance met his gaze.

"Well, enough of that for the moment. Ah, Jenkins, you've brought the champagne. Why the Taittinger? I specifically asked for the vintage Veuve Clicquot." His lordship frowned fiercely at the bottle's label as if it offended him.

"There is no more of the Clicquot, your lordship," Jenkins said placidly. "Harpers are unable to lay in any more supplies of that vintage."

Lord Duncan harrumphed. "Seems they're always running short of supplies these days. I shall complain to Harper himself."

"Yes, sir." Jenkins eased off the cork and poured the straw-colored liquid into five crystal glasses. He handed them around, and if he was aware of the tension that connected the sisters like a taut rope, he gave no sign. He bowed and left the drawing room.

The next half hour was for the sisters excruciating,

for their father a pleasantry, and for Max Ensor a period of tightly reined annoyance. At last, after the minute details of the Nile river trip had been discussed with Lord Duncan, Max set down his glass.

"Constance, we should not neglect to visit my sister," he said. "She would feel slighted if we failed her on our first day home."

"Of course," Constance said readily. "Father, I hope you'll dine with us soon."

He received her kiss with a smile. "Yes, delightful, my dear. I look forward to seeing you in your new home. Perhaps you could invite Barclay."

Constance's smile was as flat as the Dead Sea. "Yes, of course. And maybe some of your bridge cronies. We could arrange a rubber after dinner."

"Lovely, my dear." He patted her shoulder and turned to his son-in-law. "So good to have you back in town, Ensor. I look forward to discussing the new Parliament with you."

"It will be my pleasure, Lord Duncan," Max said smoothly, allowing himself to be swept on the tide of his wife and her sisters out into the hall.

Once there, he said with a peremptory nod at the stairs, "That parlor of yours, I believe."

"Now is as good a time as any," Constance agreed, moving ahead to the stairs. "We need some information, Max."

"I doubt that's all you need," he muttered, standing aside to allow Prudence and Chastity to precede him.

Chapter 4

Constance felt her husband's hand on the small of her back as she followed her sisters up the stairs. It could have been a gently proprietorial gesture, but she was not fool enough to misinterpret the pressure of the touch. Max was not best pleased.

Max closed the parlor door behind them. He glanced around and then strode to the secretaire, where lay a copy of the broadsheet. A tense silence hung over the room while he reread the article. "I had the idiotic hope that this was some deranged figment of my imagination," he muttered when he'd finished reading.

He rolled the paper tightly and stood flicking it against his thigh as he looked at Constance. "Of course you wrote this."

She nodded. "Weeks ago, before we were married."

His exasperation got the better of his composure. "For God's sake, woman, are you completely out of your mind?"

Constance lost her apologetic demeanor. "Don't use

that tone with me, Max. And I won't be called *woman* in that patronizing manner."

Prudence and Chastity exchanged a glance, then sat side by side on the sofa and regarded the bristling couple with unabashed interest.

"What do you expect me to say?" Max demanded. "Couldn't you have warned me you were going after Barclay? This is the most vitriolic attack on a respected—"

"Wait a minute—" Constance interrupted even as both her sisters jumped to their feet.

"There's nothing respected or respectable about Barclay," Prudence stated, her usually pale complexion flushed, her light green eyes alive with conviction. "Constance interviewed all three women mentioned in the article—"

"*And* I saw their children and the miserable conditions in which they were living," Constance declared. "They weren't lying, Max."

"Can you imagine what it would be like to be raped by your employer, then thrown into the street pregnant without a character reference . . . no money, no home?" Chastity weighed in with her twopence worth and Max almost physically backed away from the sisters, who were facing him like lion tamers.

"I'm not excusing him," he said. "But this is too much." He waved the rolled-up broadsheet again. "It's such a personal attack. A complete character assassination."

"It's his character we were attacking," Constance stated aridly. "The man's a philanderer, a rapist, a cheat, an embezzler—"

"Where's the evidence for that?" Max asked, a forefinger jabbing the air in front of him.

Prudence grimaced. "Rumor is all we have."

Max spun around to stare at her. "That's going to be your defense? Rumor? I'd credited *you* with more sense, Prudence." Constance stared at the carpet, hearing the inference in the emphasis. It was true she was not always as circumspect as her younger sister.

Prudence, for her part, flushed, but said stolidly, "We agree we'll have to do better than that. Once we've found a lawyer to defend *The Mayfair Lady*."

"We think we've found one," Chastity said.

"Yes, Sir Gideon Malvern," Prudence put in. "He's seeing us next Thursday. We were wondering if you knew him, Max."

Instead of answering her, Max demanded, "How are you going to keep your identities secret in a court of law?"

"We don't know yet," Constance said. "We were rather hoping that this Sir Gideon might have some idea."

"Yes. *Do* you know him, Max?" Prudence pressed. "He's a member of the Middle Temple and—"

"Yes, I know that," her brother-in-law snapped.

Prudence glanced at her elder sister, who shrugged with a gesture of resignation. They would get nowhere by resenting Max's tone at this point. They needed what enlightenment he could offer them.

"Would you like a whisky, Max?" Chastity invited with a conciliatory smile.

He regarded her with narrowed eyes, then let his gaze drift to her sisters, who were clearly struggling with the need to placate him while surging with indignation at his high-handed approach to their problem. He grinned suddenly. It was a moment to be savored. One rarely got the better of the Duncan sisters.

"What's funny?" Constance demanded, all suspicion. "You look like you did in the mews with Father's Cadillac."

"The only other occasion when I felt that I had the upper hand with the three of you," he said, his grin broadening.

"All right," Constance said. "You've had your fun at our expense. Now tell us what you know of this barrister."

"Do you have any idea how much a barrister like Malvern is going to cost you?" he asked with mild curiosity.

"We're not without resources," Prudence said tightly, her myopic gaze fierce behind her spectacles. "We have emergency funds, Max. Not that it's any business of yours," she added, and immediately regretted the addition. "I'm sorry." She pinched the bridge of her nose. "I didn't mean to be ungracious. I'm just feeling a little overwhelmed."

"You're not dealing with this alone, Prue," Constance said swiftly. "I know you bear the lion's share of the business management, but we're all in this one together."

Prudence managed a faint smile. "I *know* that. I just can't imagine what will happen if we lose."

"Well, Gideon Malvern can go a long way to ensuring that you don't," Max said, offering the brisk reassurance that he knew the sisters would appreciate more than sympathy. "He has the reputation of being the most innovative and able KC in the Inns of Court. He rarely loses a case."

That was all very well, Prudence reflected. Exactly what they wanted. But how the hell were they going to pay for what they wanted? For all her bravado, she could see no possible way of managing a top barrister's fee. The initial fifty guineas was going to be hard enough to find. If it weren't for the indigent spinsters' charity, she'd be wracking her brains for something to pawn.

Her sisters knew this intellectually, but sometimes she felt they didn't grasp the realities as clearly as she did. The management of the family finances was her responsibility. Naturally enough, since she was the bookkeeper, the mathematician, the obviously practical one of the sisters. She didn't resent the responsibility but sometimes she felt she carried it alone.

"He might suit you, because he likes challenges," Max continued. "He picks and chooses his cases; he can afford to do so," he added, watching them, not at all fooled by Prudence's defensive statements about hidden resources. "He has been known to take a case pro bono if it really appeals to him." He saw three pairs of green eyes sharpen with interest. "Or he's been known to come to a contingency agreement whereby if he wins he takes a share of the damages awarded to his client."

"Seems fair," Prudence said, frowning. "He gets paid to win."

"You'll have to persuade him that there's sufficient interest and challenge in the case to make it worth his while."

"Well, I don't think that's going to be difficult," Constance said with a short laugh. "There's got to be a more than ordinary challenge in taking on as clients three subversive women who insist on remaining anonymous."

"That problem I leave in your more than capable hands, ladies." He gave them a small bow.

"Was Sir Gideon knighted for services to the bar, or did he inherit the title?" Prudence asked quickly as Max reached to open the door.

"He was knighted after he defended a particularly difficult case that involved one of the king's rather more dubious friends," Max said, turning the knob. "Are you coming, Constance? We really should visit Letitia."

"Yes," she said reluctantly. "I suppose we should. Let's all meet at Fortnum's for tea this afternoon, Prue. We can talk strategy then."

Prudence nodded. "Max, does this Sir Gideon always defend? Or does he prosecute too?"

"He specializes in defense."

"Well, that's something," Chastity declared. "We just have to convince him that it would be a travesty of justice to find *The Mayfair Lady* guilty of libel."

"One of you," Max said. "I would most earnestly suggest that only one of you keeps the appointment."

"Why?" Constance had gathered up her gloves and now stood before the mirror above the mantel inserting pins in the mink pillow atop her russet head.

Max hesitated, searching for the most diplomatic answer. "He's a formidable man but you wouldn't want him to feel ambushed," he said finally. "I don't know how he views women in general, but I'd lay odds he's never come across any quite like you three."

"And we might put him off?" Constance asked with a sweet smile, turning from the mirror. "A trio of viragos, perhaps?"

"We are not going to have this conversation, Constance," Max said firmly, opening the door for her. "I merely gave my opinion. You may take it or leave it as you wish."

"We'll probably take it," Prudence said. "Oh, and be warned, Con. Letitia is firmly convinced that you've been camping in the desert and have a skin pitted with sand and hair matted with dust."

"Well, I daresay I shall be able to put her right on both those scores," Constance said.

"Oh, did you eat sheeps' eyes?" Chastity said, accompanying them to the stairs. "We were wondering."

"Good God! Whatever gave you that idea?" Max exclaimed, revolted.

"We thought that was a chief delicacy among the nomads of the Sahara," Chastity informed him.

"I don't think we ate any," Constance said, appearing to consider the question with appropriate solemnity. "Max actually refused to eat anything he couldn't identify."

"How unadventurous of you, Max," Prudence said reproachfully. "I would have thought when you go to somewhere as exciting as Egypt you would want to experience the culture at its richest. Mother would certainly have encouraged it."

Max knew from experience that the only way to put a stop to what could turn into a very convoluted discussion at his expense was to abandon it. "Come, Constance." He took her hand and hastened down the stairs, Constance blowing a farewell kiss to her sisters over her shoulder.

"Con, we'll see you at Fortnum's at four," Chastity called after them, laughter alight in her voice. It died fairly rapidly, however, when she saw Prue's expression.

She put a hand on her arm. "We'll get out of this, Prue. We have to."

Prudence sighed. "I know. But if Max, who's formidable enough in his own right, considers Malvern to be intimidating, how on earth are *we* going to deal with him?"

"We're considered quite formidable ourselves," Chastity said. "Even Max said as much. You'll be a match for him."

"Me?" Prudence took off her glasses and peered at her sister. "Since when did I draw the short straw?"

"It just seems obvious to me," Chastity said. "I didn't give it a second thought." She frowned, wondering why that was the case. "We'll see what Con thinks this afternoon. Maybe she's expecting to do it."

"She did write the piece," Prudence said, turning back to the parlor. But she knew from the sinking feeling in the pit of her stomach that the task of convincing Sir Gideon Malvern had her name on it. Once again she pictured him as she'd seen him in the dim light of the hall. She'd had the sense of a presence rather than any specific details about height or form or coloring. But his eyes had most definitely been gray. Gray with a certain piercing quality to them . . . a light that had fixed upon her like a torch beam. And his voice . . . now, she had liked his voice.

She was feeling in a rather more positive frame of mind that afternoon as she walked along Piccadilly to meet her sisters. Chastity had written her letter to the melodramatic miss from Wimbledon and had left early to stop at the post office to send it on its way, so Prudence was enjoying a solitary walk. It was a lovely crisp autumn afternoon, when London showed itself at its best. The trees were turning deep red and burnt orange and there was the faint scent of roasting chestnuts on the air. She passed a vendor at his brazier and hesitated, tempted by the aroma, but she was within a few yards of Fortnum's and she couldn't really walk into the tearoom with a newspaper cone of chestnuts.

How difficult could it be to persuade a barrister of the legitimacy of a case that shrieked legitimacy? So, maybe they didn't have much . . . no, any . . . evidence for the fraud accusations, but maybe, just maybe there was an obvious place to start looking. The idea so startled her that she stopped dead on the pavement. A man behind her dodged sideways to prevent a collision and passed her with a quick sidestep, staring at her.

Prudence offered a smile of apology and began walking slowly again. Why had they not thought of it before? It seemed obvious now. But perhaps they'd been blinded by their father's loyalty and dependence on his friend. She caught herself humming and relished a lighthearted feeling that had become a stranger just recently. She smiled at the doorman who held open the glass doors for her and entered the wide marble expanse of the tearoom. The usual string quartet was playing on the dais, and swallowtail-coated waiters, and waitresses in frilly white caps, moved between the crowded tables with trolleys laden with rich cakes and silver-domed serving platters.

"Mrs. Ensor and the Honorable Miss Prudence Duncan are seated in the far alcove, Miss Duncan." The maître d'hôtel bowed. "If you'd like to follow me."

"Thank you, Walter." Prudence followed him, aware of the eyes on her. Every new arrival was scrutinized in this fashion, chattering tea drinkers hoping for some intimation of scandal. Constance would have been the object of every gossiping tongue in the room since it was her first public outing since her marriage. Her clothes and general appearance would have been taken apart to the last stitch. Prudence smiled and nodded at acquaintances but didn't stop to greet anyone.

Her sisters were seated at a round table in a relatively secluded alcove behind a pillar. They waved as she came up. "There you are, Prue. We thought it better not to sit in plain sight today. To save Con some gawping and congratulating," Chastity explained.

"Oh, I think I'm already the subject of conversation at most tables," Constance said as Prudence took the chair Walter pulled out for her.

"Your dress must be," Prudence declared with approval. "It's gorgeous. I love those black and white stripes and those sleeves . . . the way they puff at the top and then are tight and buttoned to your wrists. Are those mother-of-pearl buttons?"

"Yes, aren't they pretty? What do you think of the hat?" Constance lifted the black spotted veil that covered her eyes.

"Stunning," Prudence said. "So different from that little mink thing you were wearing this morning. I love those orange plumes against the black velvet."

"I must say, I'm enjoying my new wardrobe," Constance confessed almost guiltily, drawing off her gloves. "Max is the driving force. He has the most avant-garde taste. Quite surprising, really, for someone who's always seemed so conventional."

"He married you, didn't he?" Prudence remarked. "Not the mark of a conventional man."

"Perhaps not." Constance was as unaware of the little

smile playing over her lips as she was of the glow on her cheeks, and the luminous sparkle in her eyes.

"Nice afternoon?" Chastity inquired blandly as she poured tea for her sister.

Constance gave her a sharp look and then laughed a little self-consciously. "Is it that obvious?"

"It's fairly obvious you didn't spend the entire afternoon with Letitia."

Constance changed the subject. She glanced up at the waitress who was hovering at the table. "Anchovy toast," she said. "I would like two pieces, please. What?" She looked at her sisters, who were regarding her with amusement.

"You don't usually eat tea," Chastity observed.

"I seem to be hungry this afternoon," Constance declared repressively. "And you're a fine one to talk. Look at that decadent concoction on your plate."

"Oh, it's delicious, you should try one." Chastity dipped her finger into the raspberry cream and licked it slowly. "Heavenly. Raspberry and chocolate. I can never decide whether chocolate and orange is a better combination. It all depends on which one I'm eating at the time."

"I'd like a marron glacé," Prudence said, looking the cake trolley over somewhat absently. "Thank you." She smiled at the waitress who poured her tea.

"What's the matter, Prue?" Constance inquired after a few seconds. "You've been looking at that marron glacé as if you've never seen anything like it before."

"I had a revelation on the way here," Prudence said.

"About the case?" Chastity leaned forward eagerly.

Prudence nodded. "Just a thought about this fraud business."

"Go on," Constance invited, sniffing hungrily at the fragrant plate of anchovy toast that had been placed in front of her.

"All right." Prudence took off her glasses and rubbed the bridge of her nose with a finger. "When Father threw his fortune behind that lunatic scheme to run a railway across the Sahara—"

"And lost every penny he possessed," Chastity stated.

"Precisely. Well, he didn't consult us, did he? And if he'd consulted Mother she would have put a stop to it with one soft word, but, of course, she wasn't there."

"True," Constance said, watching her sister closely.

"But who was there?" Prudence replaced her glasses. "The one person whose voice Father listened to, whose influence he bowed to."

"Barclay," her sisters said in unison.

"Yes, Barclay. The man who never left his side, who comforted him and stood his friend throughout his grief. But what if..." Prudence lowered her voice, leaning across the table, and her sisters automatically brought their heads closer to hers. "What if Barclay was preying on a man unbalanced by grief? What if he put Father up to that scheme for his own ends?"

"Father said only that it was some investment company that was behind the project," Chastity said, frowning.

"Yes," Prudence agreed. "And he said he expected the shares to quadruple in price in the first year."

"But the company went bankrupt," Constance said slowly.

"If there ever *was* a company." Prudence sat back and surveyed her sisters. "It's not difficult to counterfeit documents. Barclay could have invented the company out of whole cloth and convinced Father of its credentials. I'll bet there's some documentation somewhere among Father's papers. If we can link Barclay to the scheme, then we're home and dry. Not even the kindest interpretation could call selling shares in a trans-Sahara railway less than fraudulent."

"Oh, clever, Prue," Constance said quietly. "Not just a pretty face, are you?"

Prudence's smile was smug. "I don't know why we didn't think of it before."

"We've been too busy trying to deal with the aftermath," Constance pointed out. "The train wreck called family finances."

"The only problem is that Father's going to look an absolute fool," Chastity said. "If we have to expose his—What would you call it? Arrant stupidity? Lunacy?—in court, he'll be a laughingstock. We know it was an aberration when he was out of his mind with grief, but who else is going to take that into account?"

"Maybe we can manage to leave him out of it," Prudence suggested. "If we can marshal evidence to expose the scheme, we don't have to say who fell victim to it."

"Unless the barrister insists," Chastity said.

"You'll have to bring it up when you meet him," Constance said. "Chas and I were saying before you arrived that it has to be you. You know more about the finances than we do. And there's no way that this Sir Gideon will fail to take you seriously. People always take you seriously, even when you're not being serious."

"Yes," agreed Chastity. "Everything about you exudes gravitas and rationality, Prue."

"That sounds very boring," Prudence grumbled.

"Like some kind of Miss Prim. I'm sure it's only because of the glasses." She pushed the spectacles farther up her nose with a gesture of faint disgust.

"It's not just that," Constance said. "It's your character. Mother always said you could grasp a situation instantly and see all its ramifications long before the rest of us. There's no way this Sir Gideon is going to dismiss you as a Society fribble, an ignoramus with nothing in her head but fashion and gossip."

"I doubt he'd dismiss you on such counts either," Prudence stated.

"But he might dismiss *me* on those grounds," Chastity observed without rancor. "He might well decide I'm some flighty flirt of very little brain."

"Chas!" her sisters exclaimed. "Don't be absurd."

"It's true," Chastity said. "That's often the first impression I make. Oh, I grant you, it doesn't last. But first impressions in this instance are going to be all we've got. I agree with Con. It's up to you, Prue."

"So, I'm it," Prudence said, and finally ate her marron glacé. A waitress appeared immediately with the trolley and Prudence examined the contents. "One of those, I believe." She indicated a strawberry tart.

"I'll have a piece of that chocolate sponge," Chastity said. "What about you, Con?"

Constance shook her head. "I'm happy with my toast. Although," she added on impulse, "perhaps I'll have a scone with clotted cream and strawberry jam."

"There's Dottie Northrop," Chastity said suddenly. "On the dance floor with old Sir Gerald."

"That old roué. She won't find a match there." Constance turned in her chair to look at the dance floor. Dottie Northrop was a woman in her early forties, but dressed as if she were at least ten years younger in a tea gown of cream muslin liberally adorned with lacy frills. The neckline was daringly low for the afternoon and her face, beneath a pale pink straw hat, was a mask, thick with powder and rouge. "If she smiles, her face will crack open." It was a statement of fact made quite without malice.

"If we're going to find her a respectable husband we're going to have to transform her," Prudence said. "But how do we do that tactfully?"

"Tact is Chas's speciality," Constance said. "Together with giving advice to the lovelorn."

"You know, the ideal man would be someone like Lord Alfred Roberts," Prudence said thoughtfully. "I know he's rather older, but he seems virile enough, and he looks so sad and lonely most of the time. Dottie might enliven his life nicely."

"That's a thought," Constance agreed. "I wonder—"

"I thought you'd still be here." Max's smooth voice interrupted her from beyond the pillar and the three women looked up in some surprise.

"Max, what are you doing here?" Constance asked.

"I was hoping to have tea." He nodded his thanks to the waiter who had discreetly provided another chair. "Is that anchovy toast you're eating?" He gestured to his wife's plate.

"Yes, it's very good," she responded, spooning clotted cream onto her scone.

"Then I'll finish it for you since you seem to have abandoned it." He smiled at the hovering waitress, who had set down a fresh pot of tea and another cup. He took a piece of toast from his wife's plate while Prudence poured tea for him. "I was making some inquiries about Malvern at my club. What his courtroom style is like, that kind of thing."

"And?" Prudence prompted warily.

"He's known for his confrontational techniques," Max said. "From what I could gather, he goes for the jugular."

"I don't like the sound of that," Prudence said.

"I think you're going to have to try to get him off guard," Max said. "Surprise him somehow, so he doesn't have time to react against you."

"Ye gods!" Prudence muttered. "You really think he's going to start off prejudiced against me?"

Max bit into his toast with evident enjoyment. "I think it's possible," he said when he'd finished his mouthful. "I certainly would be straight off the bat." He glanced across at Prudence, who was looking far from reassured by this brutal candor. "You're going in as the advance guard?"

"We thought she'd be the best one of us," Chastity told him. "I don't look serious enough."

"And I'd rather not have to introduce myself as your wife," Constance pointed out.

"I appreciate your concern," Max said dryly. "But Malvern is going to know soon enough what my connection is."

"It won't hurt to delay that revelation," Constance said. "Prue's the natural choice because she manages the finances to a large extent. She'll sound very knowledgeable and serious."

"And I'll wear my thickest glasses," Prudence said, trying to sound lighthearted. "And my most earnest air."

"Dear God, what an image. I could almost find it in my heart to feel sorry for Malvern," Max declared.

"Oh, yes, Prue at her most grave and solemn is a force to be reckoned with," Chastity said.

Prudence's responding smile lacked conviction, but it went unnoticed amid her sisters' amusement.

Chapter 5

"Well, what do you think?" Prudence stood in front of her sisters on the appointed Thursday afternoon and awaited their judgment.

"You look like a cross between a nun and a schoolteacher," Constance observed.

"No, more like a librarian than a nun," Chastity said. "You have a very earnest and learned look about you."

"That was the effect I was hoping to achieve," Prudence said with her head on one side as she critically surveyed her appearance in the mirror. "I particularly like the felt hat." She lifted the navy blue veil that fell discreetly to just below her nose. The hat itself was of dark gray felt with a demurely turned-up brim.

"It goes with the suit. Dark gray serge . . . you could almost be in mourning," Constance said.

"Do you have the fifty guineas?" Chastity asked, brushing a piece of lint off Prudence's shoulder.

"Surely he'll send a bill," Prudence said, looking at Constance for confirmation. "He's not selling cabbages off a stall."

"I'm sure he will. But I should take it anyway. If he's horribly insulting and dismissive, at least you'll have the satisfaction of giving him his pound of flesh as your own parting shot."

Prudence grimaced. "I know Max meant well but I wish he hadn't found out what he did about Malvern. Just imagining his confrontational manner makes me so nervous I'm sure I'll be completely tongue-tied."

"No, you won't," Chastity said firmly. "You wouldn't let his clerk intimidate you the other day, and you won't let the barrister."

"I hope not. If he's the best there is, I can't afford to," Prudence said with a rather brave smile. "We have to net him."

Constance nodded. "By the way, you might want to pretend that we have no money worries. Once he's caught, then we can negotiate."

"It seems a bit underhanded, but I agree." Prudence pulled on navy blue gloves and picked up a capacious handbag. "I have a complete set of copies of everything I left with his clerk the other day. Just in case they were misplaced in the clerk's office," she added with an ironical shrug. "I only wish I had something concrete to back up the accusations of embezzling and cheating."

"But you can tell him we know how to go about getting such evidence," Constance reminded her.

"We *think* we do," Chastity emphasized.

"I don't intend to allow a hint of doubt," Prudence declared, and dropped the veil. "I'd better make tracks. It's nearly three-thirty."

Her sisters accompanied her in a hackney as far as the Temple Gardens. "We'll wait for you here," Constance said, kissing her.

"No, wait for me at Fortnum's," Prudence said, opening the carriage door. "It looks like rain and I don't want to be worrying about you getting wet. I've no idea how long this is going to take."

"The longer it takes, the more hopeful the outcome," Chastity said. "We'll go to Fortnum's for tea, then, but I shan't be able to eat a thing until you get there."

Prudence laughed at that. "It would be a momentous event indeed that would keep you from your cake, Chas." She climbed out of the hackney, waved once to her sisters, who were hanging out of the window, and then strode resolutely up Middle Temple Lane.

Outside the door to Sir Gideon Malvern's chambers, she paused, preparing herself. Then resolutely she turned the knob and marched up the narrow staircase to the door at its head. She knocked once and entered without waiting for an invitation. The same clerk sat behind his desk. "I have an appointment with Sir Gideon," she told him firmly, keeping her veil in place.

The clerk consulted his ledger as if to confirm this, then he looked up and peered at her. "The Mayfair Lady?" he asked.

"As you are aware," Prudence said, wondering why he always had to play games. "I believe I am exactly on time." She glanced pointedly at the clock.

"I will tell Sir Gideon that you are here." The clerk sidled from behind his desk and opened the door in the far wall a veritable crack, through which he insinuated himself with a rustle of his coattails.

Prudence waited. The door to the inner chamber opened fully and the man she had bumped into on her last visit stood in the doorway. "So, we meet again, Madam Mayfair Lady," he said in the voice she remembered, and disconcertingly the tiny hairs on the nape of her neck prickled. "Won't you come in?"

He held the door, and Prudence with a murmur of thanks entered the sanctum. The clerk gave her another appraising look, then removed himself with the slither that seemed his preferred motion.

Sir Gideon moved a chair forward for his visitor. "Pray sit down, Miss . . . Mrs. . . . ? Forgive me, I am at something of a loss."

Prudence put up her veil. "I assume everything that is said in this room is confidential, Sir Gideon? Even if you decide not to take the case."

"Whatever is said between a barrister and a client, prospective or not, is privileged communication, madam."

Prudence nodded. She had known that, of course, but she had needed it stated. "I am the Honorable Prudence Duncan," she said. "One of the editors of *The Mayfair Lady.*" She gestured to the copy that lay open on the massive oak table that appeared to serve as his desk.

He moved back behind the table as she sat down, and stood for a minute, his hand playing over the broadsheet as he regarded her with a close and unblinking scrutiny. "I seem to recall that there were two of you before."

"In fact, there are three of us."

Sir Gideon was rarely taken aback, a career in the law courts inured a man against surprise, but he was puzzled. The lady in his office bore little resemblance to the image he had taken away from their brief meeting in the hallway. Of course, it had been hard to see clearly in the gloom. The woman sitting in front of him struck him as a rather dull, plain-looking mouse of a creature. He couldn't really see her eyes, hidden as they were behind a pair of hideous, thick tortoiseshell spectacles. Her clothes were uniformly gray, unenlivened by the touch of navy blue, and he thought she looked prim and uninteresting. Which didn't sit quite right with the image of a woman who could write some of the racy and undeniably witty articles in the broadsheet.

Prudence returned the scrutiny with equal interest. She was pleased to recognize his initial surprise, but there was something in his eyes, a certain flicker, that caused her hackles to rise. He was weighing her, and unless she was mistaken, mentally dismissing her.

He was probably around Max's age, as she had calculated. Forty or so. Unlike Max, he had no gray hairs. His hair was a thick, well-coiffed dark brown mane sweeping off a broad forehead. Deep frown lines creased between his rather sculpted eyebrows, but she couldn't decide whether they were the result of a disagreeable nature or were merely indicative of hours of deep thought. He had a calm mouth beneath a long thin nose that dominated his countenance. His gray eyes were sharp and filled with intelligence, but they definitely held no friendliness in their depths. Was it her or her cause that he was dismissing? Or was that simply his habitual expression?

"And who are the other two editors?" he asked after the silence seemed to have elongated. He still did not sit down, which Prudence found even more disconcerting.

"My sisters," she said.

"Ah." He smoothed the broadsheet and she noticed that his hands were very long and white, the filbert nails well manicured. More like a pianist's hands than a lawyer's. He wore an emerald signet ring and the diamond studs in his shirt cuffs glittered, as did the pin in his lapel. Nothing ostentatious, simply an elegant, understated indication of wealth and position. Everything about his presence confirmed the impression. This was a man supremely confident in himself, and his position in the world. He was also intimidating. But Prudence had no intention of letting him know that.

She folded her gloved hands in her lap. "I left all the details relevant to the situation with your clerk, and I see that you have a copy of the article in question, so I assume you're up-to-date with the facts, Sir Gideon."

"Such as they are," he said. "Am I correct in believing that the Honorable Constance Duncan recently married Mr. Ensor, the politician?"

"You are. But that is not germane, and should not influence you in any way."

A sparkle of definitely derisive amusement showed for a second in his eyes. "I do assure you, my dear madam, that nothing influences me but my own assessment of a situation and my own inclination."

Prudence controlled her rising anger at his condescending tone. She said neutrally, "I'm glad to hear it, Sir Gideon. One would not wish to be represented in court by a lawyer who could be swayed from the truth by some personal whim."

His eyes were suddenly hooded, his countenance completely without expression, and she had no idea whether she had stung him or not. Was this his courtroom face? Giving nothing away? If so, it was a very effective weapon. She found herself resisting the urge to break the silence with some irrelevant babble.

She rose to her feet. "Forgive me, but if you choose not to sit down, Sir Gideon, I would prefer to stand too for the extent of this consultation."

His expression remained the same, his eyes still hidden under half-lowered lids. However, he gestured to the chair again, said, "Please," and sat down himself behind the table. He lightly tapped the article in the open broadsheet in front of him.

"Did you write this, Miss Duncan, or one of your sisters?"

"My elder sister, as it happens. But its authorship is not germane either. We're all in this together."

He smiled. "All for one and one for all. The three musketeers alive and well in the streets of London."

Prudence curled her gloved fingers into her palms, glad that there was nothing conveniently at hand to throw at him. She said nothing, keeping her face expressionless, aware that thanks to her convenient glasses he couldn't see the anger and chagrin she knew her eyes would reveal.

"What is it you and your sisters want me to do for you, Miss Duncan?" His voice was still quiet, but it was crisp, and now there was no mistaking the acerbity in the well-modulated tones.

"We would like you to defend *The Mayfair Lady* against Lord Barclay's libel suit." Prudence, for all her annoyed discomfiture, was aware of relief that at last the ball was in play. Maybe he had a problem doing business with women, but when they got down to brass tacks and she could steer him towards the evidence, which he must have read, he would lose his prejudices.

He said nothing for a minute, looking down at the broadsheet in front of him. Then he looked up, clasping his hands on top of the paper. "You see, Miss Duncan, I would find that very hard to do. Reading this, I am in complete sympathy with the earl. It is an outrageous, malicious piece of scandalmongering, and its authors deserve the full penalty of the law. If I were prosecuting, I would demand the maximum in punitive damages, and I would not rest until this . . ." He swept a dismissive hand across the paper. ". . . this gossip-feeding rag was put out of business."

He stood up again. "Forgive my bluntness, Miss Duncan, but there are realities that you and your sisters don't seem to have grasped. Women are not equipped to enter these kinds of battles. This is an emotional, unthought-out attack on a peer of the realm, designed to cause him maximum embarrassment, which I can see it has. He is entitled to financial redress for pain and suffering caused by this piece of rumormongering. May I suggest that in future you and your sisters confine your gossip to your social circles and keep well away from pen and ink."

He moved out from behind the desk as Prudence remained sitting, for the moment utterly stunned.

"If you'll excuse me, Miss Duncan, I have briefs to prepare." He went to the door, opening it. "Thadeus, escort the Honorable Miss Duncan to the street."

Numb, Prudence rose and allowed herself to be swept from the inner chamber, her hand given a perfunctory shake, and within two minutes she was standing in the drizzling rain outside the closed door to Sir Gideon's chambers.

She looked at her fob watch. It was barely four-twenty. In less than thirty minutes she had been roundly scolded and dismissed like a rather dim schoolgirl. Max had warned her to seize the initiative and she had let it slip. She heard the barrister's voice, that so quiet yet so clear voice, delivering the insulting, patronizing speech. No one had ever dared talk to her in that manner.

She spun on her heel to face the door again and threw it open. Not even Sir Gideon Malvern, KC, was going to get away with that.

In the gently humming tearoom at Fortnum's, Chastity and Constance sipped tea, watching through the long windows as pedestrians dodged from doorway to doorway along Piccadilly while the steady drizzle intensified to a solid rain.

"I wonder how she's getting on?" Chastity murmured for the sixth time. "I can't even eat this macaroon, and I *love* macaroons."

"Depriving yourself won't help Prue or alter the outcome of the interview," Constance pointed out, taking a cucumber sandwich from the plate on the table. "Let's think about finding a husband for Dottie Northrop instead. Have you thought any more about how to advise her tactfully on her appearance?"

Chastity welcomed the diversion. She rummaged through her handbag and produced a sheet of paper. "I thought it best just to drop a few hints in the letter." She handed the paper across the table. "I've suggested that she attend the At Home at Ten Manchester Square next Wednesday afternoon, when she should ask for an introduction to Lord Alfred Roberts, whom she might find an eligible party."

"How are we going to get Lord Alfred there?" Constance inquired. "He's a club man like Father. I can't see him holding a teacup and conducting small talk with the likes of Lady Winthrop or Mary and Martha Bainbridge."

"Father will bring him," Chastity declared with satisfied finality. "I've already asked him. I said we needed some more interesting society on Wednesday afternoons and that since Lord Alfred was a particular friend of Mother's and we think he's rather lonely, we'd like to include him."

Constance laughed. "What did Father say?"

"He hummed and hawed a little, but then said that now he thought about it, Alfred was a little less than chipper these days, and maybe he did need to be taken out of himself a little. So he's promised to bring him. As long as we have more than tea to offer them," she added, spooning sugar into her own cup.

"That's easily done. So, now we need a tactful hint about Dottie's necklines and the amount of face powder she uses."

"Oh, I've covered that. In the last paragraph." Chastity mumbled inelegantly through a mouthful of macaroon. She waved a finger at the paper her sister held.

Constance read the relevant passage and broke into a peal of laughter. "Oh, you're so good at this, Chas. It's priceless. 'The gentleman in question is rather old-fashioned, of a somewhat shy disposition, and a little alarmed by the ladies so *The Mayfair Lady* would recommend only the most decorous afternoon dress for the first introduction. The editorial staff at *The Mayfair Lady* are convinced that Lord Alfred Roberts will, with the right kind of gentle understanding and encouragement, soon lose his reticence and show himself to be a wonderful companion who enjoys all that life and Society have to offer.' "

"I thought it was quite good," Chastity said complacently. "And the more I think about it, the more I think it would be a perfect match. They can fill each other's gaps, if you see what I mean. Oh, do stop laughing, Con." She dissolved into laughter herself, choking on a cake crumb.

Constance leaned sideways and patted her on the back. "Prue will love this letter." As one, they turned to look out of the window again, hoping to see a hackney cab disgorging their sister at the curb.

Gideon almost jumped to his feet, so startled was he at the precipitate return of his visitor. But this was not the same woman who had been ushered firmly from his chambers a mere three or four minutes previously. The appearance was essentially the same but the aura was quite different. This woman crackled like a newly kindled fire. He still couldn't see her eyes behind the thick lenses but he could almost feel their heat.

"I do not understand what makes you think you have the right to treat me, or indeed any client, with such contempt and condescension," Prudence declared, setting her capacious handbag down on the barrister's table. "Since you had already prejudged the issue, I cannot understand why you would have agreed to a consultation. Unless, of course, you wished merely to amuse yourself. Women are perhaps playthings for you?"

She drew off her gloves finger by finger, each movement punctuating her words. "You did not do me the courtesy of even the pretence at a proper hearing. Did you imagine that I would come to a business meeting unprepared to discuss the evidence I left with your clerk?" She tapped the papers on the table. "We have more than enough evidence to prove our accusations against Lord Barclay. As I understand the law, if there is proof there can be no libel. I am perhaps mistaken?" She raised her eyebrows in ironic inquiry.

Gideon found a moment to catch his breath. He cleared his throat, and his visitor removed her glasses for long enough to polish them on her handkerchief. Her eyes were a revelation. A clear, lustrous light green, lively with anger and intelligence. And they were fixed upon him even as she rubbed smudges from the lenses with a derision that the lauded barrister of the King's Council had dished out often enough but never before received.

"Am I mistaken, Sir Gideon?" she repeated, setting her glasses back on her nose, resituating them with a vigorous forefinger.

"Ordinarily, no, Miss Duncan." He stood up as he found his voice. "But the anonymous nature of the accusations makes them appear less than credible and I doubt that a jury will look with sympathy on what seems . . ." He cleared his throat again. "On what could seem a cowardly stab in the back." He gestured to the chair. "Won't you be seated?"

"I don't think so," Prudence said. "Thank you. I can see that anonymity could pose difficulties, but we really have no choice in the matter. We couldn't produce the broadsheet if our identities were known, as you would have realized if you'd given it a moment's intelligent thought. You will have to find a defense that takes that into account."

He opened his mouth but she swept past his first syllables. "I assume you took the trouble to read my sister's notes taken during her interviews with the women in question. Perhaps you'd like to look at them again and refresh your memory. Of course..." She removed her glasses again and directed a challenging look in his direction. It was a look to make the bravest man wilt.

"Of course, if you continue to prejudge this issue then I will pay you your consultation fee, fifty guineas, I believe, although I would hesitate to call this little interview a consultation, and leave you to your prejudices." She took a wad of banknotes from the depths of the bag and laid them on the table with a careless flick of her hand. Her companion would never guess what the gesture cost her.

Gideon ignored the banknotes. "Do sit down, Miss Duncan, this could take a few minutes. Would you like tea?" He laid a hand on a silver handbell on his table.

"No, I thank you." Prudence did, however, sit down. High dudgeon had carried her this far, but its aftermath had left her a little shakier than she was prepared to admit.

"Oh, but I insist," he said, and rang the bell. Thadeus appeared instantly in a sliver of doorway. "Bring us some tea, Thadeus, and toast a couple of crumpets, if you would."

The man silently withdrew and Prudence declared, "I am not in the least hungry, Sir Gideon. This is not a social call."

"No, but it is teatime," he pointed out mildly. "And I'm certainly ready for mine." He selected a file from the pile in front of him, opened it, and began to read.

Prudence said nothing, merely watched him closely.

She recognized the copies of her sister's notes and felt a fresh surge of annoyance at the implication that he really hadn't bothered to read them earlier. Thadeus arrived with a tea tray, and the enticing fragrance of the crumpets swimming in butter made Prudence regret her lofty refusal.

"Shall I pour, sir?" Thadeus intoned.

"Unless Miss Duncan would do the honors." Sir Gideon looked up and gave her a smile that made her feel she was in the presence of a quite different man. The smile crinkled the skin around his eyes in a most attractive fashion, and gave to the clear gray gaze an appealing gleam.

She shook her head in brief negative and the clerk poured tea into two delicate cups that Prudence would have sworn were Sèvres china. She took the one handed to her because to refuse now would be simply churlish, but she shook her head again when she was offered a crumpet. Dealing with all that melted butter while perched on a chair in her coat and hat would detract from the dignified air of hauteur she was trying to maintain. Sir Gideon seemed to have no such reticence and ate both crumpets with relish even while he continued to read, pausing now and again to make a notation on the pad at his elbow.

At last he looked up, after dabbing the last morsel of crumpet into the remaining butter on his plate and conveying the whole to his mouth without a single drip or smear of grease.

"Very well, I admit that I saw no point in reading the background material once I had read the article. Maybe I acted in haste, but that said, I see nothing here to substantiate the accusation of financial misconduct." His voice now was as cool as it had been earlier, the smile gone from his expression, his eyes sharp and assessing.

"There is a certain lack, we all agree," Prudence said calmly. "However, we're convinced of the truth of the charge."

"Your being convinced is hardly the same as a jury's conviction," he pointed out, the tinge of acid once more in his voice.

"We have a fairly good idea where to look for evidence to substantiate the accusation," Prudence told him, setting her empty cup on the table.

He regarded her rather quizzically. "Would you care to explain, Miss Duncan?"

"Not at present," she said, thinking it might be wise to keep a few cards up her sleeve until he'd committed himself to the cause. If she told him about her father's dealings with Barclay and he still refused to represent them, then she would have exposed her father unnecessarily. It didn't matter that it would be confidential, she just didn't like the idea of this supercilious bastard looking down on her father...not unless the revelation would serve a purpose. "But I can assure you we know exactly how to go about it."

He merely raised his eyebrows and said, "You said your sister wrote the article in question, as I recall."

"Yes, Constance."

He nodded. "Is she responsible for the lion's share of the writing?"

"When it comes to political issues, particularly those relating to women's suffrage, yes."

He acknowledged this with another slight nod. "And what is your role in the production of this..." He gestured to the paper on the table. "This publication?"

Prudence detected the trace of derision again in his tone and her anger rose anew. She got to her feet as she spoke. "I take care of the business end, Sir Gideon. The finances and matters of that nature. Now, if you will excuse me, it's clear that we have nothing further to discuss, so I'll not take up any more of your valuable time. Thank you for the tea." She swooped onto the pages that contained Constance's notes and swept them into her bag in one movement, conspicuously leaving the banknotes where they were.

Gideon stood up abruptly. "It's not at all clear to me that we have nothing further to discuss."

Prudence paused as she was putting on her gloves. "You have made no attempt to disguise your contempt for *The Mayfair Lady*. I'm sure it strikes you as the work of rank amateurs. What you perhaps don't understand—"

"Don't put words into my mouth, Miss Duncan," he interrupted. "Or thoughts in my head."

"Do you deny it?" she demanded.

"I won't deny that I'm doubtful about the merits of this case," he said. "But I'm willing to keep an open mind while you attempt to prove to me that I might find it an interesting exercise." He smiled again and Prudence steeled herself against the charm. It was, she was convinced, entirely artificial, turned on as and when it suited the barrister.

"Have dinner with me tonight," he said, the smile deepening. "And do your worst." He spread his arms wide. "I swear I will come undefended, unprejudiced, open to all and any argument. What could be fairer than that?"

Prudence was so taken aback, she was momentarily

without words. He had moved the interview from a business footing to a social one, and more than that, there was something undeniably seductive in his manner. He knew the power of his smile, the deeper resonance of his voice. But why bother to turn it on her? Did he want something from her?

There was only one way to find out.

"I won't turn down the opportunity to persuade you, Sir Gideon," she said, hoping she sounded cool and collected rather than astonished and disturbed.

"Then you accept my invitation?" He looked a little peeved, she thought, at her halfhearted response, and it gave her more confidence.

"Certainly. Although I fail to grasp what a conversation at the dinner table could achieve that couldn't be achieved in your chambers."

"Then you'll have to wait and see," he responded, immediately putting her back up again. "I might surprise you. If you'll give me the address, I'll send a motor for you at eight o'clock."

It would have been more courteous of him to have offered to come for her himself, Prudence thought. She was annoyed, very much so, but common sense dictated that she swallow her annoyance in the interests of another chance to win his support. Also, he intrigued her, reluctant though she was to admit it. He was on the one hand ungracious to the point of rudeness, arrogant, high-handed, and contemptuous, yet on the other he was charming, smiled readily, judging by the crow's feet around his eyes, and was undeniably attractive when he chose. He must also have a formidable mind, a rare quality that she had always found irresistible in a man. But why was he bothering to charm a woman who had gone out of her way to present herself as a spinsterly dowd?

"Ten Manchester Square." She walked to the door, making no attempt to soften the curtness of her response with a smile of farewell, but he slid out from behind the table and reached the door ahead of her.

He took her hand and bowed over it. "I look forward to the evening, Miss Duncan. I'll show you out." He picked up a large umbrella from the stand by the door and escorted her down to the street. The rain was coming down hard and he said, "Wait here. I'll fetch a cab." Before she could protest, he had left the shelter of the doorway and was dodging puddles under the protection of the umbrella.

Prudence was yet more puzzled. From what she'd seen of his manners so far, she would have expected him to send his clerk on the errand, if he hadn't simply left her to go off on her own in the rain. A man of curious paradoxes, and he had warned her not to rush to judgment. On such slight acquaintance it was probably a warning best heeded.

A hackney cab swung around the street corner and drew up at the doorway. Sir Gideon jumped down and held the umbrella over Prudence until she was safely ensconced. "Where shall I tell the cabbie?"

"Fortnum's," she said. "I'm having a second tea."

He laughed, a soft, rich sound that she hadn't heard before. "No wonder you scorned my crumpets. Until this evening, madam." He waved a hand and Prudence lifted hers in involuntary response, aware that she was smiling.

Gideon, a thoughtful frown now creasing his brow, returned to his chambers. He stood just inside the door to his inner sanctum, tapping his lips with a forefinger.

What on earth did he think he was doing? The case was impossible, he'd known that from the first line of the article. He had no sympathy with the editors of *The Mayfair Lady*. The article in question was a piece of malicious gossip in a publication devoted to a morass of half-baked political opinions and self-righteous declarations about the unfair treatment of women. There was absolutely no way that that dowdy brown mouse, lively green eyes and termagant's temper notwithstanding, could persuade him to view the case in any other way. So, why in heaven's name had he invited her to try . . . condemned himself to an evening of crushing boredom with an inevitably unpleasant conclusion when he told her, as he fully intended to do, that he had not and never had had any intention of taking the brief?

He wondered for a second if there was any way he could rescind the invitation. He could send a note to Manchester Square, say something unexpected had come up, express his regrets, and never lay eyes on her again. His eye fell on the wad of banknotes on the table. Her voice rang again in his head, filled with angry contempt. He saw again the careless flick of her hand as she'd almost thrown the money down in front of him. Unless he was much mistaken, the Honorable Miss Duncan was not entirely what she seemed. Maybe the evening wouldn't be quite such a waste of time after all. Pursing his lips thoughtfully, he locked the banknotes in a drawer beneath the tabletop.

The cab deposited Prudence at the door of Fortnum's and she entered the now almost-deserted tearoom. Chastity waved at her from the table by the window and Prudence hurried to join them.

"Well?" they both said in unison.

"I'll tell you," Prudence said. "No, thank you." She waved the cake trolley away. "I'll have a cup of tea, though." She set her bag and gloves on the floor. "He gave me about fifteen minutes of his time, during which he subjected me to the most insulting, arrogant, patronizing speech I've ever heard. Not once did he indicate that he'd even looked at our evidence, and before I knew it I was outside in the street, staring at a closed door."

Constance whistled silently. "You went back in." It was a statement, not a question.

Prudence nodded. "I don't remember ever being so angry."

Chastity poured tea for her sister and pushed the cup across the table, reflecting that Prue rarely lost her temper, but when she did, it was a fairly spectacular tempest. "He listened to you this time?"

"Oh, yes," Prudence said, sipping her tea. "He even took the time to read the material I'd left with his clerk two days ago."

When she said nothing else for a moment, Constance prompted, "And is he going to take the case?"

"I don't know." Prudence set down her cup carefully in the saucer. "He invited me for dinner tonight." She regarded her sisters, who were now staring at her wide-eyed. "He kindly invited me to try to persuade him over dinner."

"What?" Constance's jaw dropped. "What kind of business practice is that?"

"I don't know." Prudence shrugged. "But I couldn't turn down the opportunity, could I?"

"Did you remember he's divorced?" Chastity asked. "Maybe he's not very punctilious in his personal life?"

It was Prudence who stared now. "To tell you the truth, I forgot about that."

"Divorced?" Constance said. It was the first she had heard of this interesting tidbit.

"Yes, we looked him up in *Who's Who.*" Chastity said. "He's been divorced for about six years. There's a daughter too."

"Well, I don't suppose he sees much of her," Constance said scornfully. "Legally she belongs to him, so he probably makes all the decisions concerning her life but leaves her care to her mother. It's the usual way."

"Probably," Prudence agreed. She took a cucumber sandwich and then stared at it as if wondering how it had arrived in her hand.

"What?" Constance asked.

Prudence put the sandwich down. "You know, there were times when it was almost as if he was flirting with me. Every so often he'd lose that dismissive arrogance and have an almost complete personality change. It was very strange."

"It's not unheard of for a divorced man to flirt," Constance observed. "Quite the opposite. Although I'd say it's unprofessional for a barrister to flirt with a potential client."

"Unless he has no intention of taking us on as clients. If he's a licentious libertine he could be leading Prue on." Chastity had abandoned her half-eaten macaroon. She opened her hazel eyes very wide and dropped her voice to a whisper. "To have his wicked way with her."

"Oh, Chas!" Her sisters laughed, as they were intended to, but the amusement didn't last very long.

"Now, why would a licentious libertine have any interest in me in my present guise?" Prudence demanded. "I look like a prim, dowdy, spinster governess."

"I imagine that image slipped somewhat when you got angry," Constance said with a dry smile. "Did you take your glasses off?"

"I don't know, I . . . Oh, for heaven's sake, Con. What if I did?"

Her sisters said nothing, merely regarded her with quizzically raised eyebrows. "Oh, give me strength." Prudence took the sandwich again and devoured it with two vigorous bites.

"So, you accepted this invitation," Chastity said.

"Yes, I told you," Prudence said. "I couldn't turn down the opportunity to try again to get him to take the case."

"Is he attractive?"

Prudence considered this. "Not to me," she said definitely. "But I can see how some women might find him so. I just don't fall for the superior male type."

Her sisters nodded.

"Of course, he does have a rather nice voice," Prudence said with scrupulous fairness. "And when his smile's genuine some women might think it's attractive."

"But you were never taken in by the display of charm," Constance said, taking up her teacup.

"No," her sister stated. "Not for one minute."

"Well, it'll be interesting to see what the evening brings," Chastity said neutrally.

Prudence took another cucumber sandwich.

Chapter 6

Going out, my dear?" Lord Duncan paused in the hall as his middle daughter came down the stairs that evening, her coat over her arm.

"Yes, a dinner party," Prudence said as she took the last step. She was aware of her father's rather surprised look as he took in her appearance. His daughter did not ordinarily attend dinner parties dressed for a funeral. There was something distinctly unmodish about her untrimmed gown of brown tabby. In fact, he couldn't remember ever having seen it before.

Prudence had no intention of inviting a comment on her dress and said swiftly, "Good evening, Lord Barclay." A thin layer of ice coated the polite greeting, but neither the earl nor his host heard it.

"Evenin', Prudence," the earl declared. He gave her a facetious smile. "Some eligible young man, is it?" He reached out to pat her cheek but she drew back in the nick of time.

The earl chuckled. "No need to be coy with me, Miss Prudence." He tapped the side of his nose. "A word to the wise, miss. It's all right for a debutante to be coy, but it don't sit pretty on a woman past her first few seasons."

Prudence glanced at her father and saw that he was looking with marked disfavor at his friend. It surprised her, since Lord Duncan was in general blindly loyal, but it also gave her heart. Perhaps he wasn't completely convinced of the earl's innocence, although he was loud in his denunciation of his friend's accusers. Either way, there was something acutely distasteful in the earl's veiled references to Prudence's age and unmarried situation, and Lord Duncan was both fastidious in his manners and a most loving father.

Prudence offered a chilly smile and said, "How is your libel suit progressing, my lord?"

The question had the desired effect. His lordship's complexion turned a rather unattractive shade of purple. "Damned cowards haven't responded yet... not a peep out of 'em, my solicitors say. Slippery as eels, they are. But if they think they can play mum and get away with it, they can think again."

"They're hardly going to hide forever, Barclay," Lord Duncan pointed out.

"Oh, no, we'll get 'em, and when we do I'll string 'em up, every one of 'em," he declared savagely. "I'll flay 'em alive and take 'em for every penny they've got."

"Somehow I doubt even the full penalty of the law will allow you to do all three," Prudence observed mildly. "How many defendants do you think there are, sir? You seem confident it's more than one."

"Of course there's more than one... a whole team of sissies, backstabbing men masquerading as women, up to all sorts of perversions, you mark my words." He glared at Prudence and wagged a finger very close to her nose.

"You mark my words, miss, we'll have every copy of that filthy rag confiscated and burned in the streets. I'll ruin 'em and see 'em rot in jail, every damn one of 'em."

"You don't think it's possible that these writers are *actually* women, Lord Barclay?"

He stared at her as if she'd grown two heads. "Nonsense . . . nonsense. Women, indeed!" He laughed uproariously, clapping Lord Duncan on the shoulder. "*Women*. Women writing that kind of filth, digging up those lies, going into those places . . . what d'you think of that idea, eh, Duncan?"

Lord Duncan frowned. He was thinking of his late wife. "Unlikely," he agreed. "But not impossible."

"Oh, your brain's addled, my friend," the earl declared. "No respectable woman would have anything to do with it."

"Respectable women seem to read it, though," Prudence pointed out. "My own mother, as I recall, used to find the broadsheet's articles stimulating."

This comment effectively silenced Lord Barclay, since he could hardly pour scorn on his friend's dead wife.

Prudence gave him a minute to find a suitable response, and when it seemed he would be grasping for words for rather a long time said, "Are you dining in, Father?"

Lord Duncan was visibly relieved at the change of subject. "Yes, I thought we would. Jenkins and Mrs. Hudson could rustle something up for us."

Prudence reflected that the butler and housekeeper would have appreciated some notice, particularly since the household income didn't allow for a pantry stocked with delicacies just on the off chance that their employer would decide to dine in and invite a few friends. But she and her sisters had long given up expecting their father to acknowledge the household's straitened finances.

She glanced at the grandfather clock. It was nearly eight. Chastity was dining with Constance and Max this evening, so there was no one but herself to steer Mrs. Hudson through her initial dismay when it was made clear to her she would have to produce a passable dinner in the next hour.

"I'll go and talk to Mrs. Hudson," she said. "There's a fire in the library. I'll send Jenkins with whisky." She draped her coat over the newel post and hurried into the kitchen, the skirts of her gown rustling stiffly around her.

"Is that his lordship, Miss Prue?" Mrs. Hudson had been sitting in her rocking chair beside the range in anticipation of a quiet evening with no dinner to prepare, but she got to her feet as Prudence entered the kitchen.

"Yes, I'm sorry, Mrs. Hudson. His lordship and Lord Barclay would like dinner. Do we have anything in the pantry?" Prudence opened the pantry door even as she asked the question.

"Oh, dearie me!" the cook muttered. "And I gave young Ellen the evenin' off. Mr. Jenkins will have to help me."

"I'd help you myself, but a motor is coming for me at eight." The chime of the front door rang from the row of bells above the kitchen door. "Oh, that must be it now. There are some venison chops in here, could you roast them?"

"I was a bit doubtful about those," Mrs. Hudson said, pushing past Prudence into the pantry. "I had my doubts about whether the venison had hung long enough." She picked up the chops and sniffed them critically. "Have to do, I suppose. With a few potatoes, and I've some brussels sprouts here somewhere..." Her voice faded as she moved farther into the pantry, poking along the shelves. "A drop o' red currant jelly and a glass of Madeira in the gravy, maybe..."

"And a Queen of Puddings for after," Prudence suggested.

"Oh, aye, that I can do. And there's some of that Stilton left that his lordship's so fond of." Mrs. Hudson backed out, dangling two thick venison chops from her fingers. "I'll just throw these in the roasting pan. Don't know what to do for a first course, though."

"The motor is here for you, Miss Prue," Jenkins announced from the door. "I understand his lordship and Lord Barclay will be dining in tonight."

"Yes, and Mrs. Hudson has come up trumps as usual," Prudence said. "And Father would like you to take whisky to the library. I'm sorry I can't stay to help but—"

"Just you run along and enjoy yourself, Miss Prue," Mrs. Hudson said. "Mr. Jenkins and me, we'll manage. They can have sardines on toast to start. A few springs of parsley and a little chopped egg'll dress it up nicely."

Prudence smiled. "You're a wonder. Don't wait up for me, Jenkins. I have my key."

"The chauffeur said he'd been sent by a Sir Gideon Malvern," Jenkins mentioned casually as he preceded her into the hall. He took her coat from the newel post and held it out for her. "An elderly gentleman, is he, Miss Prue?" The puzzled glance he cast over her dowdy dress was covert and yet its meaning was quite clear to Prudence. Jenkins was not accustomed to seeing any of the ladies of the house venturing outside in anything but the most stylish and elegant of dress. And Miss Prue was exceptionally meticulous in all matters sartorial.

"I wouldn't have said so," she replied, buttoning her coat.

"I heard there was a barrister of that name, Miss Prue. Quite a famous one."

"Yes, Jenkins," she agreed as he opened the door for her. "And we need him rather desperately, so wish me luck. I need to be especially persuasive tonight. I'm hoping I look very serious and businesslike, ready for an evening of grave discussion, not idle pleasure." She raised an eyebrow, inviting his opinion.

"That's certainly the impression I have, Miss Prue," he said tactfully, escorting her down the steps to where a liveried chauffeur stood beside the open door of a black Rover. "I'm sure your business will prosper."

"You have more faith in my powers than I do, Jenkins." Prudence stepped into the back seat of the car with a smile at the chauffeur and a wave for Jenkins. The chauffeur began to close the door. "Where are we going?" she inquired.

"Long Acre, madam." He closed the door and went around to the driver's side.

Prudence sat back. The car had a top but the sides were open and she was glad the rain had stopped and it was a mild and windless evening. Nevertheless, she tied the scarf she wore to protect her hair more tightly beneath her chin and turned up the collar of her coat. Covent Garden was a strange choice of venue in the circumstances, she thought a little uneasily. The restaurants around the Opera House and the theaters of Drury Lane would be very public, and there were bound to be people she knew. If she was seen with Sir Gideon, there would inevitably be talk, and maybe later, when the trial started, someone would remember seeing them together and start to wonder. It was a little too risky for comfort. It seemed stupid now that she hadn't asked where he was taking her, and yet at the time the question hadn't occurred to her. When a man asked you for dinner you either accepted or didn't. You didn't base your response on the kind of entertainment he was offering.

The chauffeur drove slowly and considerately through the puddle-strewn streets. The ripe stench of horse manure was thick in the air, stirred up by the afternoon's rain, but the rain had also settled the dust. When they turned into the thronged narrow streets around Covent Garden, Prudence drew farther back into the vehicle's interior and wished she'd thought to bring a veil.

The car drew up outside a discreet-looking house with shuttered windows and a door that opened directly onto the street. The chauffeur helped Prudence to the street and escorted her to the door. She glanced up at the house. It bore none of the telltale signs of a restaurant. In fact, she thought, it had the air of a private home.

The door opened a minute after the chauffeur had rung the bell. A gentleman in austere evening dress bowed a greeting. "Madam, Sir Gideon is awaiting you in the red room."

Red room? Prudence glanced at the chauffeur as if for enlightenment but he had already stepped back to the street. She found herself in an elegant hall with a black and white marble floor and elaborately molded ceilings. A flight of stairs with gilded banisters rose from the rear.

"This way, madam." The man preceded her up the stairs and along a wide corridor. Voices, both male and female, came from behind closed doors, together with the chink of china and glass. Prudence was as intrigued as she was puzzled.

Her escort stopped outside a pair of double doors in the middle of the corridor, knocked once, then with an almost theatrical flourish opened both doors wide. "Your guest, Sir Gideon."

Prudence stepped into a large, square room, furnished as a drawing room except for a candlelit dining table set for two in a deep bow window overlooking a garden. It was immediately obvious why it was known as the red room. The curtains were red velvet, the furniture upholstered in red damask.

Gideon Malvern was standing beside the fireplace, where a small fire burned. He set down the whisky glass he held and came across the room. "Good evening, Miss Duncan. Let me take your coat."

His evening dress was impeccable, tiny diamond studs in his white waistcoat. Prudence, as she removed her head scarf, had a flash of regret at her own carefully chosen costume. In the interests of making absolutely certain the barrister understood this meeting was not a social occasion, she had decided to preserve the image of the dowdy spinster that she'd created in his chambers that afternoon. In fact, without exaggeration, she looked a fright in a hideous brown dress she'd unearthed from a cedar closet that hadn't been opened in ten years. She had no idea where the dress came from. It certainly wasn't something her mother would ever have worn. She unbuttoned her coat with some reluctance and allowed him to take it from her. He handed it to the man who had ushered her upstairs. The man bowed and withdrew, closing the doors gently behind him.

Gideon surveyed his guest, one eyebrow lifting a fraction. He was trying to imagine how any woman, let alone one as relatively young as this one, could deliberately choose to dress with such abominable lack of taste. One had to assume she had *chosen* the gown she was wearing, just as she had chosen her costume that afternoon. Perhaps, he thought, she was color-blind as well as shortsighted, or whatever problem she had with her eyesight that obliged her to wear those thick horn-rimmed spectacles. She was certainly fashion-blind. His nose twitched. Could that possibly be a whiff of mothballs emanating from the folds of that dreadful evening dress?

"Sherry," he said. "May I offer you a glass before dinner?"

"Thank you," Prudence responded, well aware of his reaction to her appearance. It was exactly what she had intended, but it still left her chagrined. She was far more used to admiring glances than the barrister's mingled pity and disdain.

"Please sit down." He gestured to one of the sofas and went to the sideboard, where decanters of sherry and whisky stood. He poured sherry and brought the glass over to her.

"Thank you," she said again, with a prim little smile that she thought would be appropriate to her appearance. "What is this house?"

"A private supper club," he said, taking a seat on the sofa opposite her. "I thought a restaurant might be a little too public." He sipped his whisky.

"It wouldn't do for us to be seen together," she agreed, smoothing down her skirts with a fussy little pat of her hand.

Gideon could only agree wholeheartedly. He wasn't

sure his social reputation would survive being seen in public with such a wretchedly drab companion. He watched her covertly for a moment. She wore her hair twisted tightly onto her nape in an old-fashioned bun stuck with wooden pins. But the stuffy style couldn't do much to disguise the lustrous richness of the color. Somewhere between cinnamon and russet, he thought. No, something wasn't quite right. He couldn't put his finger on it, but there was something out of kilter about the Honorable Miss Prudence Duncan. He remembered that moment in his chambers when she'd taken off her glasses as she launched her attack. The image of that woman with the one in front of him somehow didn't gel. And after his late afternoon's reading he was not about to jump to conclusions about any of the Duncan sisters.

"As I recall, Miss Duncan, you said you took care of the business side of the publication. I assume you're something of a mathematician."

"I wouldn't say that precisely," Prudence stated. "I would describe myself as a bookkeeper."

At that he laughed. "Oh, no, Miss Duncan, I am convinced that you are no more a bookkeeper than your sister is the writer of Penny Dreadfuls."

Prudence looked startled. "Have you been reading copies of *The Mayfair Lady* since this afternoon?"

"I discovered an unexpected source of back issues," he said dryly. "Curiously enough, under my own roof. My daughter and her governess appear to be avid readers."

"Ah," she said. "Your daughter. Yes."

"That appears to come as no particular surprise to you," he observed.

"Who's Who," she said. "We looked you up."

He raised an eyebrow. "So you know more about me than I do about you, Miss Duncan."

Prudence felt herself flush as if he was accusing her of prying. "*Who's Who* is a matter of public record," she stated. "Besides, if we hadn't looked you up we wouldn't have been able to find you."

"Ah," he said. "Sensible research, of course."

"Does your daughter live with you?" She couldn't hide her surprise.

"As it happens," he responded shortly. "She attends North London Collegiate for her formal schooling. Her governess takes care of the wider aspects of her education. It seems that women's suffrage is of particular interest to Miss Winston, hence her familiarity with your publication." He rose to take his glass to the sideboard to refill it, after casting a glance towards Prudence's barely touched sherry glass.

This was a man of surprises, Prudence reflected, unable to deny that her interest was piqued. North London Collegiate School for Ladies, founded in 1850 by the redoubtable Frances Buss, one of Prudence's mother's female icons, was the first day school to offer a rigorous education to young women. Miss Buss, like the late Lady Duncan, had been a fervent supporter of women's rights as well as education.

Prudence took a healthy sip of her sherry. "You believe in women's education, then?"

"Of course." He sat down again, regarding her a little quizzically. "I imagine that surprises you."

"After your diatribe this afternoon about how women are not equipped... I believe I have that right... not *equipped* to enter the battleground of lawsuits and suchlike, I find it incredible. I think you advised me and my sisters to confine ourselves to the gossip of our own social circles and keep away from pen and ink." She smiled. "Do I have *that* right, Sir Gideon?" She leaned over to put her now empty glass on the sofa table.

"Yes, you do." He seemed completely untroubled by the apparent contradiction. "The fact that I support the education of women does not deny my assertion that the majority of women are uneducated and ill equipped to deal in my world. More sherry?"

He reached for her glass when she nodded and went back to the sideboard. "Were that not the case, there would be little need for my support for the cause." He refilled her glass from the decanter and brought it back to her. He stood looking down at her with that same quizzical, appraising air. Prudence was distinctly uneasy. It felt as if he were looking right through her, through the facade she was presenting, to the real Prudence underneath.

"Your daughter . . ." she began, trying to divert his attention.

"My daughter is hardly relevant here," he responded. "Suffice it to say that under the guidance of Miss Winston she's a passionate supporter of women's suffrage."

"And are you?" The question was quick and sharp. Without thinking, she took off her glasses as she often did in moments of intensity, rubbing them on her sleeve as she looked up at him.

Gideon took a slow breath. Wonderful eyes. They did not belong to this spinsterly dowd. So, just what game was Miss Duncan playing here? He had every intention of discovering before the evening was done.

"I haven't made up my mind on that issue," he

answered finally. "Perhaps you should try to convince me of its merits while you attempt to persuade me to take on your defense." A smile touched the corners of his mouth and his gray eyes were suddenly luminous as they locked with hers.

Prudence hastily returned her glasses to her nose. That gaze was too hot to hold. And there was a note in his voice that made her scalp prickle. Every instinct shrieked a warning; but a warning about what? Rationally, he couldn't possibly be attracted to her, and yet his eyes and voice and smile said he was. Was he playing some cat-and-mouse game? Trying to fool her into a false position? She forced herself to concentrate. She had a job to do. She had to persuade him that he would find their case interesting and . . .

Her mind froze. Was this part of what would make it interesting for him? An elaborate, cruel game of mock seduction? Was there some kind of quid pro quo here to which she was not as yet a party?

Prudence thought of *The Mayfair Lady,* she thought of the mountain of debt that they were only just beginning to topple. She thought of her father, who so far had been protected from the truth, as their mother would have striven to protect him. With those stakes, she could play Gideon Malvern at his own game, and enjoy the sport.

She gave her skirts another fussy pat and said with a schoolmistressy hint of severity, "On the subject of our defense: As we see it, Sir Gideon, our weakness lies in the fact that we do not as yet have concrete evidence of Lord Barclay's financial misdoing. However, we know how to find that. For the moment, we have ample evidence to bolster our accusation of his moral failures."

"Let's sit down to dinner," he said. "I'd rather not discuss this on an empty stomach."

Prudence stood up. "I'm impressed by your diligence, Sir Gideon. I'm sure you had a full day in your chambers and in court, and now you're prepared to work over dinner."

"No, Miss Duncan, you are going to be doing the work," he observed, moving to the table. "I am going to enjoy my dinner while you try to convince me of the merits of your case." He held out a chair for her.

Prudence closed her lips tightly. This was the man she had met that afternoon. Arrogant, self-possessed, completely in control. And much easier to deal with than the glimpses she'd had of the other side of his character. She sat down and shook out her napkin.

Her host rang a small bell beside his own place setting before sitting down. "The club has a considerable reputation for its kitchen," he said. "I chose the menu carefully. I hope it will meet with your approval."

"Since you've just told me I'm not going to have the opportunity to enjoy it, your solicitude seems somewhat hypocritical," Prudence said. "I would have been content with a boiled egg."

He ignored the comment and she was obliged to admit that he was entitled to do so. She took a roll from the basket he offered while two waiters moved discreetly around them, filling wineglasses and ladling delicate pale green soup into deep white bowls.

"Lettuce and lovage," Gideon said when she inhaled the aroma. "Exquisite, I think you'll find." He broke into a roll and spread butter lavishly. "Tell me something about your sisters. Let's start with Mrs. Ensor."

"Constance."

"Constance," he repeated. "And your younger sister is called . . . ?"

"Chastity."

He sipped his wine and seemed to savor this information. There was a distinct gleam in his gray eyes. "Constance, Prudence, and Chastity. Someone had a sense of humor. I'm guessing it was your mother."

Prudence managed not to laugh. She declared, "We are the perfect exemplifiers of our names, I should tell you, Sir Gideon."

"Are you indeed?" He reached to refill her wineglass and once again shot her that quizzical look. "Prudence by name and prudent by nature?" He shook his head. "If they match their names as appropriately as I believe you match yours, Miss Prudence Duncan, I cannot wait to meet your sisters."

Prudence ate her soup. She wasn't going to step into that quicksand. If he was beginning to see through her pretense, she wasn't going to help him out.

"This soup is certainly exquisite," she said with one of her prim smiles.

He nodded. "It's one of my favorite combinations."

She looked at him, curiosity piqued once more despite her intentions to stick with business. "I get the impression you're something of a gourmand, Sir Gideon."

He put down his soup spoon. "We have to eat and drink. I see no reason to do either in a mediocre fashion."

"No," Prudence responded. "My father would agree with you."

"And you too, I suspect." He twirled the stem of his wineglass between his fingers. Her appreciation of the white burgundy in her glass had not gone unnoticed.

Prudence realized that her facade had slipped. She

said with a careless shrug, "No, in general I'm indifferent to such things. We live very simply, my sisters and I."

"Really," he said, his voice flat as a river plain.

"Really," she said firmly, starting to reach for her glass, then instead putting her hand back into her lap.

The waiters returned, removed soup plates, set down the fish course, and left.

"Plaice," the barrister said, taking up his fish knife and fork. "A seriously underappreciated fish. Simply grilled with a touch of parsley butter, it's more delicate than the freshest Dover sole."

"In your opinion," Prudence murmured, slicing into the slightly browned flesh. The addendum passed unnoticed by her companion, who was savoring his first mouthful. She took her own and was forced to admit that he had a point.

"There is no way to fight Barclay's libel action without you and your sisters divulging your identities."

It was such a stunning change of subject, Prudence was for a moment confused. It was an attack rather than a continuation of their conversation. She blinked, swiftly marshaled her thoughts, and entered the fray. "We can't."

"I cannot put a newspaper on the stand." His voice had lost all trace of conversational intimacy. He pushed aside his plate. "I spent the better part of two hours reading back issues of your broadsheet, Miss Duncan, and I do not believe that you and your sisters lack the intelligence to imagine for one minute that you could escape the stand."

Prudence wondered if this was an ambush. Part of the cat-and-mouse game. "We cannot take the witness stand, Sir Gideon. Our anonymity is essential to *The Mayfair Lady.*"

"Why?" He took up his wine goblet and regarded her over the lip.

"I do not believe *you* lack the intelligence to answer that question yourself, Sir Gideon. My sisters and I cannot divulge our identities, because we propound theories and opinions that because we're women would be automatically discounted if our readership knew who was responsible for them. The success of the broadsheet depends upon the mystery of its authorship, and its inside knowledge."

"Ah, yes, inside knowledge," he said. "I can quite understand that no one would speak freely to you if they knew they could be opening themselves to the ironical, if not malicious, pen of *The Mayfair Lady.*"

"I would dispute *malicious,*" Prudence said, a slight flush warming her cheeks. "Ironical, yes, and we don't suffer fools gladly, but I don't consider we're ever spiteful."

"There's a difference between malice and spite," he said.

"It's a little too subtle for me," she responded frostily.

He shrugged, raised his eyebrows, but made no attempt to amend his statement.

Prudence took a minute to recover her composure. She knew that she and Constance had a tendency to indulge their own sharp and sardonic wit, but it was a private pleasure. Chastity was usually their only audience and even she, the gentler-natured sister, could be roused to blistering irony in the face of social pretension or arrant stupidity, particularly when someone was hurt by it. In the broadsheet they certainly made fun of such failings, but they never named names.

He spoke again while she was still collecting her thoughts. "Miss Duncan, if you cannot defeat this libel, your broadsheet will cease to exist. If, as I understand you to say, your identities are forced into the open, then your broadsheet will also cease to exist." He set down his glass. "So, now, tell me what legal help I can offer you."

So that was it. In his judgment they had no possibility of winning. Never had had. So it *was* cat and mouse. But why? Why this elaborate dinner just to watch her squirm like a butterfly on the end of a pin? Well, whatever the reasons, she was not about to accept his assessment meekly and go on her not-so-merry way.

Once again she took off her glasses and rubbed the lenses with her napkin. "Maybe, Sir Gideon, we're asking the impossible, but I was given to understand that you specialized in impossibilities. We are not prepared to lose *The Mayfair Lady*. It provides us with a necessary livelihood, both the broadsheet and the Go-Between. We would never get clients for that service from among our own social circle if they knew whom they were dealing with. That must be obvious to you."

"The Go-Between . . . that's some kind of matchmaking service that you advertise. I didn't realize you ran it yourselves." He sounded both amused and faintly incredulous.

Prudence said as coldly as before, "Believe it or not, Sir Gideon, we're doing rather well with it. You'd be surprised at the unlikely matches we've managed to make." She said nothing further as the pair of waiters returned, did what they had to, and left them with veal scaloppini on their plates and a very fine claret in their glasses.

Gideon sampled both wine and veal before he said with a slight shake of his head, "You and your sisters are certainly an enterprising trio."

Prudence, still holding her glasses in her lap, directed her myopic gaze at him. Immediately she remembered that this was a mistake. Whenever she took off her glasses his expression changed unnervingly. She put them back on and now fixed him with a deep frown between her brows and a hard glare behind her lenses. Everything in her expression indicated conviction and the absolute determination to deal with the impossible. "Enterprising or not, we have to win this case. It's as simple as that."

"Simple as that," Gideon said, nodding slowly. "I am to put a sheet of newspaper on the witness stand. Just supposing we set that difficulty aside, there is another one. Would you mind telling me exactly how you propose defending the publication's accusations of fraud and cheating?"

"I told you earlier, Sir Gideon, that we have a fairly good idea where to find the evidence."

He touched a finger to his lips. "Forgive me, Miss Duncan, but I'm not sure that that assertion is sufficient."

"You will have to find it so. I cannot at this point be more specific." She sipped from her wineglass, clasped her hands on the table, and leaned towards him. "We need a barrister of your standing. Sir Gideon. We're offering a case that you should find challenging. My sisters and I are not hapless defendants. We're more than capable of acting vigorously in our defense."

"And are you capable of paying my fee, Miss Duncan?"

He regarded her now with unmistakable amusement, his eyebrows lifted a fraction.

Prudence hadn't expected the question but she didn't hesitate. "No," she said.

He nodded. "As I thought."

Her frown deepened. "How could you have known?"

He shrugged. "It's part of my business sense, Miss Duncan. I'm assuming that your brother-in-law, Max Ensor, is not offering to support you."

Prudence felt the heat again rise to her cheeks. "Constance . . . we . . . would never ask him to do so. And he would not expect it. This is our enterprise. Constance is financially independent of her husband."

His eyebrows lifted another notch. "Unusual."

"We are not usual women, Sir Gideon. Which is why we're offering you the case," Prudence declared with sublime indifference to the realities. "If we win—and we *will* win, because our cause is just—then we'll happily divide the damages at whatever proportion you dictate. But we cannot broach our anonymity."

"You think you will win because your cause is just?" He laughed, and it was the derisive laugh she detested. "Just what makes you think the justice of your cause guarantees justice in the courts? Don't be naive, Miss Duncan."

Prudence smiled at him without warmth. "That, Sir Gideon, KC, is precisely why you will take our case. You like to fight, and the best fights are those that are hardest to win. Our backs are against the wall, and if we lose, we lose our livelihood. Our father loses his illusions and we will have failed our mother."

She spread her hands in a gesture of offering. "Can you resist a battle with such stakes?"

He looked at her. "Were you designated spokeswoman because of your persuasive tongue, Prudence, or was there another reason?"

"We divide our duties according to circumstance," she responded tartly, noticing only belatedly that he had used her first name for the first time. "Either of my sisters would have willingly tackled you, but they had other things to do."

"Tackled me?" He laughed, and this time it was with pure enjoyment. "I have to tell you, Prudence, that you'd have done a better job of tackling me without the . . ." He waved an expressive hand. "Without the playacting . . . that prim smile and that ghastly dress." He shook his head. "I have to tell you, my dear, that it's simply not convincing. Either you improve your acting skills or you give up the pretense. I know perfectly well that you're a sophisticated woman. I also know that you're educated and you don't suffer fools gladly. So I would ask that you stop treating me like one."

Prudence sighed. "It was not my intention to do so. I wanted to be certain you took me seriously. I didn't want to come across as some flighty Society flibbertigibbet."

"Oh, believe me, Miss Duncan, that you could never do." The disconcerting smile was in his eyes again, and she hadn't even taken off her glasses.

Prudence took the plunge. She had to at some point and it would at least banish that smile. "Very well," she said. "Will you take the case?"

Chapter 7

There was a moment of silence, broken by the return of the waiters. Prudence sat quietly until they had left. She was aware of a sinking feeling in her stomach, a slight quiver in her hands that were now clasped in her lap. She had hazarded everything on that one throw of the dice. If he said no, it was over. She had no other arguments, no further powers of persuasion.

The waiters left a cheese board, a bowl of grapes, a basket of nuts and fresh figs. They set a port decanter on the table at Gideon's right hand, then melted away.

Gideon offered her port, and when she declined with a quick shake of her head, filled his own glass. He gestured to the offerings on the table, and again she declined, watching as he helped himself to Stilton and snipped a small bunch of grapes from the branch with the tiny scissors.

"So," she prompted, when she could bear the silence no longer. "Will you defend us?"

"What a terrier you are," he observed, taking a sip of port.

"Will you?"

Gideon opened his mouth to give her the answer he had always intended to give, but his tongue seemed to have a life of its own. To his astonishment, he heard himself say, "Yes."

Prudence felt quite weak with relief. "I thought you were going to refuse," she said.

"So did I," he agreed aridly. "I had no intention of saying yes."

"But you can't change your mind now," she said swiftly. "You said yes. You can't renege."

"No, I don't suppose I can." He returned to his cheese and grapes with a little shrug of resignation. He was not an impulsive man. Lawyers, by definition, were never swayed by such an unreliable force. So, if his agreement was not impulsive, what was it? An interesting question to be explored at leisure.

Prudence drank the last of her claret. He didn't sound exactly enthusiastic about the prospect of the case. Did that mean he wouldn't take too much trouble over it? Would the fact that they couldn't pay him limit the amount of time he would spend?

She took a deep breath. "If you don't think you can give the case all your attention, I think it would be best if you *did* decline after all."

He looked at her, his eyes suddenly sharp, his mouth hard. "What are you implying?"

Prudence began to regret she'd brought up the subject. But since she had, she could see little choice but to continue. "You seem ambivalent," she said. "And since we can't pay you, I thought—"

He interrupted her, one hand raised in emphasis. "You thought that I would take on a case and fail to give it my full professional attention. Is that what you thought, Miss Duncan?" His tone was harsh, his voice, while still soft and well modulated, was incredulous. "What kind of barrister do you think I am?"

"An expensive one," she said, refusing to be cowed. "I wondered if you had a sliding scale of fees appropriate to the amount of effort you expended. I wouldn't call that unethical. In most circumstances one pays for the service one gets."

"I have never, *ever* taken on a case to which I did not devote every ounce of my legal knowledge, intellect, and energy," he declared, quietly enunciating every single word. "I give you fair warning, Miss Duncan. Do not *ever* impugn my professional integrity again." He flung down his table napkin and rang the little bell with considerable vigor.

Prudence could think of nothing to say. She was taken aback by the force of his reaction but supposed she had unwittingly trampled on his pride. Something to be careful of in the future. She made a mental note.

"Let's move back to the fire for coffee," he suggested as the waiters reappeared with a tray of coffee. His voice was once again pleasantly neutral. He rose from the table and drew back her chair for her.

Prudence stood up and picked up her handbag. "Would you excuse me for a minute?" She looked expectantly towards the door.

"This way, madam." One of the waiters moved to the door instantly and she followed him. He showed her to a small water closet just down the corridor, well equipped with basin and mirror, soap and towels. Again more suited to a private residence than a restaurant. She took a few minutes to compose herself, dabbing cool water on her wrists. She ought to feel jubilant at her victory. But instead she felt uneasy, even slightly deflated. This partnership was not going to be easy to manage. Gideon Malvern was not going to be easy to manage. And somehow they had to find a way to pay him for his services. The Duncan pride was a pretty fierce variety too. An idea nibbled at the corners of her mind. She found herself smiling. It was such a perfect solution. But would the barrister find it so?

She went back to the drawing room and took her seat on the sofa once more, accepting a cup of coffee from her host. She cleared her throat. "I would like to discuss the question of your fee, Sir Gideon."

"Certainly," he said promptly. "If Barclay fails to prove his case, he'll be required to pay all the legal costs, yours as well as his own. And in addition I'll be asking the court to award damages to *The Mayfair Lady,* whose reputation was damaged by his frivolous suit. If, therefore, Miss Duncan, we should win—and mind you, it's a big if—then my share over and above my fee, which will be paid by the other side, will be eighty percent of the damages awarded."

Prudence absorbed this, keeping her expression neutral. Then she said coolly, "I understand you're divorced, Sir Gideon."

He drew his head back like a startled cat. "What has that to do with anything?"

"It must be difficult to bring up a child, particularly a daughter, without a wife." She stirred her coffee.

"I don't find it so," he said, watching her with a frown in his eyes. "And I fail to see what this has to do with my terms. You accept them or you don't."

She took a sip of her coffee and set the tiny cup back

into the saucer. "Well, you see, I have a rather more equitable suggestion."

"Oh?" He raised his eyebrows. Against his will he was intrigued. He had expected some shock, if not downright outrage at his proposed split. Certainly not this cool, considered reaction. "How so?"

"An old-fashioned barter, Sir Gideon. An exchange of services." She leaned forward to put her cup and saucer on the table. "In exchange for your legal services the Go-Between will undertake to find you a wife and a stepmother for your daughter."

"What?" He stared at her, incapable of coherent thought for a minute.

"It's simple enough, surely. Of course, if we fail to find you the right partner, then the eighty-twenty split will stand." She smiled placidly. "And even if we lose our case, we will still hold true to our side of the bargain. We will find you a wife." She opened her hands again. "How can you lose?"

"How, indeed?" he murmured with a soundless whistle at this mixture of effrontery and ingenuity. "But as it happens, Miss Duncan, I am not in the market for a wife."

"You may not be looking actively, but if the right prospect dropped into your lap, surely you would not be averse. A life's companion, a mother for your daughter. It's very hard for a daughter to grow up without a mother's influence."

"Believe it or not, one divorce is plenty," he said, his lips suddenly thinned. He moved a hand in a dismissive gesture. "Plenty for me, and I'm sure more than enough for any child. But you wouldn't know, would you, Miss Duncan? Husbands have not come your way."

Prudence was unperturbed by this cutting statement. Gideon Malvern was not to know that her unmarried status was a matter of sublime indifference to her. She ignored the snub, and considered. She wanted to ask him who had been responsible for the divorce, but couldn't get her tongue around the words. It seemed far too intrusive a question under the circumstances.

"Yes," she said. "I can see that. Once bitten, twice shy. But a second failed marriage doesn't necessarily follow from a first." She steepled her hands, touching them to her mouth. "You don't have to agree to anything except to let us suggest some possibilities. As we work together and get to know you better, we'll have a much clearer idea of the kind of woman who might suit you."

Gideon was not accustomed to delivering a coup de grâce and having it ignored. He looked at her with renewed interest as he said brusquely, "It's a ridiculous idea. I have no time for romantic fantasies."

"Ah, but what I'm suggesting is the antithesis of romantic fantasy," Prudence pressed. "I'm merely suggesting that we come up with some possible candidates, you look them over. If there are any that interest you, we'll arrange a meeting. No strings. As I said before, how can you lose?"

He had a sense that Miss Duncan wasn't going to give up easily. His interest grew, although it had nothing to do with her proposition. More to do with the set of her head and that aura of firmly competent determination, he decided. So ludicrously at odds with her prim and dowdy exterior.

He supposed it could do no harm to agree to this absurd bargain. It might be amusing to play along for a while—and even useful to discover how the Duncan sisters worked. He shrugged and said, "I won't stop you trying, but I should warn you, I'm a very hard man to please. I think I'll rely on the eighty-twenty split."

"Assuming we win."

"I don't often lose," he said.

"And we don't often fail," she returned in much the same calmly superior tone. "So, we have a bargain?" She held out her hand.

"If you insist." He took the hand.

"Oh, you may think you're humoring me, Sir Gideon, but you'll be surprised," Prudence said with rather more confidence than she felt.

He inclined his head in half-laughing acknowledgment. "You'll have to forgive me if I'm skeptical. But as you say, I can't lose."

"Then I think we have brought this evening to a satisfactory conclusion," Prudence stated.

"Must we conclude?" he asked. "I hate to close a social evening on a business note." His gray eyes had gone dark as coal and Prudence found her own eyes focused on his mouth. A very sensual mouth, she realized, with a long upper lip and a deep cleft in his chin.

"It was a business evening, Sir Gideon," she declared, rising to her feet.

"Do you wear your glasses all the time?"

"If I want to see," she said with asperity. "And as it happens, I'm more interested in good eyesight than my appearance."

"That I doubt," he said. "I hope to see you in your true colors next time we meet."

"The appearance I choose to present depends upon the impression I choose to make," she responded stiffly. "Could you ring for my coat, please?"

He stepped over to the table and rang the handbell, then turned back to her, a slightly quizzical smile touching his mouth. "Is there a man in your life, Prudence?"

The direct question astounded her, and to her annoyance she found herself answering it as directly. "No, not at present."

His smile deepened. "Has there ever been?"

Her eyes flashed. "I fail to see what business that is of yours, Sir Gideon. I am your client, my personal life does not enter into our business relationship."

"I was merely interested in discovering whether you used your own services," he said. "It would be something of a recommendation, don't you think?"

There was no possible answer to that. Fortunately, the reappearance of the waiter in response to the summons made her silence unremarkable. Gideon asked for their coats and gave orders for his motor to be brought round from the mews. Then he turned back to Prudence. The smile had gone.

"So," he said, "to avoid any further misconceptions, let me make one thing clear: your personal business is about to become mine. Yours and your sisters'. No area of your lives will be immune from my questions."

Prudence stared at him. It was the most inflammatory statement, made all the more so by his manner, so relaxed, so cool, and so infuriatingly confident. "What are you talking about?"

"It's quite simple. I am now your barrister. And in that capacity I'm afraid I'm going to have to ask you and your sisters some very personal questions. I have to know everything about you. I can't risk any surprises in court."

"How could there be surprises in court when no one will know who we are?"

"I win cases by leaving nothing to chance," he responded. "And if you and your sisters can't guarantee me your complete cooperation, then I'm afraid our bargain is null and void."

Prudence frowned. She could see his point, but deeply resented his tone. "You may find it a case of the biter bit, Sir Gideon," she said. "In order to find a suitable match for you, we too will have to ask some very personal questions."

"There is one difference. I may choose not to answer yours since I'm less interested in finding a suitable mate than you're interested in preserving your livelihood. Your stakes are much greater than mine, Prudence, as I'm sure you'll agree."

Prudence recognized that that was game, set, and match. "I think we have nothing further to discuss this evening."

"Perhaps not," he agreed amiably. He took her coat from the waiter, who had returned, and helped her into it. He put on his own heavy overcoat and driving gloves as she tied her scarf around her head.

"The night's quite chilly," he commented as pleasantly as if that acerbic exchange had not taken place. "There's a lap rug in the motor." He escorted her down the stairs to the hall, one guiding hand lightly clasping her elbow.

The vehicle stood, engine already running, at the curb. He tucked the rug over her knees when she was seated and took his own place behind the wheel.

"I'll see you and your sisters in my chambers at eight-thirty tomorrow morning," he stated, guiding the motor expertly through the crowded streets. The Opera House was disgorging its clientele and hackney cabs jostled for space with private vehicles awaiting their owners.

"Eight-thirty!" Prudence exclaimed. "That's the crack of dawn."

"I have to be in court at ten," he said. He glanced across at her. "Believe it or not, Prudence, I do have other clients, all of whom at present are neither pro bono nor contingency cases... not to mention barter arrangements," he added with a touch of acid.

He was such an arrogant bastard! He was treating her offer as if it was no more than a joke... and a feeble one, at that. Prudence stared rigidly ahead, wishing she could tell him to jump in the Thames and take his conceited smugness with him. But then he'd have to take his legal expertise as well, so of course she couldn't.

"When you come tomorrow, I'll need you to explain to me how you're going to back up your accusations of Barclay's financial improprieties. I can't prepare a case until I have that evidence in my hands."

"I won't have the evidence tomorrow," Prudence said. "But we have a lead. I can explain that tomorrow."

"Then I suppose I must be thankful for small mercies," he said, drawing the car to a smooth stop at the curb outside 10 Manchester Square. He turned sideways on the seat, and before she could respond he had taken her face between his hands and brought his mouth to hers. Prudence tried to pull back but he was holding her too firmly and he was kissing her with far too much authority for resistance.

He moved one hand behind her head, displacing the scarf as he held her head in his palm, his fingers working through the tight bun at her nape. She tried to put her hands on his shoulders to push him away, but he was holding her too closely to give her the freedom of movement. She pushed her head back against his palm, trying to turn her mouth aside, but his lips merely moved to the corner of her mouth, his tongue lightly stroking her lips. She was breathless when finally he raised his head and smiled down at her. Her face was hot, flushed with anger, and for a moment she was speechless. Not so Gideon. "Well, that satisfies my curiosity," he said. "I've been wanting to do that ever since you stormed back into my chambers this afternoon."

"How *dare* you?" she demanded, outrage throbbing in her voice as she tried to tidy her disordered hair, pushing loosened pins back into the russet bun. "Without even *asking*? What gave you the right to assume that *I* wanted it?" She glared at him, and even through the thick lenses he could almost feel the sparks of rage in her eyes. He could certainly imagine them.

"What did you think you were doing?" she continued with the same fury. "Taking payment for your services?"

"Oh, you are so sharp, you could cut," he said with a soft laugh, pulling her back into his embrace. He kissed her again, his closed mouth hard against her lips, then released her as abruptly. She caught her breath on a gasp and was momentarily silenced.

"Actually," he said gravely, although his dancing eyes belied his tone, "I thought it might help you to know what kind of woman just *might* suit me when you commence your search. And it might be helpful for any prospective candidates to have some idea of the kind of lover I might make. You could probably make a more informed assessment of both issues now." He got out of the motor and came around to open her door, offering his hand to help her out.

She remained seated and said with icy deliberation, "You are a cad, Sir Gideon. We do not accept as clients men who ride roughshod over women. Men who assume that they can sweep a woman off her feet with some absurd attempt at mastery are of no interest to me . . . I mean us," she amended hastily. Ignoring the hand, she stepped down to the curb.

"There's a time and a place for every approach," he said without the blink of an eye. "And sometimes surprise is the essence of a successful campaign. Good night, Prudence." He raised her hand to his lips in a courtly gesture that shocked her almost as much as the kiss. "Don't forget. Tomorrow at eight-thirty sharp in my chambers."

She took back her hand with a jerk and without a word of farewell turned to the steps, infuriatingly aware of his soft laugh at her back.

He stood on the bottom step until she had let herself into the house, then returned to the motor. As he drove home, he began to wonder just what in hell he thought he was doing. He was *not* a man of impulse. Never had been. He'd agreed against every judicial instinct to work with the woman. Then on a pure impulse he found himself kissing her. What in hell's teeth did he think he was doing? He was beginning to have the unnerving sensation of loosing his moorings, casting himself adrift on a sea of blind compulsion.

Prudence had barely closed the door behind her when her sisters came running down the stairs to greet her.

"Con, what are *you* doing here?" she asked in surprise.

"Oh, Max had a division bell just as we were finishing dinner and had to go to the House of Commons for a vote. He might be there most of the night, so I decided to come back with Chas and hear what happened." Constance regarded her sister closely. "You look a little disheveled, love."

"In the circumstance, that's not surprising," Prudence answered somewhat sharply as she took off her coat. "Let's go up to the parlor and I'll tell you all about it." She became aware of her sisters' incredulous stares. "Why . . . What's the matter?"

"That dress is frightful," Constance said. "Where did it come from?"

"The old cedar chest. It was supposed to keep the barrister's mind on business," she added somewhat bitterly.

"And it didn't?" Chastity asked. "This is very intriguing, Prue." She followed her sister to the stairs. "But can you at least put us out of our misery and tell us if he agreed to take the case?"

"Yes, he did, finally," Prudence answered, opening the door into their parlor, where a fire burned brightly in the grate. "But I'm beginning to think it's a very bad idea to get mixed up with Sir Gideon Malvern, KC."

"Couldn't you handle him?"

"No," Prudence said frankly. "I thought I could, but I can't . . . at least not alone."

Constance closed the door and stood leaning against it, her gaze rather anxious as it rested on her sister. "You're all right, Prue?"

"Yes, just about." She touched her lips, which still

seemed to be tingling. "As well as can be expected after an assault."

"What?" Both sisters stared at her.

"What do you mean, Prue?" Chastity put a hand on her arm. "Who assaulted you?"

"Oh, that's a bit melodramatic," Prudence said with a sigh. "It wasn't an assault, it was just a kiss. But it was unexpected and he didn't ask permission and I don't like being grabbed as if I have no say in the matter."

Her sisters untangled this and came to the correct picture. "He's the masterful type, then?" Constance said with some scorn.

"He certainly likes to think so." She changed the subject abruptly. "Are you spending the night, Con?"

"Yes, in my old room," her sister replied, leaving the door to take up the goblet of cognac she had abandoned when they'd heard Prudence's return.

"Doesn't Max mind? It's a bit soon after your wedding to abandon the marital bed, isn't it?" Prudence tossed her head scarf onto the sofa, following it with her discarded coat, aware that the teasing note she had been aiming for was somehow missing. Her voice sounded rather raw.

Constance sipped her cognac, still keeping her eyes on her sister. It was generally better with Prue to let her tell her story at her own pace, so she answered easily, "To tell you the truth, I didn't actually ask him if he minded. I just left him a note. But he won't be back until close to dawn, I imagine, so I'm sure he won't mind at all."

"Well, it's a good thing you are going to be here first thing in the morning," Prudence said, examining her disordered appearance in the mirror above the mantel.

"Since we have to be at the barrister's chambers at eight-thirty tomorrow."

Her sisters exchanged a quick glance. The hostility in Prue's voice was unmistakable. "So, you said he's agreed to take the case," Chastity prompted, wondering which avenue would lead to more discussion about the unwanted kiss. Her sister was clearly disturbed, and the subject couldn't simply be abandoned.

"Yes." Prudence sat down and kicked off her shoes. She pressed her fingertips to her temples. "I have had too much wine."

"Where did you go for dinner?"

"Some supper club in Covent Garden. In the interests of privacy," she added. "Oh, and by the way, you were wrong, Con. His daughter apparently lives with him, not her mother."

"Oh," Constance said, sipping her cognac. "Well, he obviously has custody. He probably prevents the mother seeing her."

Prudence shook her head. "No, much as I'd like to agree with you, I don't think you can go off on one of your antipaternalistic diatribes in this instance. I don't know what caused the divorce, but he seems a rather enlightened parent. He sends her to North London Collegiate and allows her to read *The Mayfair Lady* with her governess and makes no objections to the governess's teaching the girl about women's suffrage."

Constance raised her eyebrows. "Well, that's novel. But to get back to the case. He's agreed to take it, so how do we pay him?"

"His suggestion is an eighty-twenty split of any damages *The Mayfair Lady* might be awarded if Barclay's case is thrown out as frivolous. Sir Gideon will ask for recompense for damage done to the broadsheet's reputation, in addition, of course, to all our legal costs, which would include his fee. Of course, we have to win for all that to happen."

"Oh, that seems a very reasonable split," Chastity said.

"Eighty for Sir Gideon, Chas. We get the twenty."

Constance grimaced, but shrugged. "We don't have any choice but to accept his terms."

"I suggested a different arrangement," Prudence said, and explained.

"That's a brilliant idea, Prue!" Chastity exclaimed. "What kind of person would suit him?"

Her sister gave a short laugh. "More to the point, what kind of woman would put up with him? You won't like him, I'll tell you that much. He's arrogant, conceited, imperious, rude." She shrugged. "You name it, he's it."

"And he has a habit of grabbing women and kissing them against their will," Constance prodded.

"He didn't hurt you, though, Prue, did he?" Chastity asked anxiously.

Her sister shook her head and tried for a reassuring smile. "Only my pride. I don't like being manhandled. I wish I'd slapped him, only he took me so much by surprise I could only gape at him like a gaffed fish."

"Is he really all bad?" Chastity pressed. "Is he attractive, at least? Or even interesting in some way?"

Prudence frowned. "Don't take this the wrong way, Con, but he reminds me of the way Max was at the beginning. You thought he was the most arrogant, supercilious bastard ever to walk the streets of London."

"I still do think that sometimes," her sister responded. "But the good qualities far and away outweigh the bad.

Besides," she added with brutal candor, "I'm no angel myself. I can be every bit as obnoxious in the right circumstances. It makes us rather a good match." She laughed slightly. "Surely this Sir Gideon must have *some* good qualities."

"So far I haven't seen any," Prudence declared. "I find him detestable. But I believe he's a brilliant lawyer, and that's all that concerns us. I'll just have to try to keep my antipathy from being too obvious."

Chastity cast her sister a shrewdly speculative glance. Was there a hint of overprotest in Prue's voice? She asked, "Does he think we have a chance in court?"

"At first he said absolutely not. Because we won't take the stand."

A short silence fell as they contemplated the ramifications of this. "It is difficult, I can see that," Constance said after a minute. "Is there a way around it?"

"He must have some ideas or he wouldn't bother with us," Chastity pointed out.

Constance regarded Prudence with raised eyebrows. "You said *at first*. Something made him change his mind? Do you know what it was?"

"Not really," her sister said. "Perhaps persistence paid off. Perhaps I wore him down." She shrugged. "Whatever the reason, he agreed. We got what we wanted." She wondered why he had not been in the least perturbed by her angry response to his kiss. Quite the opposite, he had actually laughed at her indignant rejection. *Odious creature.*

She leaned her head against the back of the sofa and yawned. "I'm exhausted and we have to have our wits about us first thing in the morning." She stood up with a groan. "And I warn you, we'll need all the wits we possess. Our barrister doesn't miss a trick, and he's already warned me that he's going to be asking some very personal questions."

"I don't suppose you warned him that we have a tendency to bite if someone crosses our boundaries," Constance said, rising to her feet with her sister.

"I thought we'd let him find that out for himself," Prudence returned, managing a smile. "Breakfast at seven? I'll leave a note for Jenkins." She went to the overburdened secretaire and scribbled a few words, setting the paper beneath her sister's empty cognac goblet, where the butler would find it first thing in the morning.

"Into the breach once more." Constance linked arms with her sisters until they separated at their own doors.

Chapter 8

Constance awoke a very few hours later in the gray light of dawn. She wasn't sure what had woken her until she heard the door click shut. She peered blearily into the dimness and smiled, brushing hair out of her eyes as she struggled up against the pillows.

"Good morning, Max. I assume it is morning. Why aren't you fast asleep in your own bed?"

"That was rather the question I was going to ask you," her husband said somewhat aridly as he set a tea tray on the dresser. "I get home to find a cold and empty bed and a scribbled note from my wife telling me she's returned to the bosom of her family."

"Only for tonight...I mean last night," Constance protested. "I didn't think you'd mind, as you'd be working most of the night."

"Well, as it happens, I think I do mind," he declared, pouring tea. He brought two cups over to the bed and sat on the edge, handing her one.

"Oh, come on," she said. "You know you don't really." She sipped gratefully of the steaming brew. "Did you make this yourself, or is Mrs. Hudson up and about already?"

"Jenkins made it. He said you'd left a note saying you wanted breakfast at the crack of dawn, so I thought I'd wake you myself."

"That was very thoughtful of you," Constance said. "But I'd have liked a good-morning kiss before the tea."

He took the cup from her and set it, with his, on the bedside table, then leaned over and kissed her, murmuring against her mouth, "Not that you deserve it, deserting me like that."

"Good morning, Con—oh, Max, are you here too?" Chastity spoke even as she opened the door and came in, followed by Prudence, carrying a tea tray.

"Since the mountain wouldn't come to Mohammed, Mohammed had no choice but to come to the mountain," Max observed, straightening slowly, turning to look at his sisters-in-law.

"I told Con you wouldn't like it," Prudence said. "We brought tea, but I see you have some already."

She poured for herself and Chastity and the two of them sat companionably in their night robes on the bed beside Max, who seemed as unconcerned as they about their dishabille.

"Actually, it's very convenient that Con's here," Prudence said, "because we have an appointment with Gideon Malvern in his chambers at half past eight."

"Did he agree to take the case?" Max took up his teacup again.

"Prue persuaded him," Chastity said. "I think he fancies her, but Prue's not saying."

"Chas," Prudence protested.

"It's only Max, and he's family," her sister said. "And I didn't say anything about your fancying the barrister."

"I told you perfectly clearly what I thought of him," her sister stated.

"And what's that?" inquired Max.

"Eminently dislikable," Prudence said crisply.

"Just the reaction Con had to—" Chastity stopped, coughing violently, the cup rattling in her saucer.

"You are so indiscreet, Chas," Prudence accused.

Max raised his eyebrows. He was far too used to the sisters to be in the least surprised or put out by anything they could say or do. He glanced at his wife for enlightenment.

"Don't give it another thought, Max," Constance instructed. "We were just being silly, as is our wont."

"I don't believe I've ever seen any of you being in the least silly," he commented. "So I'll take that as a roundabout way of telling me to mind my own business." He stood up. "I'll leave you to get dressed and keep your appointment." He put his cup on the dresser. "You will be back for luncheon, Constance." It was statement rather than question.

"Yes, of course." She gave him a placatory smile. "We'll probably have coffee at Fortnum's to fortify ourselves after our ordeal in chambers, but I'll come straight home afterwards."

He nodded, kissed her again, kissed her sisters on the cheek, and left the bedroom.

"Sorry, Con," Chastity said. "It's too early in the morning for me to think clearly."

"Oh, it doesn't matter in the least," her sister reassured. "Max knows perfectly well what I thought of him when I first met him. I still throw it in his face when we fight."

"I remember when you threw a vase of daisies in his face," Chastity said with a laugh.

Constance shook her head. "I do rather regret that," she said ruefully.

"Well, that's water under the bridge," Prudence stated, sliding off the bed. Ordinarily she would have been happy to reminisce with her sisters, but she was filled with a restless impatience this morning. "We need to turn our attention to Gideon Malvern. Did you bring a day dress, Con? Or do you want to borrow something?"

"No, I packed a skirt and jacket." Constance threw aside the covers. "It's not quite as smart as I would have brought if I'd known I wouldn't be going straight home this morning, but it'll do. I don't have a hat, though. Should I borrow one? Is he a great stickler for the niceties?"

Prudence gave a short laugh. "Not when it comes to taking liberties."

Constance pursed her lips. "He's not going to be doing that when we're all together."

"He's not going to be doing it ever again," Prudence declared, going to the door. "I'm going to keep a hat pin up my sleeve. Come on, Chas. We'll see you in the breakfast room in half an hour, Con."

In her own bedroom Prudence reviewed the contents of her wardrobe. It was time to abandon the ill-fated attempt at old-maid dowdiness. But she must still avoid all hint of frivolity. She wanted something that said . . . said what? She chewed her lip, riffling through the silks, tweeds, wools, velvets. Cotton or muslin would be too thin for a crispish autumn morning. What image did she want to project to Gideon this morning?

Definitely businesslike. Nothing too dressy that would look as if she had made a particular effort . . . but nothing too understated either. Something suitable for an everyday business appointment, but with a little extra flair to it. Much as she hated to admit it, her pride had suffered sorely under her previous disguise.

Prudence, her sisters would agree, had an infallible dress sense. She always knew what would suit a particular occasion and her sisters happily bowed to her judgment. She pulled out a rather smart black woolen suit that had belonged to her mother and had gone through several reincarnations to reach its present form. Lady Duncan, her daughter remembered, had worn it when she was in a confrontational mood. And Prudence was in a confrontational frame of mind.

She laid it on the bed and tried pairing it with a severe white silk shirt, high-buttoned at the neck, and stood back to examine the effect. No, she decided instantly. Much too funereal. She turned back to the wardrobe, and found what she sought.

The dark red silk blouse with a floppy cravatlike tie at the neck was exactly right. It lightened and softened the black suit but it was also very elegant and the color was almost indistinguishable from her hair. So, no hat; definitely no hat.

When she came downstairs to the breakfast room as the grandfather clock in the hall struck seven, her sisters were already there. "Oh, bravo, Prue," Chastity applauded.

"Yes, exactly right," Constance agreed, buttering a piece of toast. "No hat, though."

Prudence laughed and shook her head. "The pompadour is good enough, I think." She touched her hair that was piled and pinned on top of her head over pads, forming an elaborate coiffure.

"Perfect," Constance said, reaching for the coffeepot to fill her sister's cup. "Chas and I are dressed to fade into the background so that you can take center stage."

Prudence merely grinned. Constance was wearing a gray-and-white-striped skirt, tightly belted at her narrow waist, with a dark gray fitted jacket and neat buttoned boots. Chastity wore a dark green dress with a bolero jacket and full sleeves that buttoned tightly at her wrists. There was no possibility of either of them fading into the background when it came to fashion, even though both outfits, like Prudence's, had been through several makeovers.

"I would have thought you'd have abandoned your pre-Max wardrobe by now," Prudence remarked, cracking the top of a boiled egg.

"Somehow it goes against the grain to throw away perfectly good clothes," Constance said seriously.

"You could give them to charity," Chastity suggested, dipping a finger of toast into her own boiled egg.

"I haven't had a chance to go through them yet," Constance pointed out. "Anyway, this was one of Mother's favorites. Now, Prue, prepare us a little for this morning. We need to come up with a concerted attack . . . or defense. I don't know which we're talking about."

"Probably both," her sister said.

Gideon had reached his chambers soon after six o'clock that morning. The janitor had lit the fires in both chambers but the coals were still showing little life. His clerk had not yet arrived, so he lit the spirit stove, set water to boil for the strong coffee that would compensate for too little sleep, and hauled selected tomes off the bookshelves. Once settled at his desk, still wearing muffler and gloves because the night's chill took a while to disperse through the ancient stone walls despite the fires, he looked for precedents on a libel suit when the defendants were anonymous. By the time Thadeus had arrived an hour later, the barrister had found none.

Thadeus flourished his toasting fork and offered toast and marmalade.

"Yes, thank you," his employer grunted in response to the offer, heaving open another volume.

"Trouble, Sir Gideon?" Thadeus hovered in the doorway.

"Anonymous clients, Thadeus." Gideon looked up, two fingers pressed to his eyes.

"There was a libel case, sir, in 1762 I believe, when the defendants were shielded from the court by a curtain." Thadeus disappeared into the outer chamber, returning almost immediately with a plate of hot buttered toast. "More coffee, Sir Gideon?"

"Yes . . . and the precedent." Gideon bit into the toast.

"Right away, Sir Gideon." And it was right away. Within a minute, Thadeus set down the relevant volume, opened at the correct page. A nicotine-stained finger underlined the passage in question.

"You are without price, Thadeus," Gideon said without looking up.

"Thank you, sir." Thadeus was well pleased. "I'll show the ladies in when they arrive."

Gideon looked up. He examined his office and found

it wanting. "Oh, yes, and see if you can find another two chairs. I can't have two sisters standing."

"I have already done so, Sir Gideon. Sir Thomas Wellbeck's clerk has lent us two extra chairs."

"Again, Thadeus, you are without price." This time Gideon smiled. His clerk returned the smile.

"At your service, sir. Always at your service." He backed out.

Gideon finished the last piece of toast as he read, then he wiped his fingers on the napkin thoughtfully provided by his clerk and drained his coffee cup. He had the beginnings of a strategy now. He heard the door to his outer office open at precisely half past eight and rose to his feet behind the table to greet the three sisters as Thadeus showed them in.

His greeting smile was bland and courteous, no indication of his swift assessment of the sisters. He had been very curious to meet the other two and was not disappointed. They were as striking a trio of women as a man could hope to meet. And Prudence, now sporting what were clearly her true colors, had an even more powerful presence than he had expected. He was hard-pressed not to laugh at the memory of her previous incarnations when compared with this elegant, impeccably dressed woman. Her fashionably elaborate hairstyle showed off the rich, lustrous color of her hair, complemented so beautifully by the red blouse. Gone too were the thick horn-rimmed glasses. In their place a delicate pair of gold-rimmed spectacles that perched on the bridge of her nose and offered no impediment to the view of the light and vivid green eyes beneath. She was a sight for the sorest of eyes.

His swift assessment led him to conclude that there

was something almost formidable about the front they presented. Despite their very obvious individuality in both appearance and manner, they seemed to share an aura of combative intelligence. The same kind of sharp intellect that informed the content and writing of *The Mayfair Lady*. The barrister in him noted this with satisfaction. They would make excellent witnesses. Except, of course, that they were insisting he couldn't put them on the stand.

But he would meet that difficulty head-on. He became aware that he was the subject of silent scrutiny and assessment by Constance and Chastity and he couldn't help wondering what Prudence had told them about the previous evening. Prudence herself was giving nothing away. Her expression was composed and unsmiling.

"Good morning, Sir Gideon," she said formally. "May I introduce my sisters."

"Let me guess." He came out from behind the table, hand extended towards Constance. "Mrs. Ensor. I'm delighted to meet you."

Constance took the hand, her own grip as firm as his. "I won't ask how you guessed."

He merely smiled and turned to Chastity. "Miss Chastity Duncan."

"That's me," Chastity said, her handshake every bit as decisive as her eldest sister's. "Do I look two years younger than Constance?"

"Somehow, I don't think I want to step into that particular quicksand," he said, waving a hand to the three chairs. "Please . . . sit down."

They sat in a semicircle facing him, all three coolly composed, hands resting in their laps. All three of them had green eyes, he noticed somewhat distractedly.

Prudence's were lighter than her elder sister's, and Chastity's had hazel lights in their depths. The same with their hair, three different shades of red.

Dear God! What an impression they would make on the witness stand.

He cleared his throat. "Mrs. Ensor, I understand you were the author of the offending article."

"The article in question," she stated. "I did not, and indeed *do* not, consider it to be offensive."

"Nevertheless, it certainly offended Lord Barclay."

"Some people are offended by the truth."

"Yes, quite inexplicable," he observed, taking up the relevant issue of *The Mayfair Lady*. "Hard to imagine why a man would be offended at being accused in a public forum of being a rapist, a despoiler of young girls, a cheat, a thief, an embezzler." He set aside the sheet and regarded the sisters, who met his ironic gaze with unwavering sangfroid.

"I thought we'd covered this ground yesterday," Prudence said. "And we also dealt with the issue that no *one* of us is responsible for this libel suit. We are all involved to exactly the same extent. *The Mayfair Lady* is the defendant. And that publication is a composite of the Duncan sisters."

"You're not making my task any easier."

"We don't intend to make it any more difficult than it has to be," Prudence said tightly. "Our views on Lord Barclay are clearly stated in the article. If we hadn't believed in the truth of the accusations we would not have made them." She glanced at her sisters and saw that they were willing to let her lead the advance. She could also see that behind the shared calm exterior they were aware that the rude and imperious side of Sir Gideon Malvern was definitely coming to the fore.

Gideon glanced down at the paper again. "Yes, it's clear that you are all champions of the downtrodden female. I assume you are also suffragists."

"What have our political opinions to do with this?" demanded Prudence.

He looked over at her. "A jury may not find them sympathetic."

"And we need a sympathetic jury," Constance put in.

"Quite frankly, I think that's going to be very hard to find."

Chastity leaned forward in her chair. "Sir Gideon, are you so desperate that just the faintest chance of coming away with eighty percent of possible damages is sufficient motivation for you to take on a case that you clearly don't believe in?"

On the rare occasions when Chastity was roused to anger she could outdo both her sisters. Prudence and Constance exchanged a quick look but said nothing.

Gideon's nostrils flared for an instant, then he said, "I thought your matrimonial agency was going to find me a suitable wife as payment for my services." There was no mistaking the disdainful note in his voice.

"You might need to cultivate a more pleasant manner," Prudence stated. "We can't work miracles."

"Neither can I, Miss Duncan." In leisurely fashion he reached for a silver cigarette box on the table beside him. He flipped the lid. Hesitated. Some women did smoke these days, but only in private. In general it wouldn't occur to him to offer the box to a woman, but with these three . . . ? He gave a mental shrug and leaned over the desk, proffering the box first to Prudence.

"No, thank you, it's one means of shocking the world we haven't embraced," she said, her voice chilly enough to give a polar bear shivers.

"Then I hope you don't mind if I do," he responded, ignoring the chill. "I find it helps me to think." He lit a cigarette and smoked in silence for a couple of minutes, staring at a point on the wall somewhere above his visitors' heads.

"I have the unmistakable feeling that we're wasting your time," Prudence said at last.

He waved her into silence with a gesture that infuriated all three of them, and continued with his cigarette. Only when he'd thrown the stub into the fire did he speak again. "This broadsheet of yours is inflammatory even when it's not directly and personally attacking a member of Society. I am merely pointing out that an all-male jury, twelve good men and true, are unlikely to find against one of their own in favor of a group of subversive women."

"Not necessarily," Prudence said. "It's not inevitable that every man on that jury will be of the same social standing as the earl. It's possible that they might have some sympathy for the women Barclay has ruined."

"Yes," Chastity put in. "There may even be one or two who for whatever reason—envy, personal discontent—would enjoy seeing someone like Barclay get his comeuppance."

"Ignoble motives, but certainly to be considered," Gideon said. "However, I can't put together a case for the defense if I don't have some basis for a defense." He tapped the sheet and the pile of notes Prudence had left him with a flick of his fingertips. "Now, Prudence, is the moment to give me what you have to support these accusations of fraud, theft, and cheating."

Prudence took a deep breath. "At present, nothing. But we suspect that Barclay was responsible for inveigling our father into a fraudulent scheme that resulted in the loss of his entire fortune."

"And Prue is convinced she'll find evidence in support of that among our father's financial papers," Constance said.

Gideon frowned. "This smacks of a personal vendetta. That won't sit well with a jury."

"Since no one will know our identities, no one will make the connection," Prudence pointed out.

Gideon shook his head and leaned forward. "Now, listen to me." He pointed an imperative finger. "Do you really think for one minute that Barclay's legal team will allow you to remain anonymous? They will turn heaven and earth upside down to discover who you are. And when they do, they will crucify you."

"There's no need to sound so patronizing," Prudence snapped. "We're not blind to the realities."

"Forgive me," he said in much the same tone as before. "But I think you are."

He sat back in his chair for a moment, then suddenly glared at Prudence, his gray eyes hard and cold as a gravestone. "Madam, do you have any personal reasons for this vendetta against his lordship? Has he perhaps made an unwelcome advance to you?"

"No," Prudence said, sounding shocked. "No, not at all."

"Are you asking the jury to believe that this crusade against a respected member of Society was entirely motivated by a desire for the public good?" He raised his eyebrows in sardonic disbelief.

"No . . . I mean yes," Prudence said, aware that she was stumbling now, her cheeks suddenly warm. "There's nothing personal about it. Lord Barclay ruined—"

He silenced her with a raised hand. "We don't need to hear your scurrilous accusations repeated, madam. The jury should note that they are the accusations of a few servants, young girls, easily manipulated, probably more than willing to gain their employer's favor in return for favors of their own. It's a common enough situation."

Prudence jumped to her feet an instant before her sisters. "How dare you!" She jabbed a finger at him across the table. "What kind of bullying monster do you think you are? We have no need to listen to another word." She spun around to the door, but Gideon moved quickly, leaning across the table to grasp her wrist.

"Sit down again, Prudence. I want to hear you answer me." His tone was peremptory and she tried to jerk her wrist free of his grasp. His fingers tightened. "Sit down. All of you, sit down."

"You were wrong, Prue," Chastity declared. "He's a lot worse than Max ever was."

Gideon was for a moment bewildered by this remark, which seemed to have no bearing on anything. He looked from one to the other of them, and his clasp of Prudence's wrist loosened. She liberated her wrist and deliberately rubbed it, taking advantage of the barrister's momentary disadvantage.

"I'm sorry," he said in evident chagrin. "Did I hurt you?"

Prudence made him wait. Then she said frigidly, "I thought I had made clear last night that I do not tolerate being touched without my permission. If you cannot keep your hands to yourself, Sir Gideon, this arrangement is at an end."

Gideon looked so shocked, so utterly taken aback, that Prudence could almost have laughed. Finally she had the satisfaction of besting him, of making him uncomfortable.

After a minute he said in a more moderate tone, "Forgive me. I was only trying to make a point. Please sit down. All of you."

They took their seats again and Prudence, whose anger had faded under a few minutes' calm reflection, said, "I suppose you were giving us a taste of what it might be like with a hostile prosecution in court."

"I was."

"But we've already explained that we can't appear as witnesses," she said, sounding impatient again. "We're going around in circles on this one, Gideon."

"Not quite. I think I see a way to break the circle. One of you will have to appear on the witness stand." He looked at them each in turn. "I'm sure you can lay hands on a really heavy veil, one that will totally conceal features."

"I suppose we could," Prudence said, glancing at her sisters. "Would it work, d'you think?"

"You'd have to disguise your voice," Constance pointed out. "But we could practice that."

"And if Con and I wear veils too, we could sit in the courtroom," Chastity observed, frowning in thought. "At least we'll be there for moral support."

"Why me?" Prudence asked.

No one answered and she gave an accepting shrug.

She had been the main player from the start, it was logical she should continue. "It's risky," she said.

"Everything about this case is risky, Prudence," Gideon declared.

"You're being patronizing again," Prudence exclaimed. "Do try not to keep telling us what we know already and to our cost."

Gideon Malvern was one of the top barristers in the country and he was most definitely not accustomed to being taken to task for his professional manner by anyone, let alone by an indigent client. However, he resisted the impulse to put her in her place. He had the absolute conviction that an attempt to set one sister straight would bring down the wrath of the other two and he wasn't sure he could handle them in concert. One at a time . . . *maybe* . . . but definitely not all at once.

He chose the dignified course and ignored her remark, instead saying, "How would you answer the question in court, Prudence?"

She frowned. "As I recall, it was not so much a question as a repellent inference designed to appeal to a male jury."

"It was also designed to fluster you."

"As it did."

"So, give me your response." He sat back in his carved chair and folded his arms.

"I would probably say that—"

"No," he interrupted. "I want a spontaneous answer."

"We gathered sufficient evidence from the young women who had been violated and abandoned by the earl of Barclay, and from those who had assisted them, to substantiate their claims beyond any doubt. The press took up—"

"The gutter press, madam. The *Pall Mall Gazette,* which thrives on sensationalism. Did it appear in the *Times,* in the *Telegraph,* the *Morning Post*? No, it did not." Gideon leaned forward, pointing a finger at her. "No respectable person gives any credence to yellow journalism. If that's your only evidence, Madam Mayfair Lady, I can see no possible justification for the jury to find in your favor."

"Oh, I like that," Constance said. "Madam Mayfair Lady."

"Yes, a splendid alias," Chastity said.

"Just a minute, Gideon, are you saying that despite all our evidence we're not on solid ground with those accusations?" Prudence asked.

"His lawyers will certainly try to discredit your evidence." Gideon took up the legal document that Prudence had brought him the previous afternoon. "I was trying to point out how shaky the ground is even when you have fairly strong support for the accusations. Where you don't have..." He shrugged as he perused the document.

"I told you, we will get what's needed," Prudence declared.

"Yes, so you've said. I'll reserve judgment until I see it." He didn't raise his eyes from his reading.

Prudence closed her mouth firmly and gazed at the ceiling. He looked up then and the corners of his eyes crinkled. He seemed to have won that point. It was curiously satisfying, almost childishly so, he thought. He said, flourishing the document, "Falstaff, Harley, and Greenwold are as good as solicitors get when it comes to libel. And they've briefed Sam Richardson, KC, as counsel. Which was inevitable. They always work together."

"And he's good."

"Yes, Prudence, the very best."

"I thought you were."

"In some areas I am. But I've had less experience than Richardson in libel cases," he returned matter-of-factly.

"This case will, however, add to your stock," Prudence said. "A potent motive for taking it on."

"It was one of several," he responded without a flicker. He laid the solicitor's letter on the table again. "So, ladies, we go on the attack. I'll draft the letter and get it to the solicitors by this afternoon. Then we sit back and wait for a trial date. Or at least," he added, "I get on with my other cases, while you try to get me some evidence for an adequate defense." He stood up. "If you'll excuse me. I have to be at the Old Bailey by ten."

It was a firm but perfectly courteous dismissal and Prudence gathered up her gloves and handbag, her sisters following suit. In the outer chamber Gideon donned his black gown and white curly wig. "I'm lunching with Sir Donald at the noon recess. I'll be back this afternoon, Thadeus."

"I'll work on the brief for the Carter case this morning," the clerk said, handing him a thick folder of papers. "The witness statements are all there."

Gideon riffled through the folder and nodded. "If I need anything extra, I'll send a runner." He turned to his visitors. "Let me escort you downstairs."

He followed them downstairs, his gown swishing around the striped trousers of his morning dress. In the street, Prudence said, "You'll keep us informed?"

"Oh, yes, on a daily basis," he said, putting a hand to his wig as a gust of wind whistled around the corner of the building. "We have much to do to prepare you to take the stand, so you may rest assured that you will hear from me again very soon." He gave her a little nod and then turned and strode off towards the Old Bailey.

"And that last, Prue, was entirely for you," Constance observed when he'd disappeared from view. "For all his arrogance, our barrister friend is nowhere near as hostile as he makes out. I would say he's definitely interested in you."

"He has a strange way of showing it," Prudence returned rather dourly.

"Oh, but I think Con's right," Chastity said. "Even after that set down you gave him." She shook her head in awe. "I'm amazed he was able to recover from it."

"The man has the skin of a rhinoceros," her sister stated. "But if he dares put a hand on me again for *any* reason, I shall stick him with my hairpin."

"I would be a little careful I didn't get stuck back," Constance said with a laugh. "I wouldn't want to push our barrister friend too far."

Chastity chuckled. "No, indeed," she agreed. "There's something a little dangerous about him." She glanced sideways at Prudence, adding slyly, "Of course, some women might find it attractive. Some women like playing with fire."

Prudence felt an unusual flash of irritation at her sisters' levity. For some reason she couldn't find anything amusing in the situation. Ordinarily she wouldn't mind being the object of her sisters' teasing, but she didn't feel like being teased about Gideon Malvern. She said nothing.

If her sisters noticed her lack of response, they let it go. Chastity said cheerfully, "Actually, Con, he *is* worse than Max."

"Oh, they're all the same, these successful professional men," Constance said airily. "They're so sure of themselves, so ready to mow down all opposition, but to tell you the truth, I'd rather have that breed of arrogance than the aristocratic kind that's based solely on inherited wealth and doesn't need a brain to back it up. Don't you agree?" She glanced at Prudence for confirmation, then said quickly, "Something wrong, Prue?"

"No, not at all." Prudence shook her head and forced herself to join their mood. "And you're certainly right," she agreed. "I can hear Mother saying the same thing."

Chastity gave her a searching look, hearing the slight hesitation in her sister's voice. Prudence smiled and said, "It's nearly ten o'clock. Fortnum's will open in half an hour. Let's go and have coffee and cakes, and plan this campaign of investigation."

Chastity was not convinced that Prudence was her usual self, but now didn't seem a suitable moment to pry. "Good idea," she said with an easy smile. "I have a craving for a slice of Battenburg cake."

"And this afternoon we can sit down and draw up a list of suitable marriage prospects for Sir Gideon," Constance said. "Or at least decide what kind of woman we think might suit him. Now that we've all met him, we ought to have some ideas." She waved at a passing hackney, saying as she climbed in, "You'd better come to my house. I probably ought to stay in for bride visits this afternoon."

Chapter 9

"Have you had any bride visits yet, Con?" Chastity asked as she walked into her sister's drawing room that afternoon.

"Oh, this is such a pleasant room," Prudence said, following on her sister's heels. "I do like that Chinese wallpaper."

"Lady Bainbridge turned up her nose," Constance said. "She was here half an hour ago. Very supercilious she was on the subject of these newfangled tastes." She plumped up a silk cushion embroidered with peacocks. "She examined me very carefully, clearly looking for an expanding waistline."

"It would be too soon for that, even if you were thinking about it," Prudence pointed out, casting a glance at her elder sister's slender figure. "Who else has been?"

"Letitia . . . oh, and Aunt Agnes. She was very complimentary about the Oriental theme."

"She would be. Agnes has never said a critical word about anyone," Chastity said fondly of their father's sister, their favorite aunt.

"Let me get some tea," Constance said, "and then we can talk about lists." She pulled the fringed bell rope beside the fireplace. "I've been wracking my brains trying to think of eligible women for the barrister—" She broke off as a maid appeared in answer to the bell. "Could you bring us some tea, Brenda? Thank you."

"What kind of woman would suit him?" Chastity asked, settling into a corner of the sofa.

"I haven't the faintest idea," Prudence said, depositing herself into a deep armchair.

"That's not very helpful," Constance chided. "This was your idea, remember."

"I remember." Prudence sighed. "And it seemed like a good one at the time. Before I realized that I wouldn't wish him on my worst enemy."

"Don't exaggerate," Constance said, bending to clear a marquetry table to receive the tea tray brought in by the maid.

Prudence grinned reluctantly and leaned over to take a cucumber sandwich from the plate. The maid poured tea and left.

"Well, who's going to start the ball rolling?" Constance sat down on the end of the sofa opposite Chastity.

Chastity frowned and instead of answering that question posed one of her own. "Did it occur to you that it might be very difficult to find a woman willing to marry a divorced man?"

"He's rich and successful," Prudence pointed out. "He's well connected. There's nothing particularly unfavourable in his appearance."

"Talk about damning with faint praise," Constance

said with a crow of laughter. "I think he's rather distinguished-looking."

"He has good eyes," Prudence conceded. "And a good head of hair."

Chastity chuckled and spread honey on a buttered crumpet. "Nice voice too."

Constance declared with a touch of acid, "Divorce isn't the same handicap for men as it is for women."

"No," Chastity agreed.

"But we don't know who was the injured party," Prudence pointed out.

"Even if it was his wife, I'm sure he did the decent thing," Chastity said. "It would be unthinkable otherwise."

"Allowing her to divorce him?" Prudence frowned. "With most men I would agree with you, but in my experience, Gideon doesn't play by all the rules."

"He only kissed you, Prue," Chastity said.

"Without my permission!" her sister fired back. "How would you like it, Chas?"

Chastity shrugged. "It often happens to me. I just pat their cheeks and explain that I'm not interested."

Prudence surveyed her with slight exasperation. "But I'm not you, Chas. I don't flirt, and I don't shrug these things off. I expect men to leave me alone unless I invite them closer."

"This isn't getting us anywhere," Constance said. "Let's look at what qualities we think Gideon would insist upon in a second wife."

"Faithfulness," Prudence said with a short laugh.

"That goes without saying."

"A submissive type, probably," Prudence added. "One who doesn't mind being grabbed at will."

"Prue, you are not helping," Constance rebuked.

Prudence nodded. "All right," she said. "Since he believes in women's education, I'm sure he'd prefer a woman with an educated mind." She drank her tea.

"And of course someone who could hold her own in the kinds of social gatherings he frequents." Chastity rummaged in her bag for a notebook and pencil. "Let's make a list of what we see as necessary qualities and then you can show it to him, Prue. See if he has any others to add."

"We have to consider the daughter's feelings too," Constance said. "I wonder how much it would matter to him that the child should like a potential candidate."

"I think it would have to be someone who liked children, who got along well with them," Prudence said definitely. "In all conscience, we couldn't possibly promote a marriage in this case where we knew the potential bride had an antipathy for children."

"Prue's absolutely right," Chastity said, and Constance nodded her agreement.

"I would think a potential candidate's level of education would be important too," Constance put in. "If he's sending his daughter to North London Collegiate, he must be intending her for Girton, wouldn't you think? He'd want another woman in the house to be able to keep up with the girl's education."

Prudence considered. Girton, the women's college at Cambridge University, now allowed women to sit public examinations. They still weren't allowed to take a degree, but the cachet was enormous. "Then he'd be expecting her to pursue some kind of career," she mused. "Teaching, I suppose."

"Who do we know who's qualified to teach? Not a

governess, of course, but at undergraduate level, or at least in one of the good girls' schools. That would cover the necessity for getting along with children too."

"Astrid Bellamy," Chastity suggested. "She's passionate about women's education. She went to Lady Margaret Hall at Oxford."

"She's too old," Prudence stated instantly. "She must be nearly forty."

"But we don't know that age would matter to him," Cosntance pointed out. "Unless he wants more children, of course."

"He'd have been looking more actively for himself if that was the case," Prudence pointed out. "He must be forty himself."

Constance frowned. "Maybe so. But once we get him interested in this process it might become a factor."

"I suppose so," Prudence said, sounding doubtful.

"Well, we could ask him." Constance regarded her sister with the same frown.

"We could," Prudence agreed.

"You seem less than enthusiastic about this, Prue," Constance observed.

Prudence shook her head. "No, I'm not. Not in the least. Of course I'm not."

"Ah," Constance said. "My mistake."

Chastity cast a quick glance between her sisters, then returned to her note-taking. "What about looks?" she asked. "Do you think those are important to him? Must it be a beautiful woman?"

Prudence thought about this. "I would say looks were less important than brains and personality, but . . ." She shrugged. "What do I know?"

"More than we do," Chastity said, chewing the tip of her pencil. "You spent an evening with him."

"I can't see around his domineering, overbearing personality," Prudence stated. "What woman of strong character with a mind of her own would give him the time of day?"

"I seem to remember some comparison with Max," Constance murmured from the depths of her sofa. "But then, perhaps I'm not a woman of strong character with a mind of my own."

Prudence threw one of the fringed peacock cushions at her. "Max has redeeming features."

"We might find some in Gideon Malvern if we look hard enough," Chastity said. "What do you think about Agnes Hargate? She's fairly young, fairly attractive, well read, although she didn't go to university."

"She's a widow with a five-year-old son," Prudence said.

"So we know she likes children," Constance said.

"We don't know he wants a ready-made family," Prudence objected.

"Again, we could ask him," Chastity said. "I'm sure Agnes would be interested. I know she's lonely."

"Did he say anything to you, Prue, anything at all after you proposed this bargain?" Constance asked, leaning forward slightly.

"Yes," Chastity said. "Did he give any hint of the kind of woman who might appeal?"

Prudence hesitated. What had he said after he'd taken that kiss? Something about how having kissed him she would now know what kind of woman would suit him. How she would now know what kind of lover he would make. Somehow she didn't feel like sharing that with her sisters.

"No," she said. "He said only that he wasn't in the market for a wife and he was very hard to please."

"Well, that's encouraging," Constance observed aridly. "More tea?"

Prudence passed her cup. Constance was right, of course. She wasn't entering into the spirit of this exercise with genuine enthusiasm, but why not? It had been her idea to find the barrister a bride. It was a brilliant solution to the generally intractable problem of finances. But every woman who came to mind as possible struck her as impossible. She was just depressed, she decided. Depressed and oppressed. The more she dwelt on the libel suit, the more impossible it seemed to defeat it.

Constance glanced at her and then looked across at Chastity, who made a comprehending face. Something was wrong with their generally imperturbable sister. Prudence was always on an even keel, the reins of business firmly in her hands. Her sisters could take off on emotional flights of fancy on occasion, but never Prudence. She was too sensible, her concentration on the subject at hand unwavering. But not this afternoon, for some reason.

"Excuse me, madam." The maid appeared in the doorway. "Fred just delivered this for Miss Prue." She extended a letter. "It went to Manchester Square and Mr. Jenkins thought it might be important, so he sent it straight round."

"Thank you, Brenda." Constance took the letter and glanced at the envelope. "From the chambers of Sir Gideon Malvern, KC." She handed it to Prudence. "He didn't waste any time, did he?"

Prudence slit the envelope and unfolded the paper. "He says that he's received immediate acknowledgment from Barclay's solicitors that he's the barrister of record in the matter of *Barclay v.* The Mayfair Lady." She looked up. "Gideon said he'd send them a letter this afternoon. I wonder if it's a bad sign that they responded so quickly." A worried frown creased her brow.

"It'll be a relief to get it over with," Constance said.

"What else does it say?" Chastity leaned forward.

"He says they are requesting an early trial date, and he's not going to contest that. He wants to see me this evening to start preparing for the case." She handed the letter to Chastity. "You'd think that he would try to postpone as long as possible, wouldn't you? We don't have the evidence for the fraud accusations as yet."

"We haven't had a chance to search Father's papers," Chastity said, laying a soothing hand over her sister's that was twitching on the arm of the chair. "We'll do it at the first opportunity."

Prudence nodded. "I know. It's just happening too fast."

"Well, we must have at least a month to put it all together," Constance said bracingly. "Cases don't come to trial overnight."

"No, true enough." Prudence managed a smile. "So, I suppose I'd better send a message back to say I'll be there . . . which is where?" She took back the letter and read it again. "Oh, Pall Mall Place. Number Seven." She looked up with a shrug. "I'd have expected his chambers."

"Perhaps he has another office," Chastity suggested.

Prudence shrugged. "I'll find out at seven o'clock."

"He doesn't say anything about dinner," Constance observed.

"Which, I trust, means that this is a purely business meeting," Prudence declared crisply. "He's not sending his chauffeur for me either."

"So, with any luck you won't have to be fending off unwelcome advances," Chastity murmured.

Her sister ignored this. She said coolly, "If Father's not using the carriage this evening, I'll get Cobham to drive me in the barouche. And I'll tell him to come back for me at eight o'clock so I'll be home in time for dinner. An hour should be sufficient for the barrister. It'll certainly be enough for me," she added.

"Are you going to take this list?" Chastity indicated her notebook. "Or at least ask him whether he has any particular preferences?"

"I won't take the list, but I will ask him about preferences," her sister said, rising to her feet. "We should go home, Chas. It's nearly five o'clock. Are you dining in tonight, Con?"

"No, at Number Ten," her elder sister said, referring to the Prime Minister's official residence with an exaggerated sigh.

"Oh, that's an honor," Prudence said, regarding her sister with narrowed eyes. "Something in the wind?"

Constance smiled. "I don't know, Max won't say anything. But I have a feeling . . . just a feeling."

"A Cabinet post?" Prudence asked quickly.

"As I said, Max is mum."

"Well, he deserves it," Chastity said, hugging her sister.

"Let's hope it's one that doesn't clash too much with a

vocal suffragist wife," Prudence said, voicing an awkward truth in customary practical fashion.

Constance grimaced slightly. "We'll cross that bridge when we come to it."

"Yes, of course you will." Prudence kissed her. "We'll talk tomorrow . . . exchange accounts of our evenings."

Constance laughed and showed them out. Max was just drawing up to the curb outside the house as they said their farewells on the top step. He ran up the stairs. "Are you two leaving?"

"We just came for tea," Prudence said.

"Well, hold on a minute and I'll get Frank to drive you home before he puts the motor away." He kissed his wife and hurried into the house, calling for his manservant.

Just before seven o'clock Prudence stepped up into the barouche, greeting the elderly driver with a warm smile. "How are the horses, Cobham?"

"Oh, well enough, Miss Prue," he said. "Getting ready to be put out to pasture. Just like me." He cracked his whip and the two glossy chestnuts picked up their hooves and started off at a smart trot around the square.

"They don't seem ready to be put to grass," Prudence observed. "Any more than you do. You're looking very sprightly, Cobham."

"Well, that's right kind of you, Miss Prue. But I'll be seventy next birthday. Time for a nice little cottage in the country."

Prudence realized that she was being given a serious message. If Cobham was ready to retire, then he had every right to do so. And every right to the pension that would enable him to live as he chose in the little cottage in the country. But there was no provision for pensions in the budget. Her mind worked fast, adding and subtracting expenses. Adding and subtracting necessities. She scraped for Cobham's wages every week, even though in this day of motorized omnibuses and frequent hackney cabs they really could manage without a coachman, let alone the horses that cost a fortune to feed and house in London. But it wasn't remotely conceivable to turn the old man off.

However, if the horses went to pasture at the country house at Romsey, they would be much cheaper to keep. Then she could rent out the mews at Manchester Square. Mews courts were being turned into garages for the new motor vehicles all over fashionable London; it would be an income, of sorts, that would contribute to Cobham's pension. And if he took one of the cottages rent-free on the estate at Romsey, then he could live comfortably on half his London wage, which would probably be the equivalent of the rent on the mews. He could have a very comfortable retirement and the family finances would benefit.

"Had you thought where you would go, Cobham?" she asked.

"The wife's a hankering for the old village," he said, slowing the horses across a slippery patch of cobbles. "Spent enough time in London. Misses her sister."

Prudence nodded. Cobham's wife came from Romsey. It was how Cobham, a Londoner to his bootstraps, had come to work for the Duncan family at the Manor.

"There's a vacant tenant cottage on the road to Lyndhurst, if you'd be interested. Of course there'd be no rent to pay. It would be part of your pension, if that was agreeable."

There was silence while the coachman ruminated into his whiskers. After a minute he said, "Reckon so, Miss Prue. I'll talk to the wife."

"Good. Let me know what you decide and we'll settle the details." Prudence sat back with the sense of a job well done.

The barouche turned off the wide thoroughfare of Pall Mall and onto a quiet cul-de-sac of tall, narrow houses.

"Number Seven, Miss Prue." Cobham reined in his horses and looked back at his passenger.

"So it would seem," Prudence said, examining the Georgian house with its telltale fanlight above a shiny black front door, its black railings and white steps, the double frontage with the two bow windows. This was no private supper club. This, unless she was much mistaken, was the residence of Sir Gideon Malvern, KC. And once again he'd sprung a surprise that threw her off balance.

Cobham let down the step and opened the door for her. "Thank you, Cobham. Would you come back for me at eight, please?"

"Of course, Miss Prue." He closed the carriage door and put up the step again. "Since it's only an hour, I'll have a tankard in the Black Dog, just over on Jermyn Street, if that's all right with you."

"Of course," she said, heading to the front door. "In an hour." She took up the shiny door knocker in the shape of a lion's head and rapped it smartly.

It was opened immediately by the barrister, still in morning dress, as if he'd just this minute returned from his chambers. Prudence was glad that she too was wearing what she had worn for their meeting that morning.

"A carriage," he said with a smile, watching Cobham drive away. "Expensive to keep horses in London." He stepped back, holding the door for her.

"Yes," she agreed, moving past him. "But nothing compared to a motorcar. Believe me, I looked into it. My father was very keen of having one, until he realized how unreliable they were." She drew off her gloves as she took a quick survey of her surroundings. Subdued elegance, she decided.

"They can be unpredictable," he agreed with an affable smile. "May I take your coat?"

"Thank you." She thrust her gloves into her pockets and shrugged out of her coat. "Do you ordinarily conduct business in your own house, Sir Gideon?"

"Only when my business has to be conducted after-hours," he said, gesturing towards a door that stood open at the rear of the hall. "When I'm short of time, Miss Duncan, I have to sacrifice some of my leisure, and it's more comfortable to do it here."

Prudence followed the gesture and found herself in a pleasant library with a very masculine air. There was a lingering smell of cigar smoke, leather and oak furniture, an Aubusson rug on the highly polished oak floor, dark velvet curtains at the long windows, not yet drawn against the encroaching shadows of night. There was not an inch of space visible in the bookcases that lined three out of the four walls.

"Drink?" Gideon asked, closing the door behind them.

"No, thank you," she said. "I'm here to talk about the case."

"I often discuss cases over a drink," he said casually, pouring himself a whisky. "Please . . . sit down." He indicated a comfortable armchair in front of a cherry wood table on which reposed a small pile of neatly arranged papers and nothing else.

Prudence sat down. "Why did the earl's counsel respond so quickly to your letter. Is it a good sign?"

Gideon considered. "Neither good nor bad," he said, sipping his drink. "They may think their case is foolproof and just want to get on with it, or they may have doubts and want us to show our hand."

"As soon as we can look at my father's papers we'll have all the evidence we need," Prudence stated.

He leaned his forearms on the table and his eyes were now sharp, his voice clipped. "Well, as I said this morning, I'll wait until I see it before I'm convinced. Let's deal now with what we have."

He was all business, Prudence reflected. Not a hint of personal connection in his demeanor. She should find it reassuring, except that it put her back up. She shook her head in an unconscious gesture designed to banish her own inconvenient personal reactions. "Very well," she said briskly, and folded her hands in her lap. "You have questions for me."

He drew a sheet of paper towards him and took up a pen. "I need some hard and fast facts. When did the publication first come out?"

Prudence considered. "I'm not positive. My mother started it. We began to help her when Con was fifteen, I think. So I would have been fourteen."

"I don't think we want to bring your mother into this," he said, frowning. "It'll complicate matters too much. When did you and your sisters take over the sole running of the publication?"

"Four years ago, on our mother's death."

"All right. And have you been sued before?"

"No, of course not."

"There's no *of course* about it. How many adverse reactions have you had? Complaints from readers, for instance?"

"Not many."

"How many? More than ten, less than five?"

"Probably more than ten."

"So, you would agree that this is a controversial publication?" He was writing as he spoke, not looking at her as he fired the questions.

"Yes."

"Do you set out to be offensive?"

"*No.* What kind of questions are these?"

"The kind you're going to be asked in court. And if you give way to a show of petulance or indignation, you're going to lose the jury and give the prosecution ammunition. If you lose your composure, you're lost." He picked up his glass and went back to the pier table where the decanters stood. "Are you sure you won't have a sherry?"

"No, thank you. I need to keep my wits about me if I'm going to survive this ordeal."

"I don't mean to make it one." He refilled his glass.

"Yes, you do," she contradicted.

"Only for your own good." He sat down again.

"This hurts me more than it hurts you?" she scoffed.

He shook his head with a gesture of exasperation. "No." He reached for a cigarette in the silver box on the table.

" 'A cigarette is the perfect type of a perfect pleasure. It is exquisite, and it leaves one unsatisfied,' " Prudence quoted.

"That sounds like Oscar Wilde," he said.

"Yes, *The Picture of Dorian Gray.*"

He smiled a little. "I only smoke when I'm working. Now, can we get on with it?"

Prudence nodded with a sigh. "By all means, carry on. I have to leave at eight o'clock."

He looked momentarily taken aback and then as quickly his expression resumed its calm neutrality. "Do you and your sisters ordinarily consort with—" He was interrupted by a knock at the door. "Yes?" His voice was not inviting.

The door opened and a girl's head appeared. "I didn't mean to disturb you, Daddy, but Mary is out for the evening and I have all these literature quotes to identify and I just can't get them all." Gray eyes, her father's eyes, darted around the room, fixing on Prudence, who now leaned back in her armchair and prepared to discover what she could about the barrister and his daughter.

"Why don't you bring the rest of you in here," Gideon said. "I don't care to converse with disembodied heads."

"Like the Cheshire cat's smile," the girl said with a sunny smile of her own as she inserted herself fully into the room, although she stayed by the door. "It's just two references that I can't identify, Daddy. Please, can you help?" Her tone was pleading and made Prudence smile. This was one child who knew how to manipulate a compliant parent.

"I'm with a client, Sarah," her father said. "And judging by the monthly accounts from Hatchards and

Blackwell, you have a substantial library of reference books. I must ask Mary why a *Dictionary of Quotations* is somehow missing from the schoolroom shelves."

Sarah looked a little self-conscious. "I'm sure we have one, I just couldn't find it, and I have so much other preparation to do for tomorrow, Latin and French, that I thought maybe . . ." She cast him a quick mood-assessing glance, and then before he could respond, said, " 'Beauty is truth . . .' "

" 'Truth beauty. That is all ye know on earth and all ye need to know,' " Prudence said. "Keats, 'Ode on a Grecian Urn,' 1820."

"Oh, thank you," Sarah Malvern said. "And there's one other: 'Love built on . . .' "

" 'Love built on beauty, soon as beauty dies,' " Prudence said. "John Donne. The elegies, I think." She frowned in thought. "Fifteen ninety-five, I *think*."

Sarah beamed. "Thank you so much, Miss . . ."

"Duncan," Prudence said, rising and holding out her hand. "I'm a client of your father's."

The girl shook it with considerable warmth. "I didn't mean to disturb your meeting."

"No, of course you didn't," her father murmured from the far side of the table. "If your curiosity has been satisfied, Sarah . . . ?"

"It wasn't curiosity," the girl denied. "It was genuine research."

Gideon nodded. "Oh, yes, of course. Research." A smile quirked the corners of his mouth.

"Thank you for your help, Miss Duncan," Sarah said politely. She backed out of the door, asking just before she closed it, "Are you dining out, Daddy?"

His eyes glanced off Prudence, who had returned to her seat and was gazing studiously out into the now complete darkness beyond the window. "Apparently not," he said. "I'll come up and say good night in an hour."

Sarah bobbed a curtsy. "Good night, Miss Duncan. Thank you again for your help."

Prudence smiled. "I enjoyed the exercise. Good night, Sarah."

After the door had closed on the girl, Gideon observed, "So, you're something of an expert on English literature."

"We all are," Prudence said. "It was one of our mother's passions. We imbibed it at the breast."

He nodded, rising to draw the heavy velvet curtains, shutting out the night. "Sarah has a particular affinity for mathematics. She also plays the flute."

"Music and mathematics tend to be complementary talents," Prudence observed. "She seems to be an avid student. Which reminds me of some questions I need to ask you." She opened her handbag and took out her own notebook. "We were beginning to put together a list of possible brides this afternoon and there are one or two issues we'd like to clarify."

Gideon returned to his seat. He leaned back and folded his arms, then raised his eyebrows, his mouth set in an expression that was not encouraging. "I should warn you that I have very little time to spend on this brief, Miss Duncan. If you want to take some of that valuable time away from your own affairs, that is of course your business."

"It seems to me we have to work in tandem,"

Prudence said. "You have your job to do and I have mine, but they are intimately connected. Now, we're assuming you would only consider prospective brides who would be sympathetic to Sarah. Someone whom she would be able to confide in, to feel comfortable with."

"If you're asking me whether I would consider marrying again just to provide Sarah with a mother, the answer is no." He shook his head vigorously. "That seems to me to be the worst possible reason for tying oneself to someone, and I can't imagine any woman worth her salt settling for such a bargain. No, if I ever married again it would be because I met a woman who suited *me*. I would like to think that Sarah would find such a woman both likable and sympathetic."

He unfolded his arms and leaned his elbows on the table. "Now, if that answers your question, perhaps I could return to mine."

"Well, you obviously couldn't consider someone who disliked children," Prudence pressed on. "There's one possibility who might suit you. A widow called Agnes Hargate. A charming woman, very attractive. She has a five-year-old son. Would that be a disadvantage?" She looked up from her notebook and raised one hand to adjust the set of her glasses as she examined his expression.

"The prospect leaves me less than joyful," he stated. "Now, are you and your sisters in the habit of consorting with fallen women?"

"No," she said. "At least, I don't know what you mean by *fallen* women. I'm sure there are plenty of women of our acquaintance, not to mention of Lord Barclay's, who've indulged in a little extracurricular activity. And that's another question for you. Are you only interested

in prospective brides who have an unblemished reputation?"

He sighed. "I'm trying to get across to you, Prudence, that I am not at present in the least interested in any prospective brides." He glanced impatiently at the clock, and his voice was irritable as he said, "We haven't covered as much ground as I wanted to this evening. I was hoping we could have a working dinner, something simple, but since you have to leave..."

"Your message—or summons, rather—made no mention of dinner," she said. "But I would have had to decline, anyway," she fibbed blithely. "I have another engagement."

"It wasn't a summons," he said. "It was a request."

"It read like a summons."

"Then you must forgive me." But he didn't sound in the least apologetic. He got briskly to his feet and suddenly pointed a finger at her. "Are you and your sisters in the habit of consorting with women of the street, Madam Mayfair Lady?"

Prudence opened her mouth to answer a resounding and indignant negative and then realized what he'd said. "They won't know there's more than one of us," she protested. "We've agreed. It's just one representative. The Mayfair Lady. They couldn't ask that question because they won't know anything about us."

He shook his head. "Don't be so certain. They're going to move heaven and earth to track you down. It wouldn't surprise me if they employed a detective agency. I assure you, they're going to be no happier than I am at putting a sheet of newspaper on the stand." He moved out from behind his desk as the grandfather clock in the corner of the library struck a sonorous eight bells.

"Detectives?" Prudence said, sounding shocked. "Surely not." She thrust her arms into the sleeves of her coat that he was holding for her.

"Just be on your guard," he said, going to open the door for her.

Prudence went past him. "How long do we have, do you think, before the trial date?"

He shrugged. "Three, maybe four weeks. Sam Richardson has some influence on the bench and his clerks are extraordinarily efficient. They'll discover who's presiding, and Sam, I'm sure, will have a pleasant chat over a more-than-satisfactory dinner in his club, and the case will come up when he wants it to."

Prudence frowned. "But don't you have influence like that?"

"Certainly I do, but I don't intend to use it."

"But we still don't have our case put together."

"Bring me the evidence, Miss Duncan, and I believe you said that we'll have all the case we need." He opened the front door. The street lamps were now lit and Cobham sat smoking his pipe on the driver's seat of the barouche, the horses shifting their hooves impatiently as the autumnal night air grew chilly.

Gideon walked her down the steps and saw her into the carriage. "But do *you* believe that?" she asked, stung by the tinge of sarcasm in his tone.

At that he laughed, but it wasn't a particularly pleasant laugh in Prudence's estimation. "I have no choice but to do so, my dear. Confidence is half the battle. I can't go into court expecting to lose."

"But do you expect to?" She took off her glasses and fixed him with an anxious gaze, the light of the streetlamp giving her eyes a golden hue, tingeing the russet hair with touches of gold.

For an instant an arrested gleam appeared in his gray gaze; he half opened his mouth, as if about to say something, then shook his head with another slight laugh, stepped back, and waved her away.

Chapter 10

"Another letter for you, Miss Prue. From Sir Gideon." Jenkins put the long envelope beside her plate at breakfast the next morning. "If I may say so, the barrister seems an assiduous correspondent."

"I trust it means he's equally assiduous in his efforts on our behalf," Prudence said tartly. She slit the envelope with her butter knife and perused the contents.

"You have no reason to believe otherwise, Prue," Chastity protested mildly, looking over the top of the *Times*.

"No, I don't suppose I do," Prudence agreed with a little sigh. "It's just that he made me feel last night that it was a wasted effort and we had no chance of winning and basically he resented the time he was spending." She crumpled the letter and tossed it into the fireplace.

"Maybe he just wasn't in the mood to talk about brides," Chastity suggested. "You'd just met his daughter, after all. That must have been awkward for him."

"No, it wasn't," her sister stated. "He was not in the least put out. The girl was being curious and he had no real problem with it at all. It amused him. I just don't think he's serious . . . ever has been . . . about this bargain. He's going to insist on his eighty-twenty split." She shrugged and refilled her coffee cup.

"Well, we can but persevere," Chastity said with customary optimism. "I was wondering about Lavender Riley, or even Priscilla Heyworth." She regarded her sister with a raised eyebrow, waiting for the objections she instinctively expected.

Instead, Prudence shrugged again and said, "They're possibilities, I suppose."

"So, what was in the letter?" Chastity gestured with a piece of toast to the crumpled sheet that had not yet caught flame.

"A surprisingly polite request that I make myself available all day tomorrow for a more intensive preparation session."

"In his chambers?"

"No, he says he will collect me here at the house at eight-thirty in the morning."

"He does like to make an early start, even on a Sunday," Chastity commented. She folded the newspaper carefully along the crease. Lord Duncan had not yet come down to breakfast, and he abhorred an obviously previously read newspaper.

"Well, he made it clear last night he has to work on this brief in his leisure. I can hardly insist on mine, even though tomorrow *is* Sunday." She took up her coffee cup again.

"Good morning, my dears." Lord Duncan entered the breakfast parlor, his complexion ruddy from his morning ablutions, his white hair impeccably coiffed. "Jenkins has promised me kippers," he said, rubbing his hands. "A morning that starts with kippers can only lead to good things."

"You're very cheerful this morning, Father," Chastity observed, placing the newspaper at his plate. "Considering that it's pouring with rain." She gestured towards the long windows, where rain slanted against the panes.

"Oh, what's a little rain?" his lordship said. "I'm going with Barclay to meet with his solicitors and the barrister. They want me to take the stand as a character witness."

Prudence took an overly large gulp of hot coffee and choked, tears filling her eyes as she buried her face in her napkin.

"Really," Chastity said rather weakly. "How good of you."

"Good God, it's hardly good to stand by a friend in need. Oh, delicious, Jenkins, thank Mrs. Hudson for me." Lord Duncan sniffed hungrily at the aroma rising from the plate of steaming kippers placed before him. "And brown bread and butter, of course." He patted his embonpoint, where his silver watch and chain rested in state.

Prudence poured coffee for him and passed the cup. "Will it be a long meeting?"

"Oh, no idea," her father said. "Judging by the exorbitant fees these fellows charge, it ought to last all day." He attacked a kipper, scraping aside the larger bones before taking a forkful that he consumed with an air of bliss. "Manna," he murmured. "Sheer manna. Can't think why you girls don't eat them."

"Too many bones," Chastity said. "By the time I've fiddled with them, the kipper's stone cold and I've lost my appetite."

"Oh, you just chew 'em up," Lord Duncan said, suiting action to advice. "The little ones don't do you any harm." He opened the newspaper with a flick and perused the headlines.

"Will you be in for luncheon?" Prudence inquired, spreading marmalade on her toast.

"Shouldn't think so, m'dear. If we're done with these lawyer fellows in time, Barclay and I'll lunch at the club. What's today?" He glanced at the date on the newspaper. "Oh, Saturday. Odd that they work on a weekend." He shrugged. "Not to worry. It's steak and oyster pie today. We'll definitely be lunching at the club."

"You haven't forgotten we're having dinner with Constance and Max this evening?"

"Oh, no. Pity Barclay couldn't accept the invitation. Some relative or other come to town."

"I think Con's invited the Wesleys though," Prudence said. "You know how much you like to play bridge with them. Con will partner you."

"Oh, yes, it'll be a capital evening, I'm sure. Capital." He returned to his paper.

Prudence glanced at Chastity and folded her napkin. "If you don't mind, Father, we'll leave you to your breakfast. Chas and I have a few errands to run this morning." She pushed back her chair and dropped a kiss on her father's cheek as she headed for the door, Chastity at her heels.

In the hall, she paused, tapping the folded thumb of her fist against her chin. "We have to do it this morning, Chas."

"Go through the papers?"

"Yes. There's no knowing when we can be sure Father

will be out of the house again for a decent stretch of time."

Chastity nodded. "Should we send a message to Con?"

"Yes, get Fred to run around to Westminster. With three of us looking, if there's anything to find we'll find it."

Chastity hurried off to the kitchen. Fred, the errand boy and general handyman, was polishing shoes by the range and chatting amiably with Mrs. Hudson. "Lord Duncan's delighted with his kippers, Mrs. Hudson," Chastity said.

"Oh, I thought he'd find 'em tasty," the housekeeper said. "'Tisn't often the fishmonger has 'em on his cart when he comes of a Thursday, but this week he did. And they weren't too expensive neither. Twopence halfpenny apiece."

"Well, they gave his lordship more than fivepence worth of pleasure," Chastity told her. "Fred, when you've finished with the shoes, could you run around to Mrs. Ensor and ask her if she could visit this morning? As soon as she can."

Fred spat on one of Lord Duncan's evening shoes. "I'll be done here in ten minutes, Miss Chastity." He polished vigorously, working the spittle into the leather.

"Miss Con will be here for lunch, then, Miss Chas?" Mrs. Hudson inquired.

"Yes, but bread and cheese will do fine."

"Oh, I might turn my hand to a bit of pastry," the housekeeper said. "Seeing as there's no dinner to cook this evening. There's a nice piece of ham in the pantry and I think I could lay my hands on a bit of stewing veal. How would you fancy a veal and ham pie?"

"Very much," Chastity said.

"And a jam roly-poly for pudding."

"You spoil us, Mrs. Hudson . . . even on our budget."

"Oh, 'tis not difficult, Miss Chas, if you've an eye for a bargain," the woman said with a pleased smile. With an answering smile, Chastity left the kitchen, reflecting that they should all count their blessings when it came to Jenkins and Mrs. Hudson. But, of course, they did, every waking minute.

She had stopped smiling when she reached the upstairs parlor. "We have to stop Father from taking the stand," she stated as she entered. "What if he recognizes your voice, Prue. Even if you disguise it, you're his *daughter*."

"I know," her sister said. She was standing at the window watching the drumming rain and the sodden trees in the square garden. "And Gideon will be cross-examining him. It'll be hideous, Chas." She crossed her arms over her breasts.

"Everything we tell Gideon about Father will be armor for his cross-examination." Chastity shook her head. "I don't see how we can do it, Prue."

"We have to," her sister said simply. "We have to find a way. We can't lose, Chas, you know that. If we do, Father will be devastated . . . broken."

"Then you're going to have to act as you've never acted before," Chastity said, now briskly accepting the reality. "You need a voice, one that won't slip under pressure, and won't bear any resemblance to your own."

"The one thing we have in our favor is that it would never occur to Father in his wildest nightmares that we would have anything to do with the case," Prudence said, turning away from the window. "Even if he had an inkling that there was something familiar about the veiled witness for the defense, he would never associate her with one of us."

"I only hope you're right." Chastity came over to the window to stand beside her sister, and they stood looking down onto the street until a hackney disgorged Constance, under a big umbrella.

Constance didn't pause on the pavement to look up at the parlor window as she might have done on another day, but scurried up the steps to the house. The door opened as she reached the top, and she nearly ran into her father, similarly equipped with a big, black umbrella.

"Good morning, my dear," he said hastily while waving his umbrella at the cab that had just delivered his daughter. "Can't stop. I'll take your cab."

"I'll see you this evening, Father," Constance said to his retreating back. She turned to the door, shaking the rain off her umbrella.

"I'll take that, Miss Con." Jenkins deftly removed it. "It'll dry in the back scullery. Weather's not fit for ducks."

"That it's not," Constance agreed, taking off her hat in the hall. "Are my sisters upstairs?"

"Waiting for you, Miss Con."

Constance nodded, and ran up the stairs. "So, what's happening?" she asked as she opened the door. "That was a rather urgent message to someone who's giving an important dinner party this evening." She was laughing as she spoke, but her laughter died when she saw her sisters' expressions. "Trouble?"

"Of a kind. But we also need your help this morning." Prudence explained the situation.

"Damn and blast," Constance said. "He would, wouldn't he?"

"Yes, he would," Prudence agreed with a resigned shrug. "Loyalty to his friend."

"And we're going to blow that loyalty to smithereens," Chastity stated.

They were silent for a minute, then Prudence said heavily, "Well, let's go and find the evidence to do that. I asked Jenkins to light a fire in the library." She went over to the secretaire and opened one of the small drawers. "I have a key to the safe."

"When did you get that?"

"Months ago. Jenkins had it copied for me. I can't keep control of the finances if I don't know what Father is spending. All his bills are in the safe, so I see them before they come due. That way I can make sure there's enough in his bank account to cover them . . . or at least make sure that he's not too overdrawn."

Constance put a hand on her sister's shoulder. "Prue, why didn't you tell us?"

"This is my job. I didn't see any reason to burden you both with the more dubious aspects of its operation. I don't like the idea of snooping and prying into Father's personal affairs, but since he won't give me any information freely I had to find a way to get it without his knowledge." She tossed the tiny key from hand to hand, her expression hard to read.

"Prue, love, this isn't a burden you carry alone," Chastity said. "We would have supported you in this if you'd told us. You don't need to feel guilty."

"Maybe not. But I do. Let's go and dig ourselves deeper into this slough of deceit." She strode to the door.

"So, how was your evening, Prue?" Constance asked

as they entered the library. "Does our barrister seem to have a handle on the case?"

Prudence closed the door behind them, and then after an instant's hesitation, locked it. "He's very aggressive with his questions but I'm sure he's right that opposing counsel will be and I need to be forearmed." She leaned against the door for a moment. "He also says that we can expect them to put detectives onto finding our identities."

Her sisters turned to stare at her. "Detectives?" Chastity repeated.

Prudence nodded. "I suppose, if you think about it, it's almost inevitable."

"Where would they start?" Constance wondered. "Oh, *The Mayfair Lady*, of course."

"Yes," Prudence agreed. "That was what I was thinking. They could start asking questions at all the places that stock it. No one knows us, of course. When we go to collect our money, we're always heavily veiled, but..." She shook her head. "It's still alarming. Maybe on Monday we can go to some of the outlets we use—Helene's Milliners, Robert's of Piccadilly, a few of the others—just to see if there's been any unusual interest or inquiries."

"We'll do the rounds," Constance said.

"That might put our minds at rest. Help me with the Stubbs." Prudence went to the far wall and moved aside a large George Stubbs painting of a racehorse. Constance held it to one side while her sister unlocked the wall safe behind and took out its contents, passing them to Chastity.

"There's so much stuff in here... I'm sure a lot of it's out-of-date." She reached into the depths of the safe for the last few pieces of paper, then closed the safe door. Constance let the painting swing back into place.

Chastity put the pile of papers on the cherry wood desk that stood in the bay window looking out onto the walled back garden. "Shall you go through these, Prue, while Con and I go through the desk drawers?"

"Yes. We're looking for anything that resembles a legal contract. Any piece of paper that has a law-firm heading . . . or something that sounds like one."

"Jaggers, Tulkinghorn, and Chaffanbrass," Constance said, sitting at the desk and opening the top drawer.

"You're mixing your authors," Prudence observed, gathering up the pile of papers liberated from the safe and crossing to the sofa in front of the fire. "Chaffanbrass was Trollope, not Dickens."

"I know," Constance said. "They just had a nice ring to them." She drew out a folder from the drawer. "So when are you seeing our barrister again?"

"Tomorrow." Prudence leafed through her pile. "At some godawful hour. I'd like to have something concrete to show him."

"I wonder why he's not meeting you in his chambers," Chastity said, on her knees in front of the cupboard in the side of desk. "If he's preparing you for the witness stand, why's he coming to fetch you in his motor?"

"I have no idea," her sister said. "The man's a mystery to me."

"Of course it is Sunday," Constance pointed out.

She looked up, aware that Prudence wasn't listening. "What is it? Have you found something?"

"I don't know," Prudence said slowly. "There's a note here, signed 'Barclay.' No date." She turned it over. "It refers to '*our agreement*.'" She frowned. "'As per our agreement of last week, the payment schedule should be advanced to take advantage of the present favorable market. I am advised by the principals that interest rates will rise in the next month to our disadvantage.' "

"But it doesn't say what the agreement is?"

"No, Chas. Nothing specific. But it seems that he's asking for money. I wish there was a date on it."

"Let me see." Constance came over to the sofa. Prudence handed her the note. "Well, it's not recent," Constance said. "The paper's got an old stain on it . . . here, at the bottom." She indicated a brown smudge. "See how it's faded?"

"The paper's a bit yellowed too," Chastity observed, peering over her sister's shoulder. "And the ink's faded."

"We'd make very good detectives," Prudence said. "So, let's assume that this is about three years old, about the time of Father's investment in the Trans-Saharan Railway. We're talking interest rates, payment schedules . . ."

"But no indication of what for," Constance said.

"Perhaps they had a verbal agreement," Chastity suggested. "If Barclay was up to something fraudulent, maybe he didn't want anything on paper."

"Surely Father wouldn't agree to something so huge without something in writing?" Constance said.

"Wouldn't he?" Prudence responded glumly. "A man who'd believe in a chimera in the Saharan desert?"

No one could find an argument for that. "Let's just go through everything thoroughly, just to make sure we don't miss anything," Prudence said, folding the note carefully. "I'll give this to Gideon tomorrow. Maybe he can see a way to use it."

At the end of another hour, she looked at the piles of

paper with something like despair. "That's it," she said. "We've gone through everything with a fine-tooth comb."

"There must be something else we can do." Chastity threw another shovel of coal on the fire.

"The bank," Prudence said suddenly. "We have to get access to his bank records."

Constance said from her perch on the arm of the sofa, "The bank manager must know you because you do all the dealings with the household accounts, maybe he'd be willing to let you look at Father's personal records."

Prudence shook her head. "Not Mr. Fitchley. He's a real stickler for the rules, and I'm sure he'd think an unauthorized examination of a personal account would be unethical." She paced restlessly to the window and stood looking out on the rain-drenched garden, drumming her fingers on the sill. "But maybe there's a way to get Father to sign an authorization for me," she said slowly.

"How so?" Chastity asked.

Prudence turned from the window and stood resting her palms on the sill behind her. "He signs things I put in front of him," she said, sounding so reluctant, it was almost as if the words were being dragged from her. "Bills, orders for the household, those kinds of things. Usually he doesn't bother to look at them." She watched her sisters as comprehension dawned.

"It's so deceitful," Chastity said with a tiny sigh. "I really hate the idea."

"We all do, love," Prudence said. "But I don't see any other way. I'll write an authorization and slip it into the middle of a pile of other papers and catch him this evening before we go to Con's. He'll have had a good lunch with Barclay, and by then he'll probably have had a whisky while he was dressing for dinner. He won't give anything a second glance."

"It is horrid," Constance said, "but I don't see we have any choice. Once you get the authorization you can go to the bank on Monday morning."

"I'll write it now." Prudence went to the secretaire and selected a sheet of paper headed with her father's crest. She took her pen and inscribed, "To Whom It May Concern."

Her sisters sat in silence until she had finished and blotted the ink. "Tell me if that seems official enough." She held it out to them.

"It might be even more convincing if we could get Father's seal for the envelope," Constance said, going over to the desk. "He keeps it in this drawer, I think." She opened the top drawer. "Yes, here it is. He doesn't usually lock it away, does he?"

Prudence shook her head. "Not as far as I know. Why would he? He's not expecting it to be misappropriated." There was a touch of irony in her otherwise dull tone. Then she shook her head again, as if dismissing her bleak thoughts. "We're doing it for his benefit, after all."

"That's exactly right," Chastity affirmed. "This is a case where the end definitely justifies the means."

Prudence took the paper back. "I'll put together some other papers, then, and get it over with this evening."

"I'd better go home," Constance said, rising to her feet. "Since this is my first official dinner party as Mrs. Ensor."

"Oh, what happened last night, at Downing Street?" Prudence asked, suddenly remembering. She'd been so taken up with their own concerns she'd forgotten to ask if anything significant had come out of the Ensors' dinner with the Prime Minister.

Constance smiled. "This whole business put it right out of my head. After the ladies had withdrawn, leaving the gentlemen to their port and cigars, the Prime Minister offered Max the Ministry of Transport."

"That's wonderful," her sisters said in unison. "He must be delighted."

"I think he'd have preferred the Foreign Office or the Home Office," Constance said with a grin. "Maybe even the Exchequer, but you have to start somewhere."

"I think it's amazing to get a Cabinet post after only one year on the back benches," Prudence said.

"Yes, so do I. And he really does seem quite pleased with himself. He was still smiling when he woke up this morning."

"Well, we can celebrate this evening," Chastity said, accompanying her sister to the door. "Eight o'clock?"

"Thereabouts," Constance said, kissing her sisters before hurrying down the stairs.

Prudence dressed for dinner early and then waited in the parlor until she heard her father's tread on the stair. She popped her head out. "Are you going to dress, Father?"

Lord Duncan paused on his way to his dressing room. "Yes. I won't be very long. What time are we expected?"

"Eight. Cobham will bring the barouche at quarter to," she said. "When you're ready, I'd like you to sign a few orders and bills for me. There are some papers to do with the estate at Romsey, a couple of tenant roofs that need to be replaced. I'd like to get them in the post on Monday."

Lord Duncan nodded agreeably. "I'll be down in the library in half an hour."

Prudence returned to the parlor and picked up the pile of papers she had assembled. For the tenth time, she riffled through them. And as before, the one she wanted hidden seemed to stick out like the proverbial sore thumb. But that was only because she knew it was there, she told herself.

Chastity came into the parlor, also dressed for the evening. "We'll do this together," she said, seeing her sister's strained expression. "Let's go down to the library and wait for him. Jenkins will bring us sherry, you look as if you could do with some Dutch courage."

Prudence nodded. "I need something, Chas." They went downstairs arm in arm. Jenkins was arranging some late chrysanthemums in a copper vase on the hall table. He turned to greet the sisters. "Where would you like sherry, Miss Prue?"

"In the library," Chastity answered. "Lord Duncan will be joining us there in a few minutes."

"I'll bring the whisky too, then," he said, standing back to survey his flower arrangement with a critical air. "I don't know why it is, but I don't seem to have your touch, Miss Chas."

"You don't need a touch, Jenkins," Chastity said with a smile, coming over to the table. "With chrysanths, all you need to do is pick them up, like so . . ." She lifted the flowers out of the vase. "And then drop them back and let them find their own arrangement. See?" She suited action to words and the big-headed blooms fell into a natural composition.

Jenkins shook his head. "I'll fetch the sherry."

Chastity laughed and followed her sister into the

library. Prudence laid the papers on the table and stood back, looking at them. Then she approached them again, squared them off, and patted the top sheet. "It doesn't look natural," she said. "Perhaps I should just give them to him, put them in front of him when he sits down. What do you think?"

"I think that if you don't relax, Prue, you're going to make him suspect something the minute he walks in." Chastity leaned over the desk and spread the papers out a little as if they'd just been dumped there. "Where's his pen? Oh, here it is. I'll put it beside them. Now we'll both sit down, and when he comes in you can gesture to them very casually and ask him to sign them."

"Why are you so calm?" her sister asked, sitting on the sofa.

"Because you aren't," Chastity replied. "Only one of us at a time can panic."

That produced a smile from her sister just as Jenkins came in with a tray. Lord Duncan followed him. "Ah, good, Jenkins, whisky. You read my mind."

"Father you always have a whisky at this time of the evening," Prudence said lightly. "Jenkins doesn't have to be a mind reader." She rose from the sofa with a casual air. "The papers I need you to sign are on your desk. There's a pen there, I think. Oh, thank you, Jenkins." She took the sherry glass from the tray and was relieved to note that her hands were quite steady. She resumed her seat on the sofa.

Lord Duncan took a deep draught of his whisky and moved behind the desk. He didn't bother to sit down, merely picked up the pen and began to sign the papers. "Did you know that Max has been offered Secretary of Transport in the Cabinet?" Prudence asked swiftly as he set aside one signed order form and his eye ran down the paper beneath.

"Is this the farrier's bill?" he asked, picking it up and holding it close. "Don't recognize the name."

"No, he's new. He took over from Beddings," Prudence said. "Did you hear what I said about Max?"

Lord Duncan scrawled his signature on the paper and set it aside. His daughter's letter of authorization was now uppermost. It seemed to Prudence that it glared up at her father, trying to attract his attention. "Max," she said. "They were dining at Downing Street last night and the PM offered him a Cabinet post."

Her father looked up. "Well, how splendid," he declared. "Always knew he was going far. Constance did very well there. Transport, did you say?" As he spoke he scribbled his signature on Prudence's sheet.

"Yes," Chastity said, moving to the table. She leaned over and scooped the signed papers to one side, sliding the letter of authorization under the pile. "Constance joked that he'd have preferred the Exchequer or the Home Office, but of course he's very pleased." She straightened the remaining papers for him. "Just a couple more."

"Oh, yes." He resumed his task. "Better take something to celebrate this evening. How about a bottle of that Coburn's, the '20 vintage, Prudence? Ask Jenkins to bring one up."

"Yes, Father." Prudence went to the door, aware that her legs were like jelly and her palms wet. "I think there's only one bottle left."

Her father gave an exaggerated sigh. "Always the way these days. Whenever I ask for something special, there's only one bottle left . . . if we're lucky enough to have any, that is. Never mind. Bring it up anyway. It's not every day a man's son-in-law is given a Cabinet post."

Prudence left the library and stood for a minute in the hall, leaning against the closed door while she waited for her heart to settle down. She'd been frozen in her seat the minute the incriminating paper had been revealed. But it was done . . . over. Thank God for Chastity's quick thinking. Now all she had to do was visit Mr. Fitchley at Hoare's Bank on Piccadilly. There must be something there. There *had* to be.

Chapter 11

"There." Prudence pressed her father's seal into the melted wax on the envelope that contained the bank authorization. She glanced out of the library window. It was barely dawn and only she and Chastity were up in the silent house. Lord Duncan was snoring sonorously after a late night of bridge and substantial quantities of Coburn's 1820 vintage.

"Let's go back to bed," Chastity suggested, hugging her dressing gown closely around her.

"You go, I'm wide awake now," her sister said, returning the seal to its drawer. "I'll make some tea and read a little. I have to be ready to leave at eight-thirty anyway."

"It's barely six now," her sister pointed out, yawning. "I'll see you at breakfast."

"Eight o'clock," Prudence said, closing the drawer gently. She glanced around to make sure everything was in its place, then extinguished the gas lamp and followed Chastity from the room.

* * *

In the house on Pall Mall Place Gideon too was up and about at the crack of dawn. He rarely slept more than a few hours a night and he found himself even more wakeful than usual. Prudence Duncan wouldn't leave his mind. He felt challenged by her, as if she herself was a case he had to win. He had not seen her the previous day, but he had not stopped thinking about her . . . or rather, he corrected himself swiftly, about the case and her role in it. Part of his job as a barrister was to coach witnesses. And since Prudence Duncan was the only witness he was going to have, he couldn't afford any mistakes.

He ran hot water into the basin in the bathroom and began to shave. Lathering his face with slow circular movements, he contemplated the day he had planned. He had decided that their next meeting should be in different surroundings, somewhere removed from the official background of chambers and law books. Even his library in his own house was more like an office. He wanted to see what she was like when she was relaxed, in a more social frame of mind.

He drew his razor through the lather, frowning at his reflection in the mirror. He wanted to catch her off guard. Would she make a better witness if she was not on the defensive, not combative, not challenging? He had provoked this response from her, and he was obliged to admit it had not always been intentional. There was something about the way they reacted to each other, the proverbial oil and water, which he didn't quite understand because he couldn't control it. However, he had certainly intended to see how she would respond under pressure. He knew now from his own bristling reaction that a judge and jury were not going to sympathize with her in that guise.

He washed off the lather, burying his face in a steaming washcloth with a little sigh of pleasure. He peered closely in the mirror to make sure he hadn't missed a spot, before stepping into his bath. He slipped down beneath the surface of the water, wondering if the day he had planned for them would achieve his goal.

He wanted, no, needed, to soften her reactions, persuade her that she would have to appeal to the male responses in the courtroom, appeal to masculine sympathy. Convincing her of that necessity would not be an easy task, he was under no illusions on that score. She would initially see it as weakness, as evidence that her case was not just if she had to resort to acting. But if he could get her in the right frame of mind, one where she quite naturally lost her combative edge, then perhaps he'd have a better chance. So long as he didn't inadvertently put her back up. She was as prickly as a blackberry bush.

Nevertheless, he was feeling in a relatively optimistic frame of mind when he went down to the breakfast parlor. Sarah, in riding dress, was consuming a mound of scrambled eggs. She greeted him with a sunny smile. "Milton said he was bringing the motor around. Are you going somewhere, Daddy?"

"For a drive in the country," he said, bending to kiss the top of her head.

"There's deviled kidneys for you." The girl gestured to the covered dishes on the sideboard. "Are you going for a drive on your own?"

Gideon helped himself to kidneys. "No," he said.

"With a client." He sat down and took up the newspaper.

"With Miss Duncan?"

Now, how had she guessed that? He gave his daughter a rather exasperated glance over the top of the *Times*. "As it happens."

"But you don't usually see clients on a Sunday. And you don't go for drives with them." She drank from a cup of milky coffee and took a piece of toast from the rack.

"There's a first time for everything."

Sarah spread butter and then marmalade on her toast. "Do you like Miss Duncan?"

There was something deceptively casual about her tone. Her father shrugged and turned to the editorial page with a decisive crackle of paper. "That's hardly to the point. She's my client."

"Do you think she's pretty?" The question was muffled by a mouthful of toast and marmalade.

"Don't talk with your mouth full."

She swallowed, dabbed her mouth with her napkin. "But do you?"

Gideon folded the paper beneath the leader. "No," he said definitely, without taking his eyes off the printed page. "That is not a word I would use to describe Miss Duncan."

Sarah looked disappointed. "I think she is."

"Well, you are entitled to your opinion." He set down the paper and looked across at her, his tone softening. "What are your plans for the day?"

"Oh, I'm going riding in the park with Isabelle this morning. Then she's coming back here and Mrs. Keith is making us Sunday lunch of roast chicken with blancmange for pudding. Yesterday we went to Madame

Tussaud's exhibition." Her eyes gleamed. "There's a real chamber of horrors there, with an actual French guillotine. Well, it's wax, of course, but they say you can't tell the difference."

Gideon grimaced slightly. "I expect you could if you were about to lose your head to it."

Sarah laughed. "You're so silly, Daddy. Of course you could tell. The wax one would bend."

He laughed with her. "Did Mary take you?"

"No, Isabelle's governess. Mary's gone to visit her sister for the weekend. Did you forget?"

"I suppose I must have done. Hadn't you better get ready?"

Sarah pushed back her chair and came round to him. He put an arm around her waist and hugged her to him. "Don't fall off your horse, will you?"

She laughed again at the absurdity of such an idea, and kissed his cheek. "What time will you be back?"

"I'm not sure exactly. It's quite a long drive, so probably after you're in bed." She nodded cheerfully and danced her way from the room. Gideon, still smiling, returned to his kidneys and newspaper in peace.

The black Rover drew up at the curb punctually at eight-thirty that morning. "He's here," Chastity said from the parlor window where she'd been watching the Square. "Driving himself, no chauffeur. He looks very dapper this morning. You get your things and I'll run down and tell him you're on your way." She whisked out of the parlor.

Prudence went to her own bedroom, where she studied her reflection for a moment in the cheval glass. She smoothed the long jacket of her mulberry-colored wool suit over her hips and shook out the pleats of the long skirt, which was edged with darker red braid. She was aware of a certain nervousness, a slightly swifter heart-beat than usual, and her pale complexion was tinged with rose. Why she should feel so unsettled, she couldn't imagine. Gideon Malvern didn't alarm her.

Did he? Ridiculous idea. She'd handled him perfectly well from their first meeting, and while their preparation session today might be a little unpleasant, she knew that it was only intended to armor her against the much greater unpleasantness she could face in court. But she couldn't help wishing her sisters were coming along for the ride. There was strength in numbers. But what on earth did she need strength for, she demanded crossly of herself. He was just a man. A perfectly ordinary man. She'd been alone with men often enough. And she'd never felt this anxiety on those occasions.

She shook her head as if to dismiss the buzzing of her thoughts, and slipped on the fawn silk-and-alpaca dust coat that would protect her dress from the dust of the road, and tied a heavy silk veil over her felt hat. She could drop the veil over her face if the dust was really bad. But where were they going? Why had he come for her in the motor? Perhaps they were just going to his house again and he was being overly polite by coming to escort her in broad daylight. No, she decided. That was not Gideon's way.

She pulled on her leather gloves, picked up her purse, handkerchief, notebook, and pencil, and Lord Barclay's note, and dropped them all into the deep pockets of the dust coat, then went downstairs.

Gideon and Chastity were talking in the hall, the front

door ajar behind them. He was wearing a wolfskin coat and a flat woolen motoring cap with a visor. He was definitely dressed for something more than a short drive through the London streets.

He turned and smiled at her as she came down the stairs, then the smile vanished. "No," he said decisively, "that won't do at all."

"What won't?" she demanded, taken aback.

"What you're wearing. You'll freeze to death. It's sunny but it's cold."

"But we won't be in the motor for long?" she protested.

He ignored the hanging question, merely repeating, "You'll freeze to death. You must have something warmer."

"The fur, Prue?" Chastity suggested with a tiny shrug.

"It seems so unnecessary. It's only October and the sun's shining."

"If you have fur, I'd really suggest you go and put it on," he said, making a big effort to sound conciliatory. "Trust me, you'll need it."

Prudence hesitated. For a minute she almost laughed, because the effort he was making to subdue his customary imperiousness was so obvious. She was tempted to question it but then decided to honor the attempt. She turned back to the stairs.

The sisters had inherited a silver fox coat, hood, and muff from their mother, as well as three strands of matchless pearls. They shared both jewelry and furs according to whose need was greatest. Prudence took them out of the cedar chest in the linen room, where they had resided throughout the summer, and held up the coat. It smelled faintly of cedar, but unlike the dress she'd worn the other evening, not of mothballs.

She tossed aside the dust coat and slipped the fur on. Immediately she felt invested with an aura of luxury and elegance. It was a wonderfully extravagant garment with a high collar that caressed her neck. The hood fitted closely over her head, hugging her ears, but revealing the carefully arranged russet curls on her forehead. She buried her gloved hands in the muff and decided with a grin that even if she was roasting it was well worth it for the effect. She didn't need a mirror to tell her she looked stunning. She took a second to transfer the contents of the dust coat's pockets into the muff and went back downstairs.

Chastity was still in the hall, but there was no sign of Gideon. "You look fabulous, Prue."

"I know," Prudence said. "This coat always has that effect, whoever wears it. Where is he?"

"He'd left the motor running and he didn't want to leave it unattended."

"Did he say where we were going?"

Chastity shook her head. "I tried to ask but he just said you might be late this evening and we weren't to worry, you were in safe hands."

"Ye gods, he's *impossible,*" Prudence exclaimed. "Does he think women like to be pushed around like that?"

"I don't think he can help it," Chastity said, laughing slightly.

The blast of a horn from outside made them both jump. Prudence threw up her hands and Jenkins moved smoothly across the hall to open the door. "I believe Sir Gideon is waiting, Miss Prue."

"I wonder how you guessed," she said. She gave Chastity a quick kiss. "I'll see you later."

"Good luck."

Prudence hesitated. "Why would I need good luck, Chas?"

Chastity shrugged. "I don't know, it just seems that you might."

Another imperative blast of the horn sounded and Prudence raised her eyes heavenward and hurried outside.

Gideon stood beside the car, one foot on the running board, one hand resting on the horn mounted on the dashboard. His eyes widened as Prudence came running down the steps. "I should really have a horse-drawn sledge and a frozen Russian lake for you," he observed.

"The horses would have run off by now with that blasted horn," Prudence said with asperity. "There was no need for that."

"I know, I'm sorry," he said. "I do try for moderation, but I am a little short on patience, I'm afraid." He opened the door for her, spoiling the apologetic effect with the unwise addition, "But you'll get used to me."

"I'm not sure that's an overriding goal," Prudence murmured, stepping into the motor.

"I beg your pardon?" He stood holding the door.

"Nothing," she said with a sweet smile. "I have a habit of talking to myself. You'll get used to me." She tucked her legs neatly under the dashboard.

He raised his eyebrows, closed the door on her, and went around to take his own seat. "Oh, you'd better put these on." He reached into the back and felt around. "Here." He handed her a pair of tinted goggles in wide metal-and-leather frames. "They should fit over your glasses."

He put on a pair himself as Prudence examined the ones he'd given her. "Why would I need these?"

"To protect your eyes, of course. The wind can be fierce when you're driving." He put the motor in gear and the car moved smoothly forward.

"You must need very little sleep if you always start your day this early," Prudence observed, still turning the goggles around in her hands. "It is a weekend, after all."

"Forgive me if I stole your beauty sleep," he said cheerfully. "But even driving at twenty miles an hour, it'll take us nearly three hours to get where we're going."

"Three hours!" Prudence turned sideways to stare at him. "Where in the devil's name are we going?"

"It's a surprise," he said. "I told you, I think, that surprise is frequently the essence of a successful campaign."

"In the law courts," she said.

"Oh, certainly there," he agreed with a laugh. "But, as you so rightly say, today is Sunday, so we won't talk about the law."

"But I thought we were going to prepare for the trial."

"Well, we are, in a way, but not as we have been doing. We don't want to waste a beautiful day with too much stress and strain on the nerves. Besides, in general I like to keep my weekends free from excessive work. It ensures my mind stays fresh."

Prudence could think of nothing to say immediately. She was sitting in this motor going God only knew where, for reasons not vouchsafed, with a man she disliked more by the minute. "So you lied," she said finally. "Just to inveigle me into spending the day with you."

"That's a little harsh," he protested, smiling slightly. "I have told you once before that getting to know you is a very important part of my preparation."

There was really very little objection she could raise to what was a perfectly logical aim. "I would have thought you'd spend your Sundays at least with your daughter," she said.

"Oh, Sarah has better things to do this Sunday," he responded. "Her day is packed to the minute, she has no time to spare for her father."

"I see." Their speed had picked up and she was conscious now of the wind making her eyes water. Resigned, she put on the goggles and turned to look at her companion.

For some reason he was smiling, and even though she couldn't see his eyes behind the goggles, she knew the skin around them would be crinkling and there would be little dancing lights in their gray depths. His mouth had not become less sensual since she'd last seen him and the cleft in his chin seemed even more pronounced. She dragged her gaze away and stared out at the road ahead, tucking her hands deeper into her muff. "So, where are we going, Gideon?"

"Oxford," he said. "We should be there just in time for luncheon at the Randolph. Then, if it's not too cold, I thought we could take a punt along the river. But you're so well wrapped that it wouldn't matter much if it was snowing."

"We're driving fifty miles there and fifty miles back in *one* day?"

"I love to drive," he said with a complacent smile. "And I love this motor. It'll do twenty miles an hour without a problem. It's a beautiful day, if a bit nippy. Do you have any objections?"

"It didn't occur to you that I might have plans for this afternoon?" she said tightly.

"It did, but I assumed you would have sent me a message if my invitation wasn't convenient." He glanced sideways at her and his smile deepened. "I did try very hard to make it sound like an invitation and not a summons. I hope I succeeded."

Prudence was obliged to concede this point. "It was a rather more politely couched summons than your usual," she said.

"Oh, that is so ungenerous," he exclaimed. "I'm trying to reform my manner and you won't give me the least credit."

"I have no interest in your manner of conducting yourself," she stated. "I am interested only in how you conduct yourself in court. And, on that subject, I have some information that might interest you."

Miss Duncan was as tough a nut to crack as he'd expected, he reflected ruefully. Women usually responded when he took the trouble to turn on his charm. He took one hand off the wheel and held it up. "Let me enjoy my Sunday a little first, Prudence. Get the cobwebs out of my head. There'll be time enough for work later."

And there really wasn't anything she could say to that. The man was entitled to a little rest and relaxation now and again. Her fingers closed over the notebook in her muff. Ah, now, there was a topic to be explored.

"Well, maybe we could work on something else, then," she said, taking out the notebook. "Since we're going to be sitting side by side for the next three hours, we might as well do something productive." She opened the notebook and sucked thoughtfully on the end of the pencil.

Gideon looked a little alarmed. "What are you talking about?"

"Have you forgotten that we're charged with finding a suitable candidate for you to marry?" Prudence inquired in mock surprise.

He sighed. "Not that again. I'm not in the mood, Prudence."

"I'm sorry," she said. "But you agreed to consider our suggestions. If we can find you a bride it will make the difference between twenty percent and a hundred percent of our damages. And that's deadly serious business to us."

He shook his head. "You really *are* a terrier. All right, if you want to play this game, then let's play it."

"It's not a game," Prudence said. "And I insist that you treat it seriously. We've drawn up a list of qualities that we think will be important to you. If you would just assign a number, on a scale of one to five, to each one as I go through them, that would be a great help."

"Fire away," he invited, assembling his features into a suitably earnest expression.

Prudence shot him a suspicious look. She couldn't see his eyes behind his goggles but there was a telltale twitch to the corner of his mouth. "First, age," she said. "Do you have a preference?"

He pursed his mouth. "I don't think so."

"Oh, you must have some idea," Prudence exclaimed. "Does the idea of a young woman in her first season appeal, or would you rather meet someone of more mature years?"

He seemed to give the matter some thought as he

swung the motorcar around a stolidly plodding horse and cart. The driver cursed and waved his whip at them as the horse shied, and the motor sped ahead in a cloud of dust.

"One of these days people are not going to turn a hair when they see a motor," Gideon observed. "They'll be the only way to get around."

"Something will have to be done about the roads, in that case," Prudence said as the vehicle bumped violently into a muddy rut. "They're not designed for something traveling at this speed."

"The Royal Automobile Club is lobbying Parliament for better roads. Are you getting dreadfully bounced around?"

"I'm not wonderfully comfortable," she said. "But please don't let the prospect of my discomfort for the next three hours affect your plans in any way."

"It's not that bad," he said. "And we'll stop for coffee in Henley. I'll need to refill the fuel tank then anyway, and you can stretch your legs."

"How nice to have something to look forward to." She returned to her notebook. "You haven't answered my question. What age would you like your wife to be? Within about five years."

"Extreme youth is very tedious for a man my age. Inexperience is equally so. I have no interest in educating a virgin in the ways of the bedroom."

This, Prudence reflected, was rather more information than her question had sought. However, the more information they had, the better able they would be to find a suitable match, so she merely nodded in a matter-of-fact way. "So, a mature woman would suit you."

"Mature . . . now, I'm not so sure about that," he responded. "It's a word that conjures up images of desperate spinsters or languishing widows. I don't think either category would suit me. Of course," he added, "you have taken into account the difficulties inherent in matching a forty-year-old divorced father of a ten-year-old daughter with an eligible woman."

"We decided that those difficulties were more relevant for a woman than a man," Prudence said. "You have much to recommend you."

"How kind. I'm flattered."

"Don't be. I merely meant that your profession and your financial situation will probably compensate for your disadvantages with all but the most rigid adherents to the social code."

"Oh, I see. I am suitably put in my place."

Prudence was aware of a most inconvenient urge to laugh. She suppressed it sternly and said, "So, we're looking for someone in her early thirties perhaps? Not over thirty-five. I know you didn't like the sound of Agnes Hargate with her son, but are you averse to widows in general?"

"No. So long as she be not languishing in her maturity. Neither would I object to a spinster, as long as she be not desperate in hers." He glanced sideways at her. "But I think thirty-five is a little too old for what I had in mind. Maybe you could look for someone in her late twenties." He nodded. "Yes, the more I think about it, the more I realize that late twenties would be the perfect age."

"All right," Prudence said, making a note in her book. "That gives us somewhere to start." She knew perfectly well what he was doing and she was not going to allow him to do it. He would not discompose her. She took a breath and asked casually, "Now, must she be beautiful?"

"Beauty is in the eye of the beholder."

"Don't be glib. Do a woman's looks matter to you?"

"Let's leave that question. I don't know the answer," he said, sounding serious for the first time.

Prudence shrugged. "Education, then? How important is that on a scale of one to five?"

"Well, until a week or so ago I would have said about two and a half. Now it's definitely a five."

Prudence wrote it down. He looked at her again. "Aren't you going to ask what changed my mind?"

"No," she said firmly. "It's not relevant. What kind of personality do you like?"

"Oh, meek and mild," he said definitely. "A woman who knows her place, who knows when to hold her tongue, who knows that I know best."

That was too much. Prudence snapped the notebook shut and thrust it back into her muff. "All right, if you won't take this seriously—"

"But I answered your question," he protested. "Wouldn't you assume that someone as arrogant and combative and self-opinionated as myself would want a helpmeet who would revel in those qualities—"

"Qualities," Prudence interrupted. "They're not qualities, they're vices."

"Ah. I stand corrected." He turned the motor into a narrow lane at a signpost that said HENLEY, 2 MILES.

Prudence fell silent, watching the passing autumnal countryside through her tinted goggles as the wind whipped past her fur-encased ears. The fields were brown stubble, the hedgerows rich with luscious blackberries and crimson holly berries.

"And they're vices you agree I have?" Gideon's question in his quiet voice startled her out of a moment's unquiet reverie.

"I told you earlier, I'm not interested in anything about you except what relates to your ability to win this case," she stated.

"Then let's talk about you," he said. "Has marriage ever tempted you, Prudence?"

"How is that question related to our suit?"

He seemed to consider this before saying, "I would prefer it in court that you didn't come across as an ill-tempered, man-hating, embittered spinster."

Prudence inhaled sharply, but he was continuing calmly, "As I've said before, you can be certain that Barclay's barrister will do everything he can to put you in an unfavorable light. I would like to give them a warmhearted, crusading female who is out to protect the most vulnerable of her own sex from hurt and exploitation. A woman gentle of tongue but resolute. A woman who has only the softest feelings towards the male of the species, except those who are patently not deserving of softness."

Prudence shifted slightly in her seat, suddenly feeling unsure of herself. "Do I really come across in an unfavorable light?"

Again he considered before saying mildly, "On occasion. When your hackles are raised. I'd like you to be able to control that response."

"Because they will try to provoke it in court."

"I think you should be prepared for it."

Prudence was silent. He had every right to point that out, and she couldn't help but recognize its truth. But it was a wretchedly uncomfortable recognition nevertheless.

Chapter 12

They were driving down the high street in Henley-on-Thames now. The pavements were crowded with Sunday-morning strollers, the green lawns edging the river dotted with pedestrians enjoying the sunshine. A few rowboats were on the river and Prudence realized that the air was a lot warmer now. But that, of course, could have something to do with the fact that their speed had slowed to a crawl and in her fur casing she was beginning to feel like a hibernating bear.

Gideon spun the wheel and turned under an archway into the cobbled back court of an Elizabethan timbered inn. He turned off the engine and jumped down. Prudence was too eager to make her own descent to await his help and stepped down, resisting the inelegant urge to rub her backside that seemed rather numb after the jolting drive.

"Go in and order coffee," he said. "I'll join you in about five minutes when I've put more fuel in the engine." He hauled out a can labeled PRATTS MOTOR SPIRIT from the enclosed compartment at the rear of the motor.

Prudence stretched and rolled her shoulders, then took off her hood and the fur coat. "It's far too hot for these." She laid them on the passenger seat of the car. "I'll see you inside."

The Dog and Partridge had a comfortable parlor just off the saloon bar. A cheerful maid promised coffee and currant buns and directed Prudence to the ladies' lounge. When she emerged, refreshed, her hair tidied, she found Gideon already sitting in the bow window, pouring coffee. "I'd suggest we take a walk along the river but I want to be in Oxford for luncheon," he said as she sat down.

"Why do we have to go all that way? Why don't we stop here?" Prudence selected a sugar-sprinkled currant bun from the plate.

Gideon frowned, as if puzzled by the question. "I intended to drive to Oxford," he said.

"But you could change your mind," Prudence said, regarding him quizzically. It occurred to her that perhaps he couldn't.

As if in confirmation, he said, "When I've made a plan, I like to stick to it."

"Like to, or need to?"

He added sugar to his coffee with careful deliberation. It was not a question he'd ever asked himself, but the answer was immediate. "Need," he said. He looked across at her with a rather rueful smile. "Does that make me very rigid and pedantic?"

She nodded, and drank some coffee. "I would say so. I'll need to bear that in mind when I'm looking at candidates. Some women find that quite comforting . . . knowing that someone isn't going to change his mind."

"Somehow I think that you are not one of them," he observed, taking a bite of currant bun.

"Spot on," she said with a cool smile, breaking a tiny piece off her bun.

"We seem to be concentrating on my character flaws this morning," Gideon observed. "I *had* been hoping for a pleasant day of getting to know one another."

"Isn't that what we're doing? Flaws and all?" she inquired. "And on that subject, if Barclay's barrister is going to attack me, wouldn't it be better if you asked me first the hostile questions he might ask . . . spike his guns, as it were. Then I might be able to respond with proper composure."

"That was one of the tactics I was considering," he conceded. "But whenever I start to ask them, you attack with all the ferocity of a swarm of hornets."

"Ah, but that was because I hadn't realized it was a tactic. Now I know that it's just preparation and you're not expressing your own views, I'll practice moderating my responses." She took off her glasses and rubbed them on a napkin, unaware that it was a reflex action whenever she felt on her mettle. "Am I right to assume that you *aren't* expressing your own views?"

"It wouldn't matter if I were. My views are not at issue here." He pushed aside his coffee cup and sat back in the deep leather armchair. The light was dim in the low-ceilinged parlor, and the diamond-paned windows let in little sunshine. In the gloom he noticed how her hair glowed a rich copper and how her eyes were a brilliant glinting green in the smooth cream oval of her face.

"To answer an earlier question," he said, "I have decided that a woman's personal appearance is very important to me."

Prudence set down her coffee cup. "She must be beautiful?"

He shook his head. "No, not at all. Interesting . . . unconventional. Those are the adjectives I would choose."

"I see."

"Aren't you going to write that down?"

"My notebook is in the motor." She wanted to glare at him; she wanted to smile at him. But instinct told her she could do neither. Not unless she was prepared to let down her guard. He was trying to draw her into playing this game of allurement. It wasn't naked seduction, it wasn't as banal as flirtation, it was just a beguiling invitation to join the dance. And a little voice that she tried to ignore was questioning: *Why not join the dance?*

The answer, however, was as clear as day. She . . . her sisters . . . they all needed this man's complete professional attention. *She* needed his single-minded professional attention on the issue, or she'd lose her own. There was no room for anything but a purely business relationship with the barrister. And besides, she reminded herself, she disliked him excessively.

When it was clear that he was not going to get a more interesting reaction, he said neutrally, "Ready to continue?" He stood up, shoveling a handful of coins from his pocket onto the table.

"Since Oxford needs to be the destination," she said, rising in her turn.

"You will enjoy it," he promised, moving ahead of her to open the door to the bright, sunlit outdoors. "And I own, I'm curious to see how well I remember punting. It's been nigh on twenty years." He gave an exaggerated sigh. Prudence closed her lips firmly. She was not going to give him the compliment he was fishing for. She was not going to join this dance.

"I don't think I need this fur," she commented when they returned to the motor. She folded it carefully over the back of her seat.

"You'll need the hood and the goggles," Gideon said, putting on his own goggles. "And I think you'll find in a few minutes that you need the coat. Once we're on the open road." He put on his own coat then turned his attention to the crank that would start the engine. It sprang to life after a couple of turns and he stowed the crank and climbed behind the wheel, saying as cheerfully as if he was not beginning to feel disheartened, "Ever upwards and onwards."

"How far is it from here?"

"About twenty miles. We should do it in an hour, or just over. The road's quite good. I'll be able to open her up."

Prudence fastened the hood beneath her chin, reflecting that his clear enthusiasm at the prospect of bouncing along rutted roads at top speed was not something she could share. She pulled the fur coat up over her shoulders as the rushing air chilled her anew and rather gloomily contemplated the prospect of the three-hour return journey. By the time they left Oxford, the sun would be going down and the air would be even colder. Her companion, who was humming contentedly to himself, obviously had no such qualms.

"Are you ever free in the afternoons?" she asked.

Gideon stopped humming. "Unless I'm actually in court, or have a business meeting, I can be," he said. "Why?"

"We usually use our At Homes to introduce likely

couples. I was thinking that you could vet some of the possibilities one afternoon."

A terrier with a bone, no other description would do. He sighed and accepted the inevitable. "And do you have any possibilities in mind? Apart from this Agnes Whatever-Her-Name-Is."

"Hargate," she said. "And I really think you're doing yourself a disservice by not at least meeting her. You would like her very much. You haven't even listened to a description."

"I had an instinctive reaction," he stated. "The minute you mentioned her, I knew we would not get on at all."

Prudence surveyed him with growing irritation. "I don't know how you can be so certain."

"Well, I am."

Prudence opened her notebook again. She looked at the few names that she and her sisters had come up with. "All right, let's try again. You might get on well with Lavender Riley. I'm sure I could get her to come to an At Home if you were available on a Wednesday."

"No," he said firmly.

"No, you wouldn't be available on a Wednesday?"

"No, I would not be interested in Lavender Riley."

"How could you possibly know that? I haven't told you anything about her." Exasperation rang in her voice.

"You told me her name. I forgot to mention that names are very important to me. Perhaps you should write that in your little book. I could not possibly live with someone called Lavender."

"That is so ridiculous. You could give her another name . . . a pet name."

"I find the whole concept of pet names quite revolting," he said. "Besides, everyone else would be calling her Lavender. I'd never get away from it."

"If you're just going to make frivolous objections—" She stopped abruptly. She was just laying herself open to mockery by persisting, and she wasn't going to encourage him any further.

However, it seemed he didn't need any encouragement. He continued blithely into her frozen silence, "Now, the names of the virtues I find most appealing. Hope—"

"Hope is not a virtue," Prudence snapped.

"Oh, I think a hopeful character is a virtuous one," he demurred. "But Charity is an appealing name; Patience, I like. Oh, and Prudence, of course. Now, that's a very attractive name, if a rather stolid virtue."

Prudence clasped her hands inside her muff and refused to smile.

He glanced at her and grinned. "Come on," he said. "I can see you want to laugh. Your eyes are shining."

"You can't possibly see what my eyes are doing behind these goggles."

"I can imagine them very easily. Your mouth is quivering just the tiniest fraction, and when it does that your eyes sparkle. I've noticed often."

"Considering what little reason I've had to smile in your company since we first met, I find that an unlikely observation."

"It was intended as a compliment," he said rather plaintively.

"An empty one, in that case." She shrank deeper into her coat as the motor's speed increased and the wind whistled by.

"You are a very stubborn woman," Gideon said. "I

had planned a delightful day out and you're doing your level best to spoil it."

Prudence turned sideways in her seat to face him. "*You* had planned a delightful day out. Without one word of consultation with me. Without a moment's consideration of my own possible plans, or indeed of my wishes. And now you're accusing *me,* who was dragged along willy-nilly, of spoiling *your* plans. You said we were going to work on the case."

"Well, we are, but unfortunately it's not going as well as I had hoped," he said. "I wanted to see how you are when you're relaxed, comfortable, not on the offensive . . . or defensive. I had thought that if I provided the right situation and surroundings, you would show me that side of yourself. If such a side exists," he added a shade dryly. "If it doesn't, this is indeed a wasted day."

Prudence was silent for a minute. Then she said, "It does, actually. Why do you need to see it?"

"Because that's the side that's going to win this case for us," he said simply. "I want the warm, intelligent, compassionate Prudence Duncan on the witness stand. Can you give her to me?"

There was silence then between them. Prudence was absorbed in her own reflections and assumed her companion was in his. It was such a simple, reasonable explanation, and she was beginning to wonder why she had resisted the appeal of this outing, fighting his efforts to charm her, disarm her, amuse her, with such dogged persistence. There was surely no need to do so, not when his objective was so directly related to their libel suit.

Gideon broke the silence finally. "It's a lovely day, we have a delicious lunch waiting for us, followed by a quiet trip on the river. We'll stop for dinner in Henley on the way back, and then you can sleep the rest of the way home curled up in your furs. How could you possibly resist such a prospect?"

"It is irresistible," she responded, feeling the tension suddenly leave her shoulders. She hadn't even realized how tightly clenched her muscles had been, as if she had been arming herself against something. "If you promise not to annoy me, I will show you my other side."

"I can't promise," he said, turning to smile at her. "Sometimes it's inadvertent. I'll ask that you give me the benefit of the doubt if something slips."

"All right," she agreed. "Just for today. But in return I ask that you listen to two things about the case that I have to tell you. We don't need to discuss them, but you need to hear them so that you can think about what we should do."

"Fire away."

"First, my father is going to take the stand as a character witness for Barclay." She watched for his reaction but there was none. He merely nodded.

"Don't you see how awkward . . . in fact, terrible . . . that is?"

"Not really."

"But you'll have to attack Father."

"I will attempt to shake his faith in his friend's probity, certainly."

"But you won't be unpleasant to Father?"

"Not unless he makes it necessary."

Prudence absorbed this. He sounded so matter-of-fact and unperturbed by what for her was a hideous prospect. "I'm afraid he might recognize me . . . or my voice, rather," she said after a minute. "I don't know if I can disguise my voice well enough to fool him."

"What did you have in mind?" he asked curiously.

Prudence chuckled. They had decided she should adopt the accent Chastity had used when meeting their first paying client, Anonymous, at the very beginning of the Go-Between venture.

"Oh, but I am from Paris, *moi*. *En France* we do not ask ze ladies such questions. *Non, non, c'est pas comme il faut*, you comprend? Ze Mayfair Lady, she is most *respectable. Vraiment respectable*. Respectable, that is what you say over 'ere, *n'est ce pas?*"

"Can you keep it up?" Gideon demanded through his laughter.

"I don't see why not," Prudence said airily. "My French is good enough to combine the language enough to add a little confusion to the mix, while still not making myself completely incomprehensible. I thought that would be a good idea."

"A mysterious, veiled French lady," Gideon mused. "It'll certainly be intriguing. It might also make you seem more sympathetic. Your regular Englishman is fascinated by the somewhat—how shall I put it?—somewhat *uninhibited* reputation of the French female. They might be rather less hostile to the views expressed in *The Mayfair Lady* if they believe they're perpetrated by a woman not of their own kind. A woman who might be expected to be a little outrageous."

"So, it's a good strategy all around," Prudence declared.

"It'll serve if you can hold it together in the face of some fairly relentless interrogation."

"I'll practice with my sisters," she promised.

"It will also depend upon your identity remaining hidden at the time of the trial," he reminded her. "As I said before, I can promise you that the prosecution will do everything they can to discover your identity. They're probably setting a search in motion already."

"We're going to discover next week if there have been any strange inquiries at the various places that distribute *The Mayfair Lady.*"

"Sensible," he said. "So, what's the second thing?"

Prudence reached into her muff for the earl of Barclay's note, and read it to him. "It's not dated, but it's certainly not recent."

"It's not good enough," he stated. "Find this schedule of payments, find me dates, find out what your father was buying. I'm not opening this can of worms without unshakable evidence."

"You could surely question the earl about it," she said, bristling at his brusque dismissal despite their earlier compact. "Maybe rattle him a little."

He shook his head. "No, it's not sufficient even to bring the subject up. You'll have to dig deeper."

"Well, as it happens, I have authorization to examine his bank records. I'll go to Hoare's tomorrow."

"How did you get that?" His surprise was evident.

Prudence huddled deeper into the coat, turning the collar up. "It was a trick. Not one I'm proud of, so can we leave it at that?"

"Of course," he said instantly. "Are you cold?" His quiet voice was now concerned and sympathetic.

"A little," she admitted, although it was not really a bodily cold, more an internal chill.

"We'll be there in less than half an hour. See the spires?" He gestured with one hand towards a faint outline on the horizon. Oxford's gleaming spires in the valley below them.

"It's strange, but I've never been to Oxford," Prudence said, resolutely putting aside her depressing thoughts. "Cambridge, yes. But never Oxford."

"I prefer Oxford, but then I'm prejudiced."

"You were at New College?"

He nodded, then placed a hand on her knee. It was a fleeting touch but it felt oddly significant to Prudence. In fact, she realized this whole journey had taken on a significance that she couldn't identify. But it was more than the sum of its parts. A lot more.

They drove up in front of the Randolph Hotel on Beaumont Street just as the city's clocks chimed noon. Prudence stepped down and stretched her shoulders again. The sun was very warm, more like early summer than autumn, and once again she discarded her furs.

Gideon scooped them off the seat. "We'll take them inside. They'll be safer than lying on the seat in the open."

A doorman hurried to escort them into the lofty hall of the hotel. An elegant sweep of staircase led to the upper floors. "The ladies' lounge is upstairs," Gideon said. "I'll wait for you at the table." He strode off to the restaurant.

When Prudence joined him, he was perusing the wine list. A glass of champagne sat by her place.

"I took the liberty of ordering you an aperitif," he said. "If you'd rather have something else . . ."

"No," she said, "this is lovely." She sat down and took a sip from the glass. "It does seem to cheer one up."

"And I get the impression you need cheering up," he said. "Let me try for the rest of the day to do just that." He leaned over and placed a hand over hers on the tablecloth. "Will you?"

Oh, yes, Prudence thought, this day was very much more than the sum of its parts. She slid her hand out from under his quite gently and opened her menu. "What do you recommend? I assume you know the dining room."

"I know it well," he said, accepting her change of subject. If she wouldn't give him a spontaneous answer, then he wasn't going to press for one. He had his pride, and he was not accustomed to rejection, but he allowed none of his pique to show, saying coolly, "The kitchen is very good. How hungry are you?"

"Starving."

He examined his own menu. "Saddle of lamb," he suggested. "Unless you'd prefer the Dover sole."

"Lamb sounds good," she said. "I'm not feeling fishy. What should I have to start?"

"The smoked mackerel pâte is delicious, but if you're not in a fishy mood..." He frowned at the menu. "Vichyssoise, perhaps?"

"Yes, perfect." Prudence closed her menu, took off her glasses to rub them on her napkin, and gave him a smile. Gideon was not prepared for the effect of a smile that he had seen all too rarely. When combined with the luster it gave to her lively green eyes, it was quite stunning. It was something of a consolation prize, he decided, but it was not one to be sneezed at.

"Burgundy or claret?" he asked, picking up the wine list again.

"I'm more in a claret mood."

"Then, a *bon Bordeaux* it shall be."

Prudence sipped her champagne and leaned back in her chair, looking out of the long windows at the Martyrs' Memorial in the little square opposite, and the bicycling undergraduates, their black gowns flapping as they pedaled vigorously along St. Giles. Her mood had changed. She was feeling suddenly relaxed, contented, looking forward to her luncheon. Her companion's attention was entirely on the wine list and she had the opportunity for a leisurely if covert examination of his features.

The thick hair was swept back off a broad, rather knobby forehead, and she thought his hairline was probably receding slightly. In another five years that broad forehead would be even broader. Her gaze tracked down over the aquiline and very dominating nose, the mouth that she found disturbingly attractive, and the deep cleft in his chin that she found even more so. His hands with their filbert nails were delicate for a man—long-fingered, like a pianist's. She remembered that had been one of her first observations.

It had been a long time since she had consciously found a man attractive, even longer since she had found one sexually inviting. She had lost her virginity the year after her mother had died. She and her sisters had made a pact that while none of them were set on marriage, they *were* determined not to die wondering about sex. So they'd given themselves a year. At the end of that year they were none of them virgins.

Prudence's experience had been, she supposed, pleasant enough. Or at least, not unpleasant. But she had certainly felt that something had been missing. Some transport of delight or similar sensation that their reading of Victorian pornography had given the sisters cause to expect. Perhaps *The Pearl* and other books of its ilk had magnified the transcendent delights of orgasmic *spending*. But Prudence had definitely been left wondering.

Now, however, she caught herself imagining those hands on her body. Her mouth already knew about Gideon's kisses. But the deep-seated thrill of excitement in her belly was not a familiar sensation. It was a shock to admit it, but it seemed that she was attracted to Gideon Malvern.

How was it possible to be attracted to a man one disliked? Well, at least there would be no temptation to do anything about it. She needed the man's mind, not his body, and had no intention of confusing the two.

"Penny for them?" he said, looking up from the wine list.

Prudence blushed. And the more she blushed, the more embarrassed she felt, and the more she blushed. He was looking at her, his gray eyes searching as if he would read her mind. Her face was as hot as hell's fire, and, she was sure, as red as a beetroot.

Then he turned his gaze away to address the sommelier, who had appeared opportunely. Prudence breathed slowly and felt the heat in her face subside. She took up her water glass and surreptitiously pressed it to the pulse below her ear. It had an immediate cooling effect, and by the time Gideon had finished his consultation with the sommelier, she was her usual self, cool and composed, her complexion its customary pale cream.

"A St. Estèphe," he said. "I hope you'll approve."

"I'm sure I shall. I never presume to question the choice of an expert," she said lightly, breaking a bread roll and spearing an artful coil of butter from the glass dish.

"That's a sage and intelligent attitude," he observed. "You'd be surprised how many people lack the sense or are too inflicted with vanity to bow to the voice of experience."

Prudence shook her head at him. "Gideon, you may be right, but your manner of being so is sometimes insufferable."

"What did I say?" He looked genuinely surprised.

She shook her head again. "If you don't know, there's no virtue in my pointing it out."

The waiter appeared and Gideon gave their order before saying, "Point it out, Prudence. How will I ever learn otherwise?"

And that made her laugh. "You missed the irony in my statement, and you missed it because it didn't occur to you that I might be something of an expert with a wine list myself."

"Are you?"

"You'd be surprised," she said, thinking of how much she had learned about the wine trade while manipulating the contents of her father's cellars with Jenkins.

Gideon considered her with a half smile as he sipped his champagne. "You know, I don't think there's much about you that would surprise me, Prudence. Tell me how you became an expert."

Prudence frowned. She and her sisters were intensely private about their household matters and the shifts they were obliged to make to keep their heads above water. No one in their society must know that the Duncan family for close to three years had dodged bankruptcy on a near daily basis. The Go-Between and *The Mayfair Lady* were beginning to bring in an income, but they were still far from out of the woods. But then, she reflected, they had no secrets from the barrister, they couldn't have. He already knew they were in financial difficulties, and why. He just didn't know that Lord Duncan was kept blissfully unaware of the true situation.

She waited until they had been served their first course, then as she slowly stirred her soup she explained the situation in all its detail. Gideon, spreading mackerel pâte onto toast, listened without comment until she had fallen silent and had turned her attention to her soup.

"Are you really doing your father any favors by keeping him in ignorance?" he asked then.

Prudence felt a familiar prickle of annoyance. There was an unmistakable note of criticism in his tone. "We believe so," she responded tautly.

"Oh, it's none of my business, I realize that," he said. "But sometimes an outside perspective is helpful. You and your sisters are so close to the situation, maybe you're missing something."

"We don't think so," she said in the same tone, aware that she was sounding defensive, which somehow gave credence to his criticism, and yet unable to help herself. "We happen to know our father very well. And we also know what our mother would have wanted."

Gideon said calmly, "How's the soup?"

"Very good."

"And the wine. I trust it meets with your expert approval."

She looked at him sharply and saw that he was smiling in an appeasing fashion. She let her annoyance fade and said, "It's a fine claret."

After luncheon they strolled through the city and down to Folly Bridge, where Gideon rented a punt.

Prudence surveyed the long flat boat and the unwieldy length of the pole with some trepidation. "Are you sure you know how to do this?"

"Well, I used to. I assume it's like riding a bicycle," he said, stepping onto the flat stern and holding out a hand. "Step in the middle so it doesn't rock."

She took the proffered hand and stepped gingerly into the punt, which, despite her caution, rocked alarmingly under her unbalanced weight.

"Sit down," he instructed swiftly, and she dropped immediately onto a pile of cushions in the prow. They were surprisingly soft.

"I feel like a concubine in a seraglio," she said, stretching out in leisurely fashion.

"I'm not sure the clothes are quite right," Gideon observed, taking the monstrously long pole from the boathouse attendant.

A punt with a trio of laughing undergraduates was approaching as Gideon pushed off from the bank. The punter dug his pole energetically into the mud, failed to pull it up in time, and the punt slid gracefully out from under him, leaving him hanging on to the pole in the middle of the river. There was riotous applause from the spectators on the bank, and Prudence watched with some sympathy as the luckless punter did the only thing he could—dropped into the water while his punt came to a stranded stop a few yards distant.

"Are you sure you can do this?" she asked Gideon again.

"Oh, ye of little faith," he scolded. "I'm not some callow undergrad, I'll have you know."

"No," she agreed. "That you're not." She regarded him

with slightly narrowed eyes. "I wonder if you ever were."

He didn't answer, merely pushed the pole into the riverbed, let it slide back up in his hands with an instant and to-the-manor-born rhythm. Prudence lay back on the cushions, replete with lunch and wine, her eyelids drooping as the afternoon sun warmed them, creating a soft amber glow behind. Idly she trailed a hand in the cold river water and listened to the sounds of the world around her, laughter and voices, birdsong, the steady rhythmic plash and suck of the pole. London seemed many miles away, and the brisk chill of that morning's drive a mere memory.

Gradually she became aware that the sounds of other punters had vanished and now there were only the river sounds, the quack of a mallard, the trill of a thrush. She opened her eyes slowly. Gideon was watching her, his gaze intense and intent. Automatically she took off her glasses to wipe them on her handkerchief.

"Is something the matter? Do I have a smudge on my nose? Spinach in my teeth?"

He shook his head. "Nothing's the matter. Quite the opposite."

Prudence sat up straighter on the cushions. There was something lurking in the depths of those piercing gray eyes that sent a shiver of suspense up her spine and made her scalp prickle. She had a sense of imminent danger. But paradoxically, no sense of threat. Her own eyes seemed locked on his and she couldn't avert her gaze.

Dear God, what was she getting herself into?

With a supreme effort of will she broke the locked gaze and forced herself to cast an apparently casual glance at the scenery as she replaced her glasses. They had reached a point where the river branched around a small islet.

Gideon took the left-hand fork and the punt slid past a lush grassy bank with sides that sloped with gentle invitation down to the river. A small hut was set back a little on the bank. "I think it's safe enough to take this side at this time of year," he said as lightly as if that intense but silent exchange had never taken place.

"Why wouldn't it be safe?" She looked around with sharpened curiosity.

"Over there lies Parsons' Pleasure," he said with an airy gesture of his free hand towards the grassy bank and the little hut. "Had the water not been too cold for swimming, we would have been obliged to take the other side, which is not nearly so pretty."

Prudence regarded him warily. There was a distinct note of mischief in his voice, a hint of laughter in its quiet depths. "What's swimming got to do with it?" she asked, knowing she was supposed to. She felt like a sidekick in a comic routine at the Music Hall.

"Parsons' Pleasure is the private bathing spot for male members of the university. Since it's exclusively for men, bathing suits are considered unnecessary," he informed her with some solemnity. "So women are forbidden to punt on this stretch of the Cherwell."

"Yet another example of male privilege," Prudence observed. "But I fail to see how women can be *forbidden* on this piece of the river. It's a free country, no one owns the water."

"I rather guessed that would be your reaction," he said. "And you're by no means the first. I'll tell you a story, if you like."

"I like," she said, once again lying back on the cushions. The danger seemed to have passed for the moment, although she was not blind or fool enough to imagine it would not again rear its head.

"Well, on one glorious, hot summer day, while the parsons were taking their uninhibited pleasure on that bank, an enterprising group of women decided to protest this bastion of male privilege, as you put it."

Prudence grinned. "You mean they punted past?"

"Precisely. Although I believe they were rowing. Anyway, as the story goes, all the gentlemen leaped to their feet, covering their private parts with towels, all except for one notable scholar, who shall remain nameless, who reacted by wrapping his head in a towel."

Prudence struggled to keep a straight face. This was not a tale a respectable gentleman should tell any respectable gentlewoman. The image, however, was deliciously absurd.

Gideon's expression remained solemn, his voice grave as he continued, "When questioned by his colleagues as to this peculiar reaction, the scholar is said to have replied: *'In Oxford, I am known by my face.'*"

Prudence tried; she tried as hard as she could to stare at him with unmoving disapproval. "That is a most improper story," she declared, a quaver in her voice. "It's certainly not for a lady's ears."

"Maybe not," he agreed amiably. "But I doubt the Mayfair Lady would consider it anything other than delightfully amusing." His eyes were laughing at her. "In truth, I believe there is nothing ladylike about the Mayfair Lady. You can't fool me, Miss Prudence Duncan. You don't have a prim and prudish bone in your body. And neither do your sisters."

Prudence gave up the struggle and began to laugh.

Gideon began to laugh too. In his distraction, the punt pole slipped through his hands, and instead of making contact with the river bottom slid away from him. His laughter died on the instant. Swearing vigorously, he grabbed for it, swaying precariously on the stern of the punt as he tried to get control of the unwieldy pole. Water splashed over the stern, soaking his feet. Prudence was now laughing so hard, she couldn't speak. What price the elegant, self-assured barrister now?

Finally Gideon wrestled the pole into submission and resumed his firm but now rather damp stance on the stern. "That was no laughing matter," he said rather stiffly. He was clearly put out at having been made to look like a clumsy amateur.

Prudence took off her glasses again to wipe her eyes as tears of laughter streamed down her cheeks. "I'm sorry," she said. "I didn't mean to laugh at you. But you looked as if you were wrestling a sea serpent. A truly modern Laocoön."

Gideon didn't deign to reply. She took her trailing hand from the water, aware that her fingers were growing numb with the cold, and said solicitously, "Your feet are so wet. Do you have any dry socks?"

"Why would I?" he asked somewhat sourly.

"Perhaps we could buy some on our way back to the hotel. You can't squelch your way back to London. You'll catch your death. Perhaps we could get you a mustard bath at the Randolph before we start driving home. They say it can ward off a chill. You wouldn't want— Oh!" Her sweet-voiced speech was abruptly cut off by a shower of water as Gideon pulled the pole from the river with sufficient vigor to send a significant quantity of the Cherwell spraying across the punt.

"You did that deliberately," Prudence accused, brushing at the drops scattered across her dress, shaking out her booted feet.

"Not a bit of it," he said innocently. "It was purely accidental."

"Liar. I was only thinking of your well-being."

"Liar," he fired back. "You were making mock."

"Well, it was rather funny," she said. "On top of the story." Her laughter, her pure enjoyment of the last few minutes, had brought a soft glow to her cheeks, and once again, with her glasses now in her lap, the lustrous sparkle of her eyes was revealed. Gideon began to think that his momentary discomfort had probably been worth it just to produce that effect.

"Well, since we're both somewhat damp, I think it's time to turn around," he said, glancing up at the sky through the yellowing tendrils of the weeping willows that lined the bank. "It's going to get really chilly once the sun goes down."

"It's going to be a very cold drive home," Prudence observed. She replaced her glasses, well aware of his thoughtful scrutiny of a minute earlier. Thoughtful and definitely appreciative. The air between them was taut and singing with tension.

"You have your furs," he reminded her. "And we'll break the journey in Henley for dinner."

They handed in the punt and began to walk back briskly towards St. Giles. "Gideon, I can hear you squelching," Prudence said as they passed a men's outfitters. "Go in there and buy yourself some socks."

"I'm not going to admit to some shopkeeper that I got wet in a punt," Gideon stated.

"Then I'll buy them." Before he could argue,

Prudence had disappeared into the shop, setting the bell ringing. She emerged within five minutes with a paper bag. "There." She presented it to him. "One pair of black socks. Large. I guessed the size, but I don't think you have particularly small feet."

He took the bag, peered inside. "They have a pattern on them."

"It's just the ribbing on the silk," she said. "It's not really a pattern at all. You should be grateful I didn't buy you plaid."

Chapter 13

They stopped at the same hostelry in Henley where they'd stopped for coffee that morning. It was dark by then and Prudence hurried into the warm, softly lit lounge, already glad of her furs. She wondered for a fleeting instant if Gideon had reserved a table for dinner, but it was only a fleeting instant. He was not a man to leave anything to chance. They were greeted as expected guests, ushered into a cozy private room, where a fireplace gave out comforting warmth. Sherry and whisky decanters stood on the sideboard, and as Prudence shed her outer garments, Gideon poured drinks.

"They seem to know you here," she observed, taking her glass and sitting down in a deep chintz-covered armchair beside the fire.

"It's been a favorite spot of mine since my undergraduate days." He took the opposite armchair. "I took the liberty of ordering dinner beforehand."

"On the telephone?"

"How else?" He sipped his whisky. "The Dog and Partridge is renowned for its local Aylesbury duckling.

Plain roasted with a touch of orange sauce, it's hard to fault, so I hope you like duck."

Prudence thought he sounded a little anxious and found it both refreshing and surprisingly endearing that over some things he was not surging with confidence in his own supremacy. "I love duck," she said.

He smiled and rose from his chair, uncoiling his long, lean body with a slow deliberation that reminded Prudence of an indolent lion preparing itself for a night's hunting. The atmosphere in the room changed abruptly, no longer relaxed, but singing with that same dangerous tension of before. He leaned against the mantel, glass in hand, one foot resting on the fender, and looked at her.

"Prudence." He spoke her name softly, thoughtfully, rolling the syllables around his tongue. His gray gaze was once again intent and intense. She resisted the urge to take off her glasses, knowing from experience that that gaze was too hot to hold without the defense of her lenses. She began to feel rather strange, light-headed almost. Her stomach felt as if it was floating. Whatever this was, it was not supposed to be happening.

She was impaled in her chair, her body pressed back against the overstuffed cushions by some invisible weight. Gideon moved away from the mantel. He took the few steps necessary to reach her. And yet still she sat unmoving, waiting. He leaned over, his hands braced on the arms of her chair. His face was very close to hers. She could feel the warmth of his breath on her cheek, and could almost imagine that she felt the sparks that lit the gray eyes now fused with hers. She let her head fall back against the cushions behind her, exposing the column of her throat in a movement that expressed both abandonment and submission. A tiny sigh escaped her.

He kissed her. A very different kiss from the one he had first given her. The one he had first *taken* from her. The pressure of his mouth on hers was light, almost exploratory, and if she had wanted to turn her head aside, to push him away, she could have. But she didn't. His tongue stroked across her lips, and then gently but with absolute deliberation pushed into the warm velvet of her mouth. His breath mingled with hers as his tongue slid delicately over her teeth, touched the inside of her cheeks, danced with her own. Her eyes were closed, her lips parted, and she tasted hungrily of his tongue, drawing him farther within. Her body was in control now, her mind for once subservient to this unfamiliar but imperative need. She moved her hands up to clasp his head, and her tongue darted with swift serpentine movements between his lips, exploring his mouth as he'd explored hers.

It was only breathlessness that forced them apart, and Prudence finally let her hands fall into her lap, reluctant to lose the heady scent of his skin, the warm taste of his mouth. He smiled down at her, still keeping his hands braced on the arms of her chair.

"This is ridiculous," she said. "I dislike you intensely."

"All the time or some of the time?" His face was still so close to hers, his breath rustled warm across her cheek.

"Some of the time . . . it would seem," she added, sounding both puzzled and slightly indignant.

"Does it help if I tell you that the feeling is entirely mutual?" he asked, still smiling. "There are times when I dislike you every bit as intensely."

"Then this isn't supposed to happen."

"The world is full of surprises. It would be a very

boring place if it weren't." He moved closer and suddenly kissed the tip of her nose. "Don't you agree?"

"I suppose I must," she murmured. "But there are surprises and surprises, and this kind has no right to happen."

"That bad, huh?" He kissed the corner of her mouth, a light butterfly touch of his lips. Both eyes and voice were now amused.

Prudence made a movement to straighten in the chair and instantly he stepped back, but without taking his eyes off her. She took off her glasses and blinked. "I don't want things to become confused," she said. "And it seems to me that this can only lead to a morass of confusion."

He continued to look down at her, then he leaned forward and took the glasses from her hand. He said, "It doesn't have to. I don't see why lovers can't also work together."

Prudence blinked myopically at his now blurred expression. Without her glasses, matters looked rather different. The brisk, businesslike, highly focused, prudent Prudence Duncan existed behind those gold-rimmed lenses. Without them the world moved into softer focus and the hard realities of every day receded into a rather convenient mist.

When he reached down a hand to pull her to her feet, she offered no resistance. He put his hands on her shoulders and lightly kissed her eyelids. "Should we have dinner first?"

There was no mistaking his meaning and Prudence was not one to play coy games. She touched her tingling mouth with her fingertips. It happened sometimes, when the sensible, logical side of her nature was somehow driven out by rash instinct, and it was definitely happening now.

Slowly she took her glasses from him and returned them to her nose, testing. If when she could see straight her prudent nature once more gained the ascendancy, she would know this was all some kind of bad joke. But all that happened was that she could now see Gideon's face clearly and it made not the slightest difference to what she wanted.

"Will the duck keep?" she asked.

Gideon nodded, his smile deepening. "Wait here," he said, and left her in solitude.

Prudence took up her sherry glass and drank down the contents as she stood by the fire, gazing into the flames. Whatever this madness was, she had neither the will nor the inclination to stop it, and to hell with the consequences. But she jumped nevertheless at the sound of the door opening, even though she was expecting it. Her heart banged against her ribs as she turned away from the fire.

Gideon stood in the doorway, a small valise in one hand. His other he extended in invitation. She stepped across the room and took his hand. His fingers closed tight and warm over hers. "We'll be more comfortable upstairs," he said.

Prudence inclined her head in brief acknowledgment. She was no longer in control of anything, and for once in her life had no desire to be so. They walked up a shallow flight of stairs to a narrow, carpeted corridor. Gideon, still holding her hand, opened the first door they came to. It led into a bedroom, complete with four-poster bed, low beamed ceiling, and uneven oak floors. There was a fire in the grate and chintz curtains drawn across two small windows.

"How cozy," Prudence murmured.

He looked sharply at her as if he suspected a sardonic edge to the description, but there was nothing in her expression to confirm the suspicion. He was beginning to feel uncharacteristically nervous. He'd made love to a goodly number of women, and never—apart from the first few times in his youth—felt any qualms as to his ability to please.

He realized he didn't even know if Prudence was a virgin. Ordinarily he would assume that an unmarried woman of her birth and social position would have to be. But he was learning not to expect the ordinary when it came to the Honorable Prudence Duncan. He wondered whether to ask, and then decided he couldn't manage the question with any aplomb at the moment, which in itself was an unusual problem. Asking difficult questions was his stock-in-trade, after all.

"No," she said with a sudden smile. "I'm not. I'm not particularly experienced either, but I do have a pretty good idea of what's what."

He looked a little chagrined. "How did you guess?"

"It seemed an obvious thought you would have, and you were looking rather indecisive and uncomfortable." She found that instant of vulnerability she had glimpsed on his face reassuring, drawing her closer to him. He was perhaps as uncertain, as unsure of himself and his instincts at this moment as she was. And she could only like him the better for it.

She walked to the fire and bent to warm her hands, although they weren't in the least cold. The strange lightheaded sensation grew ever more powerful and she began to wonder if perhaps she was dreaming and none of this was really happening. And then she felt his arms around her, his body hard against her back, and she knew it was no dream.

He pressed his lips to the nape of her neck, his hands tracing the swell of her breasts beneath her jacket. She leaned her head back against his shoulder, so that her breasts filled his palms.

"You have too many clothes on," he murmured, moving his mouth to her ear as his fingers deftly unbuttoned her jacket, and as neatly drew it backwards off her shoulders. His fingers slid between the buttons of her cream silk blouse and explored the warm swell of her breasts through the thin chemise. He could feel her nipples hardening against the material. His tongue darted into the tight shell of her ear, and she squirmed with a tiny squeal. He laughed softly, his breath tickling her ear anew.

He unbuttoned her blouse, the tiny pearl fastenings flying apart, and he was no longer nervous, unsure of himself, and he could sense her own rising urgency for the touch of skin upon skin. The blouse fell to the floor with the jacket and he slipped his hands into the low neck of the chemise and held her breasts in his palms, surprised at how full they were. Her frame, elegant though she always looked, was thin and angular rather than shapely, but her breasts in his palms were round and smooth.

Prudence touched her tongue to her lips as her nipples grew harder and more erect under his circling thumbs. She was aware now of a clutch in her belly, a fullness in her loins, and with sudden urgency she placed her hands over his, pressing them against her breasts.

He turned her to face him with the same urgency and she began to fumble with the buttons at the waist of her long, pleated skirt. Impatiently he pushed aside her hands and did the job himself. She stepped out of the skirt and stood in her one undergarment, a combination of chemise and drawers of lacy, beribboned silk taffeta, gartered silk stockings, and buttoned kid shoes.

He put his hands at her waist, bunching the chemise, feeling her skin warm beneath the silk. It delighted him that she was wearing no corset of any kind. It made her body accessible in the most alluring fashion. There would be no ridges of whalebone etched onto her skin, and the body he felt was the same as the one he would feel when she was naked. He drew a deep, shuddering breath and removed her glasses, laying them carefully on the mantel. "You don't mind?"

She shook her head; the mist softening her vision at the moment had nothing to do with myopia. Her own hands went to the buttons of his coat. "Hurry," she whispered, her voice quivering with a surge of passionate need. "I have to see you . . . touch you."

He helped her, shrugging out of the coat, pulling off his tie, the starched wing collar of his shirt, discarding his waistcoat and the shirt. She touched his nipples and caught her bottom lip between her teeth when they hardened instantly. "I didn't know men's did that."

"We aim to please, madam," he said, a husky note now in his quiet voice. He reached for the buttons of the chemise, opening it before drawing her against him so that their bare skin touched. It was Prudence's turn to inhale with a little shudder of excitement as her sensitized breasts pressed against his chest. Her hands caressed his back, running down the clear line of his spine to the waist of his trousers.

He took the cue and stepped back an instant to unfasten his waistband and fly and push the striped trousers off his legs. "Oh, damn," he muttered as they met the obstacle of his shoes. He fell back on the bed and Prudence, with a gurgle of laughter, unfastened his shiny black shoes and pulled off his socks with his trousers. The prosaic moment interrupted the intensity, and the brief instant when passion yielded to the mundane only intensified her anticipation.

He stayed stretched on the bed, wearing only a pair of long woolen drawers, and she gazed down at him, at the hard swell of his penis. She reached down and touched it. It jumped against her hand and she closed her fingers over the jutting bulge, feeling the throb of the veins through the wool.

"Take it out," he whispered, his eyes now closed, his breath ragged.

Prudence sat on the bed and undid the buttons. She slid her hand into the opening and drew out his penis. It sprang up against her hand. With a little frown of concentration she explored the feel of it, reaching beneath to find his balls. She had never explored a man's body in any detail before, outside the anatomical pictures in the pages of a medical encyclopedia or Greek statues in the British Museum. Her only previous experience of sex had been too quick for such intimacies. She enclosed his penis in her hand, experimented with tightening and loosening her grip. She heard Gideon groan and then he reached down, took her wrist, and removed her hand.

He took a deep breath, murmured, "Let's take this slowly, sweetheart." He sat up, still holding her hand.

"I was enjoying myself," she said.

"So was I. But I'd like to share this first time." He stood up and pushed the undergarment off his hips and kicked his feet free. "Your turn now."

Prudence gazed at the long, lean length of him. For a man who spent his days studying law books and pontificating in a courtroom, he had a remarkably athletic body—muscled thighs, a flat belly, hard biceps. She put her hands on his narrow hips, running her thumbs over the sharp pelvic bones. A glow of excitement and pleasure spread through her. She slid her hands around to his backside, her fingers pressing hard into the taut flesh. "You have a beautiful body," she murmured, lightly touching her tongue to his nipples. "You could have modeled for Michelangelo."

Gideon looked startled. "I'm not sure that's a compliment."

"I think it is," she said, grazing his nipples with the tips of her front teeth.

"Then I'm suitably complimented . . . I think." He began to unpin her hair as her head remained bent against his chest. He tossed the pins in the direction of the dresser, heedless of those that missed and fell to the floor. He combed his fingers through the wavy russet mass as it fell to her shoulders and down her back. Then he cupped her face in his hands and tilted it up. He bent and kissed her eyes and said softly, "I need to see you now."

She nodded and slid the opened chemise off her shoulders. It fell to her hips, and Gideon dropped to one knee, hooking his fingers into the tops of her drawers. He pulled them down slowly, inch by inch, his lips trailing kisses over her belly, over the creamy flesh of her thighs thus revealed. She stepped out of the puddle of taffeta and lace and lifted her feet as he removed her shoes, then unfastened her garters and peeled off her stockings.

Still kneeling, he ran his hands up the backs of her legs to clasp the soft cheeks of her bottom. "That feels good," he murmured with a smile of satisfaction, kneading the silky roundness. He kissed the base of her belly, then slid his hands around to press apart her thighs.

Prudence quivered at the intimate exploration, the deep recesses of her body moistening, opening. She felt laid bare, more naked than she was, and she reveled in the feeling, her feet shifting on the wooden floor as she parted her thighs yet farther in mute encouragement as passion surged. She clasped his head, pressing it against her belly, her fingers raking through his hair. A wave of delight was building deep in her loins, swelling into a racing breaker. She bit down on her bottom lip, her fingers curling tightly in his hair as the wave crested and broke. She heard herself cry out. Her knees shook uncontrollably. Gideon stood up, holding her against him until she'd regained her balance.

"Oh," was all she could manage to say. "Oh."

He smiled down at her and kissed her damp forehead. "So passionate," he said softly, turning her towards the bed, taking the opportunity to run his eyes hungrily down her back, narrow and elegant, the nip of her waist, the flare of her hips, the curve of her backside, the long, clean sweep of her thighs.

Prudence fell on the bed, rolling onto her back, opening her arms to him. She was filled with an urgent need to share this pleasure with him. He knelt above her and she raised her legs, curling them around to press her heels into his buttocks. "Come," she demanded. *"Now."*

"At your service, madam," he said. "In just one second." She watched as he slipped a rubber sheath over his penis. Vaguely she wondered if he always carried them with him, but it seemed an irrelevant thought as he slid within her still-pulsating body and she tightened her inner muscles around him, glorying in the feeling as he filled her, pressing deep within her.

He looked down at her and she smiled up at him, her light green eyes alive with pleasure. "Don't move, sweet," he said. "I want to make this last, but I'm so close to the brink."

"You call the tune," she replied, stretching her arms way above her head in a gesture of abandonment that was so sensual, he inhaled sharply, clinging desperately to the last threads of self-control. He withdrew slowly, then as slowly sheathed himself within her again. She gasped, her eyes closing, her belly tightening as the wave began to build once more.

He withdrew again, closing his own eyes, holding himself on the very edge of her body, then with a soft cry he drove hard and deep to the very edge of her womb, and her body convulsed around him as his penis throbbed and pulsed within her.

He fell upon her with a groan, crushing her breasts so that she could feel the rapid beating of his heart, so close to her own. She clasped his sweat-slick back, lay still until her breathing slowed and her heartbeat returned to normal.

Gideon stirred and rolled off her. He lay on his back, one hand resting on her belly, the other flung above his head. "Jesus, Mary, and Joseph," he murmured. "You are miraculous, Miss Duncan."

"You're not so bad yourself, Sir Gideon," she returned with an effort. "Now I really won't die wondering."

He turned his head slowly to look at her. "What does that mean?"

She merely smiled and closed her eyes. She certainly knew now what had been missing in the past. And although she would never have admitted it to herself before, she had been just a little envious of Constance, who obviously found nothing missing in the realms of passion with Max. The smile was still on her face when she plunged into a deep and dreamless sleep.

She awoke an hour later to the sound of soft voices coming from the doorway. Lazily she propped herself on one elbow and looked towards the door. Gideon, in a dressing gown, was talking to someone in the corridor outside. She flopped back on the pillows, realizing that without disturbing her sleep Gideon had managed to pull back the covers and somehow insert her between the sheets.

The voices ceased and the door closed. Prudence struggled up against the pillows, holding the sheet up to her neck. "Where did the dressing gown come from?" It was a particularly elegant garment of brocaded silk and didn't look as if it formed part of the guest supplies of this hostelry.

"I brought it with me." He picked up the small valise that she now remembered noticing earlier.

"You mean you planned for this?" she demanded, not at all sure that she liked the idea that he had set out that morning completely prepared for seduction. Condom and all.

He shook his head. "You're so suspicious, my sweet. No, I did not plan for *this*. I've spent most of the day trying to overcome our mutual dislike. But I am a motoring enthusiast, as you probably realized."

"More of a fanatic, I would have said."

"Yes, well we won't quibble about the degree of my enthusiasm." He was opening the valise as he spoke. "However, as an experienced motorist, I know that even the most reliable vehicle can strand one in the most inconvenient circumstances on a long drive, so I'm always prepared." He took out a silk garment and shook out the folds. "This is for you."

He laid the garment on the bed. It was a dressing gown of emerald green Chinese silk, beautifully embroidered with deep blue peacocks.

Prudence fingered it. "It's lovely, but we have to go home straightaway."

"No," he said. "We have to have dinner straightaway. Roast duck, if you remember."

She pushed aside the covers, casting an agitated glance at the clock on the mantel. It was close to nine-thirty. "Gideon, I have to get back. My family will be worried out of their minds."

"No, they won't," he said with that calm assertive confidence that so often put her back up. Not this evening, though. "Milton knows the uncertainties of motoring, so he was not surprised to be told that if we had not returned by ten o'clock he should drive to Manchester Square and explain that we had been benighted and would return in the morning."

She stared at him, still with some degree of incomprehension. "But what about the morning? It's Monday, don't you have to go to work?"

"My first appointment is at noon. We'll leave early and we'll be back in plenty of time."

Prudence lay back again and pulled the covers up. "Is there any detail you've missed?"

"I don't believe so," he returned rather smugly. "I have hairbrush, toothbrush, tooth powder, and a nightgown for you. Although," he added, regarding her consideringly, "I doubt you'll need the latter."

"Perhaps not," she agreed. "If we're going to eat roast duck, shouldn't we dress and go downstairs?"

"No, we're going to eat in here. It seems like too much effort to go downstairs, and they want to close the dining room soon anyway."

"Ah." She fingered the dressing gown again. "Then I suppose I'll get up and put this on."

"That might be a good idea," he agreed. "The bathroom is right opposite. I don't think anyone else is staying on this corridor, so we don't have to share it."

Prudence put on the robe, tying the girdle at her waist tightly. "Did you say something about a hairbrush?"

"I did, but I'd like to do that myself. There's something about your hair that drives me wild." He came up to her, tilting her chin on his forefinger and kissing the corner of her mouth.

She merely smiled and padded barefoot to the door. The bathroom was small but contained the necessities: a claw-footed tub, a basin, and a water closet. Prudence began to draw a bath and while the water was running twisted her hair into a knot on top of her head and returned to the bedroom. "What happened to the hairpins?"

Gideon took a handful off the dresser and stuck them

judiciously into the piled mass. "Would you like company in the bath?"

"It's very small," she said doubtfully.

"We could wash each other's back."

"Irresistible." She reached up and caressed his cheek, observing with a smile, "You're stubbly."

"Five o'clock shadow," he said. "I usually shave in the evening as well as the morning."

"I rather like it," she said. "It adds a certain something... a *je ne sais quoi*. It gives you a more rugged look."

He bent and rubbed his cheek gently against hers. "You prefer rugged to smooth, then?"

"Depends," she said. "On circumstances. I must get the bath before it overflows."

He followed her into the bathroom, watching her cast aside the dressing gown, stand for a minute naked, aware of his gaze, offering herself to it, before she stepped into the bath.

"There really isn't enough room for two."

"Nonsense," he said, throwing off his own dressing gown and stepping into the bath at the opposite end. Water slurped over the edge as he struggled to sit down, drawing his knees up to his chin to fit.

Prudence pushed her feet under his backside and wriggled her toes. He grabbed her ankles and water cascaded over the edge of the bath onto the wooden floor.

"Stop that," he said, squeezing her ankles. "It'll leak through the floor to the ceiling below in a minute."

"I told you it was too small for two." She leaned against the back of the tub, still idly wriggling her toes against his nether parts.

Gideon heaved himself to his feet, sending a further

wave of water onto the floor, and stepped out. He grabbed a towel from the rail and threw it into the puddle to soak up the mess. "I'll shave instead," he said, returning to the bedroom for his razor and strop.

Prudence soaped herself lazily, enjoying the intimacy of their shared ablutions. It had a wonderfully sensual undercurrent, one that built on the glory of their earlier lovemaking, somehow solidified it, while creating a delicious surge of anticipation. Her toes curled and she moved the soapy washcloth to her thighs...and between them, idly visiting the sites of her earlier pleasure.

"Would you like some help there?"

The quiet voice made her jump, and her eyes, that she hadn't realized were closed, flew open. Gideon stood at the side of the bath, his own eyes darkened to a charcoal gray as they watched her.

"No, thank you," Prudence said with as much dignity as she could muster. "We've already proved the bath is no place for games."

He laughed and reached for a dry towel. He unfolded it and held it invitingly. "Out. Otherwise I'll begin to feel superfluous."

She stood up in a shower of drops and stepped out, trying to think of a snappy response to the statement and failing utterly. He wrapped the towel around her and then stepped into the bathwater.

Prudence dried herself vigorously, shrugged into the Chinese silk robe, and left him in the bath. In the bedroom she saw that a table had been set in front of the fire, with an already opened bottle of Pouilly-Fuissé, a basket of hot rolls, a dish of butter. She poured the wine into the two glasses and sat at the table, breaking open a roll, spreading butter thickly. Sex seemed to stimulate the appetite.

Gideon came back as she took the first sip of the wine. "Is it good?"

"Delicious. Haven't you tasted it?"

"No, but the landlord has made sure it's not corked." He took the seat opposite her. His hair was wet and Prudence noticed with some amusement that when wet it had a springly curl to it. It was rather frivolous, not at all suited to the fearsomely intimidating barrister she had first met.

A knock at the door heralded two waiters, who placed a three-tiered stand piled high with shellfish on the table. "Oysters, Sir Gideon, clams, cockles, shrimp, lobster claws, winkles, and smoked mussels," one of the waiters intoned, pointing with a fastidious forefinger as he listed the offerings.

"Thank you." Gideon nodded and the waiters faded from the room. He took a small pointed stick and selected a tiny shellfish. "These are quite delicious." He picked the minute winkle from its shell and passed Prudence the stick.

She popped the winkle into her mouth. Ordinarily she considered these tiny shellfish barely worth the trouble to extract, but now she realized what she had been missing. She nodded and took one for herself. She was beginning to learn that Gideon treated the business of food with utter seriousness. They ate their way through the tiers of shellfish with a dedicated concentration, punctuated by the occasional appreciative murmur and the odd remark, and when a waiter returned to clear their plates and the stripped-bare stand, they merely sat back, sipped wine, and nodded with satisfaction.

"I would never have put you down as such a thoroughgoing hedonist," Prudence said into the satisfied silence. "It doesn't go with being a barrister."

"Oh, now, there you're wrong, sweetheart," he said. "Barristers live as indulgently as the members of any other profession... and more than some. We have our own clubs, our own pubs, our own restaurants. We don't have much conversation, I'll grant you that. Mostly law talk, case discussions, but we do ease business along with the good things in life."

Prudence nodded, reflecting how easily the endearments slipped off his tongue. She liked them, they made her feel special and enhanced the sensuality of this interlude, but she was not used to them. Her father had never been one for demonstrative speech, and even her mother had used endearments sparingly. She didn't feel comfortable using them herself and wondered if Gideon would notice that she only used his name. But perhaps he would notice the different tone she had now when she spoke his name. Her tongue rolled the syllables around as she took the last sip of her wine.

Roast duck appeared, with orange sauce, succulent green beans, crispy roasted potatoes. A bottle of Nuits-St. Georges was opened, the waiters faded away once more. Gideon took the tip of his knife and slid it beneath the crispy skin of the bird. He sliced upwards and then took his fork to spear the golden brown paper-thin skin.

He leaned over, holding the fork to her lips. "Greater dedication hath no barrister than to give the best morsel of a roast Aylesbury duckling to his client."

Chapter 14

Gideon was awakened in the morning by the slither of a soft body across his recumbent form, by lips pressed into the hollow of his throat. He didn't open his eyes and he didn't move as Prudence covered his face with tiny butterfly kisses, his eyelids, his nose, his cheekbones, the corners of his mouth, the cleft of his chin.

"Don't pretend you're asleep," she murmured between darting flicks of her tongue into that fascinating cleft. "I can feel that the most important part of you is wide awake." She moved her lower body over his in emphasis.

Gideon stroked down the length of her back as she lay long upon him, languidly caressed her bottom. "My mind, like the notable Oxford scholar's, is generally considered to be the most important part of me," he murmured into the fragrant mass of russet hair.

Prudence chuckled. "That depends on the circumstances. Right now, I have to tell you that your mind is of not the slightest interest to me. This is." She moved a hand down, slipping it beneath her to grasp the jutting evidence of his wakefulness. "I'm wondering if it's possible to do it like this."

"Certainly it is." The languid note in his voice was fading fast. "Move back and raise yourself just a little."

"Like this?"

"Just like that." With a leisurely twist of his hips he entered her as she hung above him.

"Oh, this is quite different," Prudence said, sounding rather surprised.

"There are an infinite number of ways to enjoy each other," he said. "Don't tell me you haven't read the Kama Sutra, because I wouldn't believe it."

"We have read it, of course, but some of those positions looked completely impossible, not to mention tortuously uncomfortable." She pushed back onto her knees, circling her hips slowly around his penis buried deep within her. "Have you tried them all?"

"No. I've never found a partner willing to entertain the idea." He clasped her hips, pressing his thumbs into the pointy hipbones. "Lean forward just a tiny bit . . . ah, that's good." He smiled, lifting his hips rhythmically as she pressed the cleft of her body against his belly, rising and falling with him.

He watched her face; her eyes were closed, and he said softly, "Open your eyes. I want to see where you are."

She opened her eyes, fixing her gaze on his. He watched for the deepening glow in the light green depths, the spark of excitement as her pleasure grew closer to its climax, and when he saw it he touched her sex lightly with his fingertips. Her eyes widened and he thrust upwards, holding her bottom with his free hand, pressing her down hard upon him. Then, with a swift, deft movement just as she cried out in delight, he rolled her sideways to the bed, disengaging the instant before he allowed his own climax to rip through him.

Prudence felt the orgasmic shudders quiver through her body for several minutes. Her body was a weightless mass of delicious, languorous sensation, her muscles utterly powerless, her loins drained. She turned on her side, resting her head in the damp hollow of his shoulder as he lay on his back. With an effort, he reached a hand to brush strands of damp hair that were stuck to her cheek. Then his hand fell limply to her flank.

"I wonder if one could ever have too much of this good thing," Prudence murmured when she could speak. She calculated that since eight o'clock last evening they had made love four times, and judging by the light in the window, it was only just past dawn.

"Not I," he said.

"Nor I," she agreed with a complacent chuckle.

"Unfortunately, or perhaps fortunately, daily life makes other demands," Gideon said, sitting up with a groan of exertion. "We have to get on the road and get you home before your family calls out the police."

"You said they would have a message." Prudence forced her own muscles into action, struggling up against the pillows.

"They will have, but they're still going to want to see you alive and well before the morning's too much advanced," he pointed out, swinging his legs to the floor. "Shall I run your bath?"

"Please." She leaned back, exhausted by the simple effort of getting herself semiupright, and closed her eyes again. Soon she heard the sound of water running and her mind woke up to full consciousness. *Where were they to go from here?* It had been the most wonderful night, full of transcendent delights. But now what?

Almost as if he read her thoughts, Gideon reappeared. "Prudence, your bath is drawn. Get up now. We have to get moving."

Her eyes shot open and she looked at him, startled by the imperative tone. During the long hours of their loving she had forgotten that he had that tone—assertive, authoritative, impatient. Now she caught herself wondering if perhaps this manifestation was his normal self and the soft, tender lover who issued only endearments in the exciting, sensual richness of the words of loveplay was an occasional visitor.

"I'm up," she said, getting off the bed and reaching for the dressing gown. She brushed past him in the doorway and went into the bathroom. She wondered fleetingly if he would follow her, but was not surprised that he didn't. The idyll was definitely over, and reality had once more reared its demanding head.

She performed her morning ablutions quickly and returned to the bedroom. Gideon was dressed once more, and even though he was wearing the casual morning dress suitable for weekend, it was clear he had reverted to his former physical self. The charming disorder of his curly hair had been tamed, he was clean-shaven, even his posture had somehow straightened, become more rigid. He was the barrister again, utterly in control, utterly sure of himself and his superiority.

Prudence went to the dresser and grimaced at the state of her hair. It was a wild tangle that she knew would take ages to return to order. She sat down on the small stool and picked up the hairbrush, dragging it through knotted strands.

"Let me." He stood behind her, reaching over her shoulder for the brush.

She relinquished it, observing, "Since you're responsible for this mess."

The gray eyes gleamed and she caught a glimpse of the lover. "Not entirely responsible," he demurred, putting his hand on the top of her head and pulling the brush down with resolute strength. "Sorry," he offered at her wince of pain. "Is there a gentler way of doing this?"

"No. Just do your worst." She squeezed her watering eyes tightly shut, bent her head, and let him get on with it.

He laid the brush down after five minutes of tugging and pulling. "There. I think that's the best I can do."

Prudence opened her eyes and combed her fingers through the now relatively straight mane. "I'll manage from here."

"Right." He went to the door. "I'll order breakfast in the coffee room. Can you be ready in ten minutes?"

"In a pinch," she said dryly.

"Put the robe and everything else in the valise when you've finished with them. I'll send a boy up to take it to the motor."

Prudence, coiling and pinning her hair, nodded, and he went out, his step energetic, and she could fancy there was an almost military click to his heels. She dressed quickly—trying not to think of those moments when she had undressed—and packed the valise, reflecting as she closed it and snapped the locks that there was something symbolic about this putting away and closing up. It was a neat tidying up of a delightfully untidy idyll. She glanced once around the room before leaving it. Nothing was out of place, apart from the wildly tumbled bed, where the sheets and coverlets straggled to the floor. Her eye caught a couple of hairpins on the floor and she remembered how Gideon had drawn them out. With a quick shake of her head, she left and hurried downstairs.

Gideon was reading the newspaper when she came into the coffee room. He rose politely as she sat down. "Newspaper? I ordered two." He handed her a neatly folded copy of the *Times*.

Prudence couldn't help a smile. This was a man who did not like breakfast conversation. She poured tea, buttered a piece of toast, and opened her own newspaper, offering her companion no distraction from his paper or plate of kidneys and bacon.

Then they were once more in the motor, driving through the quiet early morning streets of Henley. A few shopkeepers were opening up, but there were few customers as yet. Prudence had again donned her furs and tucked her hands into her muff. Conversationally, she opened a subject that had aroused her curiosity. "Gideon, this morning we didn't use a condom, but you withdrew at the last minute. Is that uncomfortable for you?"

He shrugged. "Neither method is ideal from a man's point of view, but the possible consequences of ignoring precautions don't bear thinking of."

"Ah." Prudence absorbed this. Her fingers closed over her little notebook. He'd given her entrée into another issue. "Would you want more children . . . in the right circumstances, I mean?"

"Do you want children, Prudence?" he asked, casting

her a quick glance, but she couldn't really see his expression behind the visor and goggles.

"I asked *you*. If you were going to get married again, I mean."

He gave her a look of pure disbelief. "You've put your hands on that notebook again, haven't you?"

She felt herself flush slightly. "I just thought I'd ask since the subject had come up."

"We have just spent a night of fairly ecstatic lovemaking and you've now turned your attention to finding me a bride?" he demanded. "I don't believe this, Prudence. It's so utterly inappropriate."

"No, it isn't," she said firmly. "You said last night that there would be no confusion. We are each other's client. I expect you to do your best for me, and I will do my best for you. We agreed you would like a bride young enough to give you another child, but we didn't actually talk about whether you would want one. Obviously, if you don't I can't introduce you to a woman who's desperate to have children." She turned to look at him. "Be reasonable, Gideon, you can see that."

He stared straight ahead at the winding road and declared through thinned lips, "I don't want to have this conversation."

"You have your head in the sand," she said, throwing up her hands. "How can I do my job when you won't respond?"

Gideon only shook his head.

"All right," Prudence said, "we'll stop talking about possible brides for the moment. But surely you don't mind thinking about some factors. Would Sarah like a ready-made sibling, do you think?"

"I thought we'd put Agnes Hargate to rest."

Prudence ignored the acid tone. "I'm not talking specifics here. I'm trying to establish some parameters. You must have an opinion, surely."

Gideon, against his will, found himself considering the question. He realized he had no idea what Sarah would think about a stepmother, let alone a half sibling. Let alone a stepsibling. "I don't know," he said finally. "I'd have to ask her."

With what she recognized was now personal curiosity, Prudence asked, "How would you feel if a potential bride had, say, an illegitimate child?"

That piqued his interest. "Do you know anyone in that situation?"

She didn't, of course. Women in the circles they would be considering did not have, or at least own to having, illegitimate children. "None that would acknowledge it."

"Then why ask?"

She'd asked because she wanted to know which was the real Gideon Malvern. He cultivated the appearance of conventionality, lack of flexibility, lack of sympathy for those who didn't quite meet his standards, and yet she had seen beneath that surface, seen that he could be quite the opposite, embracing the unorthodox, open to change. But was that the right way round? Maybe the open, unorthodox side of him was an appearance to create a certain response, and the real Gideon was the rigid and aggressive barrister, with no time or sympathy for anyone who didn't play by his rules. Her own peace of mind seemed to rest on the answer to the conundrum.

"Well," she said thoughtfully, resorting once more to the lighthearted tenor of their earlier conversations, "we do know that you would like to meet a future partner who's willing to explore the delights of the Kama Sutra."

"I'm certainly willing to give some of the less extreme positions a try," he said, turning to look at her fully. And now he was smiling. "What's the point of all this, Prudence?"

"I am trying to find you a suitable wife."

"Maybe that's something I would prefer to do for myself."

"You agreed to the terms."

"I agreed to let you try."

"And I am trying. By the way, you're about to run over a farm cart," she observed. "I'm sure you're supposed to keep your eyes on the road when driving."

Gideon swore as he wrenched the wheel to the side just in time to avoid a stolid horse pulling a cart piled with manure, driven by an old man smoking a pungent pipe that was nevertheless insufficient to combat the powerful odor from the cart.

"That would have been a messy experience," Prudence said when they were clear.

"Why don't you just enjoy the scenery and let me concentrate?" He sounded as annoyed as he looked. Prudence thought of his wet socks and bit back a smile. Gideon was not a man who liked to make mistakes.

"Very well," she agreed amiably. "I'm a little short of sleep, as it happens." She huddled into her coat, drawing up the collar, and closed her eyes behind the goggles.

She had not expected to sleep but she came to with a groggy start when the engine stopped, and saw that they were outside the house on Manchester Square. "I slept all that way."

"You did," he agreed, coming around to open the door for her. "Snoring peacefully."

"I do not snore." She stepped onto the curb.

"How would you know?"

"I'll tell you something, Gideon, this habit you have of conversing in combative questions grows irksome," she declared. "It might serve you well in a courtroom, but it's annoying and uncomfortable in a social conversation." She removed her goggles and tossed them onto the seat she had vacated.

He pushed his goggles up over his visor. "Does it occur to you that I might find your way of conversing in distinctly personal questions just a little irksome?"

"I was only doing my job," Prudence declared. Then she shook her head in a little gesture of resignation. "I think we're disliking each other again."

"So it would seem," he agreed. "I imagine it will go in cycles." He put a finger on the tip of her nose, raising his eyebrows.

"Maybe so," she said, aware of a softness in her voice that she hadn't intended, but he was disarming her now, showing her the other side of Gideon Malvern. "Maybe so," she said again, "but you provoke those reactions, Gideon. I'm generally a peaceable, easygoing person. Ask my sisters."

"I don't think I'll bother. I'm sure they'll back you to the hilt. Instead, I'll concentrate on the memory of the wildly passionate lover whenever you become quarrelsome, and then I won't be tempted to respond in like fashion." He bent and kissed the tip of her nose and then the corner of her mouth. "Find me some accurate records of Lord Duncan's dealings with Barclay, Prudence. I can't do anything without them. And come to my chambers tomorrow afternoon, after five. We'll talk about how to present you in court and what impressions you have to avoid giving." He gave her a wave before she could respond, and turned back to the motor.

Prudence hesitated, words tumbling in her head, but none of them seemed adequate. One minute he was kissing her and calling her sweetheart, the next issuing brusque instructions. She waited until he had disappeared around the corner of the square and then went up the stairs to the front door.

Jenkins opened the door as she inserted her key in the lock. "Miss Prue, what happened?" He couldn't hide his concern.

"Prue, is that you?" Chastity appeared at the head of the stairs. "Did you have an accident. Are you all right?"

"No, no accident, and yes, I'm all right, love." Prudence swiftly climbed the stairs. "Motors have a habit of breaking down. We spent the night at an inn in Henley." She gave her sister a quick kiss as she hurried past her. "I have to change my clothes, Chas. They're the same ones I wore all day yesterday."

"Yes," Chastity agreed. "Did you sleep in them?"

There was something in the question that caused Prudence to stop on her way to her room. She turned slowly. Chastity was regarding her with her head tilted to the side, a slight smile on her lips.

"No," Prudence said. "I didn't."

"So, what did you sleep in?"

"If I told you the inn had spare nightgowns for benighted guests, would you believe me?" Prudence was aware now that her own lips were curving.

"Not a bit of it," Chastity said. "Are you going to spill the beans?"

"Of course." Prudence laughed. "Come and help me wash my hair. It's a mess."

She had told Chastity the whole and was sitting by the parlor fire drying her hair in a towel when Constance came in. "You're back. Thank goodness. I was quite worried when I got Chas's message last night. What happened?"

"Oh, Prue had an impulse to which she yielded, and it seems to have led to a night of unbridled passion in Henley-on-Thames," Chastity said with an airy wave.

Prudence emerged from the tent of the towel. "In a nutshell."

"That's quite a nutshell." Constance perched on the arm of the sofa. "Is he a good lover?"

Prudence felt herself blush. "I didn't have much to compare him with," she said. "But I can't imagine how the night could have been better."

Constance grinned. "That sounds fairly definitive," she said. "The question, though, is how does this—"

"Affect our business dealings with the barrister?" Prudence interrupted. "I know, Con. And don't think I haven't considered it. But I really don't believe it will make one iota of difference. Sir Gideon Malvern, KC, is not the same person I spent such a wonderfully crazy night with. He reverts with surprising ease." She picked up her hairbrush and began to brush her still-damp hair with vigorous strokes.

"That's good, isn't it?" Chastity asked doubtfully.

"Of course it is," Prudence declared, smothering her own doubts. "And on the subject of business, he's adamant that that note from Barclay isn't sufficient for him to base a case on." She sighed a little. "So, it seems there's nothing for it. I'll have to go to Hoare's first thing tomorrow morning. It's too late today."

"I thought we'd already agreed on that plan," Chastity said, throwing another shovel of coal on the fire.

"I know, but I had a smidgeon of hope that we could avoid it."

Constance shook her head. "We're in too deep for regrets now, Prue. Did Chas tell you what I've been doing this morning?"

"No, I haven't had a chance," Chastity said. "I had to stay here for you, Prue, so Con went out alone to see if she could discover whether anyone had been snooping around." She looked worriedly at her eldest sister. "Was there anything, Con?"

The sisters' lightheartedness of a moment earlier was now quite dissipated. "Tell us," Prudence said. She knew instinctively that they were going to hear nothing good.

Constance paced to the window and back again. "As we agreed, I went to some of the main outlets we use, Helene's Milliners, Robert's of Piccadilly, a few others. I tried to make it seem we were doing the usual rounds to see how many copies they had sold of last week's issue."

She paused, and her sisters waited. "Every one of them said other people had been asking questions about how the broadsheet was delivered to them, who checked on supplies, took orders, collected the money."

"Detectives," Prudence said flatly. "Employed by Barclay's solicitors. Gideon was right."

Constance nodded. "Of course, no one knows who we are, we're simply representatives of *The Mayfair Lady*. We're always veiled, and nothing can be traced to this address. But I'm thinking we should hold next week's issue."

"Not publish?" It was a concept so foreign to the sisters that Chastity's exclamation came as no surprise to the other two.

"Maybe we should cease to publish until after the court case," Constance said reluctantly.

"But that's giving in to them," Chastity said, her mouth set with unusual firmness. "I think it should be a last resort."

"What about Mrs. Beedle? They're bound to have followed up on the poste restante address," Prudence said with a worried frown. "She wouldn't betray us, but we can't have her harried."

"One of us should go there tomorrow and talk to her," Constance said.

"I can't." Prudence stood up, shaking out her hair. "I have to go to the bank. One of you will have to go."

"I will," Chastity volunteered.

"I don't suppose during your night of unbridled passion you had a chance to advance our search for a bride for the barrister?" Constance regarded her middle sister with the hint of a raised eyebrow.

"I did try," Prudence said. "He won't have anything to do with Agnes or Lavender. Quite adamant he was on that score."

"But he hasn't even met them," Chastity protested.

"I don't think that matters a whit to him. To be brutally frank, I don't think his heart is in this bargain."

"Then why did he agree to it?" Constance demanded.

Prudence shrugged. "I think he thought it was a joke, something he didn't have to take seriously."

Her sisters looked at her thoughtfully. "Of course,

matters might be a little more complicated now," Constance observed. "One lover finding the ideal bride for the other. A situation almost perverse, one might say."

"One might," Prudence said aridly.

"In fact," her elder sister continued with a speculative air, "one might wonder if *your* heart is still in the search."

"I assure you that my heart is as much in it as it ever was," Prudence declared with asperity. "A brief fling with a client does not have to affect one's objectivity."

"No," Constance agreed. "Of course it doesn't. A brief fling, that is."

Chapter 15

Prudence stood outside the narrow entrance to Hoare's Bank in a steady drizzle. She was nerving herself to go in when the glass door opened and the liveried doorman emerged, holding up a big umbrella. He bowed and came towards her. "Are you coming into the bank, madam?"

"Yes," she said. "I'd like a word with Mr. Fitchley if he's in today."

"He certainly is, madam." The doorman held the umbrella high as she took down her own, shaking the drops off. He escorted her into the hushed interior of the bank, where everyone for some reason that Prudence had never been able to fathom spoke in undertones.

"The lady is for Mr. Fitchley," the doorman said almost behind his hand to an elderly, hovering clerk.

The clerk recognized the visitor without difficulty. It was sufficiently unusual for women to transact financial business for themselves to make Miss Duncan a distinctive client. "Good morning, Miss Duncan. I'll tell Mr. Fitchley you're here." Prudence smiled her thanks. She sat down on a straight-backed velvet-cushioned chair, holding her handbag in her lap, and hoped she didn't look too self-conscious. The silently busy clerks and cashiers in their cubbyholes cast her barely a glance, but she could feel her guilt radiating from every pore.

Mr. Fitchley himself came out of his office to greet her. "Miss Duncan, good morning. This is a pleasure. Do come in, come in." He waved expansively towards his office.

"Good morning, Mr. Fitchley. A rather wet one, I'm afraid." She offered another smile as she went past him into the sanctum. It was a small, dark room with a smoldering coal fire in the grate.

"Pray have a seat." The bank manager gestured to a chair in front of the desk, where not a scrap of paper was to be seen. He folded his hands on the immaculate surface and said with a smile, "What can we do for you this morning, Miss Duncan?"

Prudence opened her handbag and took out the envelope containing the letter of authorization. Her fingers were not quite steady as she turned it over so that the earl's official seal was immediately visible. "I need to examine Lord Duncan's bank records, Mr. Fitchley. I realize it's unusual, but my father has some concerns about some past transactions. He would like me to look into them." She leaned forward and laid the envelope in front of the banker.

Mr. Fitchley put on a pince-nez and lifted the envelope. He turned it over in his hands several times. "I trust Lord Duncan's concerns have nothing to do with the service Hoare's Bank has provided. The earl's family has banked with us for four generations."

Prudence made haste to reassure him. "No, of course

not. It's just that he wants to refresh his memory on some transactions that took place about four or five years ago." She offered a self-deprecating smile. "As you know, Mr. Fitchley, I tend to manage the financial affairs of the household. My father has little time to spare for such chores."

The bank manager nodded. "Yes, your late mother, dear Lady Duncan, used to tell me the same thing." He took up a paper knife and slit the envelope, unfolding the crisp, headed vellum. He read it very carefully—almost, Prudence thought, as if he would memorize every duplicitous word. Then he laid it down on the desk, smoothing it with the palm of one soft, white hand.

"Well, that seems to be in order, Miss Duncan. If you'd like to follow me . . . we have a private office where clients may examine their effects without disturbance." He rose from his desk and led the way into the main room. Prudence followed him across the marble-tiled expanse, past the cubbyholes where diligent workers kept their eyes on their desks as the manager walked by. He opened a door and stood aside for Prudence to enter a rather cell-like room, furnished with a table and chair. Gray light came from a small window.

"A little chilly, I'm afraid," he said. "We don't keep a fire in here unless a client has made a previous arrangement to come in."

"I'm sorry . . . I should have done, of course. But this came up rather suddenly," Prudence said.

"That's quite all right, Miss Duncan. If you'd like to make yourself comfortable, I'll have a clerk bring you the ledgers. Will you be wanting the safe-deposit box as well?"

"Yes, please."

The bank manager bowed himself out, closing the door behind him. Prudence shivered in the damp chill and paced the small space from wall to wall. Within ten minutes the door opened again and a clerk came in with an armful of ledgers, followed by another with a locked box. They set these on the table. "Should I light the gas, madam?" the first clerk asked.

"Yes, please." Prudence took the key that lay on top of the box and slipped it into the lock. The gas flared, casting at least the illusion of a warm and cheerful glow over the cheerless room.

"Would you care for coffee, madam?"

"Yes, that would be lovely, thank you."

They left the cell and she sat down at the table, lifting the lid of the box. She had the feeling that if her father had anything he wanted kept secret he would put it under lock and key, not leave it in an open ledger. The box contained only a sheaf of papers. She took them out just as the clerk returned with a tray of coffee and some rather stale-looking digestive biscuits, which he set down beside her. She smiled her thanks and waited until he'd retired, closing the door once more, then she spread the papers on the desk.

Her parents' marriage certificate; the sisters' birth certificates; her mother's death certificate; her mother's will; her father's will. None of these interested her. She knew that her mother's small estate had all been spent on *The Mayfair Lady*. It hadn't occurred to Lady Duncan to charge for the publication, so her own money had kept it afloat. Lord Duncan's will was straightforward . . . everything to be divided equally among his three daughters. Not that there was anything, really, other than debt, to pass along, she reflected, without rancor. Maintaining the country house in Hampshire, with its tenants' cottages and dependencies, together with the house and staff in London, would take up whatever small revenues the country estate brought in. But that was the way it was now, so they were quite used to that. She returned the papers to the box as she looked them over and then she came to the last one.

She stared at it, feeling suddenly queasy, for a moment unable to believe what she was reading. It was a legal document. A lien on the house on Manchester Square. The house that had been owned by the Duncan family since the time of Queen Anne. She looked at the document blankly. Took a sip of coffee. Looked at it again. It was dated April 7, 1903. And the lien was held by a company called Barclay Earl and Associates.

It didn't take a brilliant mind to make the connection. The earl of Barclay held a lien on 10 Manchester Square. A house that had never in all its history had so much as a mortgage against it, at least to Prudence's knowledge. A slow burn of anger grew in her throat. *Why?* What on earth could have possessed her father to hand over the house that was his inheritance, his pride, his family's pride?

Desperation.

There was no other explanation. There could not be another explanation.

Prudence dropped the document into the box as if it was something vile. She found the ledger for 1903. The payments started in January . . . payments to Barclay Earl and Associates. Every month the sum of one thousand pounds. And then in April they stopped. But in April Lord Duncan had given Barclay a lien on his London house. No longer able to make the payments that he had presumably contracted to make, he had done the only possible thing.

She took up the ledger for the previous year. The payments started in October. But there was nothing to say what they were for. Was her father being blackmailed by Barclay? No, that was too absurd. The two men were fast friends, or at least Lord Duncan certainly seemed to think they were.

She reached into her handbag for the note from Barclay that they had found among the papers in the library. Payments . . . schedules . . . interest. She went back to the safe-deposit box, and there she found it, tucked into a slit that formed a pocket in the lining. October 5, 1902, a few weeks before his wife's death, while she lay in the agony he could not endure to see, Lord Arthur Duncan had agreed to finance a project to build a trans-Saharan railroad. He would make payments of one thousand pounds a month to Barclay Earl and Associates, who would manage the project.

And when he could no longer make those payments, he had accepted a lien on his house. She slid her hand into the pocket again. There was another sheet of paper. Half a sheet, rolled thin as a cigarette, as if the recipient hadn't been able to bear reading it. When she unrolled it, Prudence understood why.

My dear Duncan,

So sorry to bring bad news. But it's a bad business. Trouble with the Mahdi again, and people still remember the spot of bother with Gordon in Khartoum. Unfortunately, no one seems too keen on our little project at present. The rolling stock is in place, our people are set to start work. But the backers have decided to renege on our agreement. Political concerns, don't you know. We're all in the hole to the tune of a hundred thousand pounds. Just to reassure you, we won't be taking up the lien unless matters become desperate.

Barclay

Presumably, they had not yet become desperate, Prudence reflected. There was no way her father could have resumed making thousand-pound payments out of the household budget without her knowing. So the lien hung there, the veritable sword of Damocles. Her father must be in torment. And yet he was prepared to stand up in court as a character witness for this thief, this charlatan, this out-and-out villain?

It was beyond her imagining. She could understand how a man unhinged by grief could make unbalanced decisions, but her mother had been dead for almost four years. Surely their father had regained sufficient control of his senses to see what had been done to him.

Prudence sat back in her hard chair, drumming the tip of her pencil on the table. Pride would keep Arthur Duncan from admitting his mistakes or confronting the man who had fooled him. Pride would keep his head firmly buried in a dune in the Sahara.

She sat up straight again. Whatever their father's present state of mind, they did now have something to bolster their accusations of financial shenanigans. They needed to investigate the credentials of Barclay Earl and Associates. Did it exist as a legitimate entity? Had it ever? The whole idea of a railway across the Sahara had always been absurd. At least to people not crazed by grief, she amended. But to make their case, they would have to prove that it had been fraudulent from the start. That Lord Duncan had been inveigled into investing in a fraud. Investing so deeply that he handed over the family property when he couldn't meet his payments.

Prudence, no longer in the least guilty, calmly removed all the relevant papers from the box and the relevant pages from the ledger and put them in her handbag. Gideon would know whom they could use to look into the credentials of Barclay Earl and Associates. There must be a registry of companies somewhere. She swallowed the last of her coffee, relocked the safe-deposit box, tidied the ledgers, and left the cell. A clerk escorted her to the door and she went out into the rain, putting up her umbrella with a satisfying snap.

Chastity stood at the corner of the small street outside an ironmonger's and looked across at Mrs. Beedle's shop. It had been ten minutes since the man in the homburg and rather shabby mackintosh had set the doorbell tinkling on his way inside.

It was drizzling and she was both well protected and relatively invisible in a Burberry raincoat, a waterproof hat with a half veil, and a large umbrella. She had strolled down the street once since he'd gone in, but hadn't been able to see into the shop from the opposite pavement and was reluctant to cross over and risk drawing attention to herself.

The door of the corner shop opened and Chastity turned to look in the window of the ironmonger's, feigning interest in the display of cast-iron kettles. She glanced over her shoulder and saw the man in the homburg stroll down the street in the direction of the bus stop. Mrs. Beedle's shop was visible from the bus stop, and Chastity decided she couldn't risk going in to the shop until the man had boarded his bus . . . but since she couldn't stand in the open street for any length of time either without causing remark, she went into the ironmonger's, shaking out her umbrella.

A man in a baize apron emerged from the back at the sound of the bell over the door. "Mornin', madam. What can I do you for?" He surveyed her with an acquisitive gleam in his eye. Run-of-the-mill customers in this part of Kensington could not in general afford Burberry raincoats. His mind ran over the more expensive range of goods he could show her.

Chastity thought rapidly. "A flatiron," she said. "I need a flatiron."

"I've got just the thing for you, madam. Cast iron; nice, even surface. Heats up in a jiffy. Your laundry maid will love it." He hurried into the back, and Chastity stood at the window, craning her neck to see if the man wearing the homburg had left the bus stop as yet. She had no desire to burden herself with a heavy piece of totally unnecessary and probably expensive cast iron, but she couldn't leave if he was still there.

She couldn't see the bus stop, so she opened the door and peered into the street. At the sound of the bell, the ironmonger came rushing out from the back, afraid he'd lost his customer. Chastity saw the horse-drawn omnibus round the far corner of the street, and the man climbed aboard.

"Here's the iron, madam," the ironmonger said behind her. "Just the thing."

"Oh, yes." Chastity turned. "Actually, I think I'll send the laundry maid instead. Since she'll be using it, she might as well choose what she'd like. Expect to see her this afternoon." With a smile from beneath her veil, she whisked out of the shop, leaving the disconsolate ironmonger holding the flatiron.

The bus passed her as she waited to cross the street, and once it had lumbered around the corner, she darted across to Mrs. Beedle's shop.

"Why, is that you, Miss Chas?" Mrs. Beedle looked up from the counter, where she was refilling a large glass jar with peppermint humbugs. "You just missed a man asking after you. Second time he's been."

Chastity propped her umbrella against the door and put up her veil. "Did he say who he was? What did he want?"

Mrs. Beedle knitted her brow. "Wouldn't really say who he was, just that he was interested in talking to someone from *The Mayfair Lady,* and did I know where to find you. He said something about having some good news for you." She shook her head and resumed her task. "Didn't like the look of him . . . something didn't smell right."

"So, you didn't tell him anything?"

The woman looked up. "Now, Miss Chas, you know better than that. I told him I don't know nothing. I just receive the letters that come in the post."

"But he must have asked who picked them up?" Chastity was still anxious, even though she knew that by pressing she could offend Mrs. Beedle.

"Aye, he did. And I told him a boy comes every Sunday. Don't know his name, don't know nothing about him. None of my business. That's what I said, both times." She screwed the lid firmly back on the jar and wiped her hands on her apron. "You look as if you could do with a nice cup of tea, Miss Chas. Come on in the back." She lifted a hinged piece of countertop so her visitor could get behind.

"Thank you," Chastity said, dropping the top in place before following her hostess through a curtain into the cheerful kitchen beyond. "I didn't mean to imply anything, Mrs. Beedle, it's just that we're very anxious at the moment."

"Aye, m'dear, I'm sure you must be." She poured boiling water into the teapot. "We'll let that mash for a minute or two." She opened a cake tin and placed bath buns on a flowered plate that she set on the table, where Chastity had taken a seat. "Have one of those, Miss Chas. Made fresh this morning."

Chastity took one with unfeigned enthusiasm. "We think they hired detectives," she said. "They're snooping everywhere and our barrister says they'll be very determined to discover who we are, so they'll just keep coming back."

"Well, they won't hear nothing different from me," Mrs. Beedle declared, pouring tea. "Drink that down now. It'll keep out the damp." She set the cup of strong brew in front of Chastity. "Strange weather we're having. Yesterday it was almost like spring. And now look at it."

Chastity agreed, sipped her tea, nibbled her bun. "Is there any post for *The Mayfair Lady* today?"

"Just a couple." Mrs. Beedle reached up to a shelf and took down two envelopes. She handed them to her visitor, who after a cursory glance tucked them into her handbag.

"Now, don't you be worrying about these detective

folk, Miss Chas. They'll not discover nothing from me, and no one else knows about you. Apart from our Jenkins, of course." Mrs. Beedle always referred to her brother by his working title.

"And Mrs. Hudson," Chastity said. "But you're right, Mrs. Beedle. We know our secret's as safe as the grave with all of you. And we're so grateful to you."

"Nonsense, m'dear. We'd have done the same for your sainted mother, God rest her soul."

Chastity smiled, and drank her tea. The shop bell rang and Mrs. Beedle hastened through the curtain to greet her customer. Idly, Chastity listened to the conversation as she took another bath bun. A pleasant male voice with the hint of an accent that she thought was Scottish greeted Mrs. Beedle by name.

"Good morning, Dr. Farrell," the shopkeeper replied with a genuine note of welcome in her voice. "And what a wet one it is."

"Indeed it is, Mrs. Beedle. I'll take a pound of humbugs, and another of licorice sticks, if you please."

"Right you are, Doctor," Mrs. Beedle said. Chastity heard her opening jars, shaking sweets into the scales. Who would buy a pound of humbugs and a pound of licorice? Curious, she set down her teacup and walked softly to the curtain. She twitched aside a corner and peered behind. A tall man was leaning against the counter. His shoulders were as broad as a wrestler's, she thought. He had a rather rugged countenance, with the skewed nose that indicated it had once been broken. Oddly, rather than marring his face it seemed to enhance it, Chastity thought with a somewhat detached interest in her own observations. He was hatless and his wet hair clung to his scalp in a springy mass of black curls. He wore a mackintosh that had clearly seen better days, but he had the most delightful smile.

He turned from the counter as Mrs. Beedle weighed the sweets, and strolled to the magazine rack. He was a very big man, Chastity noted. Not fat at all, but all brawn. He made her feel quite small and delicate. As she watched, he picked up a copy of *The Mayfair Lady* and flicked through its pages. Something made him stop to read more closely.

"All ready, Dr. Farrell. That'll be sixpence for the humbugs and fourpence for the licorice."

"Oh, and I'll take this too, Mrs. Beedle." He laid the copy of *The Mayfair Lady* on the counter and counted out change from his pocket.

Chastity waited until he had left, setting the bell ringing vigorously, his vital step seeming to exude energy. She returned quickly to the kitchen table.

Mrs. Beedle bustled back behind the curtain. "Such a nice man, that Dr. Farrell. Hasn't been in the neighborhood long."

"Does he have a surgery around here?" Chastity inquired casually, setting down her teacup and preparing to take her leave.

"Just off St. Mary Abbot's," Mrs. Beedle said. "Bit of a rough part of town for a gentleman like Dr. Farrell to be practicing, if you ask me." She began to clear the table as she talked. "But our Dr. Farrell can take of himself, I reckon. Told me once he used to wrestle for the university. Oh, and box too." She shook her head, clucking admiringly as she put the cups in the sink.

Now why would such a man be interested in reading The Mayfair Lady? Chastity took her leave, pondering the question.

She walked to Kensington High Street and hailed a hackney, unwilling to face the damp crowds and steamed-up windows of the omnibus. She hadn't needed reassurance that Mrs. Beedle would keep their secret if she could, but the persistence of the earl's solicitors didn't bode well. They were clever; there was no knowing what devious tricks they would use to trap the unwary. Mrs. Beedle was a good, honest woman, but she would be no match for the conniving of an unscrupulous and sophisticated detective agency.

Chastity reached home just as a rain-soaked gust of wind blew across the square, almost turning her umbrella inside out. "Miserable day," she said to Jenkins as she entered the hall. "Is Prue back yet?"

"Not as yet, Miss Chas." He took the umbrella from her.

Chastity unpinned her hat, shaking out the veil. "Mrs. Beedle sends her best regards, Jenkins." She took off her mackintosh, handing it to the butler. "I'll be in the parlor when Prue gets home."

Jenkins bowed and went to dispose of the rain-drenched garments. He heard Prudence let herself into the house a few minutes later and with stately gait retraced his steps to the hall.

Prudence greeted him rather distractedly. The documents in her handbag seemed to have acquired some kind of physical weight on her journey home. All the familiarity of the hall in which she stood gently dripping seemed to waver, to take on some strange patina. Because, of course, this hall no longer legally belonged to the Duncan family unless her father could discharge his debt. *Or prove that debt fraudulent.*

"You look a little pale, Miss Prue. Is everything all right?"

Jenkins's disturbed tone brought her out of her reverie. "Yes," she said. "Quite all right. Just wet." She managed an effortful smile as she relinquished her outer garments. "Any messages?"

"A telephone call from Sir Gideon, Miss Prue."

Prudence was aware of a surge of adrenaline, a rush of pure physical excitement that, however momentarily, chased all else from her mind. "What was the message?" she managed to ask, busily unpinning her hat.

"He said that since the weather was so miserable, you shouldn't go to his chambers this afternoon. He'll send his chauffeur to fetch you at six o'clock."

"How considerate of him," Prudence murmured. "Thank you, Jenkins. Could you send a message to Con. Ask her to come around at her earliest convenience?" She hurried upstairs to the parlor. Chastity had just sat down to begin answering letters to the Aunt Mabel column of *The Mayfair Lady* when Prudence entered the parlor. She turned in her chair at the secretaire.

"Anything? I have." Her expression was anxious.

Prudence nodded. "You first," she said.

Chastity described the events of the morning. "I'm just worried they'll dig something up, however closed-mouthed everyone is. Maybe we *should* cease publication. Go to ground."

"Like the hunted fox." Prudence bent to warm her chilled hands at the fire, then straightened, a gleam in her eye that gave Chastity some heart.

"What did you discover?"

Prudence opened her handbag. Silently, she handed the documents to her sister. Chastity would need no elaboration to grasp the implications. She read in silence, laying the sheets on the secretaire as she read them. Then she looked up. "Con needs to see these."

"I asked Jenkins to send for her."

Chastity shook her head in disbelief. "Barclay basically owns our house."

Prudence opened her hands in a wordless gesture of agreement.

"There's more at stake than *The Mayfair Lady*, then."

Prudence nodded. "A stake through the heart comes to mind."

"Well, we'd better wait for Con before we talk about murder," Chastity said. "Mrs. Beedle was holding a couple of letters. Shall we look at them while we're waiting?" She reached for her handbag and took out the envelopes. "I'm almost afraid to open them."

She slit them with an onyx paper knife. "This one seems quite straightforward. It's a request for an introduction to people who have a passion for poetry. Not exactly a matchmaking request, the writer wants to set up a poetry circle." She looked up and shrugged. "What do you think? Shall we come up with a list?"

"I don't see why not," her sister said. "We do put people in contact with like-minded souls. It seems harmless enough."

Chastity nodded and tossed the letter onto the desk. She turned her attention to the other one. Silently she handed it to Prudence.

To whom it may concern:

An interested party has some information of considerable benefit to the owners and editors of The

Mayfair Lady *regarding the present libel suit. Evidence has come to light that will be of service to them in their defense. A private meeting is requested at a location of the editors' own choosing. The information we have is of the greatest importance and must be delivered in a timely fashion. Please respond to the above address without delay. And please believe us to be the most sincere admirers and supporters of* The Mayfair Lady.

Prudence looked up. "It's a trap."

"But what if it isn't?"

"It has to be." She nibbled a fingernail. "It's anonymous."

"As are we," Chastity pointed out. "If it's a friend of Barclay's, or maybe an ex-friend, he might not want to be known. Supposing he has evidence of Barclay's fraud, maybe he was a victim, like Father. Can we afford to discount it?"

Prudence tore off the piece of nail she had loosened with her teeth and threw into the fire. "I don't know, Chas."

"You could show it to Gideon."

Prudence nodded. "I'm seeing him this evening. I'll show it to him then." She folded the letter and slipped it back into its envelope.

"Oh, there's Con," Chastity said at the sound of their sister's unmistakable footstep on the stairs.

Constance entered the parlor, took one look at her sisters, and said, "We need to go out for luncheon."

"That's the best idea I've heard all day," Prudence said. "But read these first. I have to change my shoes, they're soaked." She gestured to the documents on the secretaire. "Oh, and the letter. Give it to her, Chas."

Chastity handed it over. "Where are we going for luncheon?"

"Swan and Edgar's?" Constance suggested, her eye already scanning the papers in her hands.

"Perfect," Prudence approved on her way to the door. "They do a nice luncheon and I want to buy a paisley scarf to go with my sage evening dress."

Constance looked up for an instant. "Are you seeing the barrister tonight, then?"

"As it happens. But if you finish reading you'll see that a business meeting is somewhat urgent," her sister declared. "I'll tell Jenkins we won't be in for luncheon."

"Business?" Constance murmured with a raised eyebrow as the door closed behind Prudence.

"I doubt Prue has either the time for or the interest in anything else right now," Chastity declared with unusual acerbity. "If you'd read what's in your hand, you'd realize that."

Constance's eyebrows reached her scalp but she said nothing. Her baby sister would have a reason for snapping. When she'd finished reading she understood.

"Barclay has a lien," she said in an incredulous whisper.

Chastity nodded.

Chapter 16

Prudence stepped into the motor when it arrived punctually at six o'clock that evening and gratefully accepted the mackintosh lap rug that the chauffeur provided. She was just as grateful for the leather curtains that he had rolled down over the open sides. When they reached the house on Pall Mall Place, the front door opened the minute they attained the top step, under the shelter of the chauffeur's umbrella.

"Oh, you were exactly right about the time, Milton," a childish treble declared. "You've been gone exactly three quarters of an hour."

"Unless there are unexpected delays, I am in general correct about such things, Miss Sarah," the driver said with an indulgent smile.

"Good evening, Miss Duncan," Sarah Malvern said.

Prudence smiled down at the rather untidy schoolgirl and took the small hand extended in greeting. "Good evening, Sarah." She had time for a closer examination of the girl than had been afforded by their previous unexpected meeting. Sarah's countenance was more freckled than Prudence had noticed, and she was rather skinny, dressed this evening in a conventional school tunic of blue serge with a white blouse, somewhat ink-stained on the sleeves. Two thick ropes of fair hair hung down her back, a straight fringe brushing her forehead.

"Won't you come in?" Sarah said, pulling the door wide. "I'm to entertain you while Daddy's finishing the truffled eggs. If you'd like to come in here, you could take off your coat and scarf." She led and Prudence followed into a small bedchamber leading off the hall. A dresser, a mirror, a jug and ewer of hot water, a towel, brush, and comb all lay ready for any guest in need.

"There's a water closet through that door," the girl said matter-of-factly, gesturing to a door at the rear of the room. "I found some camellias in the garden." She perched on the end of the single bed. "I thought you might like them."

Prudence noted the little vase of heavy-headed red camellias still speckled with raindrops. "They're very pretty," she said. "Thank you," she added, taking off her coat.

"Oh, it was no trouble," the child said with a sunny smile. "And I put out hot water in case you were dusty. What an elegant dress."

Prudence didn't need to look in the mirror to know that this was true. It was one of the Parisian creations that Constance had brought back from her honeymoon for her sisters, and it perfectly suited her coloring and her figure, making the most of her less-than-imposing bosom. She had decided on this occasion to dress as if she'd received an invitation for dinner, since—to put it euphemistically—experience had taught her that the barrister was sometimes a little forgetful about declaring his intentions.

Truffled eggs, though?

"It came from Paris," she said, and unpinned her scarf. She had chosen to wear her hair in a thick, braided chignon, tied with a velvet ribbon at her neck. It was a style that softened her rather angular features and made the most of the deep copper of her hair.

"If you're ready, we'll go into the drawing room," the girl said. "I'm glad you didn't get wet on the drive."

"Milton was very solicitous," Prudence said, following her diminutive hostess across the black-and-white marble-paved floor and into a long, narrow drawing room that stretched the length of the house. It was a pleasant room of soft shades of cream and gold, welcoming sofas, and floor-to-ceiling bookshelves. Unlike the library, the only other room she had seen, it didn't strike her as having anything masculine about it at all. Did it date from Sarah's mother's day, a reflection of her taste? Or some other woman's? Had there been another woman in Gideon's life since his wife?

Prudence was realizing how little she still knew about this man who had become her lover. There was the little matter of his failed marriage, for instance. That was a history she needed eventually to unravel.

An open exercise book lay on a sofa table, with pen and inkwell beside it. "I have the most pesky algebra problem," Sarah Malvern declared. "Daddy said you might be able to help me with it."

Oh, did he, indeed? Prudence merely smiled. "I wonder what gave him that idea. Let me have a look."

The girl gave her the exercise book, then flitted across to a sideboard. "May I pour you a glass of sherry?"

"Yes, thank you." Prudence sat down on the sofa with the exercise book. It took her a few seconds to figure out the answer to the problem. She took the glass of sherry Sarah had carried carefully across the Aubusson carpet. "Do you want me to help you figure this out or just do it for you?"

"That would be cheating," Sarah said, taking the exercise book from her guest.

"Well, yes, I suppose it would." Prudence couldn't help smiling as she sipped her sherry. The girl was clearly struggling with her conscience. "But then again," she said, "if I showed you how to do it and you followed along, you would learn for the next time, so it would be a lesson rather than a cheat."

Sarah considered this, her head on one side, a frown on her freckled face, then she grinned. "I don't think even Daddy would argue with that. And he argues with most things. He says it's a good mental exercise."

"What's he doing with truffled eggs?" Prudence inquired casually as she took up the pen.

"Making them," Sarah replied matter-of-factly. "They're one of his specialities. You're having quails stuffed with grapes too. They're tricky to cook because they have so many bones and Daddy has to take them all out when the birds are raw. It always makes him swear." She glanced up at Prudence as she sat on the sofa beside her. There was a rather mischievous, if speculative, gleam in her gray eyes. "He doesn't cook them very often," she said. "Only for special occasions."

Prudence ignored the significant tone and the speculative gleam and took back the exercise book. She felt on much firmer ground with algebra. "All right, here is how we do this." She began to explain the solution to the problem, Sarah leaning close to her, listening intently.

"Now see if you can do it." Prudence handed her the pen at the end of her explanation.

"Oh, it's easy now," Sarah said confidently. "Two to the power of three..." She worked quickly and neatly, impressing Prudence considerably. It was a far from simple problem for one so young. But then, she was the daughter of Sir Gideon Malvern, the youngest-ever KC. And she attended North London Collegiate. Gideon had talked of a governess too. A Mary Winston. Why wasn't she present? Why wasn't *she* helping the child with her homework?

Schoolgirls didn't do their evening homework alone in a formal drawing room—or, not in Prudence's experience.

The house was almost unnaturally quiet and there didn't seem to be any evidence of servants, except the chauffeur. There'd been a housekeeper when she'd come before. This was a puzzle beyond Prudence's unraveling, and as her astonishment at this surreal situation faded, annoyance took its place. Gideon was doing his surprise trick again, designed as always to throw her off balance. She looked up at the sound of the door opening.

"Prudence, forgive me for not greeting you the minute you arrived," Gideon said, entering the drawing room. "There's a particular moment with the eggs when one can't lose concentration. I hope Sarah has been entertaining you."

He wore impeccable evening dress, except that around his waist was a large and none-too-clean apron. Prudence stared at it.

"You forgot to take off your apron, Daddy," Sarah informed him.

"Oh, how remiss. I forgot I was wearing it." He untied the apron and threw it over a brocade chair by the door. He regarded his guest with smiling appreciation that went a long way to dissipating her flash of annoyance.

"My compliments," he murmured. "That gown has the unmistakable mark of Paris upon it."

Prudence, at her sisters' insistence, was also wearing the three strings of matchless pearls wound around her neck. They had originally belonged to their great-grandmother and the sisters trotted them out on suitable occasions. Constance had worn them for her wedding. Prudence had been a little reluctant to wear them this evening for what had, after all, been billed as a working occasion; but when she had seen how well they complemented the gown, she'd yielded without too much of an argument.

Prudence took off her glasses in the reflex that was always prompted by a moment of uncertainty. Sarah's presence seemed paradoxically to add to the intimacy of the moment while making it difficult to respond naturally.

Gideon smiled and resisted with difficulty the urge to lean over and kiss the tip of her nose. The soft glow of the gas lamps set deep fires ablaze in the copper mass on her nape and his fingers itched to loosen it. But his expression gave none of this away. He said calmly, in his low, pleasant voice, "I see Sarah gave you sherry." He went to the sideboard and poured himself a glass. "Did you manage the problem, Sarah?"

"Miss Duncan showed me how to do it, and then I did it myself," the child said with scrupulous honesty.

Gideon nodded. "May I see?" He took the exercise book and ran his eye over his daughter's work. "Nicely done," he commented, handing the book back to her. "Mary came in five minutes ago. She's waiting for you to join her for supper."

"Mary went to a suffragist meeting," Sarah said. "Do you believe in votes for women, Miss Duncan?"

"Most certainly I do," Prudence said.

"Do you belong to the Women's Social and Political Union? Mary does." Sarah's interest was clearly genuine.

"I don't, but my elder sister does. She often speaks at meetings."

Sarah's eyes widened. "Is her name Miss Duncan too? I wonder if Mary's ever heard her."

"My sister uses her married name now...Mrs. Ensor."

"Oh, I'll ask Mary if she knows her." Sarah stood up, clutching her exercise book. "I don't suppose you cooked extra quail for us, did you, Daddy?"

"No, I'm afraid not. Boning four quail is as many as I can tolerate," Gideon said. "But Mrs. Keith has roast pork and applesauce for you."

Sarah gave an exaggerated sigh. "Oh, well, I suppose that will have to do."

"The pork has crackling, I am reliably informed."

The girl's laugh was light and merry, and full of warmth. "We'll make do," she said. She gave Prudence her hand. "Good night, Miss Duncan. Thank you for helping me with the algebra."

"My pleasure, Sarah. Good night." Prudence sipped her sherry as Gideon kissed his daughter good night. Sarah responded to the kiss with a fierce hug. The bond between them was obviously so strong, so easy and affectionate it reminded Prudence of the bond she and her sisters had had with their mother. She watched the softness of Gideon's expression, the warm curve of his mouth. This was the side of the man that produced the laugh lines at the corners of his eyes, the easy way he had with endearments, the tenderness of the lover.

Sarah left with bouncing step and Prudence settled back against the corner of the sofa. "She's a delightful girl."

"Her proud papa certainly thinks so," Gideon said with a laugh, coming over with the sherry decanter. He leaned across her to refill her glass, and she inhaled the unmistakable, exotic, and earthy scent of truffles, mingled with a faint cologne that after a bare hesitation she decided was onion. Her host had been chopping raw onions.

"I seem to be getting the unmistakable impression that you cook," she declared.

"That would not be an inaccurate impression," he responded with a grin that was more than a little complacent.

"Just another one of your surprises?" She sipped her sherry, watching him with raised eyebrows.

"It's a hobby, almost a passion, really," he replied, sounding serious now. "I'm hoping you'll approve of the results shortly."

"An unusual hobby," Prudence commented. She could think of nothing else to say.

"It frees my mind," he returned, still seriously. "A man needs a break from dusty law books."

"Yes," she agreed. "I suppose he does. But I thought we were going to work this evening . . . I have something really exciting to show you." She reached for her handbag.

Gideon whipped the bag out from under her stretching hand. "Not now, Prudence. Later."

"It's evidence of Barclay's fraud," she declared.

"Good," he said, placing her bag out of reach on top of the mantel. "After dinner we will discuss it."

But Prudence was not to be put off. "We'll need to check into the records of a company calling itself Barclay Earl and Associates . . . whether it legally exists. Do you know how to do that?" She leaned forward eagerly.

"Yes," he said calmly. "I do. We will discuss it later."

Prudence stared at him in frustration. "They've got detectives asking all over town about us. And they sent a letter to the publication . . . oh, let me show you." She jumped up and went to the mantel, only to find her way barred.

"After dinner," he said, placing a finger decisively over her lips. "I have just spent the better part of four hours creating a masterpiece for your delectation and I refuse to have it spoiled. There's a time and a place for everything, and right now is the time and place for truffled eggs."

Prudence gave up. "What happens to truffled eggs?"

He shook his head. "Once you've tasted them I'll tell you. Let us go in to dinner." He took her hand and laid it firmly on his proffered arm.

All right, Prudence decided, if he wouldn't talk business then they would discuss something else. "Does Sarah live with you all the time?"

"Yes," he said, escorting her across the hall.

"It's somewhat unusual, isn't it? Girls tend to live with their mothers in such circumstances," Prudence persisted.

"That would be a little difficult in this situation, since I have no idea where Sarah's mother is." He ushered her into a square dining room.

"How could that be?" Prudence demanded, no longer concerned that she might be prying. She *was* prying, in fact, but in the face of these bland responses she had little choice.

"When Sarah was three, Harriet ran off with a horse trainer." He pulled out a chair for her to the right of his own at the head of the table.

"And you've not heard from her since?" Prudence couldn't conceal her shock at this cavalier explanation offered in a tone that was so matter-of-fact it sounded almost bored. She stood holding the back of her chair, looking up at him.

"Not since the divorce. She remembers Sarah's birthday, that's sufficient for me . . . and it would seem for Sarah too. Would you please sit down?"

Prudence did so. "Divorce must have been difficult," she persisted. He had to have some emotional response to this.

"Nowhere near as difficult as realizing that you hadn't noticed that your wife had developed interests elsewhere," he said aridly.

Prudence was quiet for a moment. However dry his statement, it had revealed some indication of hurt. If his noncommittal attitude earlier had been a simple defense mechanism, then it would be unforgivable to dig at a still-open wound.

Soft candlelight lit the room and a round bowl of the same red camellias that Sarah had put in the guest room formed a fragrant centerpiece. Again Prudence was struck by the feminine touches, the delicate lace edging to the table napkins, the silver bowl of potpourri on the sideboard.

"Sarah has a nice touch with flower arrangements," she observed. "At least I assume it's Sarah."

"With a fair amount of help from Mary," Gideon responded. "Mary, for all her suffragist leanings, doesn't disdain the gentler arts of her sex. You'll meet her soon, I'm sure. You'll like her."

"I'm sure I shall," Prudence said carefully. He was making some very broad assumptions, she thought with a prickle of apprehension. It seemed as if he was expecting her part in his life to become larger, as if it was going to be quite natural for her to become friends with Sarah's governess, as if it was quite natural for her to help the girl with her homework, or have a tête-à-tête dinner in his house. A dinner that he himself had cooked. As if somehow this was not in his eyes the brief fling she had so casually called it when talking to her sisters. And if it was more than a brief fling, then what happened to the bride hunt? Not to mention their working relationship.

If Gideon noticed anything unusual about her abrupt silence, he gave no sign. He rang a small handbell at his elbow before pouring champagne into two glasses, and said conversationally, "I think champagne works best with the eggs, but if you dislike champagne with food . . . some people do . . ."

"No, not at all," Prudence hastened to reassure him as the door opened softly and a maid entered with a tray.

"You gave them just three minutes in the bain-marie, Maggie?" the barrister asked, sounding uncharacteristically anxious.

"Yes, sir, exactly as you said." The maid set a small dish in front of Prudence and the second in front of Sir

Gideon. "And the melba toast is just out of the oven, cooked nice and slow, just as you said." She set a toast rack between the diners. Her tone, Prudence thought, was rather soothing, as if she was accustomed to her employer's culinary anxieties.

"Will that be all, sir?"

"Thank you." He took up a tiny silver spoon. *"Oeufs en cocotte aux truffes,"* he announced. "The secret lies in getting them to set to exactly the right consistency." He dipped the tip of the spoon into the dish, and Prudence hesitated, waiting for the verdict.

"Ah, yes," he said. "Perfect."

Prudence took this as permission to taste her own. She dipped her spoon and conveyed its contents to her mouth. "Oh," she said. "Ah," she said. She gazed at him. "Unbelievable." Her tongue roamed around her mouth, catching every last elusive hint of truffle and caviar.

He smiled a most self-satisfied smile. "It will do." He passed the toast rack towards her. "Melba toast."

Prudence could not imagine that the astounding dish in front of her could benefit from toast but she bowed to the expert and took a fragile crisped piece. She broke off a corner and dipped it into her dish, following her host's example. *Oeufs en cocotte aux truffes* definitely needed melba toast.

She sipped her champagne and savored every tiny spoonful of the delicacy in front of her. It struck her that this was not a suitable moment for conversation of any kind, let alone of the business or personal varieties. This was a moment for awe and reverence. And it was over all too quickly.

She looked sadly into the empty *cocotte* and gave a little sigh that was part utter delight and part regret. "I have never tasted anything like that."

"Good," said her host, refilling her champagne glass. "The sole will be a few minutes." He smiled at her and laid a hand over hers.

Prudence twined her fingers in his. She hesitated, but without the distraction of culinary delight, her restless mind had turned back to the personal. She desperately needed to know the full story of his marriage. "How did you fail to notice that your wife had interests elsewhere?" she asked finally.

Gideon sipped his champagne and then gently but deliberately disengaged his hand. "I suppose you're entitled to ask, but in general I prefer not to talk about it."

"I'm sorry," she said. "But it seems very important to me to know."

He nodded. "I didn't notice for the same reason that Harriet found outside interests. I was too busy, too engrossed in my profession." He shook his head. "A barrister doesn't make KC without sacrifices, certainly not before his fortieth birthday. Harriet, with some justification, resented my absorption. She was—I assume still is—very beautiful. Very desirable . . . and the only man who failed to acknowledge that was her husband."

"But she had a child."

"Yes, but motherhood didn't suit her enough to substitute for the lack of a husband's attentions."

He looked across at her. "I blame Harriet for very little. She gave me a divorce without a murmur. I keep her in some of the luxuries that the racehorse trainer can't quite manage, and I prefer that her contact with Sarah be limited to birthday cards. Can we leave it at that now?"

He rose from the table, went to the sideboard, and

took up a bottle of Chassagne Montrachet. "This will go very well with the sole. I have a fine Margaux for the quail. I trust you'll approve."

Prudence sat back as he filled her white-wine glass. "I didn't mean to open old wounds," she said, then fell silent as the maid reappeared to clear away the first course and place delicate fillets of Dover sole in front of them. She placed a sauceboat at Prudence's elbow.

"Champagne sauce," Sir Gideon said. "I can't take credit for this dish. It's one of Mrs. Keith's specialities."

Prudence dribbled sauce onto her fish. "I imagine you had your hands full with the cocotte and the quail." She took up her fish utensils and cut into the fillet. He had asked her to drop the subject, and without being insensitive to the point of discourtesy she could only accede. "To produce this in addition to a full day at work is impressive, to say the least." She smiled at him. "Were you in court today?"

"I was. Quite an interesting case. A property dispute. Usually I find them rather tedious, but this had some unusual aspects." He talked about the case, making relaxed and urbane conversation throughout the remainder of dinner.

"The quail were wonderful. And that gâteau basque..." Prudence set down her spoon and fork with a little sigh of repletion. "I have no idea how you could put something that delicious on a table."

"Cooking is not your forte, then?" he teased.

Prudence shook her head. "I'm afraid, unlike Miss Winston, that I lack many of the gentler arts of my sex."

He looked at her sharply, as if hearing a note of criticism in her repetition of his description of Mary Winston.

She continued, with an attempt at lightness. "My forays into the kitchen are usually only to discuss with Mrs. Hudson the cheapest way to put a meal on the table that will satisfy my father and not arouse his suspicions that we've cut corners. It's not easy to do."

"No, I can imagine," he said. He laid his napkin on the table. "Let's return to the drawing room for coffee." He pushed back his chair and moved behind hers, pulling it out for her.

"Can we talk business now?" Prudence asked as they entered the drawing room. She headed for the mantel and her handbag.

Gideon sat down on the sofa and patted the seat beside him. "Show me what you've got." He leaned forward to pour coffee from the tray set ready for them on the low table in front of the sofa.

"The good news or the bad news first?" She sat down beside him, opening her bag.

"Try me with the good."

She handed him the documents she had liberated from the safe-deposit box and began to explain, but he waved her into silence with one of his gestures that so exasperated her.

"Let me come to my own conclusions, Prudence. Drink your coffee and help yourself to cognac if you'd like."

"No, thank you," she said.

"Then pour me one, would you?" He didn't look up from his reading, either as he made the request or when she set the goblet in front of him.

Prudence took up her coffee cup and wandered over to the bookshelves. She felt dismissed as an irrelevancy, and although she now assumed that hadn't really been his intention, it was annoying nevertheless.

Chapter 17

Prudence remained with her back to the room, scanning the titles on the bookshelves, doing her best to appear nonchalant. It seemed her only defense against the feeling of being irrelevant to proceedings that touched her so nearly.

"Well," Gideon said at last.

Prudence turned very casually. "Well what?" She went over to the table and set down her empty coffee cup.

"I'll put Thadeus onto discovering the legal standing of this Barclay Earl and Associates first thing tomorrow," Gideon said, tapping the sheets that he still held on his knee. "You did well."

"Praise indeed," Prudence said with a sardonic little curtsy. "I'm overwhelmed to have satisfied the exacting standards of the most famous barrister in town."

"Wasp," he accused. "How did I just put your back up?"

Prudence folded her arms. "I suppose it didn't occur to you that I might have gone through hells of conscience getting that information. I had to falsify authorization from my father, deceive the bank manager, and then dig into Father's most private papers."

"But without it your case would have been lost," he pointed out. "Needs must, my dear." He tapped the papers again. "With this I can promise that the earl of Barclay will be squirming on the stand. I think you'll find the unsavory methods you had to use worth it then."

"So it will serve?" Prudence looked at him closely.

"I believe so." He put down the papers. "And it came none too soon. The trial date has been set for two weeks tomorrow."

"Two weeks!" she exclaimed. "Can we be ready by then?"

"We have no choice," he said. "I trust you can perfect the French maid imitation in that time."

"At least it doesn't give them too much more time for snooping," Prudence murmured, half to herself. Her stomach seemed to be turning somersaults, not a good response to truffled eggs and quail.

Gideon watched her for a second, guessing at her reaction. What had been a long-distance threat was now present reality. No wonder she looked a little green. He stood up. "Come here. I've been longing to kiss you all evening."

"You've been too busy eating to think of kissing," she retorted, but she allowed him to tilt her face up to his.

"There is, as I've so often told you, a time and a place for everything. Now is the time for kissing." He brushed her lips lightly with his own, tantalizing her with a sudden flick of his tongue into the corner of her mouth.

An instant before she was lost in the scent of his skin, the taste of his tongue, the firm yet pliable feel of his lips,

Prudence pulled back her head. "No, Gideon. Before we get into this, what are we to do about the letter to *The Mayfair Lady* offering information for the case? It's so urgent now. Should we answer it?"

He frowned down at her, his fingers still closed over her chin. Then he shook his head as if in resignation and said, "I would suspect a trick."

"But supposing it *is* genuine?"

"You must do what you think best."

"That's not very helpful," she said, stepping back from him. "I need a better answer before we can move on to other things."

Gideon groaned. "How could I have fallen for a veritable Lysistrata?"

Fallen for? Prudence steepled her hands, pressing her fingertips against her mouth. There was no reason to be alarmed by such a statement, she told herself. Of course, he was not the kind of man to make delirious love to any woman who crossed his path. Any more than she was the kind of woman to fall into any man's bed. There was an attraction between them. The attraction of opposites, if nothing else. Silly to read more into it than that.

"Give me your answer," she demanded.

"Don't touch it with a barge pole. It's not worth the risk. Even if it is genuine and there is some information out there, we don't need it," he said crisply. "Now, could we go back to where we were, please?"

"Yes, sir. At your service, sir." Prudence moved into his arms, putting her own around his neck as she lifted her face imperatively. His mouth was wonderfully hard on hers, his lips at first closed then opened, pressing her own apart as his tongue drove deep into her mouth with a predatory possession that sent arrows of lust darting through her loins. In the still-sensible recess of her mind, she knew this would have to stop soon. There could be no logical conclusion to this kiss in Gideon's house, with his daughter asleep upstairs, but she was too hungry *now* to worry about the inevitable letdown to come.

The banging of the front door knocker, loud and imperative, broke their private, passionate circle. Gideon raised his head, frowning, running a hand through his already disheveled hair. "Who the hell could that be? I'm not expecting anyone. The staff have gone to bed."

The banging came again. He strode out of the drawing room. Prudence followed, standing in the drawing room entrance as he opened the front door. She couldn't see anything in the shadows of the hall, where all but a single lamp had been doused. There was a long silence.

There was a quality to the sudden silence that made her scalp crawl. Slowly she took a step into the hall.

"Harriet," Gideon said without inflection. "This is a surprise."

"I thought I'd better surprise you, Gideon," a woman's voice said with a little trill that sounded nervous to Prudence. "If I warned you I was coming, you might have refused to see me."

"Hardly," he said in the same expressionless tone. "You'd better come in."

Gideon's ex-wife stepped into the hall. She wore an opera cloak of black velvet. As she glanced curiously around, she raised a gloved hand to her black taffeta hat, adjusting one of the white plumes. Her eyes fell upon Prudence, standing now in the light streaming from the drawing room at her back.

"Oh," she said. "You're entertaining, Gideon. How

inconsiderate of me not to have warned you of my arrival." She crossed the hall towards Prudence. "Good evening, I'm Harriet Malvern."

Prudence took the extended hand belonging to one of the most classically beautiful women she had ever encountered and shook it. "Prudence Duncan," she said.

"Oh, Gideon, could you find someone to take up my valise?" Harriet said over her shoulder. "I was sure you wouldn't mind if I stayed for a few days. I do so want to see Sarah. Where is she? She's not in bed yet?"

"It's nearly midnight," Gideon said in the same expressionless tone. "Where did you think she would be?"

"Oh, don't be disagreeable, Gideon," Harriet said. "I don't know what time children go to bed, and she must be almost grown up now."

"Go into the drawing room, Harriet," Gideon instructed. "I don't know what's going on here, and you're certainly not seeing Sarah until I find out."

Harriet pouted a little. "He's so stern sometimes, have you noticed?" she said in a conspiratorial undertone to Prudence.

This was not a conversation Prudence was about to have. She stepped around the elegant figure and said formally, "It's time I left, Sir Gideon."

"Oh, don't go on my account," trilled the visitor. "I'm so tired anyway. I'll just go up to my room. Perhaps Mrs. Keith—You do still have Mrs. Keith?—could bring me up a little soup."

"Mrs. Keith is in bed," Gideon said. "Now do as I say." His lips were very thin, his eyes hard. He turned to Prudence. "Would you mind waiting in the library for a few minutes? This won't take very long."

Prudence looked at him in astonishment. *Won't take*

very long. He was intending simply to dismiss this woman, the mother of his child, who'd just turned up on his doorstep with bag and baggage. He was prepared to give her a few minutes of his time, and then presumably send her on her merry way.

"No," she said, shaking her head. "I'm leaving now. You have other things that require your attention."

"Daddy?" Sarah's girlish treble came unnervingly from the head of the stairs. "What's all that banging?"

"It's nothing, Sarah. Go back to bed. I'll come up in a minute," he called, laying an arresting hand on his ex-wife's arm as she made to move past him towards the stairs. "Not yet," he said through his teeth. "Go into the drawing room."

And this time she obeyed. Gideon turned back to Prudence. "Let me deal with this. It won't take a minute."

"What do you mean, it won't take a minute?" she demanded in an incredulous undertone, aware of Sarah now awake and curious upstairs. "That's your ex-wife, or am I mistaken?"

"No, you're not," he said wearily. "I just need to find out what she's doing here."

"Yes, you do," Prudence said, making for the guest room and her coat and hat. "And I cannot imagine how you can do that in three minutes. This is no time for me to be here." She picked up her coat from the bed and then stood in front of the mirror to put on her hat. Her hands were trembling and she hoped that Gideon, who was standing rather helplessly in the doorway, couldn't see them.

"Excuse me." She walked past him towards the front

door, stepping around the pile of valises that seemed to indicate a stay of a more than transitory nature.

"Prudence." He came after her, catching her arm as she stepped out through the still-open door. "This is not your affair. It doesn't concern you at all. Leave now if you must, but nothing's changed between us."

"What do you mean, it doesn't concern me?" she demanded, trying to keep her voice low. "We've spent an entire night in bed together. That woman is a part of your life. The mother of your child. How could you possibly be so obtuse, so . . . so insensitive . . . as to dismiss her *and me* as somehow irrelevant to your own concerns? Are you suggesting we simply carry on as if nothing has happened?"

She shook her head in disbelief, shook off his arm, and waved at a passing hackney carriage, its driver nodding sleepily on the box. "Good night, Gideon."

The cab drew to a halt at the bottom of the narrow flight of steps. Gideon made no further attempt to stop her. He waited until she was in the cab, then turned back to the hall, his expression grim.

Prudence sat back against the cracked leather swabs and tried to sort out what had just happened. It wasn't Gideon's fault that Harriet had arrived, but how could he possibly think he didn't have to deal with it . . . that in a few minutes everything would be back to normal? *What kind of man was he?*

How was Sarah going to respond to her mother's abrupt reappearance? Surely he had to realize that that would take more than a few minutes to deal with.

It defied belief.

* * *

Prudence was as incredulous the next morning as she had been when she had finally fallen asleep. Recounting the incident to Chastity had not helped to clear her mind, and neither had the hours of restless tossing in hot sheets. She awoke headachy and as tired as if she had not slept a wink.

A bleary-eyed look at the clock told her it was barely seven. She rolled over and tried to go back to sleep, but without success. A knock at the door surprised her.

"Miss Prue?" Jenkins called softly.

"What is it, Jenkins?" She sat up.

The door opened, but instead of Jenkins, Gideon walked in, dressed impeccably in morning coat and waistcoat, carrying an attaché case. Clearly on his way to work, Prudence thought, even as she stared at him.

"What are you doing here?"

"I need to talk to you," he said, setting his attaché case on a chair.

"Sir Gideon insisted on coming up, Miss Prue," Jenkins said apologetically. "He said he would open every door until he found you if I didn't show him up."

"That's all right, Jenkins," Prudence said. "I know how very *persuasive* Sir Gideon can be. Could you bring me some tea?"

"At once, Miss Prue. Should I fetch Miss Chas first, though?"

"I don't need a chaperone, Jenkins," she said. It was a little late for that, but she kept that reflection to herself.

Jenkins left, leaving the door half open. Gideon closed it, then turned back to the bed. "Good morning."

"Good morning."

He swung a chair around to face the bed and

straddled it, resting his arms along the back. "You don't look very refreshed," he observed.

"I'm not. Where's your ex-wife?"

"In bed and asleep, I assume. Harriet is not in the habit of greeting the day until the morning's well advanced."

"In bed in your house?"

"Where else?" he asked, sounding genuinely surprised. His eyes narrowed. "Not in my bed, if that's what you're asking."

"It wasn't."

"Just why did you run off like that, Prudence? I told you I had everything under control. All I needed—" He broke off as Jenkins came in with a tray of tea that he set down on the bedside table. He gave Gideon something approaching a glare and left, again leaving the door ajar.

Gideon got up and closed it.

"There seems to be only one cup," Prudence observed, taking up the teapot. "Jenkins does not look kindly upon intruders at any time of the day."

"No matter. I prefer coffee anyway. As I was saying, I needed to find out what had brought Harriet to my doorstep so that I'd know what I was getting into. Then you and I could have discussed it openly and we could at least have had a civilized good-bye. Why did you just up and run like that as if there was something to run from?"

Prudence took a sip of tea. It was impossible to have a conversation with someone so absolutely blind to another point of view. "I wasn't running from anything, Gideon. I was leaving you to your own business. I assume it's not every day that your ex-wife drops in on you?" Her eyebrows lifted. "I seem to remember you'd said she'd been absent for six years. Tell me, was Sarah pleased to see her mother after such a time?"

Gideon frowned at her tone. "I told you last night, it's no concern of yours. I have my own business well in hand." He passed a hand across his jaw, aware of her angry eyes, the set of her mouth. This was not going the way he'd intended, but she had to see reason. He made an effort to moderate his tone. "Sarah seemed puzzled by her mother's arrival more than anything," he said. "I would have preferred to have given her some warning. Harriet, however, doesn't think of other people when she's acting on impulse."

"How long is she going to stay with you?" Her voice was clipped, her expression unwavering.

He shrugged. "Until she finds somewhere else, I suppose. She's left her horse trainer and has nowhere to go at present."

She watched him over the rim of her cup. "You're not obligated to shelter an ex-wife, are you?"

"No, not legally. But ethically I think I am," he said. "Harriet isn't very good at taking care of herself. She doesn't have a practical bone in her body. But there's no reason why that should affect us, Prudence."

"Of course it affects us!" she exclaimed. "Either you're divorced or you're not, Gideon. I'm not having an affair with a man who's living with another woman, whatever the circumstances. How is Sarah going to make sense of it? Her mother has taken up residence again, but her father is seeing another woman?" She shook her head and set down her empty cup.

"Sarah's a sensible girl. She'll accept what I tell her."

"It's her *mother,*" Prudence stated. "That's a relationship you clearly know nothing about. She's going to have a loyalty towards her just by the very fact of Harriet's being her mother." She held up her hands in an almost defensive gesture. "I'm not going anywhere near that, Gideon. It's not my business. It seems to me you have more than enough on your plate right now without complicating matters with a love affair. Let's just walk away from it, *now*."

"I'm not going to allow Harriet to interfere with my life," he said tautly, his mouth thinned. "Any more than she already has done. You are in my life, Prudence, and you're going to stay in it."

"Not at your say-so." She threw aside the covers and sprang to her feet, her nightgown swirling around her ankles. "I have had enough of your ultimatums, Gideon. I make my own choices, and I do not choose to be involved in your life at this moment. Or possibly at any moment," she added. "We're so different. You can't even begin to see my point of view." She shook her head, setting her hair swirling in a copper cloud against the white of her nightgown. "You're not even entertaining the possibility that I might be right... that I might know more about daughters and their mothers than you do."

He stood up, caught her shoulder, his fingers pressing through the thin cotton, feeling the sharp bone beneath. "If you insist, I'll send Harriet away."

"You're not listening to me," she cried, jerking away from his hold. "I don't insist on anything. Do you really imagine I would encourage you to throw a dependent woman onto the streets? Who do you think I am?"

She stalked to the window, unconsciously rubbing her shoulder where the warmth of his fingers lingered. She stood with her back to him, staring out at the dim light of dawn. "I am not involved in your life. I cannot be. As you so rightly said, it is not my concern. Only not the way you mean, it's the way I mean. I want no part of it . . . and no part of a man who thinks a simple statement that there's nothing to worry about is all that's needed to keep a nice little love affair humming smoothly."

She spun around to face him. "I am not a nice little love affair to be kept on the sidelines."

"Oh, for God's sake," Gideon said, his own anger now riding high. "You're not making any sense to me."

"No, I'm sure I'm not," she said bitterly. "That's exactly the point I'm making."

"I have to go to work." He grabbed up his attaché case. "We'll talk about this later."

"There's nothing to talk about," Prudence said. "Are you still prepared to be our barrister?"

He had his hand on the door. He turned and stared at her, a white shade around his mouth, a little muscle twitching in his cheek. "Are you suggesting I would allow my personal feelings to interfere in my professional life?"

Big mistake, Prudence realized belatedly. She'd forgotten that whatever else she chose to impugn, she should steer clear of his professionalism. "No," she said. "I was just thinking that it might be difficult if you had hostile feelings towards your client."

"Don't be ridiculous. I don't have hostile feelings towards you." The door banged on his departure.

And that was a piece of gross self-deception, if ever she'd heard one. Prudence flopped down on the bed again. Everything about that encounter left a sour taste. She had not expressed herself clearly and Gideon had in his habitual fashion tried to carry the issue on the tide of his own confidence and sense of superiority. They were not made to be lovers.

She lay back against the pillows, closing her eyes. She didn't blame him for wanting to protect Harriet—indeed, she applauded him. But she could certainly blame him for not beginning to understand that it might be a problem for her. Oh, it was all part and parcel of what was wrong with this relationship. Two people who had such vigorous differences of opinion and character were doomed as a couple from the start. Maybe it was good to break it off before they were in too deep. But she still felt hollow and disappointed, and in a strange way rather lost.

"I'm so confused," Prudence said to her sisters later that morning. "He talks about *falling* for me, about how much I'd like his daughter's governess, he takes it perfectly for granted that I should help Sarah with her homework, he cooks dinner for me, for God's sake, and then his ex-wife turns up and he tells me not to worry my pretty little head over it because it's none of my business, he'll take care of it all, and we should just carry on as before."

She refilled her coffee cup. "How could he not see the essential contradiction in that?"

Her sisters had run out of responses to a question that had been repeated in various forms throughout the morning. "I think from now until the case is over you have to see him only when it relates to the libel suit," Constance said, as she had done before. "It'll clear the way to keep things professional. Let him sort out his own domestic affairs, and when the case is over and his situation has been resolved, then you can decide how you feel."

"However it's resolved," Chastity said rather gloomily, "we can forget about finding him a bride. He's not going to be open to the hunt if he's got an ex-wife living in his house. I suppose we'll have to settle for the eighty-twenty split."

"Twenty percent is better than bankruptcy," Prudence pointed out. "Anyway, for all we know there may be no damages. We might just count ourselves lucky to manage a successful defense with no damages awarded."

"That is dismally true," Constance said. "But at least the barrister will get paid by the other side if that happens, so I suggest we let him get on with his work and Prue should put her feelings about the whole business aside until it's over."

Prudence sighed and flung herself against the sofa cushions. "I know how I'll feel," she stated. "It was a mistake ever to get involved with him, and I knew it from the word *go*. I just didn't listen to my rational self. We're totally incompatible, we see the world from opposite poles. So now I'll stop obsessing about it, it's just that—" She broke off. "No, I'm not going to say another word. Let's practice my French accent. Try to think up some really unpleasant questions about the publication, make them really aggressive, and see if I can hold up."

They worked until luncheon and Prudence forced herself to concentrate, but the image of Harriet Malvern would not leave her. Such an exquisitely beautiful woman. How could any other woman hope to compete? But she wasn't competing... of course she wasn't. She had no interest in extending her brief fling with Gideon. Particularly now.

She'd brought one thing away from it, after all. She'd discovered the joys of sex.

"Prue? Prue?"

"Oh, sorry. Where were we?"

"Your eyes were closed," Chastity told her.

"I must have been dozing."

"Dreaming, rather," Constance observed.

"Well, any luck?" Gideon asked his clerk as Thadeus came into the inner chamber.

"Oh, yes," Thadeus said. "I could find no records anywhere of the legal existence of a company called Barclay Earl and Associates. I checked with the solicitors who drew up the lien on Ten Manchester Square. They are, of course, not the same firm the earl is employing in his suit . . . the solicitors who have briefed Sir Samuel. Their reputation is, of course, impeccable." He coughed discreetly into his hand. "The other firm . . . from the shady side of the street, I would have said, Sir Gideon."

Gideon nodded and lit a cigarette. "Good," he said. "Go on."

"They were a little reluctant to be forthcoming, but I managed to convince them that my principal in this case would take a lack of cooperation amiss, that maybe there were aspects of their practice that might not stand up to scrutiny . . . I mentioned the faint possibility of a subpoena in the case."

"Ah. A useful stick, Thadeus." Gideon leaned back in his chair and blew a careful smoke ring. "Any holes in the document?"

Thadeus shook his head a little sadly. "Not exactly, sir. But if the company that holds the lien is not a legal entity, then . . ."

Gideon nodded. "Then the document is a fraud. Anything else?"

"I did discover that this particular firm had been involved in several previous dealings for Barclay Earl and Associates. They did have documents showing the establishment of the company, but, as I said, nothing to indicate that the company was legally registered." He laid a folder on the table in front of the barrister. "In fact, they as good as admitted that they had failed to register the company as a legal entity."

Gideon glanced down at them. "So, these papers were merely a blind to fool the unwary, or the unaware."

"That is my conclusion, Sir Gideon."

Gideon sat forward abruptly. "All right. That's good, Thadeus. It gives us what we need. Thank you." He opened the folder as the clerk backed discreetly from the chamber.

Gideon flipped through the documents, then he pushed the folder away from him with an impatient gesture. *Of all the intransigent, stubborn women.*

Maybe she did know more than he did about mothers and daughters, but from the mess the Duncan sisters were in at the moment, they all appeared to know remarkably little about what constituted a good relationship between fathers and daughters. Trust came to mind.

Of course Harriet's reappearance was a nuisance, but the fact that he both saw it and treated it as no more than that was no reason for Prudence to start prattling about the care and feeding of dependent women.

She had to be one of the most exasperating, opinionated women he'd ever met. Harriet seemed almost restful in comparison. One couldn't possibly contemplate living with a woman whom one disliked most of the time. Except that the rest of the time . . . and maybe it wasn't *most* of the time. And anyway, where had the idea about living with her come from?

With a muttered oath, he pulled paper and pen towards him. He was her barrister and at this moment that was *all* he was. And all he wanted to be.

"What does he say?" Chastity asked somewhat tentatively after her sister seemed to have been spending an inordinate length of time reading a one-page script. "It's from Gideon, isn't it?"

Prudence scrunched up the envelope and tossed it onto the hall table. "Yes," she said. "Just details about the trial."

"In that case, may we see?" Constance asked, turning from the mirror, where she'd been putting on her hat before leaving for home.

"Certainly," her sister said with a shrug. "There's nothing personal in it. He does stop short of calling me Miss Duncan and signing himself Malvern, but that's as personal as it gets." She held out the letter.

"That's good, isn't it?" Chastity asked, as tentatively as before.

"Yes, of course it is," Prudence said on a rather testy note. "It's business only, as we agreed."

Constance refrained from glancing at Chastity. Prudence would be bound to intercept the look and she was as sensitive at the moment as if she'd lost a layer of skin. Indeed, if Constance had been asked for her opinion, she would have said her younger sister was frightened out of her mind. And not about the court case. But then, she hadn't been asked for her opinion.

She perused the contents of the letter. "It looks promising, if you can decipher the legalese," she said. "Barclay's so-called company had no legal standing, and therefore had no legal basis for demanding payments from Father. Gideon seems to be saying that he's fairly confident he can go after Barclay on the stand and rattle him enough to get some kind of an admission." She passed the letter over to Chastity.

"Yes, that was my impression," Prudence agreed.

Chastity looked up from the letter. "He doesn't suggest seeing us again until the actual morning of the trial. Don't you need more preparation, Prue?" She looked anxiously at her sister.

Prudence shook her head. "I know what he wants, he made it very clear. A warmhearted, sympathetic woman who will appeal to the hearts and minds of twelve jurymen, and will absolutely refrain from offending them in any way. I'll have to bat my eyelashes and mutter of lot of *oo-la-las* and *oui, monsieurs*."

"They won't see you batting anything under the veil," Chastity pointed out.

"No," Prudence agreed. "But I'll flutter my hands in a very Gallic fashion and wave a perfumed handkerchief around when I want it to seem that I'm distressed by the questions."

"You'll need some indignation," Constance said. "To be credible."

"Oh, I'm leaving that to Gideon," her sister stated, walking to the stairs. "His role is the fire and brimstone, mine is the honey." She turned, her foot on the bottom step. "I am not to come across as a bitter, ill-tempered, man-hating spinster, you see." Then she walked up the stairs before her sisters could close their mouths and marshal their responses.

Chapter 18

"You're up early this morning, Father," Prudence observed as she entered the breakfast room. Her father, in the most formal of morning wear, was already at the breakfast table, and judging by his empty plate had just finished his meal.

Lord Duncan regarded his daughter with a somewhat testy air. "Have you forgotten it's the first day of Barclay's libel suit? I'm to appear in court this morning."

"Oh, yes," Prudence said casually, going over to the sideboard. "It slipped my mind." She looked at the dish of kedgeree and her already rebellious stomach gave a queasy lurch.

"Well, it's a very important day," her father declared, setting aside his napkin and pushing back his chair. "I shall not be in for luncheon, you may tell Jenkins."

Neither would his daughters. But Prudence merely nodded agreeably and sat down, reaching for the toast rack. Maybe a piece of dry toast would ease the nausea.

"Good morning, Father." Chastity passed her father in the doorway. "You're up early."

"It's Father's day in court," Prudence said before her father could reply. "Did you forget?"

"Oh, yes, sorry," Chastity said. "Good luck."

"I can't imagine why you would think luck is necessary," Lord Duncan stated. "It's an open-and-shut case. By the end of today, that disgraceful rag will be off the streets and out of business. You mark my words." He gave a decisive nod and strode off.

"Oh, God, I hope not," Chastity said, heaping kedgeree on her plate. "How are you feeling, Prue?"

"Sick as a dog," her sister confessed. "How can you eat, Chas? This morning of all mornings."

"To keep up my strength," Chastity said. "And you should eat something more than dry toast, Prue. You're the one who's going to need the most strength."

Prudence shook her head. "I can't eat a thing. Even tea makes me want to vomit." She pushed away her cup and plate. "I'll go and get ready to leave."

Chastity glanced at the clock. It was only seven-thirty. "We have an hour and a half before we have to be at Gideon's chambers."

Prudence merely shook her head and left the breakfast room. In her bedroom she examined her face in the mirror. Pale and wan was about the kindest thing that could be said for her complexion at present. Her eyes were heavy-lidded and black-shadowed. Even her hair seemed to have lost some of its vibrancy. Not that her physical appearance was in the least important at the moment. No one was going to get so much as a glimpse of it beneath the thick black-spotted veil.

Gideon, of course, would see her unveiled when they met this morning. But then, her appearance was no concern of his. His sparse communications over the last two weeks had dealt only with the upcoming suit, and were implicitly addressed to all three of them. He never mentioned Harriet, or Sarah, or indeed anything personal. They had made the clean break she had asked for. She was heart-whole. Not hurt, not diminished in any way by that momentary flight of passion.

It was not at all surprising that the strain of the last two weeks of waiting should show on her face, Prudence told herself. They had been looking over their shoulders for spies and detectives, suspecting every piece of mail that came into the house. They had ceased publication of *The Mayfair Lady* for the duration. She and Chastity had barely shown their faces outside the house, and Constance had performed only those social duties that her position as Max's wife made necessary, even giving up her speaking engagements for the WSPU for these two weeks. They had sat for hours in the parlor, going over and over every detail of the case, anticipating hostile questions, as the barrister had demonstrated, Prudence practicing her fake accent until her tongue felt so thick and huge it barely seemed to fit her mouth anymore.

The door opened behind her and she spun around, feeling for some reason rather self-conscious, as if caught in an embarrassing activity . . . as if there was something odd about self-scrutiny. Chastity gave her a rather puzzled look. "Do you have any spare hairpins, Prue? I can't seem to find any and I need to fix this veil to my hat." She half lifted the black veil on her arm.

"Yes . . . yes, of course." Prudence rummaged through a drawer in her dresser. "I had a new pack in here somewhere."

"Father's just left," Chastity said.

"That's a bit early isn't it? The court doesn't even open until ten." Prudence found the pack of pins and handed them to her sister.

"I think he's as nervous as we are," Chastity said, tucking the pins into her skirt pocket. "I got the impression he'd rather walk around the square for an hour than hang around the house."

"I share the feeling," Prudence said. "Do you mind if we leave a little early? I'm going crazy just waiting."

"No, of course not. I'll be ready in ten minutes." Chastity whisked herself from the room and Prudence returned to her mirror, this time to put on her hat and try the effect of the veil for the umpteenth time.

They took a hackney to the Embankment and then walked up and down the Temple gardens, saying little to each other until it was time to meet Constance. It was a cloudy day, the river gray and sluggish, a sharp wind blowing the last remaining leaves from the trees. Prudence huddled into her coat, turning up the collar, but she still shivered.

"Are you nervous about seeing him?" Chastity asked suddenly.

Prudence didn't pretend not to know what she was talking about. "No, why should I be?"

"I don't know. I just thought you might be."

"He's our barrister, Chas. I'm only nervous that he won't succeed in defending us."

"Yes, of course," Chastity agreed. "Ah, here's Con." She gestured to where their sister was hurrying across the leaf-strewn, damp grass towards them.

"Am I late?"

"No, we were early. I couldn't stand to stay in the house another minute," Prudence said.

Constance looked at her sister. "Are you ready for this, Prue?"

Prudence knew she was not referring to the court appearance. "You're as bad as Chas. Of course I am. Gideon is our barrister. Other than that, he's nothing more to me than the memory of a brief fling in Henley-on-Thames that I've had two weeks to get over. And I'm sure it's the same for him. Let's go."

Big Ben chimed nine o'clock as they reached the street door to the barrister's chambers. They climbed the stairs in single file. The door at the top stood open and Thadeus was on his feet, clearly awaiting them, his eyes on the wall clock.

"Good morning, ladies." He bowed. "Sir Gideon is waiting for you."

But Gideon was already opening the door to the inner chamber. "Good morning," he said pleasantly. "Come in. Thadeus, bring coffee, will you?"

And Prudence knew that she was over nothing. The sound of his voice was all it took to bring memories surging to the surface. Unconsciously, she stiffened her shoulders and said neutrally, "Good morning, Gideon."

They filed past him and took the three seats awaiting them. Gideon went behind the table and took his seat, but not before he had given them all a swift, assessing glance. His gray gaze lingered for a minute longer on Prudence. She was aware of it and resisted the ridiculous urge to look away, instead forcing herself to meet his eye until he turned his attention to the papers on his desk.

He looked tired, she thought. Almost as tired as she felt.

Gideon thought that Prudence looked exhausted. He was weary himself, but she looked dead on her feet. The last two weeks had been the worst he could ever remember passing, and not only because of the chaos Harriet's reappearance had wreaked on Sarah's equilibrium. Prudence had certainly been right on that score. Keeping himself away from Prudence had been one of the hardest things he had ever made himself do. But she had made her wishes clear. Instead he had thrown himself into the libel case, working longer hours on it than he would normally devote even to a case that would guarantee him a substantial fee. Prudence would not have an opportunity to question his professionalism again.

"Forgive me for saying so, Prudence, but you don't look very robust this morning," he observed.

"It's been a stressful two weeks," she said. "I haven't slept well. And to be brutally honest, I'm quite sick with nerves this morning, as you might imagine." There was faint accusation in the last statement.

"That is only to be expected," he said so calmly, she once again had the urge to throw something at him. "Have you eaten this morning?"

"Not really," Chastity answered for her. "She ate barely a crumb of dry toast."

Prudence shot her sister an annoyed look. "So I have no appetite. That's no one's business but my own."

"Now, there I beg to differ," the barrister said. "If you faint in the witness box, it becomes mine."

"I will not faint," she retorted.

"Would you eat some toast and honey now?" he asked, his tone both conciliatory and sympathetic. A tone, Prudence decided, carefully calculated to achieve his objective.

She sighed, unwilling to appear petulant. "I'm not hungry, but if you insist..."

"No, I don't insist. I merely advise," he said, rising from the table and going to the door to make the request of Thadeus. He returned to his seat. "Now, let me explain what will happen this morning."

They listened as he gave them the order of business. Prudence was so absorbed that she had eaten most of a piece of toast and honey before she realized it, and rather to her chagrined surprise, she did feel stronger and less queasy.

Gideon wisely refrained from comment. "So, to sum up," he said. "Sir Samuel has notified us that he'll be calling *The Mayfair Lady* as a hostile witness. He's going to try to discredit the publication in the eyes of the jury before I get a chance to put on a defense. You can expect some very aggressive questioning, Prudence, but if he does any significant damage, I will have the opportunity to rectify it under my cross-examination."

Prudence, who was wondering what kind of damage he was anticipating having to rectify, merely nodded.

Gideon gave her an encouraging smile. "If I can damage Barclay's credibility sufficiently under my cross-examination, it's possible you might have a relatively easy ride."

"Unless they know who we are," Prudence said. "We don't think they do, but we can't be sure."

"They don't," he said.

"How do you know?"

He smiled. "There are ways in this business to find out certain germane facts."

"I suppose it didn't occur to you that it would have made life easier for us if we'd known that?" Prudence asked.

"I had to wait until the last minute to be certain. Things can change up until the eleventh hour."

"I see your point," Constance said, drawing Sir Gideon's attention away from Prudence. "But we've been on tenterhooks."

"I understand, but there was nothing to be done about it before." He lifted his fob watch and glanced at it. "We'll talk about how the morning's gone at the luncheon recess."

Prudence nodded, willing simply to be relieved that they didn't have to worry about their identities coming out. She found she had no thought now for inconvenient memory surges. "Should we go?"

He stood up. "Yes, we should. Constance, you and Chastity should sit in the gallery at the very back. Try not to be visible to anyone in the witness box, I don't want you to distract Prudence, even inadvertently. I'd prefer it if she almost didn't know that you were there."

"I will, though," Prudence said. "I couldn't possibly do this without them being there."

"No, I understand that. Nevertheless, you have to accept what I say. I do in this instance know what I'm talking about." He was putting on his gown and wig as he spoke.

There was the faintest emphasis on *in this instance* and Prudence wondered what it meant. It couldn't be a reference to anything personal between them, he'd given not the slightest indication this morning that they had any kind of shared history. And her own first reaction to seeing him had been an aberration, one best forgotten.

* * *

The libel case was being heard in a small courtroom in the Old Bailey, a location that limited spectators, which, as Gideon had told them, was all to the good. There were bound to be some press, some gossip columnists, maybe even some inquisitive members of London society, but there couldn't be too many of them. He did not tell the sisters that Thadeus on his principal's instruction had arranged this with his colleague, the clerk of the court responsible for allocating courtrooms.

In a small antechamber, the sisters donned their veils. The time for words was over now. They merely touched hands briefly and then Constance and Chastity left Prudence and went up to the gallery, which was already filled with a whispering, shifting crowd. They sat behind a pillar in the very back row.

Prudence waited for Gideon to come for her. She no longer felt sick. She no longer felt nervous. It was as if she had entered some quiet space quite separate from the bustling world around her.

"Are you ready to go in now?" Gideon had opened the door so quietly, she hadn't heard him, and she turned from the little window where she'd been standing staring at the blank wall visible beyond.

"Yes. How is my veil?"

"Impenetrable," he said. "How's the accent?"

"Thick," she said.

He nodded and smiled, hearing the attempt at humor in her voice. "Come." He put a hand on her shoulder and she was glad of the touch, of the sense it gave her of support. Gideon would not let her down. *Not in this instance.*

She banished the mental addendum. He would not let her down and she must not let *him* down.

The courtroom was busy and the people on the long benches turned to look at them as they walked down the narrow aisle to the defense table. Prudence heard the buzz of whispers rising to a low murmur but she looked neither to the right nor the left, merely took the chair Gideon held for her. He sat beside her, laid his papers on the table in front of him, and sat back, as calm and relaxed as if he were in front of his own fireside, except for the white curly wig and the black gown.

"May the court be upstanding."

The assembly scrambled to its feet as the judge entered and took his seat on the high dais. Prudence for the first time glanced sideways at the opposing table. Lord Barclay had an air that was both complacent and vicious, she thought, from a deep well of loathing. Sir Samuel Richardson looked rather older than Gideon, but in the same antique costume it was hard to distinguish them until they spoke. Then it was easy. Sir Samuel's voice was cracked and gravelly against Gideon's quiet, smooth tones. And they had quite different courtroom manners. Prudence was astonished to see that Gideon in his opening remarks was completely nonconfrontational, almost to the point of sounding conciliatory. He smiled, acknowledged his opposing colleague with a polite bow, and a murmured "My learned colleague" suggested that it was quite understandable that Lord Barclay should feel maligned by the publication in question, and sat down again.

Sir Samuel, on the other hand, ranted. His voice reached the rafters as he accused the publication of deliberate fabrication to dishonor the reputation of one of the most esteemed members of "Our society, m'lud."

"Like hell," muttered Prudence, and received a jab in the elbow from her companion. She looked studiously into her lap. Anger was now her friend. She had seen her father sitting in the row behind Barclay and his counsel, and at the thought of what had been done to him, her anxiety vanished. She could almost feel herself baring her teeth like a fox protecting her cubs. She could almost feel her mother's spirit on her shoulder. An absurd fantasy, she told herself, but she was willing to take any help she could get.

Barclay's testimony only strengthened her resolve. He was sanctimonious, hypocritical, and he lied through his teeth. And yet she couldn't feel the slightest reaction from Gideon, sitting so close beside her. He made the odd scratch on a piece of paper, but otherwise simply sat and listened.

Until Sir Samuel had bowed to the judge and the jury and stepped back with a nod to his learned colleague.

Gideon rose, smiling. He greeted Barclay with a bow. "Good morning, my lord."

"Morning." It was a surly response.

"You are under oath, Lord Barclay," Gideon said pleasantly. And from then on he was up and running. And this was the barrister Prudence had expected, the one she had herself experienced. Ruthless, brutal, letting nothing go until he had wrung the answer he wanted from the witness. There were objections from Sir Samuel, some sustained by the judge, but Gideon simply muttered a form withdrawal and swept on.

Prudence froze when her father's name first came up. She saw him raise his head higher with a jerk of surprise, and then she couldn't look at him again as Gideon exposed the fraudulent scheme, the lack of legal registration for the company, the demand for a huge monthly payment, and finally the lien on 10 Manchester Square.

And when the earl was a mere grumbling, muttering, sweating hulk in the witness box, Gideon reverted to his original smoothly charming manner and said, "May I suggest, Lord Barclay, that there was never any intention of building a trans-Saharan railway? I would ask you to consider how many other of your friends have been persuaded to invest in what now seem to be somewhat doubtful enterprises. How many other friends have been obliged to give your unregistered company a lien on their properties?"

"This is calumny, sir," the earl blustered. He looked up at the judge. "I appeal to you, my lord."

"Sir Samuel?" the judge suggested.

Barclay's barrister rose heavily to his feet. His gravelly voice was now rather weary and resigned. "I would ask for a recess and time to confer with my client while we examine the documents in question more closely, m'lud."

The judge banged his gavel. "We'll reconvene at two o'clock."

Prudence glanced up at Gideon as he returned to his chair. He had no expression on his face at all. His eyes were almost blank. And she realized with a chill that this was the face Barclay had been subjected to throughout his interrogation. It was enough to terrify the strongest, most righteous witness. And then it was gone, and he was smiling again, touching her hand lightly as he went around the table.

"That went well, I think," he said. "I'm afraid we can't go anywhere decent for luncheon since you can't take off that veil in public, but I've arranged a pleasant picnic in my chambers."

"My sisters?"

"Of course. Thadeus will bring them as soon as the court has cleared and there are no spying eyes around."

Prudence again refused to look anywhere but ahead of her as they walked out of the court. A few questions were shouted in their direction. Gideon ignored them and held her elbow until they were out in a street where a hackney waited. Not by accident, it was clear. Gideon gave no instructions to the cabbie and as soon as they were inside, the driver cracked his whip and the horse trotted off.

Prudence took a deep breath and put up her veil. "It's stifling behind this thing," she confided. "It is safe now, isn't it?"

"Safe enough." He turned sideways on the bench, examining her in the dim light of the carriage. "How are you bearing up?"

"Better than Barclay," she said with a shaky laugh. "You destroyed him."

"Only almost," he said gravely.

"But you can finish it?" she asked, a flutter of anxiety setting her heart racing.

"I need your father to finish it for me."

"Oh." Prudence understood now. Her father had to confirm that he had been inveigled by a man he thought his friend to invest in a fraudulent scheme designed purely to line the pockets of that so-called friend. If he insisted that he stood by his friend, that his friend had never led him astray, that he had always understood every nuance of the deal and had willingly given him a lien on his house, then their defense would crumple. It couldn't be called fraudulent if the one who was supposed to have been defrauded maintained that he was not.

Constance and Chastity listened in silence as their sister explained this. Gideon kept his offerings to dressed crab-and-lobster sandwiches, glasses of a Chablis Premier Cru, and comment when asked. But he watched Prudence closely and was glad that she took barely a single sip of her wine.

And finally he said, "Prudence, I'm guessing that Sir Samuel will call *The Mayfair Lady* as his next witness. He can't risk calling your father immediately after Barclay's breakdown."

"And with my testimony I have to get Father to switch sides." It was the flat statement of one who had already accepted this conclusion.

He nodded. He wanted to take her in his arms and kiss the lurking panic from her eyes. But if there ever would be a time again for a lover's gesture, this was not it.

"Very well," she said. She looked at her sisters, then back at him. "I'd like to talk to my sisters alone, if you don't mind."

"Of course." He rose from his chair and went to the door, then he hesitated. "You will need to tell me if what you discuss has anything to do with your testimony. You can't spring surprises on your barrister."

"We understand."

He nodded and went out.

The sisters sat in silence for a minute, then Prudence said, "We all know what I have to do."

"The question is how, without revealing your identity to the world at large," Constance said.

"I have an idea." Chastity leaned forward in her chair.

* * *

The courtroom that afternoon seemed hotter to Prudence than it had that morning. She thought she could detect a different, more alert note to the conversational buzz around her while they waited for the judge to reappear, and she was acutely conscious of the glances cast her way. Her heart was banging and the confines of the veil seemed even more stifling than before. She was sure her cheeks were scarlet, perspiration beading her forehead. Gideon, however, was as relaxed as ever as he sat beside her and she tried to draw some of that calm ease into herself by osmosis. It didn't seem to be working.

Her one glance at Lord Barclay had shown her that he too was crimson-hued, but that, she suspected, came as much from an excessively liquid lunch as anything. He was certainly huffing and puffing and having frequent vigorously whispered exchanges with his counsel. Her father looked paler than usual and was sitting very erect on the bench behind Barclay, staring straight ahead at the judge's dais.

"Please be upstanding."

The court rose, the judge took his chair, adjusted his wig, and looked out expectantly at the court below. "Sir Samuel?"

The barrister rose and intoned, "We call the Mayfair Lady to the box, m'lud."

"The publication itself?" The judge peered incredulously at the barrister.

"A representative of the publication, m'lud. A . . ." There was the barest hesitation to accentuate the insult. "A *lady,* as we understand it, m'lud, who prefers to be known simply as Madam Mayfair Lady."

"Unusual," the judge observed. "Can a publication take the oath?"

Gideon rose to his feet. "A representative of the publication can do so, m'lud. I would cite *Angus v. The* Northampton Herald, 1777."

The judge nodded slowly. "Do you have any objection to a representative, Sir Samuel?"

"No, m'lud. The witness is a member of the human race, I believe." This produced a titter around the courtroom. Prudence stared stonily ahead through her veil. Gideon didn't twitch a muscle.

"Very well." The judge nodded. "Call this Madam Mayfair Lady."

Prudence rose and walked steadily to the witness box. The clerk administered the oath and she sat down, folding her hands in her lap.

Sir Samuel approached the box. He looked like a malevolent crow, Prudence decided, with his black gown flapping around him and a look on his face that was almost a leer.

"You are responsible for this publication?" He waved a copy at the courtroom with an air of dismissive disgust.

"*Oui, m'sieur*... uh, yes, forgive me. I am one of ze editors."

"And you are from France, I gather."

"From *la France,* yes." Dear God, how was she going to keep this up? It was one thing in the parlor with her sisters at home, quite another here. For the first time, she looked towards the jury box. Twelve good men and true. At least they didn't look bored.

"Is it a habit of your publication to dishonor the reputations of members of our society, *madame*?"

"No," Prudence said simply. She caught the slight nod of approval from Gideon. His maxim had always been Keep it simple. Don't elaborate unless you must.

"And what would you call this article about one of the most respected members of our aristocracy, *madame*?"

"Ze truth, *m'sieur*."

"I would call it a deliberate attempt at character assassination," he said smoothly. "But, of course, citizens of your country are not unused to assassinating their aristocracy."

A ripple of laughter went through the spectators. Prudence glanced at Gideon. He was expressionless.

"We stand by our research, *monsieur*," she said. "And others have done so too."

"Others!" he boomed suddenly. "The *Pall Mall Gazette*, perhaps. And we all know the sensationalist penchants of that particular broadsheet. Your unfounded accusations, *madame*, have merely provided fodder for a known piece of yellow journalism."

"Zey were not unfounded, *m'sieur*," she stated. "We 'ad witnesses. Women who also spoke to ze *Pall Mall Gazette*."

"Women! Fallen women. Women of the streets! Has society come to this? We put the word of a woman no better than she should be against that of a peer of the realm?" He spun around with a swirl of his cloak and gesticulated at the jury, before continuing a circular spin back to face the witness box.

"Ah, Sir Samuel, that is what you call women who are abused by their so-called betters. Fallen women, harlots, whores, prostitutes—" She broke off abruptly, aware both that her accent had slipped and that she had broken Gideon's cardinal rule. She had let indignation rule her and shown her true colors.

"And these women are to be defended by harpies, it would seem," Sir Samuel said, turning again to nod at the jury, confirming her fears.

Prudence took a steamy breath behind her veil. "Revealing society's injustices, *m'sieur,* is part of our publication's mandate. I maintain that we 'ad ample evidence for our accusations against Lord Barclay."

"And these accusations of financial impropriety." He changed the subject with such an aggressive sweep of his hand that Prudence involuntarily flinched. "What could you, *madame,* what could this rag . . ." He waved the copy again. "What could you know of the intimate details of business between two friends . . . two very close friends of many years standing. I would suggest, *madame,* that you and your fellow editors for some reason known only to yourselves had a personal vendetta against the earl of Barclay and made up whatever facts suited you."

"That is not true," she stated.

"Is it not true that you made advances to his lordship? Advances that were rejected?" He put both hands on the rail of the witness box and peered at her as if he could see the pale frame of her face beneath the veil.

Prudence laughed. She couldn't help it, and even as she did so she saw her father's gaze swing towards her, his eyes vividly alert. She could not, of course, disguise her laugh. She hadn't practiced that. But in this case, all to the good.

"You find that amusing, *madame*?" It was clear that her laughter had discomfited the barrister. His accusation, however wild, had been intended to fluster her.

"Very much so," she said. "I was taught by *ma mère*—forgive me, my mother—to find male pretension . . . 'ow you say . . . amusing . . . ridiculous." She produced a very Gallic shrug and another careless laugh. It might not make her any friends among the jury but her father had gone very pale and his eyes remained fixed upon her.

Had he understood?

Sir Samuel, of course, had not. He was beaming now, certain that he had the jury in the palm of his hand. "Male pretension," he said, tapping the broadsheet against the rail. "Quite so, *madame*. Eloquently put. So you maintain that you have no personal knowledge of his lordship. So I ask you again, what could you know of the private business dealings between two men, friends for many years? Two men with whom you have had no dealings, whose characters you know nothing about."

He turned again to the courtroom. "Lord Duncan sits here, gentlemen of the jury, prepared to stand up as a character witness for his friend. Would he do so if that so-called friend had been dealing the cards behind his back? Would he give a man whom he distrusted a lien on his house? I ask you, gentlemen of the jury, ladies and gentlemen, isn't that a little far-fetched?" He turned back to the witness box, bowed at its occupant with a mocking flourish, and strode to his table with a nod towards Gideon.

Gideon rose. "I have no questions of this witness, m'lud."

There was a little collective gasp in the courtroom. The only witness for the defense had just been destroyed and her barrister was doing nothing to repair the damage.

Prudence rose and returned to her seat. Gideon

touched her knee, a fleeting gesture, but it told her all she needed to know. She had not dared to look at her father during Sir Samuel's declamation, but Gideon had been watching him closely.

Sir Samuel declared, "I call Lord Arthur Duncan, m'lud."

Lord Duncan walked to the witness box.

Chapter 19

Prudence could barely watch as her father took the oath. His voice was controlled and courteous, and when he sat down his hands rested unmoving on the rail of the witness box.

Sir Samuel approached the box. "Good afternoon, Lord Duncan." He smiled.

"Good afternoon."

"You are here to testify on behalf of your friend Lord Barclay."

"I am here, sir, to testify in a libel suit against a publication known as *The Mayfair Lady,*" Lord Duncan said steadily.

Sir Samuel looked startled. Then he recovered and said, "Quite so, m'lud. That is the business that brings us all here today. Would you tell the gentlemen of the jury how long you and Lord Barclay have been friends."

"I have known the earl of Barclay for close to ten years."

"And he is one of your closest friends." Sir Samuel was now regarding his witness much as a ferret might regard a rabbit hole from which a fox might appear instead of the rabbit.

"I would have called him so, yes."

Sir Samuel closed his eyes briefly and changed tack. "You and his lordship have shared several business ventures together, as I understand it."

"Only one of any significance."

"The matter of the trans-Saharan railway?"

"Yes. A venture that I was persuaded would bring a considerable return on investment."

"Such ventures often fail, unfortunately." Sir Samuel shook his head regretfully. "All the investors suffered losses in that instance, I understand."

"To my knowledge, the only investor involved was myself, sir. And, yes, I suffered losses of some magnitude."

Again the barrister shook his head. "As indeed did Lord Barclay himself."

"That I doubt, sir, since at the time of the apparent collapse of this venture, he held a lien on my house. That could not be called a loss."

Sir Samuel looked up at the dais. "M'lud," he began, but was interrupted.

"Testimony not going quite as you expected, Sir Samuel?"

"No, m'lud. I request a recess until the morning."

The judge shook his head. "No time for that. Dismiss the witness if you wish and call your next."

"I cannot dismiss the witness, m'lud, without making him available to my learned friend, Sir Gideon," the barrister pointed out in pained tones.

"No, that is certainly true," the judge said. He sounded as if he was enjoying himself, and Prudence decided she liked him even less than she liked Sir Samuel, even if he did appear to be ruling on their side.

Sir Samuel cleared his throat. "Lord Duncan, you surrendered a lien on your house willingly?"

"I did, because at the time I thought I had no choice. I was unaware, you must understand, that the company I had invested in had no legal standing. My *friend* failed to mention this." This emphasis was so slight and yet it rang through the now intent and silent courtroom like a peal of bells.

"No further questions, m'lud." Sir Samuel returned to his seat.

"Sir Gideon?" the judge invited.

Gideon rose. "No questions for this witness, m'lud."

"You seem to be having rather an easy time of it today, Sir Gideon," the judge remarked genially.

Gideon merely bowed and sat down.

Lord Duncan left the witness box and walked straight from the courtroom, ignoring the rising whispers, the interested looks that followed his progress.

Prudence half rose as if to follow him, and then resumed her seat when Gideon took her elbow.

The judge looked around the courtroom. "Any further witnesses, Sir Samuel?"

"No, m'lud."

"Then, Sir Gideon, the court is yours."

"I have nothing further, m'lud."

Prudence didn't hear the rest of the formalities. She paid no attention to the closing arguments to the jury before they were sent off to deliberate, and she registered only distantly the judge's advice that if they the jurors found the publication not guilty of libel, they could consider awarding *The Mayfair Lady* punitive damages for the distress caused by a frivolous suit.

Prudence could think only that for the last four years they had tried to protect their father, do for him what their mother would have done, and now in the most public and humiliating situation imaginable they had forced reality upon him. It had been Chastity's idea to use a phrase that their mother had used so often.

Male pretension. The phrase had always made her husband protest with one breath and laugh in the next. It had told Lord Duncan who was in the witness box. And, of course, it had explained exactly how his private shame was now public knowledge. Would he ever forgive them?

She became aware of Gideon's hand on her arm. He was ushering her out of the courtroom and into the small antechamber again. Chastity and Constance were already there. They hugged one another fiercely.

"Will he forgive us?" Chastity asked, echoing her sister's thought.

"How long could he go on living a lie?" The question came from Gideon, who still stood beside the door. They turned on him with livid eyes. He raised his hands defensively and backed out of the chamber. No man in his right mind would face the combined wrath of the Duncan sisters.

"It's true, though," Prudence said after an instant's silence. "How long could it go on?"

"It was already over," Constance pointed out practically. "Without his testimony we were going to lose and then he'd have to face reality, and with it . . . well . . ." She blew her nose vigorously.

The door opened and they all three spun to face it.

Lord Duncan came in, letting it swing shut behind him. "That barrister told me I'd find you in here." He regarded his daughters in a silence that seemed to stretch like elastic. "How dared you?" he demanded finally. "My private papers? What possible right did you think you had?"

"We didn't think we had any," Prudence said. "But we *knew* that we had no choice. Any more than Mother would have had."

"*The Mayfair Lady* was Mother's publication," Constance said gently.

He gave a short laugh. "I realize that now. I should have known it all along."

"We couldn't lose it to a man who—" Prudence fell silent as he held up an imperative hand.

"I don't want to hear it. I've heard enough for one day. I'll see you at home. You too, Constance." The door closed quietly behind him.

The sisters gave a collective sigh, then Prudence said, "This may sound perverse, but I feel the most amazing sense of release . . . now that he knows, I mean."

"Yes," Chastity agreed soberly.

"I imagine Jenkins and Mrs. Hudson will feel it too," Constance said, just as a tap at the door heralded Gideon's return.

"The jury's coming back. Prudence . . ." He gestured to the open door.

"That was quick. Is that good or bad?" she asked.

"I prefer not to speculate. Come along." His tone was brisk and she sensed for the first time today that he was not as nerveless as he appeared.

The jury filed in. The verdict was read.

"We find the publication. The Mayfair Lady, *not guilty of libel, my lord."*

Prudence went limp as if she'd lost her skeletal structure. She stared down at the table, at her hands intertwined on its surface. She barely heard the rest of it. The award to the defendant of all costs and one thousand pounds in damages.

Only when it was over did she realize that they were free and clear. All legal costs would be borne by Barclay's side, so Gideon would get his fee. Presumably. rather more than an eighty-percent share of a thousand pounds would give him, she thought as she tried not to stumble on their walk from the court. People crowded them, questions were shouted at her, but she was barely aware of her surroundings. Gideon's hand was under her arm, supporting her, and then they were outside in the gray afternoon, and once again a hackney awaited them.

"Get in," he said, thrusting her inside as a gaggle of newspapermen pressed close, shouting their questions. Prudence half climbed, half tumbled into the gloomy interior, and realized only when she was inside that her sisters were already seated. "How did you get here?"

"Thadeus," Constance said.

Gideon leaned in through the window and said softly, "The cabbie will take you to a hotel first. We don't want you followed home. I imagine your father is already besieged. When it's dark and they've given up for the night, Thadeus will escort you home."

"You think of everything," Prudence observed.

"That is part of my job. On which subject, if it's convenient I'll call upon you in the morning to conclude our business."

"Oh, yes," Prudence said. "Our bargain. Of course."

"Precisely." He closed the door on them.

"Not much of a bargain for the barrister," Constance remarked.

"Well, his fee's covered by Barclay's costs. I doubt he's concerned," Chastity said.

"No," Constance agreed. "But if not, why's he so anxious for his pound of flesh?"

"I daresay he wants to put the entire affair behind him completely," Prudence said from the darkest corner of the cab. "Once the last piece of business is settled, it will be over and he can get on with his normal life without worrying about three contentious and subversive sisters."

"You mean *one* contentious and subversive sister," Constance stated.

Prudence shrugged. "What if I do? I'll not be sorry to have it all over and done with, once and for all."

"I'm sure it will be a relief," Chastity agreed in soothing tones. Her eyes sought her eldest sister's in the dimness. Constance raised her eyebrows in silent comprehension.

Gideon went back to his chambers. He felt none of his usual euphoria after winning a case—in fact, he felt more as if he was about to start trying one. He discarded wig and gown, poured himself a stiff whisky, and sat down at his desk. He had a plan of campaign, just as he always had before starting a trial, but he had no backup plan. There was none to be had. It was a high-stakes throw. All or nothing. And there had been nothing in her manner to encourage making such a move at this juncture. He had hoped for something. He didn't know what exactly, but some small sign that she had missed him. But she'd given him nothing.

He reached for his cigarette box. He had to make allowances for the fact that she had had so much on her plate today, she probably had no mental or emotional energy for anything else. But all the same, he had watched her like a hawk when she'd first entered his chambers, and she'd given him nothing but that cool greeting. She hadn't looked well and she was clearly troubled, but that was hardly surprising. She was facing a courtroom and the possible loss of her livelihood and a great deal else besides. Her mind had definitely not been on matters of the heart.

He sighed and stubbed out his cigarette. He couldn't remember when he'd last felt this anxious.

"You look as if you could do with a sherry, Prue," Constance said when they were ensconced in a private parlor in a discreet establishment in a side street off Piccadilly.

"There seems to be everything here," Chastity said, turning from her examination of the sideboard. "There's tea, if you'd rather. Sandwiches and fruitcake . . . cheese and biscuits . . . sherry, wine, even cognac."

"It's a little early for cognac," Prudence said. "But I'll have a glass of sherry."

"You were magnificent, Prue," Constance said, tossing her hat and gloves on a console table. "I don't know how you managed to keep that accent going without it sounding like a Feydeau farce."

"I think it did," Prudence said, taking the sherry Chastity handed her. "It's the *ze* that always gets to me.

I want to laugh every time." She took a sip of sherry. "Not this afternoon, however. I've never felt less like laughing."

"No, none of us have." Constance poured sherry for herself. "But it's over. We won. *The Mayfair Lady* and the Go-Between are safe. And no one knows us from Adam."

"Except Father."

"Except Father," she agreed.

"There's a pack of cards here," Chastity said. "How about we play three-handed bridge? We've got to do something to pass the time if we're not to fall into a slough of despond."

They had been playing for two hours when Thadeus came for them. "There are no newspapermen around the house anymore," he said.

"And Lord Duncan?"

"He had not left the premises when I came to fetch you," the clerk said. "He might have gone out since, of course."

"No, he's waiting for us," Prudence said, sliding the cards back into their silver case. "You're coming back with us, Con?"

"Of course," her elder sister said. "I'd hardly leave you to face him alone. Max will know what happened in court by now, so he'll assume I'm with you."

"The carriage is at the back door," Thadeus informed them. "I thought it best to avoid the front just in case anyone's lingering."

"You think of everything, Thadeus." Prudence smiled wanly at him. He merely bowed.

They sat in silence during the short ride to Manchester Square. "We'll go in the back way,"

Prudence said as they turned into the square. "Ask him to go to the mews entrance, Thadeus."

"I have already done so, Miss Duncan."

"Yes, of course you have," Prudence murmured.

"Sir Gideon wished me to give you this, Miss Duncan." Thadeus handed her an envelope as she stepped to the ground.

"Oh, thank you." She looked down at it, puzzled. "What is it?"

"The lien on the house, madam. He thought you would know best what to do with it."

Prudence tucked it into her handbag. "Yes, I think I will."

They went into the house through the kitchen. "Oh, my goodness," Mrs. Hudson said as they came in. "What a to-do there's been. Men ringing the doorbell, asking questions, Lord Duncan in the worst mood I've ever seen him in. Locked in the library, he is. What's been going on?"

"I trust the enterprise went in your favor, Miss Prue?" Jenkins appeared in the doorway, his face drawn with anxiety.

"Yes... yes, Jenkins, it did," Prudence said swiftly. "I'm sorry we couldn't get home earlier, but Sir Gideon thought we should avoid the newspapers. He was afraid the press would follow us here, even if they weren't already here trying to get at Father."

"They were here, all right," Jenkins said grimly. "Banging the knocker. I threatened to call the police. His lordship locked himself in the library. I tried to ask him what had happened but he cursed me to the devil. I thought it best to leave well enough alone."

"Wise of you, Jenkins," Constance said with a faint

smile. "We did win the case, but in order for us to do so, Lord Duncan had to find out the truth."

"Ah," Jenkins said, "that explains it, then." Mrs. Hudson nodded gravely.

"It should make the house a little easier to manage," Prudence said. "If we don't have to pretend and cover up."

Jenkins shook his head. "I don't know about that, Miss Prue. Somehow I don't see his lordship settling for leftovers and inferior wine."

"No," Prudence agreed. "We'll still have to make shift, but at least we won't feel we're creeping around behind his back."

"I think we'd better go to him now," Chastity said. "We can't put it off much longer."

"There's no putting anything off," announced Lord Duncan from the kitchen door. "I assumed you conspirators would all be in here." He glared at the assembled group. "Don't pretend you didn't know about this Jenkins, or you, Mrs. Hudson."

"Father, it's nothing to do with either of them," Prudence protested. "You can blame us all you like, but Jenkins and Mrs. Hudson have only tried to help and make your life easier."

A dull flush mounted on Lord Duncan's cheeks. "For some reason my entire household seemed to find it necessary to shelter me from the consequences of my own folly. I do not find that a pleasant thought." He turned on his heel. "We will discuss this further in the library."

His daughters exchanged a look, shrugged in unison, and followed him. "There's no need to close the door," he said as they entered the library. "It's clear there are no secrets in this household from anyone but myself."

His daughters said nothing.

"How did you persuade Fitchley to let you examine my private papers?" he demanded.

Prudence sighed and told him. "You cannot blame Mr. Fitchley," she said at the end.

"Clearly not. Of all the deceitful . . ." He turned away from them and he seemed suddenly a very old man. "Go away, all of you. I can't face any of you at the moment."

They left him, closing the door softly. "He can't face us, or he can't face himself?" Constance muttered.

Prudence was staring at the closed door, then abruptly she said, "No, we're not bearing all this guilt. Come on." She opened the door and stalked in, her startled sisters behind her.

"I told you—"

"Yes, Father, and we heard you. However, you might want to burn this." She opened her handbag and took out the envelope. "I doubt very much that the earl of Barclay will be pursuing it after this afternoon." She held it out to him.

Lord Duncan opened the envelope, stared down at the lien on his house. "He has no legal claim, then?" he said, almost in disbelief.

"No," Prudence stated. "And he never did have. Since Barclay Earl and Associates is not a legal entity, they can't hold property in its name. Burn it, Father. *Now.*"

He looked at them as they stood in front of him, presenting a united and determined front. And he thought of his wife, and of how like her they all were. And he thought of how much he missed her, every minute of every waking hour. And he knew that his daughters missed her as deeply, if in different ways. And he thought how they were her living embodiment.

Deliberately, he tore the sheet in two, then turned and threw both pieces into the fire. He stood watching as the paper curled, caught, and fell into ash.

Lord Duncan heard the door close behind him as he remained staring into the fire, acknowledging his grief.

Chapter 20

"Prue, are you sure you don't mind seeing Gideon alone?" Chastity asked the next morning, standing on tiptoe to see in the high hall mirror as she adjusted the brim of her hat.

"Of course I don't," her sister said carelessly, sweeping into the palm of her hand fallen petals from the vase of fading chrysanthemums on the hall table. "We need to get *The Mayfair Lady* out on the streets again as soon as possible, and we haven't picked up the post from Mrs. Beedle in more than two weeks. Con's writing up the account of the trial this morning, so it's my task to deal with the barrister. It has been all along, after all."

"I suppose so," Chastity said, still sounding doubtful, but it was clear that her sister had her mind made up and it was the most sensible division of labor, since it would only take one of them to dispose of Gideon. "Very well, then, I'll be off. I'll only be a couple of hours, if that. It depends if Mrs. Beedle wants to chat."

Prudence waved her away and picked up the vase of flowers. She carried it into the kitchen to dispose of them and was returning with the empty vase to the hall when the doorbell rang.

"Shall I get that, Miss Prue?" Jenkins had appeared as usual as if by magic carpet.

"It'll be Sir Gideon," she said, smoothing down her skirts. "Show him into the drawing room."

Jenkins went to open the door and Prudence went into the drawing room, where she turned her attention to a bowl of late-blooming roses that seemed to require some rearranging.

"Good morning."

She turned slowly at the soft voice. "Good morning." She moved towards the sofa. "Do sit down."

"Thank you." He took an armchair and waited for Prudence to alight somewhere. She perched on the arm of the sofa.

"So, I take it you've come to settle our business?" she said.

"That was what I had in mind."

Prudence folded her arms. "You don't think it's a little premature?" she asked testily. "We haven't even received our thousand pounds as yet." She got to her feet abruptly. "I don't understand why this couldn't have been dealt with by letter. Presumably once the damages are paid the money will go to you. Why couldn't you simply subtract your eight hundred pounds and send us our two?"

"Well, you see, I don't think I could do that," he said.

"Well, I'm very sorry, but we don't have the money. I can't give you eighty percent of nothing, can I?" Her green eyes glared, and he could see dark emerald sparks in their depths. Miss Duncan was clearly rather irritated.

He had the feeling that it had little to do with his supposed reason for this visit.

"Unfortunately, I find myself in dire straits," he murmured apologetically.

She stared at him. "What on earth... How could *you* find yourself in financial straits? Don't be absurd, Gideon. You can't possibly expect me to believe that. I don't believe for one minute that eight hundred pounds would make one iota of difference to your bank balance."

"Oh, it wouldn't," he agreed, shaking his head. "Not one iota."

"Then what the hell are you talking about?" She was growing more irritated by the minute, and his calm demeanor wasn't helping.

He rose to his feet, murmuring, "Since *you* won't sit down—"

"There's no reason to sit down. I've explained the situation, and that concludes our business. You will get your share when we get ours." She folded her arms again.

"Well, you see, I don't think it does quite conclude our business," he explained in the same slightly apologetic tone.

Prudence was suddenly wary. "What do you mean?"

"As I recall, there was another aspect to our business agreement," he said. He walked to the window and looked down at the winter-bare garden. "A bride, wasn't it? You—or rather, the Go-Between—were going to find me a bride in exchange for my defending you in the libel suit."

Prudence was now even warier. There was something palpably dangerous in the air. She reminded herself that this man was adept at the art of ambush. She'd seen him in court, and experienced it herself once or twice. Sudden moves on her part were not advisable. She said slowly, as if speaking to one a little short on mental acuity, "You were just toying with us, with the whole idea, Gideon. You remember that."

"Oh, no," he said, turning around from the window. "I was not toying with you or the bargain. I did, as I recall, say that I might prefer to find my own bride, but I was certainly open to suggestions that would widen the field."

"Oh," Prudence said, frowning. "Would you consider meeting Lavender Riley, then? I'm sure you would like each other."

Gideon crossed the room in three strides. "Never have I known you to be obtuse, Prudence. No, I would *not* under any circumstances consider meeting Lavender Riley."

"Perhaps Heather Peterson—" she began, and then said no more because it was impossible to do so when her mouth was suddenly otherwise and somewhat forcefully occupied.

"Have I made myself clear?" he demanded when he finally raised his lips from hers, his hands still, however, holding her firmly against him.

"I'm not sure," Prudence said. "You haven't really said anything yet."

He put his hands around her throat, lightly encircling the slender column. His eyes were dark as charcoal as he held her gaze, and she could feel his thumbs against the pulse in her throat, a pulse that was beating so fast, she could hear it in her ears.

"The Go-Between fulfilled its side of the bargain. It

introduced me to the only woman who could possibly be my bride. Prudence Duncan, will you marry me?"

"Harriet?" It was the only word she seemed capable of uttering.

"Her horse trainer came back for her last week." He released her and ran his hands through his immaculately groomed hair in a gesture that expressed frustration. anxiety, and that flash of vulnerability that she found so endearing. "Sarah . . ." he said, "I need your help, Prudence. I was wrong—hell, I'm often wrong. I admit it. But I really need you."

"You're not the only one who's often wrong," she said softly, touching his face, moving her other hand up to smooth down his hair. "I admit it freely."

He grasped her wrists, held her hands tightly against his face, then turned his lips to kiss the inside of her wrists. "Will you marry me, sweetheart?"

She smiled. "I think you're supposed to produce a ring and go down on one knee."

"The ring I can do," he said, "but I'll be damned if I'm going down on one knee, even for you, sweetheart."

She grinned. "I didn't really expect you to."

"Do I have my answer?"

"Well," she said consideringly, "I suppose it would save us eight hundred pounds— No . . . no, Gideon." She danced away from him as he came after her with a look in his eye that she wasn't at all sure about. "I'll call Jenkins."

"Call him." He grabbed her arm, swinging her to his body. "You are a wasp and the most impossible woman I've ever met."

"Yes," she agreed. "And I dislike *you* intensely too."

"Then that seems like an equitable agreement."

* * *

It was an hour later when Constance and Chastity met on the steps of the house. "Well met," Constance greeted her sister. "Did you see Mrs. Beedle?"

"Yes, and a whole stack of letters. Did you write your article?"

Constance smiled. "Just wait until you read it."

"But you didn't hold Father up to ridicule?" Chastity asked with a worried frown.

"Chas!"

"No, of course you didn't. I'm sorry. I'm just so anxious."

"Prue? Did she see him alone?"

Chastity nodded. "I imagine he's gone by now. But you know how she tries to hide how she feels . . . if she's hurt, I mean. I really thought that . . ."

Constance put an arm around her. "So did I. But they aren't compatible, Chas. Prue knows that."

Chastity nodded as she put her key in the door. The hall was deserted when they went in, and they looked at each other in puzzlement. It was unheard of for Jenkins not to respond to the turn of a key, wherever he was in the house.

"I expect she's in the parlor," Chastity said, heading for the stairs. She stopped halfway across the hall as the stealthy figure of Jenkins suddenly appeared in the shadows of the stairs. He put a finger to his lips and beckoned with the other hand. Fascinated, the sisters followed him into the kitchen.

"Miss Prue is in the drawing room with Sir Gideon," Jenkins informed them.

"Still?" Chastity exclaimed. "He was supposed to come two hours ago."

"Yes, Miss Chas. But Miss Prue hasn't rung for anything."

"And you're certain Sir Gideon didn't leave . . . when you weren't looking maybe? Oh, of course he didn't," Constance corrected herself when she saw his outraged expression. "How could he have slipped past you?"

Jenkins nodded, appeased. "I thought it best not to inquire if they needed anything," he stated.

"Yes," Chastity said. "I would have done the same thing." She looked at her sister. "What do you think, Con? Shall we go in?"

"And risk in flagrante delicto?"

"Oh, don't be absurd, Con. It's the drawing room."

"Well, I think we'd better make a great deal of noise," Constance said. "Kettle drums. We need kettle drums."

"We don't have any," Chastity said through her reluctant laughter. "But we could try banging a couple of Mrs. Hudson's pans together."

"Oh, give over, Miss Chas, do," Mrs. Hudson said, although she, like Jenkins, was trying to stifle a smile.

"I suggest you knock upon the door, Miss Con," Jenkins said, once more his stately self. "And maybe wait a few minutes before you open it."

"Of course, Jenkins, the perfect solution," Constance said. She winked at him and he turned discreetly to one side, not quite managing to hide his smile.

The sisters returned to the hall. They walked around heavily for a few minutes, opened and shut the front door several times, and then approached the drawing room. Constance raised her hand to knock, but the door opened before she could do so.

"I could hear you from ten miles away," Prudence said. "Come in. We need your advice."

"Oh." That was unexpected, Constance reflected. "Good morning, Gideon. Are you still finishing up business?"

"No, I believe we're only beginning," Gideon said, coming forward with outstretched hand. "Good morning, Constance . . . Chastity."

They shook his hand and then turned as one to their sister. "Prue?"

"It seems," she said, "that Gideon has decided to take up the alternative to our bargain."

"Oh," Chastity said with a smile. "And did we find him a bride?"

"It would seem so," Prudence said. She moved her hand into the light. A circlet of emeralds threw green fire against the ray of sun piercing the window.

"The stones seemed appropriate . . . matched your sister's eyes," Gideon said, waving his hands in a slightly uncertain manner. He hadn't realized that he would think he needed the sisters' approval of his choice of gems. But he realized he needn't have worried. They were not in the least interested in the ring. They brushed their sister's hand aside as they embraced her in a hug so fierce, so all-encompassing, he couldn't help the slightest prick of jealousy.

And then they broke apart, and he found himself embraced by Constance and Chastity, and the prick of jealousy disappeared. He thought that perhaps it would be a good idea to talk to his soon-to-be brother-in-law about what he should expect of a life married to one of the Duncan sisters.

"You said you wanted our advice," Constance reminded them when the hugging was over.

"Oh, yes. I was thinking we should elope," Prudence said.

"The anvil at Gretna Green is not my idea of a wedding," Gideon said.

"But just think, we could take the overnight train to Edinburgh, it's wonderfully romantic, and then—" Prudence stopped. "You really hate the idea."

"I see no reason why we should hide in corners. Haven't you been doing enough of that?"

Prudence knew this was no ambush. He was facing her with such a question when she had her sisters around her. She could only commend his courage. "Yes," she said. "But something feels wrong about a grand spectacle at this moment. Constance's wedding was magnificent, but that wouldn't feel right now. We're all too raw." She looked at her sister for confirmation.

Constance said, "This is your wedding, love. Whatever you want to do, Chas and I will be here to support you. We'll leave you to talk it through." She nodded at Chastity, who nodded back and followed her to the door.

With her hand on the knob, Chastity turned back. "I do think Gretna Green is a really terrible idea, Prue." Then they left.

"If we could wait a year," Prudence began. "No, I don't want to either. How small . . . ?"

"As small as you like. Your family, Sarah, you and me."

"You don't have any family?"

"My parents are dead and I was an only child. If you wanted a big wedding, then I could produce a reasonable showing on my side, but only Sarah really needs to be there."

"And Mary Winston?"

"Yes," he agreed. "Mary needs to be there."

"Then we're agreed."

He took her in his arms again. "Sweetheart, we are going to agree some of the time, and disagree much of the time."

"Yes," she said against his mouth. "It won't be too difficult to remind myself that I dislike you intensely."

He moved his mouth from hers, brushed his lips along the line of her jaw, and then raised his head. "I'll get a special license. We can be married within the week."

"Yes," Prudence said. "Best to do it before I change my mind." Her smile gave the lie to her words.

"Wasp," he accused again, pinching the end of her nose. "I had better talk to your father now."

Prudence grimaced. "He's in the library. But bear in mind he's had more than his fair share of shocks in the last two days. He might not be exactly . . ." She shrugged.

"I can manage your father, if you can manage Sarah," he said.

Prudence nodded, all gravity now. "I'll do my best, Gideon."

"She's a little uncertain about things at the moment . . . after Harriet, you understand."

"I understand."

He nodded, ran his hands through his hair again, then kissed her quickly and left.

Epilogue

"Chas, are you ready?" Constance stuck her head around the door of her youngest sister's bedroom. "Prue and Father are leaving in five minutes."

"Yes, I'm quite ready." Chastity put down the letter she was reading. "I was only running through the last batch of mail for the Go-Between."

"Oh?" Constance gave her a rather quizzical look. "Strange thing to be doing on Prue's wedding morning."

"No, it's not." Chastity got up from the dresser chair. "You know how Mother used to say that a minute wasted was a minute lost forever. I'm ready, and I had a minute."

"Yes, of course," Constance said agreeably. "You look lovely."

"As do you," Chastity returned. "And Prue looks sensational. Let's give her the finishing touches." Constance nodded and left. Chastity hesitated for a minute before following. She picked up the letter she'd discarded on her dresser and looked again at the signature.

Dr. Douglas Farrell.

It seemed that the good doctor was in search of a wife. A helpmeet. A woman who would want to be involved in his work. Was it the same Dr. Farrell she'd seen at Mrs. Beedle's?

A question for another day. She grabbed her handbag, took a quick look in the mirror to make sure her hat was straight, and hurried to Prudence's bedroom.

"I don't know if I want this veil," Prudence was saying as Chastity came in. "It seems too bridal. I'm not walking down the aisle to the wedding march."

"Then wear it up," Constance suggested. "Lift it and put it back. Like so . . . then it frames your face."

"And you *are* a bride," Chastity chimed in. "It may not be the most conventional wedding, but it still has a bride and groom."

"I know. But I wish we'd gone to Gretna Green," Prudence said. She turned in front of the mirror. She could find no fault with her oyster-colored silk dress that had been refashioned from one of their mother's afternoon gowns. Something old. No fault with the mink pillow that Constance had lent her as a hat. Something borrowed. No fault with the diamond bracelet that Gideon had given her. Something new. And no fault with the turquoise earrings that her father had given her that morning. Something blue.

"You forgot the sixpence," Chastity said, dropping the shiny coin onto the dresser.

"Oh, yes." Prudence laughed, and much of her tension dissipated. She sat down, slipped off her ivory silk slipper, and slid the coin into the toe.

"Something old, something new, something borrowed,

something blue, and a sixpence in your shoe," Chastity recited. "And now you're ready to get married."

"Oh, but am I?" Prudence asked, standing up, curling her toes around the sixpence. "*Am* I?"

"As ready as you'll ever be," Constance declared. "Gideon is the only man you could ever marry, Prue. If you don't know that by now, then nothing Chas and I can say will persuade you."

"Of course I know it." She smiled a little dreamily. "I love him, but sometimes I could pour boiling oil on him."

"That's normal," Constance said from the benefit of experience. "I don't see any way that Duncan women can marry men strong enough for them without accepting boiling oil and cannon fire as part of the bargain."

"I'm ready," Prudence declared. "Let's get married." She paused in the doorway and said with a slightly tremulous smile, "At least Gideon has Max to stand up with him. I'm sure he's as scared as I am."

Chastity looked at her anxiously. "No regrets, Prue?"

Prudence took a deep breath. "No . . . none. Let's go."

Gideon and Max stood at the altar in the side chapel of the small church in Westminster. Sarah and Mary Winston sat in the front pew. Constance and Chastity sat on the opposite side. Lord Duncan had insisted that he walk his daughter down the aisle.

The organist began to play. Gideon looked towards the door. Prudence, his bride, the woman who once upon a time he could never have dreamed of as a life's companion, was now the only woman he could imagine sharing his life. And she was walking towards him, her step as strong and decisive as always. And yet he could see the slight tremor of her lips, the hesitancy in her eye, and he knew she was as terrified and yet as certain of the rightness of this as he was.

He stepped forward as she reached him. Max touched his shoulder in brief masculine reassurance and then went to sit beside his wife. Lord Duncan kissed the bride's cheek and stepped back also to take his seat. Gideon took Prudence's hand and her fingers twined with his. The words were said. He put the gold band on her finger. He kissed her. And it was done. They went into the small registry to sign the book, and when they went back to the church, they were alone.

"Never," Gideon whispered, bending towards her ear, "will I let you go. *Never*. You understand that?"

"And that goes double for me," she returned in the same whisper. "Whatever happens, we belong together. Through boiling oil and cannon fire."

"I'm not going to ask where that came from. But yes, through boiling oil and cannon fire. We belong together." He kissed her again, and there was nothing formal about this kiss. It was an affirmation that ignored their surroundings, the incense-scented gloom, lit only by the altar candles.

Prudence looked around at the deserted church and Gideon said softly, "You wanted Gretna Green. I agreed with your sisters on a compromise. We'll have a family celebration tomorrow, but for now, there are only the two of us."

She smiled up at him. "Where are we going?"

"A bride is not supposed to know her honeymoon destination," he said. "You have to trust me."

"I do," she said. "Now and for always."

"Boiling oil and cannon fire notwithstanding?" he teased.

"Trust can withstand the occasional spark," she returned.

About the Author

Jane Feather is the *New York Times* bestselling, award-winning author of *The Bachelor List, Kissed by Shadows, To Kiss a Spy, The Widow's Kiss, The Least Likely Bride, The Accidental Bride, The Hostage Bride, A Valentine Wedding, The Emerald Swan,* and many other historical romances. She was born in Cairo, Egypt, and grew up in the New Forest, in the south of England. She began her writing career after she and her family moved to Washington, D.C., in 1981. She now has more than ten million copies of her books in print.

And look for the next two tales of the delightful and vivacious Duncan sisters . . .

Jane Feather's

The Bachelor List

Con's story

On Sale Now

and

The Wedding Game

Chastity's story

On Sale April 2004

Read on for previews . . .

NEW YORK TIMES BESTSELLING AUTHOR
JANE
FEATHER
THE
BACHELOR
LIST
"An accomplished storyteller...rare and wonderful."
—Daily News of Los Angeles

NEW YORK TIMES BESTSELLING AUTHOR
JANE
FEATHER
THE
WEDDING
GAME

The Bachelor List

On sale now

Max Ensor gazed thoughtfully after the three sisters as they left Fortnum and Mason. He was convinced now that not only he but also Elizabeth Armitage had been exposed to a degree of gentle mockery. He wondered if Elizabeth had noticed it. Somehow he doubted it. It had been so subtle, he'd almost missed it himself. Just a hint in the voice, a gleam in the eye.

They were a good-looking trio. Redheads, all three of them, but with subtle variations in the shade that moved from the russet of autumn leaves to cinnamon, and in the case of the one he guessed was the youngest, a most decisive red. All green-eyed too, but again of different shades. He thought the eldest one, Constance, with her russet hair and darkest green eyes, was the most striking of the three, but perhaps that was because she was the tallest. Either way, there was something about all three of them that piqued his interest.

"Are they Lord Duncan's daughters?" he inquired.

"Yes, their mother died about three years ago." Elizabeth gave a sympathetic sigh. "So hard for them, poor girls. You'd think they'd all be married by now. Constance must be all of twenty-eight, and I know she's had more than one offer."

Tiny frown lines appeared between her well-plucked brows. "In fact, I seem to remember a young man a few years ago . . . some dreadful tragedy. I believe he was killed in the war . . . at Mafeking or one of those unpronounceable places." She shook her head, briskly dismissing the entire African continent and all its confusions.

"As for Chastity," she continued, happy to return to more solid ground. "Well, she must be twenty-six, and she has more suitors than one can count."

Elizabeth leaned forward, her voice at a conspiratorial volume. "But they took their mother's death very hard, poor girls." She tutted sorrowfully. "It was very sudden. All over in a matter of weeks. Cancer," she added. "She just faded away." She shook her head again and took a cream-laden bite of hazelnut gâteau.

Max Ensor sipped his tea. "I'm slightly acquainted with the baron. He takes his seat most days in the House of Lords."

"Oh, Lord Duncan's most conscientious, I'm sure. Charming man, quite charming. But I can't help feeling he's not doing a father's duty." Elizabeth dabbed delicately at her rouged mouth with her napkin. "He should insist they marry—well, Constance and Chastity certainly. He can't have three old maids in the family. Prudence is a little different. I'm sure she would be content to stay and look after her father. Such a sensible girl . . . such a pity about the spectacles. They do make a woman look so dull."

Dull was not a word Max Ensor, on first acquaintance, would have applied to any one of the three Duncan sisters. And behind her thick lenses he seemed to recall that Miss Prudence had a pair of extremely light and lively green eyes.

He gave a noncommittal nod and asked, "May I see that broadsheet, ma'am?"

"It's quite scandalous." Elizabeth opened her bag again. She lowered her voice. "Of course, everyone's reading it, but no one admits it. I'm sure even Letitia reads it sometimes." She pushed the folded sheets across the table surreptitiously beneath her flattened palm.

Max Ensor doubted that his sister, Letitia, read anything other than the handwritten menu sheets presented to her each morning by her cook, but he kept the observation to himself and unfolded the papers.

The broadsheet was competently printed although he doubted it had been through a major press. The paper was cheap and flimsy and the layout without artistry. He glanced at the table of contents listed at the left-hand side of the top page. His eyebrows lifted. There were two political articles listed, one on the new public house licensing laws and the other on the new twenty-mile-an-hour speed limit for motorcars. Hardly topics to appeal to Mayfair ladies of the Elizabeth Armitage or Letitia Graham ilk, and yet judging by its bold title, the broadsheet was addressing just such a readership.

His eye was caught by a boxed headline in black type, bolder than any other on the front page. It was a headline in the form of a statement and a question and stood alone in its box, jumping out at the reader with an urgent immediacy. WOMEN TAXPAYERS DEMAND THE VOTE. WILL THE LIBERAL GOVERNMENT GIVE WOMEN TAXPAYERS THE VOTE?

"It seems this paper has more on its mind than gossip

and fashion," he observed, tapping a finger against the headline.

"Oh, that, yes. They're always writing about this suffrage business," Elizabeth said. "So boring. But every edition has something just like that in a box on the front page. I don't take any notice. Most of us don't."

Max frowned. *Just who was responsible for this paper?* Was it a forum for the women troublemakers who were growing daily more intransigent as they pestered the government with their demand for the vote? The rest of the topics in the paper were more to be expected: an article about the American illustrator Charles Dana Gibson and his idealized drawings of the perfect woman, the Gibson girl; a description of a Society wedding and who attended; a list of coming social events. He glanced idly at the Gibson article, blinked, and began to read. He had expected to see earnest advice to follow the prevailing fashion in order to achieve Gibson-girl perfection, instead he found himself reading an intelligent criticism of women's slavish following of fashions that were almost always dictated by men.

He looked up. "Who writes this?"

"Oh, no one knows," Elizabeth said, reaching out eagerly to take back her prize. "That's what makes it so interesting, of course. It's been around for at least ten years, then there was a short period when it didn't appear, but now it's back and it has a lot more in it."

She folded the sheets again. "Such a nuisance that one has to buy it now. Before, there were always copies just lying around in the cloakrooms and on hall tables. But it didn't have quite so many interesting things in it then. It was mostly just the boring political stuff. Women voting and that Property Act business. I don't understand any of it. Dear Ambrose takes care of such things." She gave a little trill of laughter as she tucked the sheets back into her handbag. "Not a suitable subject for ladies."

"No, indeed," Max Ensor agreed with a firm nod. "There's trouble enough in the world without women involving themselves in issues that don't concern them."

"Just what dear Ambrose says." Elizabeth's smile was complacent as she put her hands to her head to check the set of her black taffeta hat from which descended a cascade of white plumes.

She glanced at the little enameled fob watch pinned to her lapel and exclaimed, "Oh, my goodness me, is that the time? I really must be going. Such a charming tea. Thank you so much, Mr. Ensor."

"The pleasure was all mine, Lady Armitage. I trust I shall see you this evening at the Beekmans' soirée. Letitia has commandeered my escort." He rose and bowed, handing her her gloves.

"It will be a charming evening, I'm sure," Elizabeth declared, smoothing her gloves over her fingers. "Everything is so very charming in London at the moment. Don't you find it so?"

"Uh . . . charming," he agreed. He remained on his feet until she had billowed away, then called for the bill, reflecting that *charming* had to be the most overworked adjective in a Mayfair lady's vocabulary. Letitia used it to describe everything from her young daughter's hair ribbons to the coals in the fireplace and he'd lost count of the number of times it had dropped from Elizabeth Armitage's lips in the last hour.

However, he would swear that not one of the Honorable Misses Duncan had used it.

Women taxpayers demand the vote.

It would be both interesting and enlightening to discover who was behind that newspaper, he reflected, collecting his hat. The government was doing everything in its power to minimize the influence of the fanatical group of headstrong women, and a few foolish men, who were pressing for women's suffrage. But it was hard to control a movement when it went underground, and the true subversives were notoriously difficult to uncover. Unless he was much mistaken, this newspaper directed at the women of Mayfair was as subversive in its intended influence as any publication he'd seen. It would definitely be in the government's interest to draw its teeth. There were a variety of ways of doing that once its editors and writers were identified. And how difficult could it be to uncover them?

Max Ensor went out into the muggy afternoon, whistling thoughtfully between his teeth as he made his way to Westminster.

The Wedding Game

On sale April 2004

The gentleman who was standing at the top of the steps of the National Gallery closely scrutinized the assumed art lovers ascending towards the great doors of the art museum at his back. He held a prominently displayed copy of the broadsheet *The Mayfair Lady*. He was looking for someone flourishing a similar article.

A cloud of pigeons rose in a flurry from Trafalgar Square as a figure hastened across the square, scattering corn to the birds as she came. She crossed the street directly below the museum and paused at the bottom step, crushing the paper bag that had held the corn in her hand as she gazed upwards. She held a rolled-up newspaper in her free hand. The man made a tentative movement with his own broadsheet and the figure tossed the scrunched bag into a litter bin and hurried up the steps towards him.

That the figure was small and female was about all the gentleman could discern. She was swathed in a loose alpaca dust coat of the kind that ladies wore when motoring, and wore a broad-brimmed felt hat, her face obscured by an opaque chiffon veil.

"Bonjour, m'sieur," she greeted him. "I think we are to meet, *n'est-ce pas*." She waved her copy of *The Mayfair Lady*. "You are Dr. Douglas Farrell, is it not so?"

"The very same, madam," he said with a small bow. "And you are . . ."

"I am ze Mayfair Lady, of course," she responded, her veil fluttering with each breath.

With the phoniest French accent he'd ever heard, Dr. Farrell reflected with some amusement. He decided not to call her on it just yet. "The Mayfair Lady in person?" he questioned curiously.

"The representative of ze publication, *m'sieur,*" she responded on a note of reproof.

"Ah," he nodded. "And the Go-Between?"

"One and the same, sir," the lady said with a decisive nod. "And as I understand it, sir, it is ze Go-Between that can be of service to you." *This damnable French accent always made her want to laugh,* reflected the Honorable Chastity Duncan. Whether she was using it or one of her sisters, they all agreed they sounded like French maids in a Feydeau farce. But it was a very useful device for disguising voices.

"I had expected to meet in an office," the doctor said, glancing around at their rather public surroundings. A chill December wind was blowing across the square, ruffling the pigeons' feathers.

"Our office premises are not open to ze public, *m'sieur,*" she said simply. "I suggest we go inside, zere are many quiet places in ze museum where we can talk." She moved towards the doors and her companion hastened to open them for her. The folds of her alpaca dust coat brushed against him as she billowed past into the cavernous atrium of the museum.

"Let us go to the Medieval gallery, *m'sieur,*" she suggested, gesturing towards the stairs with her newspaper. "Zere is a secluded alcove with a bench where we may talk in private." She moved authoritatively ahead of him and Dr. Farrell followed obediently, both intrigued and amused by this performance. In the long gallery she hurried down the aisle between massive canvases of atrocious martyrdoms, pietas, and crucifixions without so much as a sideways glance at these cultural icons. At the far end she turned aside into a deep window embrasure flanked by marble columns and occupied by a stone bench.

" 'Ere it is quiet and we may be private," she declared, settling herself on the bench and gathering her skirts close to her to give him room to sit beside her. When he had done so, she turned her veiled head towards him. Chastity had the advantage of Dr. Douglas Farrell in that she had seen him once before when he had visited Mrs. Beedle's corner shop to buy a copy of *The Mayfair Lady* and Chastity had watched the transaction unobserved. He was as she remembered him, a very big man, certainly not easily forgotten. Both tall and broad, with the muscular heft of a sporting man. A boxer or a wrestler, she thought. The prominent bump on a once broken nose seemed to support the guess. His features were strong and uneven, his mouth wide, his jaw of the lantern variety. His eyes were the color of charcoal beneath thick black eyebrows that met over the bridge of his nose. His hair was as black, rather curly but cut short and businesslike. Everything about him indicated someone who cared little for the nuances of appearances. He wore an unexceptional greatcoat, buttoned to the neck, with muffler and gloves, and he held a plain trilby hat on his lap.

She became suddenly aware of the length of the silence that had accompanied her assessment of her companion and said quickly, "Now, 'ow exactly can ze Go-Between 'elp you, *m'sieur*?"

He glanced around with some interest. "So this is the office of *The Mayfair Lady*?"

She detected the faint Scottish lilt to his voice that she had noticed when she'd first observed him at Mrs. Beedle's. "*Non,* but we do not see clients in our office," she informed him firmly. Chastity kept to herself the reflection that their office was either the tearoom at Fortnum and Mason or the first-floor parlor of her father's house that had been the Duncan sisters' mother's sanctum. Neither space was conducive to official client interviews.

"Why is that?" he inquired.

"It is necessary for ze Mayfair Lady to be anonymous," she stated. "Could we proceed with business, *m'sieur*?"

"Yes, of course. But, I confess, Madam Mayfair Lady, that I am curious. Why is this anonymity necessary?"

Chastity sighed. "'Ave you read ze publication, *m'sieur*?"

"Yes, of course. I would not have known to seek the services of the Go-Between otherwise."

"You can read advertisements without reading the articles," she pointed out, forgetting her accent for a second.

"I have read the articles."

She gave a very Gallic shrug. "Zen surely you must see

that the opinions expressed are controversial. Ze editors prefer to remain anonymous."

"I see." He thought he did. "Of course, creating a sense of mystery must add to the publication's appeal."

"That is true," she conceded.

He nodded. "As I recall there was a libel case several months ago. *The Mayfair Lady* was sued for libel by . . ." He frowned, then his brow cleared. "By the earl of Barclay, I believe."

"A suit that was dismissed," Chastity stated.

"Yes." He nodded. "So I remember. I also remember that the publication was represented by an anonymous witness in the witness box. Is that not so?"

"It is so."

"Intriguing," he said. "I'm sure you saw the volume of your sales increase considerably after that."

"Maybe so," she said vaguely. "But it is not for zat reason that we choose to conceal our identities. Now, to business, *m'sieur*."

Douglas, fascinated and curious though he remained, accepted that for the present, question time was over. "As I explained in my letter, I am in need of a wife."

She drew out the letter in question from her handbag. "That is all you say, 'owever. We would need to know more details of your situation and the kind of wife you are looking for before we can know whether we can 'elp you in your search."

"Yes, of course," he agreed. "As it happens there are only two essential qualities I require in a wife." He drew off his gloves as he spoke, thrusting them into his pockets. "I am hoping in your registry you will have someone who would serve my purpose. Apart from the two essential issues, I am not unduly particular." His voice was very cool and matter-of-fact as he laid out the situation for her, tapping off the points with a finger on his palm as he made them.

"As I mentioned in my letter I am a member of the medical profession. I have recently arrived in London from Edinburgh, where I received my medical degree and where I practiced for some years. I am in the process of opening a surgery on Harley Street, one that I trust will generate considerable income once I have become well enough known in London society."

Chastity made no response, merely clasped her gloved hands in her lap and regarded him through her veil. She was beginning to get a bad feeling about this interview, and her intuition rarely failed her.

The doctor unwrapped his muffler. He seemed to find it too warm in the small embrasure despite the hard stone upon which they sat and the cold December wind rattling the glass of the window behind them. Chastity, who was growing chillier by the minute, envied him. She reflected that perhaps such a large man generated his own bodily heat.

"Anyway," he continued, "I must find myself a wife who is first and foremost rich."

And at that point Chastity realized that her intuition had indeed been absolutely correct. But again she made no response, merely stiffened slightly.

"As you will appreciate," he continued in the same detached tone, "it's an expensive business setting up such a practice. Harley Street rents are very high, and wealthy patients expect to be treated in surroundings that reassure them they are receiving only the best of care from a practitioner who treats only people who expect and can afford the best."

Chastity thought she could detect just a hint of sarcasm in his voice. She said distantly, "In my experience doctors who practice on Harley Street generally do very well for themselves. Well enough to support a wife, I would assume."

He shrugged. "Yes, once they're established, they do. But I am not as yet established and I intend to become so. To do that, I need some help. You understand me?"

"I am not generally considered obtuse," she said.

If her frigid tone disconcerted the doctor he gave no sign of it. He continued as calmly as before, "I need a wife who can bring to the marriage a certain financial stability in addition to having the social graces and connections that would enable her to advance my practice. A lady, in short, who would be able to persuade the..." He paused as if looking for the right word. His lip had curled slightly. "The ladies with megrims, with the imaginary ailments that arise from having nothing to think about, nothing sensible to do with their lives, and the gentlemen with gout and the other ailments that arise from a lazy and overindulged existence. . . . I need a wife to fish for those patients for me and to instill them with utter confidence in her husband's medical skill."

"In short, *m'sieur*, what you require is not so much a wife as a banker and a procuress," Chastity stated. She wondered for a minute if she had been a little too offensive in expressing her outrage, but she need not have feared.

"Precisely," he agreed equably. "You understand the situation exactly. I prefer to call a spade a spade." He peered at her. "Is it possible to see your face, madam?"

"*Absolument pas,* m'sieur. Absolutely not."

He shrugged. "As you wish, of course. But apart from

the fact that I prefer to do business with someone whose identity is known to me, this mystery seems a trifle unnecessary. Could you at least drop the fake accent?"

Chastity bit her lip behind her veil. She hadn't expected him to believe in it for a minute, but she also knew that it successfully disguised her voice and when the time came for her to meet him face-to-face, as it would if they took him as a client, then he must not link the lady from the National Gallery with the Honorable Chastity Duncan.

She chose to ignore the question and asked coldly, "Is ze Go-Between to assume then that you 'ave no interest in a marriage where affection or respect are of any *importance*? It is only money and social status zat matter to you?"

This time he couldn't fail to hear the asperity in her tone. He slapped his gloves into the palm of one hand. "They are my priorities," he said. "Is it any business of the Go-Between to question those priorities? You are an agency that provides a service."

Chastity could feel her cheeks grow hot beneath her veil. "In order to serve you, *m'sieur,* we must ask the questions we consider necessary."

He frowned, then shrugged again as if in acceptance. "I would prefer to say that my choice of a wife is a simple matter of practicality." He regarded her now with a measure of frustration. What had seemed simple enough to him was becoming difficult for some reason, and made all the more so when he had no visual clues to work with.

Chastity watched him through her veil. She could see him quite clearly and could read his mind with some accuracy. Her instinct was to refuse the man as a client without further ado. Her finer feelings, of which she had more than her fair share, were revolted by the idea of simply finding some blatantly mercenary individual a rich wife. But she couldn't make such a decision without consultation with her sisters and she knew that they would scoff at such fine principles. They ran a business and could not afford to turn away a paying client, however much they despised him. Chastity knew she had to listen to Prudence's coolly pragmatic voice rather than her own immediate emotional response. And she could hear too how Constance, whatever she might think of the good doctor, would say that a paying client was a paying client. And there were women desperate enough for a husband who would probably find such a proposal convenient. Constance would say that such women needed to be educated to a degree of self-reliance, but until they were, then one had to deal with them on their own terms.

And both Prudence and Constance would be right. *The Mayfair Lady* and the Go-Between ensured the independence of the Duncan sisters and kept their father in relative comfort. While Prudence and Constance now had husbands well able to take care of them financially, neither woman was prepared to give up that independence.

At the thought of her father, Chastity gave an involuntary sigh. One that her companion heard, even as he saw the slight puff of her veil.

"Is something the matter?"

"No," she said. "Our business for today is concluded, I believe, *m'sieur*. I will go back to my office and consult with my si... my colleagues. You will 'ear from us by letter within ze week." She stood up, holding out her gloved hand.

He took it. "How will I meet suitable prospects?"

"You will be told," she said. "Always assuming that we can find a woman as willing as you to settle for a convenient marriage devoid of respect and affection. Good afternoon, Dr. Farrell." She left him in the embrasure before he had time to recover his wits.

He took a step after her, anger replacing incredulity at her tart tone as much as her words, but she was hurrying through the crowded gallery and he couldn't see himself arresting her to demand an apology in such a public place. But he would have one nevertheless. Of all the stiff-necked, self-righteous statements. How could she possibly know the realities of his work?

Of course, a little voice reminded him, he hadn't told her of those realities, of the other side of his work, but that was not something he chose to broadcast to all and sundry. And besides, it was not relevant to the service the Go-Between was offering.

For all the progressive views put forward in *The Mayfair Lady,* it was clear that its writers and editors were people, women he assumed, of means as well as education. They would know nothing of the dismal streets of Earl's Court, the tumbledown row houses where rats ran freely and the stench from the outhouses poisoned the air. They would know nothing of the realities of the tuberculosis and dysentery that lurked in every dark corner; of the desperate mothers trying to scrape together a penny for milk for their rickety children; of the men out of work, many of them drinking away whatever coins they could get in the noisome public houses that littered every street corner. Oh, no, it was one thing to pontificate about women's suffrage and equal rights under the law, quite another to pit such grandiose views against the grim realities of the underclasses.

Douglas Farrell strode from the gallery, still seething. Growing up fatherless in a household that comprised his mother and six older sisters, a household of chattering, squabbling yet smothering women, he was inclined to sympathize with fellow Scot John Knox and his complaint about the monstrous regiment of women. True, Knox was referring to the queens who three hundred years ago had ruled England and Scotland, but Douglas, as he had threaded his way through the maze of womanhood that had dominated his youth, took a certain savage satisfaction in applying the comment to his own situation. An abundance of love could be as much of a disadvantage as too little, he had decided some years ago, and had managed to reach the age of thirty-five without succumbing to the trap of matrimony. Now, however, he was ready to sacrifice the peace of bachelordom to the interests of his passionate commitment to the poor of London's underworld, and whose business was that but his own?

He could see no reason why the wealth of some privileged aristocratic woman shouldn't go towards improving the lot of the suffering men, women, and children whose existence he was certain she would barely acknowledge. And he could see no reason why he shouldn't put his considerable medical skills to work to the same philanthropic end exploiting the hypochondriacs who could well afford to pay for his services. So by what right did that undersized veiled creature with that ridiculous fake accent prate to him about love and respect in a marriage? She advertised a service and it was none of her business why her clients chose to avail themselves of it. If he'd wanted a love match he'd have gone and found one for himself.

Fuming, he stalked down the steps of the museum and marched off in the direction of St. James's Park, hoping that the cold air would cool his temper, as indeed it did. By the time he'd crossed the park and reached Buckingham Palace his customary sense of humor had reasserted itself. He had learned from the age of five that when dealing with women a sense of humor was essential if a man was not to court insanity.